A

by Craig Schaefer

Copyright © 2020 by Craig Schaefer.
Publisher's Note: This is a work of fiction. Names, characters, places, and incidents are a product of the author's imagination. Locales and public names are sometimes used for atmospheric purposes. Any resemblance to actual people, living or dead, or to businesses, companies, events, institutions, or locales is completely coincidental.

Cover Design by James T. Egan of Bookfly Design LLC.
Author Photo ©2014 by Karen Forsythe Photography
Craig Schaefer / A Time for Witches
ISBN 978-1-944806-23-1

CONTENTS

I: The Magician	1
Chapter One	3
Chapter Two	11
Chapter Three	19
Chapter Four	27
Chapter Five	35
Chapter Six	45
Chapter Seven	53
Chapter Eight	61
Chapter Nine	69
Chapter Ten	75
Chapter Eleven	85
Chapter Twelve	93

Chapter Thirteen	101
Chapter Fourteen	113
Chapter Fifteen	121
Chapter Sixteen	127
Chapter Seventeen	133
Chapter Eighteen	141
Chapter Nineteen	149
Chapter Twenty	159
II: Queen of Swords	167
Chapter Twenty-One	169
Chapter Twenty-Two	177
Chapter Twenty-Three	185
Chapter Twenty-Four	197
Chapter Twenty-Five	205
Chapter Twenty-Six	215
Chapter Twenty-Seven	225
Chapter Twenty-Eight	233
Chapter Twenty-Nine	241
Chapter Thirty	249
Chapter Thirty-One	257
Chapter Thirty-Two	265

Chapter Thirty-Three	273
III: The Chariot	281
Chapter Thirty-Four	283
Chapter Thirty-Five	289
Chapter Thirty-Six	299
Chapter Thirty-Seven	307
Chapter Thirty-Eight	317
Chapter Thirty-Nine	325
Chapter Forty	333
Chapter Forty-One	345
Chapter Forty-Two	355
Chapter Forty-Three	365
Chapter Forty-Four	373
Chapter Forty-Five	381
Chapter Forty-Six	391
Chapter Forty-Seven	399
Chapter Forty-Eight	407
Chapter Forty-Nine	417
Chapter Fifty	427
Chapter Fifty-One	435
Chapter Fifty-Two	443

Chapter Fifty-Three	453
Chapter Fifty-Four	461
Chapter Fifty-Five	469
Afterword	477
Also by Craig Schaefer	479

I: The Magician

CHAPTER ONE

"I knew there was going to be a sequel."

Lionel recognized the face of the dark-eyed woman at the hors d'oeuvres table. The name, he had to reach for. She tossed him a lifeline.

"Jerrica Winter," she said. "We met at the press expo in DC last year."

"Right."

He took her hand. She had a soft grip, and her fingertips slid along his palm as they parted. She lifted her hand to her face, flicking at her raven bangs while she looked him up and down. He'd thrown a sports coat over his ivory button-down and faded pale jeans, but he still felt underdressed for this party. Black tie was the rule of the evening, and the faux-sandstone floor of the Griffith Museum's gallery hall hosted a whirl of Savile Row suits and shimmering couture gowns. At least he wasn't alone, lingering at the unfashionable edge of the room; Jerrica had shown up in an off-the-rack pantsuit and sensible flats.

"I finished reading your book on the flight," she said. "Good stuff. When you went on 'indefinite leave' from Channel Seven, I figured you had to be working on a follow-up. Publisher must have handed you one hell of an advance to make you give up a steady TV gig."

"Something like that," he said, craning his neck and scoping out the room. Still hoping he'd see one particular face in the crowd.

He had left New York a month ago. Now he was living on his dwindling savings, driving a rust-spotted Corolla hatchback he'd bought with cash on the Jersey border. His mission was fueled by intuition and gas-station coffee.

Jerrica studied him with a fresh eye, like something had just occurred to her. "You're not going after Spears, are you? I know you like hunting big game, but you're wasting your time. He's so clean he squeaks when he walks."

Cordell Spears. Invisible fingertips riffled through the who's who in the back of Lionel's mind. Billionaire, philanthropist, made his cash in medical technology and slapped his name on a dozen children's hospitals from coast to coast. No. Lionel had made his journalistic bones taking down quacks, charlatans, and peddlers of mystic woo. As far as he knew, Spears was on the level.

Then again.

"Everybody's got skeletons," he said, keeping his tone neutral and his eyes on the snack spread. Small plates, deviled eggs, blocks of white cake like imported Athenian marble. The gnawing in his belly reminded him that he hadn't eaten since that morning, when he drove into Indiana with a cardboard cup of black coffee and a stale glazed doughnut in the center console.

"Not him. None worth writing about." Jerrica pursed her lips, like she disapproved of the lack of scandal. "Two ex-wives, but hell, me too. He pays his alimony on time. No disgruntled employees with receipts, no whistleblowers.

Spears Biomedical employees get a full year of paid maternity leave and an honest-to-God pension fund. Guy dedicated his life to eradicating childhood diseases, and when he's not working medical miracles he's funding charity shindigs like this one out of his own pocket. He's one of the good guys. A real-life superhero."

Lionel's eyebrows went up. "A superhero, even?"

"The *Post* called him 'Tony Stark with a stethoscope.'"

"I'm not sure there's any such thing as a 'good guy' billionaire. Not when you scratch deep enough."

"Cynic," she said.

"It's a bad habit. I'm trying to quit."

He reached for a Mediterranean pinwheel, a tortilla spiral stuffed with sundried tomatoes, spinach, and cream cheese. It was cold on his tongue, fresh, with a hint of Parmesan.

"If you figure out the trick," she said, "teach me how. So if you're not doing background on Spears, why *are* you here?"

Good question.

He was here because his lover kept a promise she had made to him. She'd made it with bloody tears on her cheeks, clutching the horn-handled knife she used on her arm sometimes when she needed to let the pressure out. *You know what happens next? You wake up one morning, and I'm gone. I'm just...I'm just gone. Because I always leave.*

He was here because he woke up alone in their bed, on the houseboat they'd rented up in Montauk, with nothing to see but an empty toffee wrapper on the counter and an empty patch of closet where she kept her rolling suitcase. Her patroness—*their* patroness now—had given Lionel a simple choice. His odyssey to New York had plunged the professional skeptic into a world of ghosts and horrors. He could leave it all behind. Go back to Chicago, back to the cameras and the spotlight, and his illusions of a rational world. In time, the memories might even fade.

Or he could choose Maddie. Choose her, chase her, following her trail across a haunted America. His teacher, masquerading as an elderly heiress named Regina Dunkle, couldn't promise him victory. All she promised him was struggle and pain. And magic.

He chose Maddie. He never looked back.

But now his teacher was gone. "Regina" disconnected her phone number and had been methodically erasing any trace of her existence. She was done wearing that particular mask. Lionel didn't feel abandoned. Sometimes, lying half asleep in the tail of a forgotten dream, he thought he could feel her. Watching, curious, eager to see what he'd do with the tools he'd been given.

The goddess Hekate—titan, witch-queen, keeper of divine mysteries—was a strong believer in the sink-or-swim method of education. And Hekate had chosen him for her own, just as she had done with Maddie centuries before.

So he trusted his intuition and drove. He followed billowing clouds of starlings and charted a course based on train-car graffiti. Lionel was new to this whole "being a witch" business—he still didn't like speaking the word out loud and never claimed it for himself—and he wasn't sure if he was hearing the whispers of the universe or just flipping a metaphorical coin and imagining a signal in all that noise, but until he found a concrete lead, that was all he had to go on. His intuition had landed him in a cheap hotel on the edge of Bloomington, where the cleaning staff had missed a tourist brochure for the Griffith Museum left behind by the previous occupant. He'd looked it up. Tonight marked the North American debut of a new traveling exhibit, *Treasures of the Mycenaean World*.

Dangling banners lined the great hall, encircling the edges of a glass ceiling that rose up like a circus tent, open to the murky night sky. A bone-white sliver of moon peered down, veiled behind wispy, ragged clouds. This was exactly the sort of show that might draw Maddie's attention: she was a treasure of the Mycenaean world herself. So far, though, no sign of her.

Lionel was still trying to answer Jerrica's question when a deep, confident voice jarred his thoughts.

"Jerrica Winter *and* Lionel Page? How much trouble am I in here?"

Jerrica greeted the new arrival with a quick, tight hug. "You know you're safe from me."

He was statuesque, chiseled, built like a Greco-Roman wrestler in a thousand-dollar suit, and he had an easy, generous laugh. He turned to Lionel and offered his manicured hand.

"Said the scorpion to the frog. Lionel! You don't know me, but I know you. Big, big fan. Cordell Spears, pleasure to finally meet face-to-face."

The man of the hour. Lionel couldn't miss the private security, hovering at a respectful distance but close enough to jump in at a moment's notice. They wore Secret Service earpieces, and judging from the cut of their jackets, they were packing more than muscle underneath.

"Same," Lionel said. "I understand you're the person to thank for this exhibition?"

"Well, our archaeologists in the field did the *real* work. I just foot the bills. It's a good cause. History is important to me. Should be important to all of us. We can't chart a clear course to the future if we don't know where we've been."

"Agreed," Lionel said.

Cordell flashed a gleaming smile. "That's why what you do is so important. Chasing down frauds, exposing snake-oil salesmen. Take it from me, my game is medical science, and it feels like every week there's some new con man slinging a miracle cure—"

He paused. An elderly woman, bifocals dangling from a chain around her neck, was waving a brochure at him from across the room.

"Looks like I've got to get up there and battle my stage fright. A thousand public appearances and it always feels like my very first time. Jerrica, Lionel, catch you two after the show."

Lionel watched him go, the silent security guards drifting like phantoms in his wake. He felt Jerrica's eyes on him while he loaded up a tiny plate of vegetarian appetizers.

"You're looking for a reason not to trust him," she said.

"I don't dislike him—"

"But you don't *trust* anybody," she said. "Like I said. Cynic."

"It's a bad habit."

"I think it's sexy." She tilted her head. "You doing anything after this? Want to grab a drink, do some catching up?"

It sounded like she had more than catching up in mind. "I'd have to ask my girlfriend."

"Oh? She here?"

No. She wasn't. Lionel took one last look across the sea

of faces, hunting for the curve of her chin, her bright-eyed glow. Maddie wasn't here. He'd followed his intuition and come up empty. Maybe he was fooling himself.

"We're kind of doing a long-distance-relationship thing at the moment," he said.

Jerrica shook her head. "Get out now, save yourself a world of heartache. Those things never work out in the end."

The wall sconces dimmed. Through the glass circus-tent canopy, skeleton moonlight shimmered down. A microphone let out a heartbeat of feedback squeal as Cordell Spears took the podium. He stood there for a moment, a wall of stony silence, all eyes on him.

"Are we...great?" he asked the gathering.

He was answered with faint murmurs, uncertain noises.

"America was built," he said, "on the foundations of the past. Our forefathers looked to the Mediterranean, to the traditions of Greece and Rome, when they laid the first stones of this nation. Why? Because they drew upon history, and they had studied a grand civilization that endured for centuries. What did they see there? Greatness. A model to be emulated, a promise of enduring glory."

Cordell's patter was well rehearsed and he had the room in the palm of his hand, but Lionel was more interested in a new arrival. Lionel didn't fit in with this crowd, but she was a piece from an entirely different puzzle. Frizzy orange hair, bags under her shell-shocked eyes, long and sallow cheeks. She wore a housecoat and combat boots.

And as she made her way through the heart of the open gallery, no one—no one but Lionel—seemed to notice her at all. The pale moonlight wreathed around her, stealing the color from her skin, turning her to glass.

New York had given Lionel scars to last a lifetime, inside and out. It had also given him a witch's eyes. The newcomer felt him looking. She turned as she passed, and her mouth moved in silence. Maybe he felt the words echoing inside his skull, or maybe he just read her lips: *Don't try to stop me.*

Maddie would have known what to do. But Maddie wasn't here. Just him. Lionel set his plate down on the edge of the snack table. He braced himself, shoulders tight, knees limber. Whatever was about to go down, he was going to have to pick a side and move. Fast.

CHAPTER TWO

Oblivious to the woman prowling toward the podium, just like everyone else in the crowd, Cordell Spears was waxing rhapsodic about the glories of the ancient world.

"Why do we pack multiplexes to watch super-powered titans battle it out on the silver screen?" he asked. "Because humanity doesn't change. Human needs, human hungers, don't change. Just as it was thousands of years ago, we need our heroes. People need to be reminded that the children of gods walk among us, and when humanity is weak and fearful, lost and alone, there are heroes prepared to step up and protect them. Not everyone can be great, but everyone can stand under the radiance of—"

She silenced him with a word. Her voice rang out across the gallery.

"*Murderer.*"

They saw her now. Every head turned her way at once, a low murmur rippling through the crowd. Behind the podium, a pair of Cordell's bodyguards were already moving in like smooth and efficient automatons. Their boss looked shaken, for just a second, and then he buried his discomfort under an easy smile.

"I...think this lady is in the wrong place. Security, could

you—? Thank you. Be gentle, please. She's clearly in some distress. Let's see if we can get her the help she needs, all right?"

She stood her ground. Lionel saw one of her hands drop, moving toward the waist of her housecoat.

"You're lying to these people," she said. "Everything about you is a lie. And heroes can die. Heroes die just like everybody else."

Cordell shook his head, solemn now.

"No, ma'am. Heroes live forever, as long as their story does."

They locked eyes. The gallery froze.

"Yours ends tonight," the woman said.

She whipped back her coat and drew what she was carrying underneath. Off to her side, in mid-pivot, Lionel saw it: a flask of white clay, long and thin, daubed with glyphs in scarlet paint. A clot of blood-red wax sealed the cork in place.

"*Gun!*" shouted one of the bodyguards, and they both pulled theirs.

Lionel grabbed Jerrica's shoulder and hauled her to the floor. People dove, scattered, and the only thing louder than the screaming was the synchronized *pop-pop-pop* of slim automatics firing. Muzzles flashed like camera bulbs and the woman staggered backward, doing a herky-jerky dance while red craters erupted in her chest.

She hit the floor on her back, eyes wide and glassy and staring straight at Lionel.

The clay bottle slid from her open palm. It thumped from her pale fingers to the sandstone and rolled free. Another suit was hustling Cordell away from the podium, fast, while the crowd stampeded. One of the museum

A Time for Witches

flacks got onto the PA system, calling for calm, promising the danger was past. No one was listening.

"Jesus," Jerrica said, crouched at Lionel's side. "That was *nuts*. What were they thinking? We could have gotten hit!"

They were thinking about protecting their boss. Private security. Lionel wasn't surprised. He was more focused on the white clay flask as it rolled between running feet, gathering momentum like it had a mind of its own.

He reached down, and the flask rolled to a stop against his fingertips. Lionel scooped it off the sandstone and slipped it into his inside breast pocket.

He rose up, an island in the heart of the chaos. Long before Lionel knew anything about monsters and magic, back when he was an iron-clad skeptic who exposed supernatural frauds for a living, this was always where he felt most at home. Panic washed over him like warm waves on a sandy beach; he kept his head cool and focused, snatching details from the stampede, drawing a picture of clarity. There was Cordell, head down, being hustled out the back through an employees-only door. The two shooters stayed behind, their smoking guns holstered and hidden away. One was trying to calm the crowd, waving his open hands, while the other looked down at the dead body with a thousand-yard stare on his bloodless face.

Lionel knew the man's story. The bodyguard had trained for this moment, probably spent a thousand hours on the shooting range, but all the training in the world couldn't teach you what it felt like to take a human life. You had to learn that the hard way, and then you had to learn to carry the weight.

Lionel had.

He looked back to the corpse. In all the commotion, the viral confusion turning the genteel partygoers into a panicked mob, someone had rewritten this story.

Now the dead woman had a gun in her hand.

Lionel flicked on a hot lamp in his mind and interrogated his own memories. He knew, better than most people, how your eyes could lie to you. He'd busted faith healers and mediums who fooled the masses with dime-store magic tricks; sometimes the simplest deceptions were the most convincing. He played it all back in slow motion. The reach, the shout—the man had seen a gun, or *thought* he had seen a gun...

Or he wanted the crowd to think he had. Because Lionel knew what he'd seen, and his eyes weren't lying. It was the woman's left hand. She'd pulled the flask with her left hand, been shot, fell, and the flask rolled to Lionel. Her left hand was empty. And now a tiny .32 revolver, scuffed and dirty, lay nestled in her open palm.

Drop piece. He had met cops who carried one, a just-in-case weapon to turn a wrongful shooting righteous. No reason a bodyguard wouldn't do the same. He knew something else, too: he wasn't going to let them get away with it. He needed backup, someone to corroborate the facts; he looked to his fellow journalist with a question in his eyes.

"Did you see her hand?"

Jerrica shook her head, not following. "What about it?"

"The flask. Did you see the flask in her hand?"

"What, her other hand? Was she drunk?" Jerrica held out her open palm, watching it quiver. "Fucking adrenaline. How are you this calm right now? You're like one of those war-zone reporters."

He was asking the wrong question. He was treating this situation like a normal crime, from his old and normal life. He'd drawn a stark line through his history, breaking it into two parts: *before New York* and *after New York*. The woman nobody saw, the clay flask...he needed to start treating this like an *after* situation.

"When she pulled her hand from her coat," he said, "just before they shot her, did you actually *see* a gun in her hand?"

Jerrica looked from her trembling fingers to the dead woman on the floor.

"It's right there," she said.

"Yeah, but did you actually see it before they shot her? Or did you see a flask?"

Or did you see both at the same time? he wondered. Jerrica squinted. Something was sparking behind her eyes, synapses misfiring as she struggled to reconcile two competing versions of the truth. Cognitive dissonance could do that to a person.

And so could witchcraft.

"I saw..." Her voice trailed off. Whatever had a hold on her—the same force that had a hold on everyone in the room, Lionel was willing to bet—wouldn't let her finish the sentence.

Cops waded against the crowd, making it to the scene in record time. A woman held a badge high, establishing a perimeter around the body with sheer force of will. Another, in plainclothes, was talking to the shell-shocked bodyguard, gently collecting his gun and outlining the facts on a spiral notepad. At Lionel's side, Jerrica was saying something. He turned and blinked.

"Sorry?"

"I asked if you'd reconsider getting that drink with me," she said. "Because I don't know about you, but it's going to take me two or three just to stop my hands from shaking."

"Sorry," he said.

"Right. Long-distance girlfriend." She gave his shoulder an uneasy pat. "Like I said, rip the bandage off and break up now. It'll only end in tears."

Maybe. Lionel only knew one thing for certain. He'd coasted his way here on a wave of intuition and coincidence, not sure if he was following the winds of magic or random chance. But there was nothing *random* about this. He'd come hunting for Maddie, but the universe had something more ironic in mind.

Now he was going to have to do Maddie's job.

~~

Emergency lights painted the sea-scallop curves of the Griffith Museum in whorls of winter blue. Lionel shrugged his jacket higher on his shoulders, hunched against a bitter night chill, and walked away from the scene of the crime. He had saved himself the parking-lot fee by leaving the Corolla on a hardscrabble patch of bad road three blocks away. It wasn't like anyone was going to steal it, and there wasn't anything inside but a couple of crumpled junk-food wrappers and an empty coffee cup.

The commotion and the lights faded behind him. The sounds of the city at night filled the gulf. Bloomington was sleeping, but sleeping rough, grumbling as it tossed and turned. Mostly it left him alone with his thoughts. A lone dog barked in the distance, its anger echoing off dark windows and drawn-down shades.

The night was laced with the tang of sour magic, and it

all boiled down to the clay flask riding snug in his breast pocket. He thought about uncorking it to see what was inside. Then he thought twice. The dead woman didn't have a gun, but she'd clearly aimed to bring Cordell Spears to account for something he'd done, and the flask was her weapon of choice. Until he knew more, he'd treat it like it was packed with nitroglycerin. He was writing a to-do list in his head, leads to follow, possibilities to consider, when a voice croaked out from a darkened doorway.

"Hey, brother. Help a vet out? I'm just tryin' to get something to eat."

The man sat slumped in a stone arch, beneath a broken light bulb. His cheeks were long, dripping with bristle, and he wore oily fatigues that might have been crisp and green in another lifetime. Lionel stopped. He reached for his wallet, doing quick math and figuring out how much he could spare. His savings were running out fast—serving as an unofficial field agent for an ancient Greek goddess was a surprisingly less-than-lucrative gig—but it was cold and late and he couldn't walk on by.

He leaned down, reaching out with a five-dollar bill curled around his fingers. The homeless man looked up at him, eyes bleary.

Then his hand, shrouded in a ragged and fingerless glove, fired up and clamped down on Lionel's wrist.

"You better watch out," he growled in a voice too deep to come from his frail body. "You better take care, son, and you better watch out for the Holy Roller."

Lionel didn't pull away. Couldn't. The man's grip was tight as a steel vise, and his eyes—blazing now, awake and sharp and glittering—pinned him where he stood.

"He built himself a monster for a monstrous road," he

told Lionel. "A chariot of bloody steel, a death coaster, a highway killer supreme! Holy Roller's on a mission, and your main squeeze...she's hot on his trail."

"Madison?" Lionel leaned closer. "What do you know about Madison?"

"Those two are looking to put each other six feet underground. You want to help her? Then you'd better run fast, young lion. But watch your own back while you do it. You got trouble of your own, coming in hot. Kind of trouble that'll eat you alive—"

Now Lionel grabbed him back. His free hand latched on to the man's arm and he gave it a shake.

"What do you know? Maddie. *Where is she?*"

The fire in the old man's eyes faded away, like a light switch flicked off behind his eyes.

He let go of Lionel's wrist, sagged back against the cold stone archway, and stared into the darkness over Lionel's shoulder.

"I don't know nothin' about nothin'," he said. His voice was a million miles away. He slowly looked down at the bill in his hand. "Thanks for the cash, brother. 'Preciate it. God bless."

CHAPTER THREE

Lionel had lost count of how many times he'd slept at the Starlite Motel. Well, not this exact one, not by this exact name in this exact town, but he'd been here. It was a faded relic of the seventies built alongside a lonely highway, nothing but open farmland and cornfields on the far side of the road, nothing in either direction but pitch-black sky. Dirt clung to the plastic shell of the parking-lot sign, and the bulbs inside hummed and flickered through the night.

He'd been to places just like this, all over the country, back when he was a road warrior chasing down one hot story after another. A hundred names, a hundred cities, but it was always the same motel. He knew what he'd find even before he pulled into the lot: a key on a fat plastic tag, his room number printed in faded gold on black. Beyond the paper-thin door, paper-thin walls, with the muffled audience laughter of a late-night talk show drifting from the next room. A flowered bedspread, overstarched sheets, and a pastoral print on the wall that had probably been bought out of somebody's car trunk.

His curtains were open. He moved in the dark, circling a tiny window-side table, and reached for the lamp. Out in the night, across the lot, across the highway, a scarecrow dangled on a leaning cruciform post at the heart of the open field.

Lionel flicked on the light and made the world outside the window disappear. Then he pulled the curtains shut.

He set the white clay flask on the table, next to his open laptop. Careful, taking his time, he turned the flask and snapped cell-phone photographs from every angle. It was the first chance he'd had to really study the thing, to note the precision of the scarlet paint, how even the smears were artfully, carefully applied, smudging the pigment this way and that, according to some unknown law of symmetry. He didn't know what the sigils meant. Maybe "handle with care" or "do not open." He gave the flask one last quarter-turn, to snap the final angle, and froze.

There was lettering there, tiny, precise, down at the base of the flask. Greek. He couldn't read the language, but he recognized the letters. A single word, maybe.

It was Maddie's handwriting.

He put his memories back under the interrogation-room lights, making sure he wasn't just jumping at a coincidence or surrendering to wishful thinking. It was Maddie's distinctive style, he was sure of it. Whatever had gone down at the museum tonight, whoever that woman was, whatever she was trying to accomplish before Cordell's men gunned her down, Maddie was part of it. She had come this way, before Lionel. He was only a few steps behind her.

Which meant he needed to close the distance, fast.

Lionel was a journalist from the old school. He valued the internet—he mostly valued how he could find records in minutes that used to take a day of rummaging in some musty county clerk's office, plus the occasional bribe—but as far as he was concerned, there was no substitute for shoe leather and face-to-face interviews. Nobody broke front-page news by sitting behind a desk.

All the same, it was past midnight. He was raring to go, to hunt down the dead woman and crack into her history, but the doors of this county were locked up tight until sunrise. There wasn't much he could do but try to get some sleep.

Well, one thing. He had set up a string of social-media accounts in the last week or two, aimed at keeping tabs on the stranger corners of the net. As expected, he mostly found a tangled web of conspiracy theorists, fantasists, and hucksters, but there was a grain or two of truth nestled under all that illusion. Like the meek, reclusive classics professor from Toronto whose poetic essay about the muse Melpomene perfectly matched Lionel's lived experience, down to the very words she spoke to him when they met. Or the Arkansan mythpunk songstress sharing photos from her show at a certain ghoul-haunted NYC nightclub, in a way that made it clear—if you had been there yourself and lived to talk about it—that she knew exactly who she'd been entertaining that night.

These were Lionel's people now. He logged on with his alter-ego account, *Fool333*, and uploaded a picture. Not the smeared scarlet glyphs; if they were dangerous, he didn't want them floating around online. Just the last one, a tight close-up of the Greek letters at the base of the flask.

Can anyone read this and let me know what it says? he typed. *Thanks in advance.*

He clicked *Post*, powered down the laptop, and closed

the lid. Hopefully morning would yield answers, and another clue to chase.

~~

Lionel hunted sleep. Tossing, turning, tangling up the over-starched sheets like a rope knotted around his naked body. Something was chasing him in the dark. It was a monster made of moments: a gunshot, a rolling clay flask, a dirty-nailed hand wearing a fingerless glove. Sounds and flickers grew teeth in his dreams.

He woke to the hum of the motel air conditioner, vintage gears grinding. No good. He slung his legs over the side of the mattress and his feet touched down on worn, faded carpet.

On an impulse, he pulled back the curtain. Dark inside, dark outside. It was 2:14 in the morning and the ribbon of highway stood empty, marked by a string of distant and pale lampposts. He looked to the cornfields across the road. He could barely see the leaning cruciform post the farmer's scarecrow had dangled from.

The post stood empty now. Lionel let the curtain fall back into place.

On the table, the clay bottle stood, cork sealed with a blob of scarlet wax, inviting him—daring him—to crack it open. The painted Greek letters, in Maddie's careful hand, floated in his night vision.

He shambled across the room. The motel provided packets of cheap instant coffee, plastic cups, a dubious plastic carafe, laid out on the edge of the TV stand. He needed to improvise.

~~

"I'm going to teach you a spell," Maddie said.

They were up in Montauk, on a rented houseboat,

A Time for Witches

recovering in each other's arms. They didn't talk about magic, much. They'd ride bikes along the shore or just walk the beach, savoring each other's company, Lionel getting his strength back day by day after his stint in the hospital. When the sun went down, turning the peaceful waters to rippling, hammered gold, they'd drink wine on the back deck and then turn in early, making love like newlyweds, wearing each other out and then tumbling into dreamless sleep together.

He almost tricked himself into thinking life was perfect. The truth was—and he saw it later, clear as the ocean sunrise—that this wasn't life. They were on vacation. And vacations weren't meant to last forever. Maddie had a job to get back to, a higher calling, and he had to make some hard choices.

Then there was the night he found her in the bathroom, perched on the closed lid of the toilet seat, her horn-rimmed knife in her hand and her arm out, showing rows of pale puckered scars like tick marks on the wall of a prison cell. She hadn't cut herself, yet. She was fighting it. She let him take the knife away, as he'd done once before, and guide her back to bed. They didn't talk about it the next morning.

Lionel wasn't naive enough to think that he'd "fixed" Maddie, or cured her. He wasn't Prince Charming, and he hadn't swooped in and erased centuries of her pain with a noble kiss. He couldn't banish the ghosts behind her eyes; he could only keep them at bay for a while. He could be there for her, when she needed him, when she let him. That was good enough.

All the same, he should have taken that night as another

sign. Should have taken this spontaneous lesson in magic as a sign, too. She was getting him ready for the inevitable.

"I don't know," he said with a smile, washing the morning's breakfast pan in the houseboat's tiny sink. "You really think I'm ready for even more cosmic power? It might go to my head."

The cabin smelled like fresh roasted tomatoes. Maddie stood behind him, curling her hands around his waist, and nuzzled her forehead against the back of his neck.

"I think I can keep you humble," she said. "Besides. This is a simple one. Apprentice level, an oldie but a goodie. I know the boss taught you some war magic that nobody's busted out since the fall of Troy, but that was a special one-time situation. So you wouldn't, y'know, die. As far as I'm concerned, you're still at the 'learn to walk before you can run' stage. You need to get more of the basics down before I can turn you loose."

He pivoted on his heel, turning his back to the sink, facing her now. His fingertip, dripping with glistening suds, drew a wet line along the curve of her jaw.

"Turn me loose?"

She scrunched up her nose at him.

"You're still my apprentice," she said. "My responsibility. So grab the nice bowl from the cabinet, the lacquered one. And a candle. I think my lighter's in the rummage drawer."

~~

Lionel sat alone in the dark, on the scratchy cheap carpet. The coffee carafe was filled with tap water from the motel bathroom sink, set out next to an empty plastic cup. He had a couple of votive candles, short and ivory white, knocking around in his rolling luggage.

A Time for Witches

He held Maddie's lighter. It was cheap pink plastic, from some forgotten gas station somewhere out on the endless maze of highways. She had left it behind.

"*You won't always have exactly what you need,*" he heard her say, "*and that's fine—*"

~~

Maddie held up her freshly scrubbed hands.

"A real witch knows how to work dirty."

They sat on the smooth laminate of the cabin floor, with a dark lacquered bowl and a pitcher of water fresh from the pier's edge resting between them. Lionel nodded back over his shoulder to the bed, the rumpled purple sheets.

"How dirty are we talking here?"

Maddie laughed. "Not that kind. I told you, sex magic is *work*. There's actual math involved. No, what I mean is we might use things to help focus our craft. Ocean water, a consecrated bowl, a candle. Stones and herbs known to have particular useful properties."

She held up her lighter, the seventy-cent gas-station special. Fluid rolled beneath the translucent pink plastic.

"But that's just stuff. Props. They help, a lot, but don't lose sight of where the power really flows from. If you don't have what you need, improvise, and trust in your own abilities. You can still get the job done. I've made consecrated candles out of melted crayons in a pinch and substituted moonshine for ceremonial wine. Xiulang can do scary-accurate tarot readings with blank pieces of paper."

Lionel fluttered his eyelashes and clasped his hands to his chest. "You mean...the real magic was inside me all along?"

"Jerk. But true. Well, mostly. There are times when you

can get things done on your own tank of gas—like when you learned how to banish death energy—and there are times when a smart witch turns her eyes to Olympus."

"I was never really religious."

She shrugged. "Well, Hekate claimed you, so you're religious now."

"Fair point," he said.

"Being a witch is all about bargains. Negotiations, trades and concessions. That includes dealing with the gods." She held up a finger. "Always show respect. A little piety and a little respect go a long way."

Lionel thought back to his encounter with the muse Melpomene. Quick negotiations on Maddie's part, and a gesture of trust on his, had saved both of their lives.

"I serve and adore Hekate," Maddie said, "but before I go out on the ocean, I make a sacrifice to Poseidon. When I'm on the hunt, I offer gratitude to Artemis. And my shots land on target."

"But you actually *know* these gods—and you can't believe how weird it still feels for me to say something like that. I mean, I didn't even believe in magic before...two weeks ago. If I'm the one calling, I don't think Mount Olympus has any reason to pick up the phone."

Her smile was soft, faintly indulgent.

"You might be surprised what a little respect and an open heart can reap. Hence today's lesson. I'm going to teach you a very simple spell of protection. Because...because I might not always be around."

CHAPTER FOUR

Sitting cross-legged on the motel carpet, alone in the dark, Lionel flicked the lighter's wheel. It rasped, sparked, then glowed with a shifting plume of fire. The light smeared his night vision, turning the room into a sphere of inky darkness with nothing but him and his improvised tools at its heart. He spoke the words from memory.

"Fair Aphrodite, lady of *agape* and *eros*..."

~~

"Fair Aphrodite," Maddie whispered, her empty hand passing over the empty bowl, "lady of *agape* and *eros*, of *philia* and *ludus*, of love in all names and all forms. Let love be my shield and desire drive my footsteps."

Lionel watched her, curious, reflecting. She caught his look.

"Do you know these words?" she asked.

He shook his head.

"My language—my first language—has many names for love. This modern notion of being 'in love' with someone would have struck us as strange back in the day. It's such a big concept, the most important one in the human experience, distilled down to a single word. *Agape* is selfless love, love you give to everyone, even perfect strangers. It's...charity, and empathy, and kindness."

"Not a lot of that going around these days," he said.

"So work to bring more of it into the world. Without *agape*, everything falls apart. Now, *eros*—"

"That one I know," Lionel said, adding another nod to the rumpled bedsheets.

An impish look danced in Maddie's eyes. "You might think you do. But real, genuine *eros* isn't about *knowing* anything at all. It sweeps you up, starves your mind, and strangles your reason. I knew a priestess back in Cyprus who referred to her mistress as *Tymborychos*. That means 'gravedigger,' and she meant it as a term of absolute respect. You don't fuck around with *eros*. You surrender to it, and let Aphrodite's will be done. Even if it means your absolute ruin."

Lionel blinked. "Admittedly I'm going off vague memories of my middle-school education, but I thought Aphrodite was, you know, the nice and sparkly goddess of love, with the hearts and cherubs."

"Welcome to the real world," Maddie said, deadpan. "It took you a while, but I'm glad you were able to join us here. Moving on, *philia* is friend love. I'm not talking about your social media followers, either. It's the love of real, deep friendship."

"'Drive you to the airport at two in the morning' friendship?"

"Or 'help you pack and move on short notice' friendship. It's loyalty, it's caring, it's celebrating their victories or hurting because they're hurting. Friendship is love, powerful love. I think that's often forgotten in this age. People are taught that love and sex are entwined, that you can't love your friends because that means you must expect something more or different from them." She hooked her fingers to make air quotes. "'Friend zoning.' Don't even get me started on how much I hate that shit. Friend love *is* love, as true and valid and vital as any other form. That's why we have words for this stuff."

Lionel thought back, testing his memory. "And...*ludus?*"

"*Ludus* is the epitome of 'hard to explain, but you know it when you feel it.' *Ludus* is playful love. Light, and teasing, and delightful. It might become *philia*, and it might become *eros*, or it might just...be what it is. Ever flirt with a complete stranger?"

"Yeah," Lionel said. "I seem to recall her name was Madison Hannah. We met over a cup of coffee, my first night in Manhattan. Typical romantic comedy meet-cute sort of situation."

"How'd that work out for you?" she asked.

"Pretty swell. No complaints."

"Good to hear. Now, there are other words for love. *Philautia*, that's a good one. Love of self, but not in a narcissistic way. It's more about being...self-sufficient. I know you've met people who really hate themselves, deep down inside."

"Sure," Lionel said. "Jimmy V. Sloane, traveling typewriter salesman."

Maddie pursed her lips like she'd just taken a bite of something sour. Then she nodded.

"Perfect example. Everything Sloane did, everything he grasped for, everyone he hurt—it was all because he couldn't find anything good about himself. So he went looking for love and acclaim out in the world, and that just doesn't work. Without *philautia*, you turn into a black hole. A hunger that can never be fed. But real, genuine self-love means you don't depend on others for validation, and you can take that love inside of you and share it with the world. Which brings us back to the spell at hand."

Lionel gestured to the empty lacquered bowl, resting on the laminate cabin floor between them.

"Right. Didn't you say this was a protection spell? Sounds like we're doing a love charm here."

She flashed a playful smile and reached for the pitcher of ocean water.

"Why can't it be both?"

~~

A pale white votive candle glowed on the motel carpet, carrying the flame from Maddie's lighter. Tap water from the coffee carafe rained down into the disposable plastic cup, a steady lukewarm stream. Lionel took deep breaths, focusing the way he'd been taught, his heart slowing to a firm, strident beat.

"Fair Aphrodite," he whispered, "lady of *agape* and *eros*, of *philia* and *ludus*, of love in all names and all forms. Let love be my shield and desire drive my footsteps."

He positioned the votive, sliding it across the carpet until its tiny flame was reflected in the cup. The water rippled and the fire danced, twin lights in the darkness.

"*The first part is the invocation*," Maddie's voice echoed in his ear. "*Now, the visualization. Picture someone you love. Any flavor, or any combination, but think of how you love them. The blind charity of agape, the whirlwind heat of eros, the trusting bonds of philia, the dance of ludus. Meditate on this while you picture their face in the water. You might see them in the reflected shadows, at the edge of the candle's flame.*"

~~

Lionel focused. The houseboat fell away, the sounds of passing motors and the lapping waves and the traffic from the pier road all blending into a muffled, meaningless hum. He was alone, meditating, his attention and his breath and the rhythm of his pulse all fixed upon the reflected flame.

There was only one person he'd see there. She was sitting right across from him, her physical body a shadow while he gazed into the water. He saw her face there, a ghost beside the fire's glow.

"Here is a secret," Madison whispered. "There's only one flame."

He saw it then, a mystery unfolding. He saw the candle, by his side, and the reflected light in the water, cradling the vision of Madison's face. He thought of all they'd been through together, the hardships they'd endured hand in hand, the war they'd fought and won. They were bound together, by *philia* and *eros* and all the rest, just like the reflection of the flame was bound to the candle.

One.

"Even when you and your love are apart," Madison said, "separated by miles, or years, or even death, you can conjure them with this trick. And they're right here with you, like they never left. You aren't alone. Remember that."

~~

Lionel gazed into the plastic cup of water, swallowed by the candlelight and the thrum of the motel's AC unit. He felt Maddie there, too, right beside him. He spoke the words from memory.

"In darkness, may my light find her. In cold, may the

warmth of my fire find her. May my strength be her strength and shield her from all terrors. Aphrodite, Queen of Desire, my heart is true. Smile upon my petition, and lay your graceful hand upon her path."

"*Now we seal the spell,*" Maddie instructed. "*Take the index finger of your dominant hand and touch the skin of the water. The dove is Aphrodite's messenger, so draw one, and make it so.*"

It was a simple thing. Abstract, two inverted *U*'s to symbolize the wings of the dove and lukewarm water rippling beneath his fingertip. Sending Lionel's spell to Maddie, wherever she was. He spoke the final words she had taught him.

"Fly, your heart to me."

And then it was done.

~~

"See?" Maddie said. "Simple."

Lionel had woven the barbarous words of the *voces mysticae* to banish death energy. He'd fought a rampaging, traitorous witch, armed with curses unspoken for centuries, while the restless dead whirled across their battleground. The rationalist in him hated to admit it, but he was getting used to the special effects. This was simple by comparison, a tiny charm, but...

"Still powerful," he said, finishing the thought out loud. Maddie nodded her approval.

"The simplest techniques often are. Remember lesson one: witches use what works. Period. We're about getting results. Especially those of us who serve Hekate. She's all about results. Excuses, not so much."

"I noticed." He glanced down to the candle. It sat cold and still. Had he snuffed it out, or had she? He couldn't recall. "I thought this was a spell for protecting yourself, though. It's all about the person you focus it on."

"Is it?" That impish smile again. "Love is a force multiplier. It spreads and grows. And it protects everyone it touches. Besides, you've been down in the dark enough times to know one thing is true."

He cocked his head. "What's that?"

"When things are at their worst, when you're all alone and lost and feeling afraid, and you don't know which way to turn? Sometimes the best way to push through the darkness and keep fighting is to be strong for someone else."

CHAPTER FIVE

Shards of dry and dusty light wedged their way around the motel curtains, carrying the slow-spreading warmth of an Indiana dawn. Trucks rumbled along the highway, the rattling thrum of their tires following Lionel into the bathroom. He shaved, nicking his cheek, and stanched the blood with a wadded-up tissue while he waited for the shower to heat up. Same routine, same just-another-morning-on-the-road energy he'd felt on a hundred trips back when he was chasing stories as a freelance journalist.

He was still chasing a story, he figured. Same old ball game. New team.

And someone from the reserve bench had left a message on his laptop, time-stamped an hour ago. He tugged on a pair of worn jeans and buttoned a soft cotton dress shirt, fixing his cuffs as he sat down at the table. Two clicks and a tiny electronic envelope blossomed into a new window.

It's a name, his scholarly acquaintance wrote. *Tisiphone. So whatever's in that bottle, I'd think twice about breaking the seal, or at least have a hazmat team and the poison-control center on standby. Just saying. Happy hunting, Q.*

The name was on the tip of his tongue. He'd heard it once, somewhere. He fired up his web browser. The name conjured sketches and woodcuts, images of leathery bat wings and serrated teeth and girdles made of squirming, venomous serpents.

Tisiphone. One of the three Furies. Tisiphone, a chthonic deity, is charged with avenging crimes of murder.

Lionel was standing on the sandstone gallery floor, under the glass circus-tent dome, watching the disheveled woman making her way through the crowd. She had silenced Cordell Spears with a single word: "*Murderer.*"

"The Furies were granted the divine right to pursue and punish mortals who offended the divine order by committing heinous crimes," he read aloud, scrolling his way down the page. "Their victims would be tortured, driven to madness, and finally slain, their souls dragged to the pits of Erebus to face eternal judgment."

He gave the white clay flask a sidelong glance. *Yeah. Definitely not opening that.*

Before he could figure out what the dead woman was trying to accomplish—and what crime she was avenging—he had to find out who she was. That part was easy. Local news stations had taken the story and run with it, featuring breathless coverage of the Griffith Museum shooting. The reports were more about Cordell Spears than the woman who came gunning for him. Lionel clicked past column after column, hunting for some real news amid the public-relations puffery. It was just like Jerrica told him: Cordell wore the cape of a real-life superhero, curing childhood diseases with one hand and financing his archaeological passion projects with the other, all while jet-setting between charity gala balls.

Looks like he can do no wrong, which immediately makes

me think he must be doing something wrong, Lionel thought. But let's be fair, that's just how I'm wired.

Besides, his hair is perfect. I don't trust any man with perfect hair.

He found the name of the victim, three layers deep, and read it aloud to the empty room. "Kayla Lambert, forty-three, postal worker."

He thought back to when people made dark jokes about *going postal*, back before they learned how a mass shooting could happen anywhere, anytime. For any reason, or no reason at all. He was still trying to figure out what kind of weapon was nestled inside Kayla Lambert's flask. Poison? Acid? The outside was clay, but the inside could be reinforced, shielded against corrosion. Three brisk steps and she would have been close enough to fling it right into Cordell's face.

He ran her name through a battery of research sites, building a paper trail. LexisNexis, TLO, and Tracers opened their databases wide for him. Well, not for him, exactly; they opened up for the Channel Seven News credentials that had been conveniently left untouched after he went on an indefinite sabbatical. They might have ended up walking different roads, but Brianna, his ex-boss-slash-ex-girlfriend, still had his back.

Kayla drove a Toyota pickup, registered to a trailer park twelve miles down the highway. Lionel needed some fresh air. He jotted down the address and grabbed his keys.

~~

Kids were outside, throwing a foam football and kicking up rocks in a weed-infested vacant lot. *Right*, Lionel thought as he pulled off the main road and down a long access corridor, *it's Saturday*. Keeping track of time had been a challenge ever since New York. The days melted together, and the old schedules that kept him pinned to his old life—his shift at the station, drinks after work, deadlines and bills and due dates—had all fallen away.

The trailer park was moored in time. Heavy RVs sat with their tires half-sunken in dried mud, so deep it would take a tow truck to haul them out again. Dead flies caked the bonnets of dead engines. Crooked aerial antennas poked at the sky, trying to snag transmissions from stations that had gone off the air when Lionel was a kid.

Nothing moved here, and nothing moved on. The mud was too thick for that.

He kept to a broken pavement path and found Kayla Lambert's mobile home. "Mobile" was aspirational; its faded shell sat rooted on a foundation of splintered, moldy wood, and what might have been a trailer hitch was nothing but a broken hub of rust. The only thing sturdy about it was the lock on the door. Lionel glanced back over his shoulder. No one was outside, no one watching.

Didn't matter. Maddie was the one with the collection of lock picks, and she'd left before teaching him the trick. Kicking the door in would make too much noise. He considered his options, turning back to Lesson One.

Witches use what works. Okay, strip away the hocus-pocus, treat this like any other lead. How would I normally get inside?

The park's "management office" was a half-size camper sitting behind a tour bus on cinderblocks. The manager on duty, a kid in his early twenties who had never outgrown his teenage acne, held his place in an Economics 101 textbook with one curled finger. He looked at the twenty-dollar bill, pinned to Lionel's palm with his thumb, like it might bite him.

"Ten minutes," Lionel said.

"The police called ahead," the kid told him. "They, uh, said they'd be sending a detective over sometime today to take a look at the place. You know what she did, right? She tried to kill that rich dude."

No, Lionel thought, *I have no idea who she is. I just like paying bribes so I can wander through random people's homes.* He forced a pleasant smile and took a breath.

"Ten minutes," he said. "I'm in and I'm out. I go in empty-handed, and I leave the same way. I won't take anything but photographs."

"What if they show up while you're in there?"

"That's my problem."

"What if you touch something?" He fidgeted with his textbook. "You know. Fingerprints."

"Also my problem."

Least of his worries. Lionel spent years working the crime blotter before he got into the professional-skeptic game. He knew how investigations like this worked. Contrary to the cop shows on TV, most regional police departments didn't have the resources or time to fingerprint actual crime scenes, let alone run forensics on a mobile home where a perp might have hung her hat once.

The manager hesitated. Lionel waggled the bill at him.

"College is expensive," Lionel said. "Buy yourself a new textbook."

He looked down at the fat hardcover in his lap, then back to Lionel.

"This one cost two hundred dollars."

"Then buy yourself a pizza. You can still get a pizza for under twenty bucks, right?"

"Well, actually, I mean, the only really good pizza place around here is Delmonico's, and their medium pan starts at—"

"Kid, you're killing me here."

He took the money, eventually, and sent Lionel back across the park with a spare key on a plastic fob. Lionel kept one eye on the parking lot, watching for new arrivals in unmarked cars. A cop coming around "sometime today" could mean tomorrow afternoon or five minutes from now. He'd have to assume the worst and move fast.

He didn't need long to explore Kayla's life. There wasn't much of it, not here at least. She'd lived a stripped-down existence, small and spare. A framed photograph showed Kayla on a tropical beach—Hawaii, maybe—with a sunburned man, both of them lifting coconut drinks and beaming for the camera. A cheap gold wedding ring sat on the bedside table. One pillow on the bed, one side of the sheets rumpled, left unmade on the morning Kayla set out to die. Lionel studied the mobile home twice: once with his naked eyes, once through the viewfinder of his cell-phone camera, snapping pictures from every angle. More than once in his career, a photograph had shown him a clue he missed on first inspection.

A box of tarot cards—a classic Rider-Waite deck—sat out on the kitchenette counter. The old cardboard box was scuffed, yellow ink faded to bone-white along the flaps, obviously well used and well loved. Kayla had been reading the cards. For reasons she took to her grave and beyond, she'd left them out when she locked up for the last

A Time for Witches

time. It was a three-card spread: face up, side by side, next to the facedown deck.

I. The Magician. A man in white robes, draped in red, stood upon the first card and raised his ivory wand high. The tools of magic—a pentacle, a chalice, a sword, a rod—sat arrayed on a table beside him, and flowers bloomed at his feet. The card took Lionel back. Back to Manhattan, back to one long, bad night. Back to the first time he came face-to-face with Jimmy Sloane, the man who killed his mother. Jimmy wanted to know if Lionel had any experience with the tarot.

"*First card in the major arcana's called the Fool,*" Jimmy had explained in his folksy drawl. "*Now, the Fool is not a fool, not like we use the word. He's not stupid—he's new. Empty of experience, taking a fresh start and setting out on a journey. All the same, there's a crumbling cliff at his feet. He might be going on to great things, or he might just be going down. That's you. You're the Fool.*"

Lionel couldn't be insulted; he'd just had his eyes opened to magic, and everything felt new. The city air was raw on his skin and there were fresh wonders, fresh nightmares, down every alley.

"*Second card up, that's the Magician. A man of magic, strong in his powers. He knows things, and he can make things happen. A lot of people think that it's the same man on both cards. Sometimes he's drawn that way—depends on the deck. You follow?*"

"The Fool becomes the Magician," Lionel had replied.

"At the end of his journey." Jimmy contemplated his glass of bourbon. "If he doesn't fall off the cliff first."

Lionel looked to the second card in Kayla's spread. *Queen of Swords.* A regal woman sat upon a throne of ivory. She wore a cloak of clouds, upon a bright blue sky, and brandished a sword in one hand. Her other hand was lifted, poised in a gesture that might have been an invitation to approach. *Or a challenge*, Lionel thought, studying the cold confidence in the woman's expression. *Bring it on.*

The final card was labeled *VII. The Chariot*. A powerful man with flowing blond hair and laurels, clad in silver armor over black, stood in the driver's seat of a chariot. A canopy over his head bore images of a night sky and silver stars, counterpoint to the Queen of Swords' sky-cloak. Instead of horses, a pair of Egyptian sphinxes—one white, one black—pulled the noble knight to victory. Lionel could read it in the man's face: victory was the only outcome he'd settle for.

The voice of the homeless man in the doorway drifted back to Lionel: *"You better take care, son, and you better watch out for the Holy Roller."*

He didn't know what the cards meant, lined up like that. Wasn't sure if this was a winning hand or a losing one. He took another photograph.

The bathroom was so small he almost missed it. He squeezed into the nook and gave it a quick once-over, feeling the minutes ticking away. A tiny oval window gave an oblong view of the parking lot, and he scouted for any new arrivals before going back on the prowl. A shallow medicine cabinet hung over the sink; he opened it up, gaze drifting between prescription bottles. Zoloft, Luvox, Doxepin for sleepless nights…each bottle had a different doctor's name, and none of them were prescribed to Kayla. She had been shopping around, buying drugs secondhand, mixing the ingredients of her own medicinal cocktail.

Depression can lead to that, Lionel thought. *So can grief. The kind of grief that doesn't heal on its own.*

He closed the cabinet, the mirror swinging back into focus, and stared into a pair of eyes too blue to be real. Jimmy V. Sloane, traveling typewriter salesman, murderer, was standing in Lionel's reflection.

CHAPTER SIX

"You still ain't him, kid. You get that, right?"

On the other side of the glass, Jimmy Sloane stood in Lionel's place, still wearing the cream-colored Stetson hat he had died in.

"Him?" Lionel said.

Jimmy solemnly mimicked the pose on the tarot card, lifting one hand high.

"The Magician. You ain't him. 'A man of magic, strong in his powers'? You really think *any* of that defines you?"

"I didn't claim that it did."

"You're thinkin' it, though. Almost daring to hope. Because if you're the Magician, that means you're ready. Ready for the storm you know damn well is coming. And if you're not...well, you're just the Fool, same as always. And that cliff edge is real, real close. Maddie ain't gonna be here to catch you when you fall, not this time."

"Maybe I'm trying to catch her," Lionel countered.

Jimmy snorted.

"Why? So she can kick you to the curb again? You're like Charlie Brown with the goddamn football. Woman slips out of your bed in the middle of the night, stone cold *abandons* you without so much as a Dear John letter, and you're dropping everything to chase her across the country."

"I'm not sure that she did."

"Come again?"

"Abandon me," Lionel said. "Hekate gave her a mission. I know that much. It had something to do with her ex-husband. She didn't want me involved."

"Not hearin' a contradiction so far," Jimmy said.

"I don't think Maddie was trying to leave me. I think she was trying to protect me."

"By ghosting you? That's wishful thinking."

"No," Lionel said. "Because Maddie knows me. I would have wanted to go with her, no matter what we were up against. And if she said it was too dangerous, I would have dug my heels in twice as hard. I'm stubborn that way. The only way she could stop me from coming with her was by...well, doing exactly what she did."

Jimmy chewed that over.

"That's one possibility," he said. "Here's another. How are you gonna feel when you finally catch up to her and she tells you she wasn't trying to protect you at all, she just wants you out of her life for good? How are you gonna feel when she says you're her *ex*-boyfriend, one of a long, long line of exes who she dumped the exact same way she did your sorry ass, and you're just the only one too dumb to take a hint?"

Even at his most optimistic, Maddie's bloody-teared confession was never far from his memories. The night she tried to push him away. The night he took the knife from her trembling hand and eased her back to bed, chasing her ghosts away until the sunrise.

"*You know what happens next? You wake up one morning,*

and I'm gone. I'm just...I'm just gone. Because I always leave."

"I don't have time to get into pointless arguments with dead assholes," Lionel said.

"Nice deflection, kid. Does it make the truth any easier to swallow?"

A car door slammed. Lionel's head turned, gaze jerking to the oblong window. A police cruiser had pulled into the lot, and two uniforms were getting out, heading this way.

He looked back to the mirror. His own reflection stood in the glass, silent and haunted.

~~

Lionel slipped out of the park, passing the spare keys back to the manager just ahead of the cops who were coming to pick them up. They were making their way into the trailer as he pulled out of the lot.

He had to focus. He could do the next bit of legwork from the motel room, all he needed was his laptop and an internet connection, but he felt claustrophobic just thinking about it. Lionel drove to the next town over, found a big, airy coffee shop down the block from a college campus, and handed over seven bucks for a steaming mug of black coffee and the Wi-Fi password.

One fact led to another. There was a single pillow on Kayla's bed. She had a photo of a man on her bedside table, a wedding ring, tangible echoes of a past life when two people slept side by side. She had a medicine cabinet full of antidepressants, all of them prescribed to strangers, suggesting she was self-medicating to make her pain go away. And she accused Cordell Spears of murder.

Natural next questions: who was the man in the photograph, and was he still breathing?

Another dive into the journalistic databases, care of his gray-market credentials, turned up a marriage certificate. Then a death certificate. Jurgen Lambert had been Kayla's husband of three years. Wedding-reception pictures, courtesy of a niece's Instagram page, confirmed he was the man in the frame on the bedside table.

Jurgen was an archaeologist, with his doctorate in linguistics. He had worked as a field researcher with WSP's Cultural Heritage Program, written guidance papers for an upcoming Harvard-backed excavation in the Sudan, and then landed the starring role of his career, heading up something called the New Cyclades Century Project.

His browser chugged, a photo slowly downloading over the spotty wireless connection. The man on the right was Jurgen, a stout Dutchman with a nicotine-stained smile and a liver spot on one side of his nose. The man on the left, eagerly pumping his hand, was Cordell Spears.

"The New Cyclades Century Project," Lionel murmured, "entirely funded by generous donations from Cordell Spears and the Spears Biomedical Charitable Foundation."

A string of pieces in archeology review journals, trailing the project's work over the past two years, filled in the blanks. They'd found a mother lode of pristine and preserved artifacts. That cache came to the States in triumph as a traveling museum exhibition, the first leg of a global tour in the making: *Treasures of the Mycenaean World*. Her appearance at the museum hadn't been random chance; Kayla had intended to kill Cordell Spears in the heart of her husband's crowning glory.

Not that he was here to celebrate the win. The treasures came home; Jurgen never did. Lionel found his final bow at the bottom of a Greek newspaper's obituary column,

A Time for Witches

translated by machine. That lead pointed the way to a couple of articles that filled in more of the picture. Jurgen was out alone—late, said one reporter, just before dawn, said another—maybe he was drunk, maybe he was jogging, in a stretch of town that both writers implied was a bad place for foreign tourists to explore without a guide. The one thing everyone agreed upon was that a street sweeper found him facedown in an alley. His wallet and phone were never recovered.

A connection was missing. Lionel opened a notebook app, to get his thoughts in order, and stared at the flashing cursor.

There was a straight line between Kayla Lambert, her husband, and Cordell Spears. Jurgen died on an expedition funded by Cordell. Kayla accused Cordell of being a murderer and came bearing a flask—presumably with something seriously nasty inside—bearing the name of Tisiphone, the Fury in charge of punishing killers.

It all looked solid on the surface, but Lionel didn't need to set one foot on that foundation to know it was riddled with holes. Nothing drew a direct thread between Cordell and the murder; it looked like Jurgen had been killed by a mugger when he wouldn't give up his wallet. Lionel knew perfectly well that a contract hit could be disguised as a random street crime, but all he had was a hypothesis with no actual evidence to back it up. Did Kayla? Or was she running on empty hunches too, with grief in the driver's seat?

He wasn't entirely sure Cordell was the villain of this story. He wasn't sure there was a villain at all. All he knew for certain was that Kayla and Maddie had crossed paths at some point, and Maddie had given her that flask.

No, he thought, *bad reporter.* He didn't know that at all. He *wanted* it to be true, because that meant he was hot on Maddie's trail. But the woman was literally immortal; she could have painted that flask anytime, anywhere, forgotten it, maybe lost it. It might have sat in a chest in someone's attic or been buried in a building's foundation for a hundred years before making its way to Kayla's hand.

But he didn't think so. His intuition told him there were more connections here, links he hadn't found yet. He'd keep digging. He'd reached the limit of what he could accomplish with a keyboard, though: it was time to pound the pavement and knock on doors. *I'll work the vic,* he thought. *First thing tomorrow morning, I'll dig into Jurgen's life. Then his family and coworkers. Somebody had to have been close to him, maybe closer than his own wife. And if he died for anything bigger than a stolen wallet, somebody out there knows the reason why.*

~~

The sun was starting to simmer down when Lionel returned to the motel. Its dying rays cast long, rippling fingers over the cornfield across the highway, mingling with a dry and dusty wind.

The motel had drawn new clientele. An eighteen-wheeler's air brakes let out a disgruntled hiss as the tractor rolled to a stop along the outer curve of the lot, flush to the curb. The trailer was robin's-egg blue with a long yellow stripe and a shipping company's name lettered in side-by-side English and Chinese. Lionel had never heard of the outfit. He had a fresh distraction, rolling in right behind him, sliding into the open space four doors down from his.

Bouncy pop metal blared from the wide-open sides of a

A Time for Witches

Jeep Wrangler. The Wrangler was caked with road dust and dried mud, a ride built for the open road. California plates. *And California girls*, Lionel thought, shifting his car into park and glancing out the side window. The driver of the Jeep hopped out. She was a tiny thing, peering through garish green plastic sunglasses that were bigger than she was, her straw-blond hair dyed with snow-cone streaks of blue and scarlet. Two more young women followed in her wake. They couldn't have been more than twenty, dressed for summer in halter tops and cut-off jeans. One circled around to grab a beer cooler from the back of the Jeep; the other, her hair worn in Lolita-esque pigtails, suckled a lollipop while she surveyed the motel lot.

Lionel chuckled to himself as he got out. *All right, that's enough looking for you. Eyes forward and keep moving.* Even if he wasn't seeing someone at the moment—technically—he knew when he was out of his league. *And way too old to be messing with college girls*, he thought.

The trucker was older than Lionel, in his forties with wind-burned cheeks and a gap-toothed smile, but he fired his shot anyway as he ambled across the lot. "Hey, sweet things! Looks like we're gonna be neighbors tonight. Any of y'all get lonely, come and knock on my door."

The blonde in the sunglasses smiled back, pushing her hip out to one side to strike a pose, and leaned forward as she gracefully flipped her middle finger at him. Lionel snickered.

He was standing at his door on the far end of the motel, jiggling his key in the stubborn lock, when a prickling sensation ran down the back of his neck. He glanced left.

The girl with the pigtails was staring at him. She eyed

him, standing motionless beside the Jeep, as her tongue played over the curve of her hypnotic-swirl lollipop. The other passenger—the tallest of the three, with coltish legs, vintage sneakers, and a pair of old headphones draped around her neck—paused with the beer cooler in her hands. She followed her friend's eyes, spotting Lionel, and asked a question.

Lionel read her lips from across the lot. One word in response: "*Him*."

Then she turned, breaking his line of sight, and said something else. Both girls broke into hysterical laughter, waving the blonde over, sharing the joke.

The door finally relented, opening wide, and Lionel headed inside.

CHAPTER SEVEN

Lionel was a bloodhound when he got going; he couldn't stop the hunt, and it wasn't like he had anything else to do until morning. He set his laptop up, plugged in the charger so it could match his own energy, and kept digging. Around seven, his stomach started to growl. *Right. Food.* He vaguely remembered a fast-food place down the road that served salads. He made it as far as the door, put his hand to the knob...then stopped.

He had a couple of meal bars in his suitcase. Allegedly they were peanut-butter flavored, with a hearty dose of "stale marshmallow" and "chalk" thrown in for good measure. But one bar and a plastic cup of tap water got the job done, quieting the hunger and keeping him fueled. He wasn't sure why he didn't leave. It just felt like the wrong choice.

Not that sticking around got him anywhere. He couldn't work on Jurgen Lambert's side of the equation until morning, so he turned his eye to Jurgen's legacy. *Treasures of the Mycenaean World* was an odd duck. The Griffith was a big museum, but it was still nestled in the heart of Indiana, and Chicago's Field Museum—twice as big, four times the patronage—was only a couple of hours' drive from here. The "tour" itself was just a handful of quick stopovers as the collection of artifacts headed east, for a big official debut at the Metropolitan Museum of Art.

New York, Lionel thought. *Everything comes back to New York.*

And it wasn't meant to, originally. He kept running across cancellations, last-minute changes, a couple of stray message-board posts on an archeology forum, the scraps building a picture. The charity board sponsoring the exhibition had laid plans for a yearlong, coast-to-coast tour, starting in LA and ending in Manhattan. Then, at the last minute, everything changed.

Cordell stepped in. Or his money did. The new grand debut coincided with his own personal charity gala.

"What's the biggest story of the season? What's *the* social event, the hottest ticket?" Cordell asked, a video clip rolling on Lionel's screen. He was casual in a blazer over a white T-shirt and blue jeans, sitting on an interview set. "The Met Gala. Biggest fundraiser of the year. Know how much it costs to get in? Thirty-five thousand dollars. Look, I've got nothing against the Gala—I have a seat on the Met's board of trustees, I've been a supporter for over a decade. But at the end of the day, it's a party for celebrities only."

The interviewer, a thin-faced woman with a notepad balanced on her knee, hung on his every word. "And your response is...?"

"The Gala for the People. I wanted to call it 'Party for the People,' but the money guys told me I had to make it sound a little more highbrow. Picture this: New York City, Central Park. The permits just came through; we've got the park, we've got a soundstage, and we've got a lineup

A Time for Witches

of musical acts, presenters, and special surprise guests you won't believe. And every last one of them is donating their time and talent to make this happen. The Spears Foundation is working hand in hand with area food banks and homeless shelters to make this the biggest charity event in New York history."

"It wouldn't be the first time you've made history," she pointed out.

He chuckled into his hand and shook his head.

"You're going to make me blush, Marsha. Look, some people are called to step up, some people are called to give more than others, and I've been blessed with the power to do just that. But this event isn't about me: it's about helping the hungry, stretching out a hand to your neighbors in need, and enjoying one hell of a great party. A minimum ten-dollar donation gets you in—of course, more is appreciated if you're in a position to give—and we'll keep the festivities going until the NYPD kicks us out. And not to brag, but the police commissioner is a friend of mine, so we *might* have a little wiggle room there."

She checked her pad. "And I understand the event is going to be live-streamed?"

"Absolutely. If you can't make it in person, get online and crank your speakers up. We're even partnering with Facebook and Oculus to bring in some hot new virtual-reality camera technology. Just pop your cyber-goggles on, and it'll feel like you're standing right next to the stage."

Cordell shifted in his chair. He played straight to the camera, as if he was staring into Lionel's eyes.

"I'm throwing a party for the whole world," he said. "And I want you to come."

Lionel stopped the playback. The video froze on Cordell's confident smile.

Two events—the artifact exhibit and the 'Gala for the People'—in the same place, same weekend. No connection between the two, not that he could draw. *But Cordell wants that exhibit in New York on the same night as his party in the park*, Lionel thought. *Could just be convenience, if he's making another speech like he tried to at the Griffith, but the guy probably owns a small fleet of helicopters and private jets. Getting around isn't a problem for him.*

And through it all, Cordell stubbornly refused to turn into a bad guy. No scandals, no sinister plots, no whispers of corruption. The more he read about him, the more Lionel wanted to have a drink with the man. *Still don't trust his hair*, he thought, shutting down the laptop. But he knew he was clinging to his cynicism out of old, stubborn habit. It was looking more and more like Jurgen had been the victim of a random crime, wrong place, wrong time, and his grieving widow had turned her fury on the man whose money sent him overseas in the first place.

The mystery would keep until morning. His eyelids were getting heavy, and the bed was calling to him, over-starched sheets and all. He clicked off the light and undressed on his way to the mattress.

He had been lying there for a while, floating in the dark, drifting in and out around the edges of a deep sleep, when someone knocked on the door.

Lionel's eyes snapped open. The crimson numbers of the bedside clock hovered in the gloom: it was 1:14 in the morning.

Another knock. He tossed back the covers, got up, and lightly padded to the door, craning his neck to check the peephole. It was the Jeep driver, the tiny blonde with the snow-cone streaks in her hair. She stood in a puddle of light on the other side of the fish-eye lens, hands cupped behind her back and one knee bent, shifting her hips from side to side as she waited for a reply.

"Hello?" Lionel called out. He wasn't sure what else to say, under the circumstances.

"Hey." Her muffled voice drifted through the door, and she gave the peephole a perky smile. "Me and my girlfriends are partying, thought you might want to join us. We've got beer, a little coke, some shrooms. I mean, you seemed cool, so I thought I'd ask."

He had to admit it wasn't the weirdest random invitation he'd ever gotten, but it was up there.

"Uh, sorry," he called back. "I've got to be up really early in the morning. I appreciate the offer, though."

"Aw. Bummer. You're kinda cute, you know? You've got that scruffy-hot college professor thing going on. It works for you. You sure you can't come over for just a few minutes? One beer."

"Sorry. Really, I can't."

She flashed a peace sign at the peephole. "You're missing out, professor."

He pulled away, turning to go back to bed, when she spoke up again.

"My girlfriend Mindy thinks you're hot. She's mostly into girls, but she gets with guys sometimes. She'll suck your dick if you want."

Lionel froze. He wasn't sure he'd heard her right.

"Excuse me?"

"I said," she repeated, "she'll *suck*. Your *dick*. Come on. Just open the door, and we can have some fun."

He looked through the peephole, one last time. Her voice was still cheerful, but she wasn't smiling anymore. And now he noticed the shadow off to her left, a dark smudge at the edge of the light. She wasn't standing out there alone.

"Open the door, professor. Open up and let us in. *Now*."

He slowly eased backward, the paper-thin carpet rasping against the soles of his feet. He didn't answer her, his voice locked by a surge of fight-or-flight adrenaline that turned his muscles to cords of frozen steel.

Lionel knew that there were things in this world that only masqueraded as human. He had long, ragged scars—one just above his left nipple, one along his forearm—from the teeth of the Manhattan ghouls who had tried to eat him alive. He didn't think the California girls were ghouls; he didn't know *what* they were, only that everything about this situation was wrong.

The old Lionel would have guessed they were itinerant thieves working a classic honeypot scam, angling to rob him blind. Experience and instinct told him that they were after more than his wallet. Opening that door would be the last thing he ever did.

He stood there, bracing for a fight in case they tried to bash it down. They gave him nothing but silence. He looked to the clock, scarlet numbers floating in the dark. Two minutes passed. Three. Four.

He edged back to the door and checked the peephole. The girl was gone.

Lionel grabbed the table's edge with both hands and hauled it across the carpet, propping it in front of the door. A lousy barricade, but it would buy him a little extra time if they came back. He got back into bed, eventually, and sank into a fitful sleep.

~~

Lionel woke to sun and sameness, the rattle of the AC unit, the grind of wheels on the highway, as if last night's strange encounter was nothing but a dream. He half doubted his own memories. All the same, he left the table blockade in place and showered fast, skipping his morning shave. He wanted to be gone, and put some serious miles behind him, before the next sunset. He didn't think the California girls would try to chase him down—they'd given up and gone away last night, after all—but he didn't feel like tempting fate.

He made plans while he tossed balled-up socks into his rolling suitcase. He could spend the morning in the area, tracking down anyone who might have been tight with Jurgen Lambert. Around lunchtime he'd pick a direction to drive in, leaving it to the flip of a coin if nothing else guided his path, and start hunting for a new motel. Ideally a place like this one, where they didn't demand ID and the night clerk was willing to accept a "cash deposit" in lieu of a credit card. Cash-only motels were getting harder and harder to find, but he was trying not to leave too much of a paper trail. The people who really needed to find him already knew how to get in touch.

A gust of warm wind kissed his cheeks as he stepped outside, tugging his suitcase behind him. It was a new day, a dry one, and the roadside air smelled like hot tar and diesel. A construction crew was at work down the highway, one lane blocked by a mixer truck, yellow-vested workers taking jackhammers to the old asphalt.

The big rig was still there, parked where the trucker left it last night, but the Jeep was gone. The occupants had taken off in a hurry, judging from the fresh black tire marks where they'd pulled a doughnut in the heart of the parking lot. More black streaks marred the curve at the mouth of the lot; it looked like they'd taken a hard right turn.

Then I'll go left, Lionel thought. Easy decision. He tossed his luggage in the trunk and strolled toward the office, looking to turn his key in.

He stopped. The door to room 6, right next door to his, was open. Just a crack.

CHAPTER EIGHT

Lionel told himself that this wasn't his business. He almost kept walking. Instead, he put his fingertips to the warm, grainy wood and gave the door a gentle push.

The television was on, tuned to a dead channel. Someone had poured a jar of strawberry jam over the screen, rivulets rolling down, the congealing wet sheet turning the bright blue of the screen sickly and pale.

Then the stench hit him, and bile surged from the pit of Lionel's throat. Not strawberry. Not jam. The carpet was sodden, a red swamp gathering black flies. One buzzed past Lionel's ear, slipping through the open doorway to join the feast. There were bits of torn clothing scattered across the floor. Bits of torn skin. A single, splintered rib bone.

The rest of the trucker was on the bed. Maybe. Lionel couldn't be sure, couldn't make sense of the jigsaw puzzle they'd made of him, and he felt like he was falling backward even as he stood perfectly still. *That's a leg with a hand on the end of it. How did they attach his hand to the stump of his leg—*

Someone had propped the trucker's head up on a pillow, the brim of his hat slung low over his eyeless, toothless face, and positioned it to face the doorway. Twin slices along the lips gave the head a permanent grin.

They wanted someone to see this, he thought. *They thought it would be funny—*

No.

Not "someone." They wanted me to see it.

He pulled the door shut, leaving the flies to their work. He wiped the doorknob with the side of his sleeve.

Under normal circumstances he'd be dialing 911, telling the cops everything he'd seen since last night, and sitting down with a sketch artist. If he thought he was dealing with a trio of mundane, *human* thrill killers, he would have done just that. He knew better.

Magic had brought him here, had guided his footsteps since he left Montauk. Someone—Hekate, the Fates, he wasn't sure—wanted Lionel in this exact spot. He only knew one thing for certain, down in his gut: bringing outsiders into the mix would just get them killed. They couldn't handle something like this.

Which didn't mean he could handle it, either.

Maddie would know, he thought, trying to keep his shoulders from clenching as he approached the front office. She'd know what those things were, and she'd know how to stop them. Probably take them out with one hand tied behind her back.

But Maddie wasn't here. He was.

He didn't recognize the daytime clerk behind the counter. He didn't tell her about room 6. He just handed over his keys and told her he was checking out. She rattled a few keys on her desktop computer and gave him a customer-service smile.

"And if you enjoyed your stay here," she added, reading

a rote script by memory, "we'd appreciate a positive review on Yelp."

I don't think that's going to help, he thought.

They had an old-style sign-in book on the desk. He'd signed it as "Walter Winchell," and the night clerk—the one who had taken a twenty-buck bribe to forget about the customary credit-card deposit—hadn't batted an eyelash. Lionel leaned over and gave it a look. The blond pixie had signed in last night, leaving her name in a fluttery, glitter-gel cursive right under his.

"Nikki Manson." It was a made-up moniker for a punk rocker, or a late-night horror movie hostess. At least he had a name to know her by now, even a fake one. And she had his.

All the more reason to go full-speed in the other direction, he told himself.

Maddie would know how to handle this. And he was already on her trail. If she'd given that clay flask to Kayla, he was *close*. He was maybe a day behind her, maybe even less. All he had to do was close the distance and catch up to her.

And in the meantime, he thought, crossing the parking lot and reaching for his car keys, *"Nikki Manson" and her two pals can find another motel and another lonely trucker come sundown and pull a repeat performance.*

He got into the driver's seat. Sitting there, staring at the exit from the parking lot, the fading black tire streaks, he had a decision to make: left or right?

This couldn't wait. They'd kill again. He didn't know how he knew it, but he knew, deep in his gut. The authorities wouldn't be able to stop them. This was all on him now.

So he'd find them. He'd find them, and—

Lionel drummed his fingers on the steering wheel.

"Who the hell do I think I'm kidding?" he asked out loud. Nobody answered him. He wasn't sure what he'd expected.

And he wasn't sure what he was supposed to do. The only force offering him any guidance on this road trip was the ghost of Jimmy Sloane, and he was fairly sure that had been a hallucination. Real or not, the dead man wasn't making an encore appearance.

He didn't need to. Lionel still heard him, loud and clear: "*You still ain't him, kid. You're just the Fool, same as always.*"

"All right," he said, "let's break it down. These are...some kind of monsters. And I don't know what kind. And I don't know what can hurt them. Or if anything can hurt them. Maddie will know, and I'm already right behind her. I just...keep doing what I'm doing, stay the course, and we'll fix this together."

He didn't speak the counterpoint out loud: *And if I do that, somebody is going to die tonight.*

He was barely a witch. He still didn't feel comfortable using the word, let alone embracing the mantle. He knew one really potent spell for banishing death energy, which had come in handy...once, and didn't work on anything living. He had a few tricks, a couple of charms. The war magic he'd learned for his battle with Jimmy Sloane, taught to him in the heart of a frozen rain and buried in a magically sealed memory, had slipped back below the skin of his mind during his recovery in the hospital. It was inside him, he *knew* it was, but it was like trying to grasp the fine details of a half-forgotten dream.

A Time for Witches

"And none of that matters," he said. He fired up the engine.

None of it mattered because that Jeep was on its way to another motel and another victim, and he was the only person in a position to try to make a difference. Paramedics didn't get to choose which accidents to stop for, and ER surgeons didn't get to choose which lives to save. That was the job they chose. The one they signed up for.

Just like Lionel had chosen this one, signing his name and his soul on Hekate's dotted line. This was a witch's work. Didn't matter if he was ready. Didn't matter if he could win. He still had to try.

Back when you were a journalist, every time you jumped in and got involved like this, you got your ass kicked.

He met his eyes in the rearview mirror.

"Yeah," he said, "but I always got a great story out of it."

He followed the tire marks, already fading to ghostly scuffs, and went on the hunt.

~~

Lionel drove like he'd been driving since Montauk: fueled by intuition and caffeine, vision sharp, mind open, trying to tune his brain like a radio on a deep country road. There was a frequency here, a station that would play loud and clear if only he could find it. He tried letting his eyes slip out of focus, to pull the psychic caul down and see the world the way Maddie had taught him.

He'd seen a flash of it, back at the motel. The only thing thicker than the blood in room 6 was the violent purple light splattered across the shreds of skin and bone, clinging like a quick-growing mold. Death energy.

He saw it out here, too. Drips, and streaks, and splashes

on the black asphalt. Fresh. *It's them*, he thought. *Either they took a piece of the trucker as a souvenir, or they didn't clean up after they tore him apart.*

He was literally tracking them by the blood on their hands. But the spots were fewer and farther apart, the trail drying up as the sun rose high. He passed one off-ramp, then an interchange, and now he wasn't sure if he was still on the right road.

His quarry helped him out. He saw a violet bloom in the distance, big as a man, and his stomach clenched. He held his breath until the body came into sight, tossed off to the side of the road. Not a human. A young deer, its antlers just fuzzy buds on its broken skull, had picked the wrong time to cross the road. Lionel pulled over, sliding onto the shoulder, and stopped the car a short walk from the remains.

It smelled like an open-air sewer. The wind shifted as he got out, washing over the roadkill and hitting him with the full-on stench of torn intestines and raw wet meat. The deer's belly was open, and it lay in a puddle of its own spilled guts.

They'd been driving fast. The crumpled front license plate, *California* in lipstick red on white, lay a few feet away amid the scattered shards of a broken headlight. No other signs of damage. The accident might have slowed them down a little, but it didn't stop them.

He turned to go.

The deer kicked.

He spun, catching the movement in the corner of his eye, seeing one matted hoof jerk. Now it lay perfectly still, same as it was a moment ago.

It's dead, he thought. *Might have been a...what's it called, when dead animals have muscle spasms?* He couldn't remember the word for it. He watched the carcass, just in case. It didn't move again.

But he didn't feel alone out here. Death and the dead had been dogging his footsteps since he chose to chase after Madison, and he couldn't shake the feeling that something was trying to get his attention. He just had to listen. Find the frequency.

He scooped up the license plate, bent double in one corner, flecked with dried blood. He stood over the deer and held the plate in front of its glassy eyes.

"Show me," he said.

Dead bodies don't bleed. He knew that much. But this one did.

A thin ruby trickle seeped from under the deer's fallen hoof. And rolled, drawing a line across the asphalt. It followed the bumps along the rough surface, guttering left, then hard left, then drawing a curving diagonal in the other direction. Then it stopped, the trail of blood ending an inch from the toe of Lionel's shoe.

Hot wind ruffled his hair as he circled the line of blood, studying it. He thought it might spell something out if he read it from the right angle, but it hadn't been drawing letters. Just a single hard line, still and congealing now, that bent and curved along its journey.

Bending, but still heading in one direction. Almost like...

He took his phone out. Two finger taps brought up Google Maps, and he pinched the screen to zero in. The deer blood was a trail, a trail that perfectly matched the road he was standing on. Lionel traced it along the screen. The first bend matched an off-ramp, two miles ahead.

Then another turn, and the long curving bend mapped onto a suburban boulevard.

He knew where they were going.

CHAPTER NINE

A Frisbee sailed through the air, slicing a lazy arc under the lush green boughs. Boynton Park was a little wedge of nature in the heartland, a sleepy park in a sleepy three-street town. Families came out to soak up the weekend sun, tossing balls or laying out picnic blankets, and a squad of sweaty-faced teenagers in the yellow-and-green uniforms of the local high school soccer team were racing torturous laps around the rolling lawns.

Not the kind of place you'd expect to find a monster. And yet, there one was.

Lionel had just found a place to park when he spotted her. The one in pigtails, no sign of her friends, emerging from a public restroom at the edge of the green. He kept his distance, circling behind a row of cars, trying to stay out of her line of sight.

A little boy, maybe four or five years old, went tearing across the park with his arms pinwheeling. He nearly collided with her, jolting to an ungainly stop at the last second and falling onto his butt. She leaned over him. Lionel's stomach clenched. He started to move, closing the distance, preparing to charge and tackle her if he had to.

She beamed, pulling the boy to his feet, then ruffled his hair with an affectionate pat. Lionel stayed back. Holding his breath, uncertain. She said something to the kid—he couldn't make it out from there—and pointed to where his parents were having a picnic. He turned and ran back to his family.

Pigtails watched him go. Then she crossed the lawn, strolling without a care in the world, and rejoined her friends. The three of them were having a picnic of their own, sitting out on a checkered blanket with an antique wicker basket and a spread of foil-wrapped sandwiches. The tiny blonde opened a screw-cap bottle of cheap merlot and splashed dollops of red into a trio of plastic cups. The women toasted, laughing, while Lionel watched from the shade of a leaning oak tree.

No one would guess, looking at them, that they'd spent their night committing a brutal murder. There was something perverse about this, watching them giggle and make small talk over a picnic lunch, that turned Lionel's stomach sour.

Well, I'm here, he thought. *Mission accomplished. Now what?*

He had never stopped being a reporter, not really, probably never would. He needed information, hard facts. The more he knew—starting with figuring out what they were, under their human disguises—the closer he'd be to stopping them. His first instinct was to go straight for the primary source. He could walk up and introduce himself, and see if they felt like talking.

They might feel like killing, too, but Lionel had a hunch that he was safe in public. The monsters he'd met so far had all kept their violence hidden behind closed doors;

a sleeping world was easier to hunt in. He even had credentials, just like his old press badge. The Sisterhood of New Amsterdam might be seven hundred miles away, but dropping their name could buy him a little respect.

Or they might just slit his throat and leave him bleeding out on their picnic blanket.

Leap of faith. The alternative was letting them finish their lunch, get back in their Jeep, and go kill again. So Lionel weighed his odds and decided he was okay with the risk. He steeled himself and got ready.

Two steps from his patch of shade, and a furtive movement turned his head. Bushes rustled, and a shadow darted behind a squat tree trunk. He figured it was another kid playing around, or one of the soccer players stealing a break from the team's marathon run. Then he saw a blink-fast glint of sunlight, gleaming off a telephoto lens.

Lionel took the long way around, sticking to the low part of the green, moving from tree to tree along the outskirts of the park until the creeper was dead ahead. He was crouched with his back turned, fixated on the viewfinder of his black Nikon camera. *D750*, Lionel thought. *That's a professional's model. Not cheap.* The elongated screw-on lens was made for long-distance surveillance, and as far as Lionel could tell, he was documenting every move the killers on the picnic blanket made.

He stood behind the photographer and cleared his throat. "Get any juicy pictures?"

The man jumped up, wild-eyed, and pressed his back to the tree. The camera dangled from a nylon lanyard around his neck, but he still gripped it with both hands, protecting it like it was his baby. He had wire-bristle hair and a scraggly attempt at a mustache.

"Public place, man! I got every right to shoot here."

Given his gear, Lionel had a hunch. He also had a few of his old business cards in his wallet, kept on hand in case he needed a little leverage. He fished one out and handed it over.

"It's cool," he said. "We're birds of a feather."

The photographer's beady eyes flicked between Lionel's face and the crisp black print on the card.

"Channel Seven. Nice gig. Yeah. Page. I heard of you. Didn't you write a book or something?"

"Or something." Lionel nodded toward the rolling green. "You picked a dangerous subject."

"The subject picked me. And I can handle myself. I've been following these chicks for two weeks now. They haven't spotted me yet. They aren't that bright."

"You know they murder people, right?"

He pocketed the card and waggled his hand from side to side.

"The evidence I've seen is circumstantial at best. My guess is they've got a stalker. Big guy. Sexually frustrated serial killer type. He follows 'em, jerks his pud in the bushes, and when he can't get off he finds a random vic to vent his rage on."

"What makes you say that?"

"Because I lost my breakfast at a crime scene over in Gary last week. Paid a C-note to this rookie to slip me past the police cordon. Let's just say that three college chicks don't have the physical strength to do what was done to that poor bastard. And women don't kill like that, doesn't fit the profile. Hell, even Aileen Wuornos used a gun."

The photographer eyed him again, with fresh suspicion. "You're a long way from Chicago. What's your angle?"

"Field research, for a new book. Special project."

Something behind the photographer's eyes shifted, his expression changing, flickering through a handful of possibilities. A little yearning, a little fear. When he spoke again his voice was lower, a library hush, like they were a pair of monks sharing a mystic secret.

"Do you speak the language?"

Lionel tilted his head. "The language?"

"The road language. The highway talk. That's how you found them, right? You're like me." He reached up, touching one finger to the side of his forehead. "You've got the eyes. You're awake. Like me."

Lionel kept his tone noncommittal but curious. "I've been some places, and I've seen some things. Was that what you meant, when you said the subject chose you?"

He pursed his lips. Debating, waffling. Then he nodded back over his shoulder.

"You need to come with me. My studio. It's an hour away, maybe an hour fifteen. People don't get it, they don't get what I'm doing, what I'm working on. Hell, my girlfriend dumped me, my friends think I'm crazy. I'm not crazy. You're—you're the first person I've seen since this all started who has the eyes."

Lionel had no idea what the "road language" was, but he was pretty sure the photographer was right about one thing. He wasn't crazy. *Guy looks like he had a head-on collision with the real world, just like I did in New York. Except nobody was around to explain things to him.*

He felt for him, but he still shook his head. "I can't leave. I can't lose sight of *them*."

"What, the college chicks? Brother, I told you, I've been following them for two weeks. They can't get away from me, not for more than an hour or two. Come to my studio, let me show you what I've got. And if you're interested in them, you *want* what I've got. When we're done, I'll put you right back on their trail, no sweat."

Lionel folded his arms. "How?"

"I got tricks. C'mon. Are you parked close? You can follow my car. Just...give me one hour of your time, okay? One hour. I just..." His scraggly mustache twisted as he scrunched up his lips. "I need somebody to believe me. Please."

Leap of faith.

"Okay," Lionel said.

The photographer thrust out his hand, eager as a puppy. "I'm Bill."

"Hi, Bill."

CHAPTER TEN

The photographer led him north on I-65, up into the heart of Gary, Indiana. A chemical tang hung over the fallen steel town like a cloud, seeping through Lionel's car windows, leaving faint black flecks on his windshield. The color green became a distant memory. He wove around potholes on roads that hadn't been serviced for a decade, past vacant lots and fields of wilted brown grass where homes once stood. Abandoned houses slouched and sank, their gray and rotting bones exposed under peeled paint, slowly swallowed by the barren earth.

There were spirits here. He thought he saw one, flitting behind a boarded-up window.

At the end of the road, Lionel nuzzled his car up to the curb, beside the husk of a caved-in tree. Tiny insects roiled inside the dead tree's belly, scavenging the marrow. He wasn't sure what this place was, originally. Not a house; it was long and narrow, cinder blocks coated in eggshell white with rectangles of red paint here and there for no apparent purpose. The windows were grimy scalloped glass, shot through with cracks.

Bill waved him around the back. A pair of heavy-duty

padlocks secured the rear delivery door, and he fumbled with a ring of keys.

"I don't like to be out here in the open for too long," he said. "I'm technically not paying rent on this place."

"You're squatting?"

The photographer shrugged. "I like to think of it as homesteading."

Inside the doorway, he rushed to kindle a pair of battery-powered lanterns. Hard white light shone across an abandoned storefront. Hot plates, sacks of groceries, a clutter of professional cameras, and a couple of mismatched backpacks had replaced the sales displays along the dusty counters, and the floor was a ragged patchwork of torn-up linoleum. Bill had an air mattress in one corner of the room, raised above the dirty floor on a pair of scavenged wooden pallets, and a sleeping bag on top of that.

And then there were the pictures.

Twine, like laundry lines, hung in bending arcs from every corner of the room. The lines were strung with photographs, dangling from clothespins. Hundreds of them. Hundreds upon hundreds, a forest of captured moments. Lionel had to duck under them as he followed in Bill's wake, navigating a maze of zigzagging lines and glossy snapshots.

"I needed a place with a basement, see," Bill told him. "For my darkroom. And film's not cheap."

"Don't you use a D750? Isn't that a digital camera?"

Bill slapped his palm on a sales counter in passing, swerving around it, sending a photograph line waving like a curtain.

"I use everything. Digital, film, I got a D750, I got an

F4S. Look at this—" He scooped up a vintage camera from the counter, a tall dirt-brown plastic box with a four-shot flashbulb mounted on top. "Kodamatic instant camera. Original, in perfect working condition. You have no idea how many thrift stores I had to hunt through just to find this baby. See, photography—you're capturing a moment in time. Freezing it. Stealing it. And some things don't want to be captured. So you've got to be sneaky, mix things up, change your technique."

"Tell me about the road language," Lionel said.

Bill led him under a low-hanging string of Polaroids and down a row of eight-by-ten glossies. Lionel eyed them in passing. Parks, parking lots, rest stops along anonymous highways. A few crowd photos, snapped with a telephoto lens. He didn't see the three young women, or their Jeep, in any of them.

"I used to work for TMZ," Bill said. "I was on assignment, chasing this celebrity who had a thing for anonymous sex in public bathrooms."

"Paparazzi. We hated you guys over at Channel Seven."

"We hate ourselves. So there I was, following this heartthrob singer—whose name you would know well, trust me—while he's wearing this ridiculous disguise and trying to get a little strange in a park toilet. And I'm lying in wait, with nothing to do but read the graffiti on the wall."

Graffiti. That's what he'd captured, in this stretch of the forest of pictures. Stall walls, scratched and painted brick, sheets of wooden laminate scarred by penknives and Sharpies.

"I'd been to five different bathrooms that day, chasing this dude's quest for oral gratification. And I'm squatting there, camera in hand, and it just..." Bill stared up at the photographs, searching for the words. "I saw it. I saw the pattern. Look. Look at this."

"'Here I sit, all brokenhearted, came to—'" Lionel read aloud. "Uh, yeah, I've heard this one before."

"No. Look." Bill reached up and poked at the picture, his fingertip making the line of photos dance. "This one. Stick figure, sitting in an outhouse. I saw that...here. Two photos down. Almost the same, but not. In this one, the stick man has one arm, raised up. In this one, stick man has two arms, both pointing down and to the left. Now look at the limerick: not the words, the *letters*. The *I*, the *l*s, the spurs of the *k*. They bend in different directions. That's not how a normal person writes letters. You see a *consistent* tilt, and that's not what this is."

Lionel saw it now, too. A deliberate sequence hidden in plain sight.

"Like...semaphore flags," he said.

Bill's head bobbed. "That was my first thought. But it didn't match up to semaphore or any other code I could find. I needed more samples. I hit rest stops, outhouses, gas-station restrooms, truck stops—"

He dashed between rows of dangling photographs. They caught the air in his wake, glossy paper rattling and swaying.

"I needed *more*," he called to Lionel, waving him through the rows. "When I closed my eyes, I could still see the code. Not code. Language. That's when I figured it out. It's pictographs, like ancient Egyptian. The lines make sounds. The sounds make words, in a language only the road people know. I tried showing it to this professor of linguistics, up at Notre Dame. He said I was crazy, that

I was seeing patterns that weren't real—apophenia, he called it. But if that's true, *how can I read the language?*"

His hand clamped onto Lionel's shoulder. Squeezing hard, clinging like Lionel was a life preserver in a stormy sea.

"You get it, right? You've got the eyes. You understand. Please, tell me you understand."

Lionel understood. He'd been taught words in a special language, too.

He remembered the back alley behind a coffee shop, chasing the trail of a dead playwright with Maddie. That was where they found the first evidence of Jimmy Sloane's plan, the occult machines—the deadcatchers—he'd been seeding across the city. And that was where she taught Lionel his first bit of magic.

"*Now we add the words. The* voces mysticae. *It's a language no human culture ever spoke. Spirits know it, though. And when you use it correctly, they have no choice but to listen. There are seven thousand words that I know of. For this, we only need three...*"

Bill saw what the professor couldn't because something—random chance, a brain spark, a bolt from the heavens—had cracked his mind open. Just like Lionel, but he had no teacher, no guiding hand to steer him away from the brink of madness.

"Bill, going to ask you a weird question."

"Shoot," he said.

"Do you believe in magic?"

The photographer's scraggly mustache twitched as one corner of his mouth went tight. He started to answer, caught himself, bouncing between responses like a fly bouncing off a window when the way out was just an inch away. Lionel knew that reaction; something inside him wasn't ready to accept the truth, wasn't ready to open his eyes more than halfway. Bill was fighting a war inside his own head.

He didn't answer the question. Instead, he led Lionel to another string of photographs. People, this time, though nothing seemed unusual about them. Random families, or loners getting in and out of parked cars. Lots of RVs and campers.

"There's a...you could call it a subculture. I call them the people of the road. They're nomads. Tribes of actual nomads, in modern-day America. I think they've always been here. They just changed with the times, upgraded from wagons to Winnebagos."

"Like...Romani?" Lionel asked.

"Different. These tribes, they use rest stops and bathrooms as a sort of bulletin-board system. I didn't get it at first. I mean, why not use the internet like everybody else? But you can't hack a piece of graffiti. They're trading meet-up notices, routes, warnings, in a language nobody knows, right out in the open."

"Warnings?"

"That's what set me onto the Jeep girls," Bill said. He walked the row, hunting now, looking for one particular shot. "I've been tracking one of these nomad convoys, following them through the Midwest. They're big enough that their followers sometimes splinter off on the highway, so they leave messages to the outriders, telling them what campground they'll be landing at next. Two weeks ago, they started warning people off particular roads, or telling them to stay away from certain motels."

"Motels like the one you checked out, here in Gary? The

murder scene. So the girls in the Jeep, they're nomads too?"

"Yeah. They're a tribe of three, and these people want *nothing* to do with them. The gist of the warnings boils down to 'stay the hell away, and if you see them, don't interfere.'"

"So you immediately started stalking them and taking their picture everywhere they went. Smart."

"I'm a *journalist*," Bill shot back, his eyes suddenly manic. "I'm documenting everything. This is all for...this is..."

He raised his arms to the forest of photographs, taking it all in, the crazy-quilt lines and countless clothespins. Then he froze. His momentary euphoria deflated, his face falling as his hands sagged to his sides. He looked lost.

"Lionel?" he said. "I don't know why I'm doing this."

I gotta get this guy some help, Lionel thought. He put his hand on Bill's arm. "It's okay. It will *be* okay."

"Everyone just..." Bill raised his face to the pictures. "Everyone just left me. My girlfriend, I was going to pop the question, right before I saw the language. She disconnected her phone and I didn't even notice. I just...I can't stop. I'm doing this and I can't stop and I know that something is *wrong* with me. But I can't stop. I just keep chasing the words and taking pictures, like...like I'm the camera. I'm the camera, and someone is using me to capture all these moments."

"Bill? Listen to me. I know some experts, okay? They're back in New York. I'm going to take you there, I'll introduce you, and they'll help you sort this shit out. They helped me, and they can help you too. But right now I've got to deal with the girls in the Jeep before they hurt anybody else. What else did the messages tell you?"

"One thing."

Bill waved, motioning for him to follow as he ducked under a low-hanging line of glossies.

"There was a word. One word, right around the time of the first murder. The first one in the tri-state area, anyway. I got the impression that the person who wrote the warning was in a panic. They saw something that scared the hell out of them. Again, supporting my theory."

"That the girls aren't the ones committing the murders?"

Bill glanced over his shoulder. "C'mon, did they look scary to you? No. I think this person saw the real killer. And they wrote down a name."

He pointed to a black-and-white photograph. The inside of a toilet stall, so dirty it was a crime scene in its own right. Lionel could pick out the code now, the precise slant to the letters on a wall of otherwise innocuous graffiti.

Down at the bottom of the shot, someone had taken a knife to the particleboard wall and carved five letters in a jagged, frenzied scrawl.

KERES.

Lionel took out his phone. He shot out a group message to his social-media contacts, keeping it short and tight. *One word: Keres. I need to know everything. The real scoop.*

Bill side-eyed him. "That name mean anything to you?"

"No, but it sounds Greek."

"So?"

"I don't believe that everything happens for a reason," Lionel said. "But sometimes, every once in a while, you find yourself exactly where you're meant to be."

He shot a glance to the grimy scalloped-glass windows and added a line to his post: *Preferably before sunset. Time-critical.*

CHAPTER ELEVEN

"Tell me about these other nomads," Lionel said. "The ones you've been tracking."

"This is going to sound crazy." Bill paused. Frozen, with a smile that looked like a grimace, trapped in a moment of cruel self-awareness. "But go with it. They're Amazons."

"Come again?"

Bill led him to a string of photographs, long-range shots taken at an RV park. At first blush, Lionel might have dismissed them as a normal campground gathering. Then he noticed, in the group of twenty-odd people, that all of them were women.

And all of them were armed. Distant sentinels watched from under the eaves of camper sunshades, cradling hunting rifles. A stout woman in the foreground, hanging out washing on a line, rose up on her tiptoes; her windbreaker had slid back, baring the glint of a revolver. A small pack of teenage girls were captured in mid-stride, following an elderly woman like ducklings. Some carried long plastic archery cases, while others slung their bows over one shoulder along with quivers of arrows.

"I mean, obviously they're not *the* Amazons," Bill amended, "but that's what they call themselves."

"Have you reached out to them directly? Requested an interview?"

"They caught me snapping pictures when I trailed them out to a campground near Shipshewana. One of them shot at me. No words, no warning, just took aim and *blam*, a bullet splintered a tree branch right over my head. And let me tell you, brother, I'm pretty sure she missed on purpose. That branch was a harder target than I was."

"She wanted you to know she could have killed you."

Bill nodded. "I took off running and didn't look back. Right after that, I started following the Jeep girls. Felt like a safer project."

"I wouldn't take that bet."

Lionel's phone buzzed. He tilted the screen in his hand.

Mr. Page, the message read, *I hope this finds you in good health. Has Ms. Dunkle sent you on an overseas assignment?*

Online, he called himself Zookeeper. Offline, Lionel knew him as Julian Whitcombe, the proprietor of a rare bookstore in Hell's Kitchen. The man's disfigurements and crippling injuries didn't stop him from serving Hekate's interests, acting as one of "Regina Dunkle's" faithful field agents.

I'm in Indiana, Lionel texted back.

Then you scarcely need worry about encountering the Keres.

Tell me everything, he wrote.

Bill led Lionel down the string of frozen memories. More telephoto shots, more images of daily life on the road. The modern Amazons, fueling up RVs and stopping for a big family lunch at a truck-stop diner. There were a lot of bright-eyed smiles in the pictures. A lot of laughter.

"Far as I can tell," Bill was saying, "they roll into a

campground for a few days—never more than a week in one place—and they go looking for piecemeal work in the area. Day jobs, construction, more than a few are buskers and entertainers. All the money goes into a common pot, to pay for whatever they need."

Lionel had one eye on his phone. A moment later, Julian's response came in.

The Keres—Ker, in the singular, though they always travel in packs—are death-spirits. They haunt battlefields, and come for the bodies of the dying.

Valkyries? he texted back.

No. Vikings believed that Valkyries came to bear valiant warriors to their just rewards in Valhalla. The Keres are killers. They are cruel, violent horrors, and care nothing of a soldier's valor, only the joy of tearing his beating heart to shreds and savoring his last moments of suffering. They are, if you will forgive me waxing philosophical, a much more accurate embodiment of the true nature of war.

And they're real? Lionel typed.

I saw one in Cambodia, many years ago, Julian wrote. *But as I said, you needn't worry. The Keres are bound by divine law, as are we all. They are only permitted to manifest upon the battlefield. Unless Ms. Dunkle is dispatching you to a war zone, consider yourself safe.*

"Then there's the shrines," Bill said.

Lionel glanced up from his phone. "Shrines?"

The only picture Bill could offer was from a nosebleed perch, so far from the edge of a lake he had to squint to make out any details. There were women in the picture, seven of them, clad in long flowing dresses and what looked like—flowered sashes? Garlands?—draped like flowing bandoliers. The photograph captured them in a dance, heels and hands high, hair flying, as they ringed a cairn of stones.

"They set 'em up when they make camp, and take them down when they leave," Bill said. "But they've got some kinda weird hippie pagan thing going on."

"They shot at you, Bill. Hippies don't shoot at people."

Bill rubbed the back of his neck, sheepish.

"Yeah, well, I mean, I don't have another name for it. I got close enough, come dark, to get pictures of one of the shrines, but none of 'em came out. I was shooting on digital and the memory card fritzed on me. I looked up what I saw, though, the symbols balanced on the stones. A bow and arrow, an ivory moon. Y'know what that stands for?"

"Enlighten me."

"Artemis. Virgin goddess of the hunt. I mean, they don't just call themselves Amazons, they're going the whole nine yards: they actually worship some old Greek god."

"Probably shouldn't call her 'old,'" Lionel muttered. He was typing again. *Humor me. If I ran into a Ker, hypothetically, how could I stop it?*

Stop it? Julian replied.

Bind it, trap it— Lionel almost wrote *kill it,* but something stayed his hand. *How do I keep it from hurting anyone?*

"Near as I can tell," Bill said, "they're moving westward. Slow, but I'm guessing they're making their way to the West Coast before the fall comes. I mean, that's what I'd do. These are the last pictures I was able to snap, before they caught me in the act."

Lionel followed him along the aisle, his gaze drifting over more still pictures of nomad life. Then he stopped, feet rooted to the torn-up linoleum, a breath frozen in his throat.

Bill had an eye for composition. Five women sat at a picnic bench in a public park, some tan, some dark, most in their forties, a couple younger than that, all of them carrying an air of confident authority. *The Amazons in charge*, Lionel thought. One stood, a booted foot up on the wooden bench, cradling a rifle in her arms as she cast a protective eye over the campground. A strong wind was in the air, bending tree boughs, turning the women's hair into wild and flowing manes.

More guns, pistols, sat out on the table; one of the nomads was methodically breaking down and cleaning them. And at the center of the bench, two women were reaching out to one another, passing a familiar white clay flask from hand to outstretched hand. One woman, he didn't recognize.

The other was Maddie.

"When did you take this photo?" he asked, leaning close. It was the same flask as the one in his rolling suitcase, but this one was pristine, without Maddie's painted sigils or the name of Tisiphone. It was also open at the top, uncorked and unsealed.

"Couple of weeks back maybe," Bill said.

Maddie looked good. Healthy, vibrant. Fierce. Lionel recognized the look in her eyes. It was the look she got when she saw something unjust or unkind, something that fired her anger, and she planned to do something about it.

He walked through the timeline, step by step. *Somewhere between Montauk and Indiana, you hooked up with the Amazon caravan. Traveled with them for a while.*

They gave you the flask. You...did your thing, put something nasty in there and corked it up tight. Then you passed the flask over to Kayla Lambert, who tried to use it to kill Cordell Spears, as payback for her husband's murder.

The timeline worked. Still didn't bring him any closer to figuring out if Spears was actually guilty of anything, though.

Didn't matter. He saw a moment of hope and latched on to it with both hands.

"So...you can read their messages. You know where they've been—"

"And where they're going," Bill said. "For a while, anyhow. I've got their whole trajectory mapped out."

"You could tell me how to find them."

He shrugged. "You aren't that far behind. I mean, they put down stakes for a few days at a time, and they move slow. I could pull together all the info I've got, make a map—if you pulled an all-nighter, I bet you could catch up with 'em by noon tomorrow."

Less than a day. If Maddie had ridden with them this far, there was a good chance she was still with them. And if she wasn't, they could tell him where she was headed. He could do this. One long drive, through the night and into the morning.

His phone trembled against his palm. He glanced down at the screen.

The Keres are the living embodiment of violent death, Julian wrote. *Don't stand in their way. I don't doubt your heart, Mr. Page, but this is a storm you are not prepared to face.*

"So, uh," Bill was asking, glancing back over his shoulder. "You want me to get that map ready for you?"

More than anything. Maddie was close enough to touch. She'd have answers, solutions, an easy fix for all of this.

And while he was on a westbound highway, driving through the night, the killers in the Jeep would be taking another life. A murder he *might* have been able to stop, if he stepped up to the plate and tried his hardest. And no matter how this nightmare ended, Lionel knew he'd feel the blood on his own hands, sticky and wet, for the rest of his life.

He slumped against the old sales counter. Took a breath, held it, let it go.

"You said you'd been following those girls for two weeks now. That you had a way to find them."

"Sure," Bill said. "They have a toll booth transponder in their Jeep. Indiana's part of the E-ZPass network, along with maybe a dozen other states. I waited until they parked one day, slipped in, and copied down the transponder number."

"You broke into their car?"

Bill spread his hands. "It's an old Jeep Wrangler. It doesn't have *doors*. Technically, that's not breaking in. Anyway, like I said, I used to work for TMZ. I've got a binder stuffed with contact numbers for people willing to leak useful info, you know, in exchange for a little financial remuneration. One of 'em works for the toll company, and he can pull transponder data anytime I need it."

"So you know which toll booths they've passed through, and when."

"Exactly. They're always moving, but they've got certain tastes. Like they always stop for the night at fleabag motels, they don't go anywhere that's got security cameras or anyplace close to a police station, and they usually stop driving when the sun goes down. Put all that data together, and it's not hard to make a short list of places where they'd hole up."

Lionel looked to the scalloped windows. The light outside was fading, turning sepia against the blurry glass.

"Okay," he said. "I'm going to need that short list."

"What are you going to do?"

He had to think about that.

"Back in my old job," Lionel said, "I had a reputation for jumping into stories with both feet. Getting directly involved, instead of standing back and reporting on what I saw."

"How'd that work out for you?"

"Oh, lousy. Got my ass kicked a lot and drove my boss nuts. Landed in the hospital twice."

"And yet," Bill said.

Lionel sighed. "And yet."

"What about the Amazons?"

Lionel tapped out a quick thank-you text to Julian and put the phone back in his pocket.

"Do me a favor. Put the map together, figure out where they're probably headed, and hold on to it for me. If I'm still alive come sunrise, I'll be back for it."

CHAPTER TWELVE

So what the hell are you? Lionel wondered as he drove, on his way to check the third motel on a list of five. The question had him in a loop. These modern-day Amazons thought the girls in the Jeep were Keres, death-spirits hunting fresh victims for the sheer pleasure of the kill. He had to assume they knew what they were talking about, especially since Maddie was riding with them; she wouldn't waste her time with pretenders.

But Julian Whitcombe knew his stuff too. And he said they *couldn't* be Keres, that the creatures only appeared on battlefields and in war zones. Indiana was about as far from a war zone as they could get.

Lionel even contemplated the photographer's theory, that the young women were exactly what they appeared to be, innocent road-trippers, and a serial killer was following them from stop to stop. Leaving them untouched, for reasons of his own, and murdering random victims to satisfy his unfulfilled lust.

He didn't buy that one. They had come to his door in the night, tried to lure him out with a siren song of beer and sex, and only settled for the trucker when Lionel wouldn't give in. He remembered the icy look in the blonde's eyes, the way she shifted from coquettish come-ons to imperious demands in a heartbeat. If they weren't doing the killings, they were at least picking the targets.

The Motel 6, nestled up against a highway off-ramp, had been a bust. So was the La Quinta. Next on the list was the Lincoln Lodge, down a long stretch of forest road. The Jeep's transponder said they left the highway between a pair of toll stations—triggering one, but not the next—so they were somewhere in the vicinity.

And the sun was down now, the sky an overcast gray mire with storm clouds rolling in. Lionel's headlights cast stark beams of white down the empty ribbon of road, carving through the darkness. He tabled his questions for now and focused on the bigger problem.

Step one, he thought, *find the Jeep. Step two, figure out what room they're staying in. Step three...*

The third step, he figured, was the one that took him right over the cliff's edge.

Charging in like an action hero feels like a great way to die, he thought. *But do I need to? What am I really trying to accomplish here? I just need to stop them from killing anyone tonight. That's it. If I can keep them busy until morning, that'd buy me time to speed west, catch up to the convoy, find Maddie, and get some heavy-hitting backup on my side. Then we can circle around and find a more long-term solution. If I can get them to chase me, even better. The Amazons shot at Bill for taking their picture. I imagine they'll have an even colder reception for a trio of supernatural slashers.*

Violence wasn't going to solve this problem, but creativity might.

As he cruised through the parking lot, he eyed the sprinkler spigots spaced along the first-floor walkway, built into the balcony overhang. A fire. Not a real one, he couldn't risk any bystanders getting hurt, but a flick of Maddie's plastic lighter would be enough to set off the alarm. They'd have to evacuate the motel and keep everyone outside until the fire department checked it out and gave the all clear.

That'll buy me...maybe an hour. Bomb threat? He couldn't use his own phone for that; nothing would break his stride like getting arrested for a false report. *So I layer the distractions*, he thought. *Set off the alarms, and hope somebody leaves their room unlocked when they rush to evacuate. Slip in, use the phone in their room to make the call. The cops will get here before the firefighters are even finished. Enough chaos could keep this place tangled up in knots for hours.*

Still wouldn't get him to sunrise, but he was getting closer. He was working out the details when his phone chimed.

"I'm at the La Quinta," Bill told him. "Where are you?"

"The Lincoln, I left the La Quinta twenty minutes ago. Why are you following the list? That's my job."

"Uh...because you told me to?"

"Excuse me?"

"Your text," Bill said. "You told me they were here, room fifteen. And I quote, 'get your ass over here pronto, and bring your camera.' And I mean, they're here. I'm perched on the far side of the lot, watching from the bushes, and the Jeep's right where you said it'd be—"

Lionel spun the wheel around, cornering hard. His hatchback wobbled on its unsteady suspension as he rocketed toward the open road, heading back the way he'd come.

"Bill, get out of there, *now*. It's a setup. They know you've been following them. They must have known all along."

"Hold up." His voice became a rustle of leaves. "It's fine. I'm hunkered down, watching through the zoom lens. They've got their curtain open, I can see them moving around in there, and they've got no clue. I used to stalk celebrities for a living, brother. If I can handle professional bodyguards, I can handle some bimbo co-eds on a road—wait."

"Get out of there. *Run*."

"One turned to the window and she's...waving to me. How can she see me? She's standing in a lit room. I'm seventy feet away, in the dark, kneeling in a goddamn bush. How can she see me?"

The Corolla thudded across a patch of bad asphalt. Lionel gripped the phone with one hand and the wheel with the other, knuckles clenched. The needle on the dash was kissing seventy miles an hour and climbing.

"Start yelling," Lionel told him. "Run and yell. Make noise. They don't want attention. Start screaming and they might—"

"Too late," Bill said. Then he chuckled. "I get it now. You asked if I believed in magic. I get it now."

"Bill?"

"There's only two of them in there. They tricked me, moving in and out of sight so I wouldn't realize there are only two of them. But now they're both standing there, waving and smiling, and they took their faces off, just for me. I can read the muscle and bone underneath, just like I read the road language. And now I know what they reminded me of, the first time I laid eyes on them."

Another sound came over the line: the rustling of bushes.

"Velociraptors," Bill said.

Two quick staccato *thumps*, and the line went dead.

~~

Lionel veered into the La Quinta's lot, catching a dizzy stomach-lurching second of air time as the hatchback fired over a dip in the road. He slammed on the brakes outside the door to room 15. The Jeep was gone. The door was open. Just a few inches, electric light burning inside, the curtains drawn tight. An invitation.

He left the engine running.

Lionel nudged the door with his foot. It groaned open, showing him the room beyond. Two beds, still made, no luggage left behind. An empty can of Coke and a crumpled Snickers wrapper sat in the wastebasket, the only sign that anyone had been here.

He knew there was more to see. He held his breath, his own heartbeat a steady thrum in his ears as he forced himself—willing his frozen muscles into action—to step inside. And then to slowly cross the room, taking each step like there might be a land mine underfoot, and make his way to the bathroom door.

He knew what they'd left for him. The coppery stench in the air told him before he got there. He still had to look.

They'd propped Bill up on the toilet seat, stripped him, and ripped him open from his collarbone on down, all the way to where his legs spread wide. The toilet bowl was a soup of scarlet, overflowing, bits of torn-away things floating in the broth. They'd taken his eyes with them when they left.

Lionel stood on the threshold, transfixed. The bleat of a

car horn jolted him like an electric shock. He turned and strode, fast, back to the motel-room door.

The Jeep was in the parking lot, waiting for him. The halogen beam of one cyclops-eye headlight, the other shattered, pinned him in the doorway. A peal of giddy laughter washed over him. Then the Jeep lurched forward, tires squealing as it spun, and took off.

He was right behind them. Lionel raced to his hatchback, jumped in, and threw it into reverse, peeling out of the parking spot. He slammed the stick into drive and stomped on the gas. They rocketed onto the open road and he was right behind them, locked onto their tail, a quarter mile behind and gaining fast.

It's a trap, he told himself. Of course it was. He knew that. Just like he knew he couldn't walk away.

The Jeep sped up, matching his pace, keeping him on a long leash. The highway wound south, deeper into the country, away from the urban lights. Wheat fields became a wavering dirty-gold blur, living canyon walls. Then the fields surrendered to forest, the road hemmed in by tangled, gnarled trees that snuffed out the moonlight. Lionel's high beams captured the broken road and the distant specter of the Jeep as it led him on like a will-o'-the-wisp.

The country road curved through thick woodland. Lionel gripped the wheel harder as it rattled under his grip, tires bouncing on the cracked and pitted pavement. He fought to keep it steady, under control, his foot on the gas. Up ahead, the Jeep slipped out of sight, swallowed by the arc of the road. He had to keep up. He was doing eighty on a road built for forty-five, but he poured on a little more speed, pushing the needle, feeling the curve shove him back against his seat like an invisible hand against his rib cage.

The road straightened out, then dipped. He picked up more speed. No sign of his target. *Where the hell did they go?* he thought, squinting into the darkness.

He got his answer a second later. The flash of the cyclops halogen beam, flooding his mirrors with white-diamond light, was his only warning. They'd slipped off somewhere, veered onto an access road he hadn't spotted in the nighttime tangle, running parallel to the main road. Now they were back, behind him, the Jeep's engine roaring like a lioness uncaged.

The Jeep fired up, swung in, and sideswiped him. Metal screamed and his door crumpled, his side-view mirror tearing off and sparking off the pavement as it went tumbling away in the dark. The impact ripped the steering wheel from Lionel's grip. His car fishtailed, nose swinging out of control, veering for the muddy ditch at the side of the road. He hit the brakes, trying to wrestle the car back under control. Then the front wheels kissed the air, sailing over the edge of the ditch, and pitched nose-down in a roller-coaster dive.

Lionel's forehead slammed against the steering wheel. He felt his skin split open, blood guttering down one side of his nose, coating his lips with salt, as his vision went fuzzy gray. Then he heard the *crump* of the airbag, hitting his cheekbone with a heavyweight punch wrapped in hot canvas, and the world turned off like a light.

CHAPTER THIRTEEN

"Wake up, bitch."

Lionel opened his eyes halfway. His vision swam, painting the forest in nauseous smears. His back was cold, wet. He felt muddy grass under his hands. He tried to push himself up.

A high-top sneaker stomped down on his aching ribs, knocking him flat and pinning him like a bug. The sloe-eyed, coltish young woman, bulky headphones draped around her neck, stared down at him and wrinkled her nose.

"I said *wake* up, not *get* up. Pay attention and learn to follow instructions. You'll live longer."

"Not that much longer," the blonde said, looming over him on the other side. The one with the pigtails—unwrapping a new lollipop and eyeing Lionel with detached curiosity—joined her two companions. The blonde turned a business card in her hand, the back smeared with fingerprints the color of rust. "Lionel Page, Channel Seven News. And I thought your name was Walter Winchell. You lied in the sign-in book, back at the Starlite Motel. Naughty."

Lionel tried to squirm his way out from under the shoe.

She pressed down harder, squeezing the breath from his lungs.

"Yeah, well," he managed to say, "I'm guessing your name isn't really 'Nikki Manson,' either."

The blonde gave a careless shrug.

"It's what I'm going by this week. My sister, currently using you as a footstool, is Beth, and this is Mindy."

Mindy put her lollipop to her lips and gave a casual wave with her other hand. "Hey."

"Let's be frank," Nikki said. "You're gonna die. And not in the 'everyone dies eventually, hopefully at a ripe old age and remembered with love' sort of way."

"More like…screaming in agony while we take turns fucking your intestines with a hunting knife," Beth added.

Nikki snapped her fingers and pointed at her.

"That. Exactly like that. By the way, if you do feel like screaming at any point, go for it. We're in the middle of nowhere, and even if we weren't, we've got a way of shutting that whole thing down." She wriggled her hand at him. "Magic."

"We're also open to begging and crying," Beth said.

"And if you piss your pants, we promise we won't make fun of you. We're here for the agony and death. We're not into humiliation."

"I am," Beth said.

"Okay, she is. She really is. The point is"—Nikki raised her arms, stretching, then stifled a yawn behind the back of her hand—"these are all extremely natural reactions, and we want you to feel free to express yourself. You only get one death, and it should be a quality experience with maximum drama. But here's the thing, Lionel Page from Channel Seven News: we've got some questions."

"Shoot," he said. "I've got nowhere else to be tonight."

"You've got a good attitude. I like that. Okay, so, we knew all about the TMZ reject stalking us—"

"Like a total creeper," Mindy said.

"I thought it was kind of funny. We were saving him for later. Like a snack, but one that follows you around. You, though? You're not part of the plan. And you're not here on official business. We Googled you. So what we really want to know is…who sent you?"

Lionel dug deep and he stared her in the eye, mustering his last scraps of defiance.

"Hekate," he said.

Nikki's smile faded. The three women looked at each other, sharing silent back-and-forth glances.

"Bull," Nikki said.

"Try me and find out."

"She knows our business, and she's never gotten involved. She doesn't intervene in our affairs. Do you even know what we are?"

He couldn't fight them off. Couldn't even sit up straight, with the heel of Beth's sneaker grinding into his bruised rib cage. The only thing keeping him alive was his wits. That, and maybe one hell of a bluff. He thought back to everything he'd learned—the road language, Julian's explanations, and the apparent impossibility of these creatures, adding it all together.

"You're the Keres," Lionel said, rolling the dice. "The reapers of the battlefield. And the reason she never interfered before was because you were fulfilling your purpose. But you left the battlefield, and you've been preying on innocent people. That's a violation of the divine order. So she sent me to deliver a message: go back where you belong, right now. Leave in peace or face the consequences."

The women shared another set of back-and-forth glances, silent. Then they burst into laughter. Hysterical peals of laughter, almost doubling over. Nikki wiped tears from her eyes.

"Oh my...wow. *Wow*. You almost had us nervous for a second there. You got me, Lionel. You really got me. Good one."

"I'm serious," Lionel said. "This is your last chance."

"Aw. Sweetie." Nikki crouched down beside him. She jutted out her bottom lip in a sympathetic pout. "You tried. You really did."

"But," Mindy said. She stared down at him, thoughtful, sucking on the rim of her lollipop.

Nikki glanced over at her. "But?"

"He does smell like her."

Nikki leaned in, sniffing at the side of Lionel's face. The tip of her tongue slid along his cheek, leaving a wet trail before she pulled away.

"Oh, yeah," she said. "He's marked with a capital M."

Beth frowned. "I searched him before he woke up. No key. No symbols or signs."

"So he's somebody's apprentice. Wayward apprentice. Probably won't be missed." Nikki rose, slapping a bit of damp grass from her knee. "Your goddess didn't send you, did she, Lionel? No, you stumbled across our trail, got all fired up, and thought you were going to ride in and save the day like a cowboy. Rookie mistake. Unfortunately, not the 'live and learn' kind of mistake."

"She won't save you." Beth's heel found a fresh bruise to torment, rocking back and forth on his chest. "How does that feel? Knowing you've been abandoned by your own goddess?"

"She saved me once," he croaked. "Well. She gave me a way to save myself."

And you can do that again, any time you feel like it, he thought, sending up a prayer to the overcast sky. *Any second now would be great, boss.*

"Why did you do it?" Mindy asked him.

"Do what?"

"Stand in our way, knowing you couldn't win?"

Beth snorted, answering for him.

"Same reason sailors chase sirens over waterfalls," she said. "Because men are stupid and weak."

"No. Not this one." She looked to Nikki. "I don't feel right about this."

Nikki's brow furrowed. She was clearly the ringleader here, but she suddenly seemed unnerved.

"Do you speak prophecy, sister?"

Mindy suckled her lollipop. She shook her head. "Just a feeling. A bad one, though."

"We can't let him live," Beth said.

"No, but..." Nikki balled one hand into a frustrated fist, resting it on her hip as she contemplated Lionel. "Her feelings are often prophecies, too."

Lionel circled around. He sensed a crack in the ranks, an opening just wide enough to drive a wedge of doubt through.

"Like I said," he told them, "you don't belong here. And how long do you think you can keep this up? I found you out. Others will, too. You're supposed to be war spirits. There are wars all over the world. Pick one and *go* there."

Mindy's sigh gusted down at him.

"Here. There. Mortal, you don't understand."

Beth sneered. "Accusing us of breaking divine law. We didn't break shit."

"Open a newspaper," Nikki told him. "Every month, every week, more blood spills. Not our doing. Yours. You people have turned your shopping malls, your churches, your *schools* into battlefields. In every place where man levels weapons against man, in every place where there is suffering and death, you will find the Keres. How dare you pretend to be surprised to find us here?"

"We didn't break the rules," Beth said. "*You* did. Know what that means? It means we get to go wherever we damn well please."

Nikki crouched down once more. The backs of her fingers drew along Lionel's cheek, feather-light, her steady gaze almost turning kindly now.

"You humans opened the door. You invited us in, and we graciously accepted. Sweetie, you think we're monsters, but we're not. Know what we really are? Consequences."

Beth shot a glare at her sister. "We can't let him live."

"No. But...if our resident soothsayer has a sour stomach about it, we have to be careful." Nikki tapped the side of her head. "I've got an idea. Hon, did you park the Jeep close by?"

Mindy's head bobbed. "Uh-huh."

"Good. I need a couple of things from the back."

~~

They bound Lionel's wrists behind his back with a loop of rough, scratchy hemp, tight enough to rub his skin raw. The rest of the rope coil, cut to size with the flash of a hunting knife, became the slipknot of a noose.

Lionel held his breath, what little breath he could draw

A Time for Witches

with his head wrenched back and his throat snared, and stood very, very still.

They'd balanced him on a broken step stool. Three legs, mismatched and wobbly, set upon a patch of muddy ground. The rope of the noose was taut, dragged up and over the stout limb of a dead tree, and the opposite end wrapped around its rotten trunk. Nikki tied it off with a festive bow.

"Like I said, scream all you want, if you can manage it. You're miles away from anyone's help. See, we're going to abstain from our usual nocturnal fun times and mix things up a little. You're still going to die tonight, but not at our hands."

"We'll let the Fates decide," Mindy said, gazing up at him. Her lollipop was wearing down, the hypnotic swirl of color fading.

Nikki shrugged. "Or anybody else who wants to. See, Lionel, I said no one was going to *help* you. Doesn't mean this patch of forest is uninhabited. There are...things out here. Ghouls, and worse. Things that never say no to a free meal. And you've got just enough of a magical spark that I bet you'll draw them like ants to a honey pot."

"Or you could take one step, any direction you like, and end it right now," Beth said.

"Or that. Of course, it's not going to be a quick neck snap. No, hung up like that, you'll just...dangle. And slowly suffocate as your windpipe is crushed by your body's own weight. Agonizing, but probably not as painful as being eaten alive by whatever kind of night-roamer decides to turn you into a snack."

The stool wobbled dangerously under his feet. Lionel shifted, desperately clinging to his balance.

"Or you might slip," Beth said. "Or, eventually, your body will finish the job. You can't stay awake forever."

"No matter how it happens," Nikki told him, "we'll be miles away. If anyone out there is sore about you shuffling off this mortal coil—which I doubt—our hands are clean. There's no loophole better than a cosmic loophole."

The trio turned to leave. Lionel's thoughts scrambled, clawing for purchase. Survival, he'd worry about in a minute. This was his last chance to learn the truth, and he couldn't let it slip away. He just had to ask the right questions. Even with a noose around his throat, he had his reporter hat on.

"One answer," he called out. "For one question. You can give me that much."

Nikki turned back. She arched an eyebrow.

"Curious. You know what happened to the curious cat, right?"

"I'm dying anyway."

"True. Sure. I'll answer. Maybe. Go for it."

"When you asked who sent me," he said, "you said I wasn't 'part of the plan.' You weren't being figurative. You're not stupid: you know you can't just spree-kill your way across the country forever. I doubt the mortal cops can stop you, but there are people like me—more powerful, more experienced—and they can and will."

"Is there a question in that statement?" she asked.

"This tells me that you're here for a reason. You feed on death and pain. The killings are food, they keep you going, but they're not the reason you're on this road."

Nikki looked away for a moment. Weighing her response in silence. Then she smiled up at him.

"We were called here on a promise. A feast like we

haven't had in centuries. We're on our way to meet with the man of the hour, so he can tell us the price of admission. He needs a little expert help before he can kick off the festivities."

"That's us," Beth added.

"There's going to be mass casualties, bloodshed, gnashing of teeth and heartbroken wailing…really, *super* fun. Sorry you're going to miss it."

"The man of the hour," Lionel said. "You're talking about the Holy Roller?"

Nikki squinted at him. "Never heard that name. But epithets pile up over the ages. I've got, like, forty or fifty different names that mortals gave me, and I stopped keeping track a thousand years ago. Anyway, we're still not sure what he needs us to do, exactly, but it's been a great road trip so far. Even if we end up turning him down, this was all worth it."

Lionel saw it, then. Bill had made a mistake. He had been reading the writing on the wall, tracking two of the nomadic tribes: the modern-day Amazons who Maddie had hitched a ride with, and the Keres. He found the marks warning of the Keres' passage. But he'd gotten it wrong.

"It wasn't the Amazons who made those marks," Lionel murmured to himself. "And they weren't warning each other away. The marks weren't there to show where you've been. It was where you were *going*."

Nikki tapped the toe of one muddy sneaker against the grass. "Speak up, Lionel. Mumbling is rude. I know it's hard, with the crushing pressure on your throat and your imminent death and all, but show some basic courtesy here."

"The man who wants to hire you. He's been telling you

where to go. What roads to drive down, what motels to stay at."

"What about it?"

He wasn't sure. He could chalk it up to caution. Whoever their patron was, he'd know that they'd kill and feed along the way, and they weren't locals. He might have crafted a route just for them, to keep them out of sight and away from potential trouble. After all, their overnight stays were chosen with the same criteria he used: out-of-the-way spots with no security cameras, and cash payments under the table.

His intuition, the carefully honed nose he'd cultivated his entire career, told him there was more to it than that. *Keep digging.*

They weren't going to let him, though. Before he could reply, Nikki turned and waved her hand over her shoulder.

"And we can't be late, so, uh, bye? Have a good death, Lionel. Seriously, consider the asphyxiation option. It's better than the alternatives."

"Maybe," Beth added, following at her side.

Mindy lingered behind. Quiet, staring at Lionel over the curve of her lollipop. She waited until her sisters were out of earshot, fading shadows in the forest, before speaking up.

"I don't want to give you false hope," she said, "I'm not that cruel."

"Mighty kind of you," Lionel rasped. He felt like someone had poured gasoline down his windpipe.

"But if you survive this...I'm not saying there's even a chance that you will, but *if* you do, will you do something for me?"

"No promises."

"Don't pursue us," she said. "Don't try to stop us. Don't even come looking. Be thankful for the second life you've been granted, and walk away."

He tried to laugh. It hurt too much.

"Second life? I think I'm on my fourth or fifth right now."

"I'm serious. I sense the machinations of the gods here. Hands are working against other hands and moving us all as pieces upon their game board."

"All the more reason for you and your sisters to leave while you still can."

Mindy shook her head, crestfallen.

"You still don't understand. You're confusing your own sense of morality with divine right. You think that you're the noble protagonist of this story. You think that we're the villains."

"From where I'm standing?" His knees shifted his weight, fast, the noose going tight as the stool wobbled beneath him. "Yeah. I'm pretty sure about that."

"Lionel, *we* are here to serve the will of Olympus. Not you. We were chosen for this duty, and you stand in heaven's way. The world is about to change, a new era born. And there will be blood, and pain, just like any other birth. But when the suffering is over and done, the outcome will be a thing of beauty and love."

She turned to leave, paused, and looked back at him one last time.

"This is a time to celebrate, Lionel. The age of heroes is returning to this world. But you...you are not a hero."

She turned her back and left him to die.

CHAPTER FOURTEEN

Lionel stood alone in the dark.

If he breathed as little as he could, every inhalation searing his throat with an open flame, and if he kept his hips and shoulders perfectly still, he could hold his balance. The stool wobbled, this way and that, threatening to pitch to one side and end it all.

His wrists were raw, scraped bloody by the knotted rope. His first try at wriggling his way loose nearly capsized the stool. By the third, every near miss sending his heart lurching, he knew he wasn't going to be able to get free on his own. So he spread his feet as wide as he dared, got his balance back, and...

...he wasn't sure. He listened to the night birds, to the cool wind rustling through the boughs, the scampering dance of prey and predators in the underbrush. He didn't see a way out of this trap, not a way out that he wanted. But he wasn't ready to give up.

Everything was connected. As he stood on death's doorstep, his mind had time to twist and turn the pieces before him into new patterns. He was back in the gallery of the Griffith Museum, listening to the opening lines of Cordell's polished speech.

"*...humanity doesn't change. Human needs, human hungers, don't change. Just as it was thousands of years ago, we need our heroes.*"

"*The age of heroes is returning,*" the Ker had told him.

And something was calling to the monsters of the world. Conjuring Keres and who knew what else, leaving road maps in mystic code on gas-station toilet walls. Drawing them across the country, while a homeless man spoke prophecy and warned Lionel about the threat of the Holy Roller.

Who was on a collision course with Maddie, who had hitched a ride with a caravan of modern-day Amazons, stopping just long enough to put a poisonous flask in the hands of a grieving widow. Who, in turn, tried to use it against a billionaire before she was shot to death, before a glimmer of dark magic planted a gun she never owned in her cold and outstretched hand.

Everything was connected.

Hekate had sent Lionel here, and he didn't believe she had sent him all this way just to die. He was a part of her design. She was counting on him to play his part and solve this puzzle. And so was Maddie.

He dug deep, grabbing onto every last scrap of strength he could, dragging it to the surface. And with it, he gave his aching muscles and bruised body one singular command: *live through this*.

A new wind rolled in from the east, colder now, and tinged with mist. He felt it sink under his skin, into the marrow of his bones.

He wasn't the only one out here.

He saw movement now, flitting through the woods. Small, and floating, and quick. Lionel let his eyes slide out of focus. He fought his panic and concentrated. Now he caught glimmers, shapes: contorted faces in the dark, trailing streamers of vapor like gossamer mist. The disembodied heads were drawing a circle around him, keeping to the clearing's edge but inching closer as they darted amid the trees.

One opened a bony, distended jaw, unhinged like a serpent's, and showed him its jagged teeth.

The Keres had promised him monsters. Opportunists who wouldn't turn down an easy meal.

"Going to have to disappoint you," he called out, bracing himself. "I can still get at least one good kick in. You might win in the end, but I *guarantee* I'm going to make you work for your supper."

One of the faces turned his way, jaw wide, its eyes smoldering pits of blue fire. It streaked toward him—and then veered away, trailing silver smoke as it slammed to one side, rebounding like a bird hitting a plate glass window. Another tried from his left, scorching through the clearing. It let out a keening wet hiss and careened into an invisible wall, spinning off into the underbrush.

A crack broke in the clouds, and moonlight shimmered down. A woman was standing like a sentinel at Lionel's side. Her shoulders pushed back, chin tilted high, he recognized her by her silhouette. And as another hungry mouth bore down on them, mist turning to boiling vapor in its wake, she raised her open palm in defiance. The creature collided with a shield of pure concentrated will and erupted in a shower of black-light sparks.

The shade of Kayla Lambert was here. And she wasn't alone.

He had never met the woman on his left, not in life,

but he knew her from photographs. Chandra Nagarkar had been a phenom, a young playwright with her whole career ahead of her, until she became one of Jimmy Sloane's victims. Lionel never had a chance to save her, but he had avenged her and returned her spirit to the muse she worshiped and loved. Now she held up her hand and drove the swirling, hungry things back to the clearing's edge.

They were joined by a third figure, extending his frail, hooked, and withered fingers, adding to the shield's strength. He turned and met Lionel's eye. He stood translucent in the moonlight, as ethereal as the things around them, but there was no mistaking his sparse black hair, his snowy whiskers. Ernest Valdemar still dressed in the vintage suit he had worn on the day he died.

Valdemar inclined his head, a gesture of solemn respect, and turned back to the silent battle.

Kayla was trying to get Lionel's attention. She pointed to her left eye.

"Eye," he said. "Seeing. You want me to see something?"

He felt a pressure inside his sinuses. Building fast, swelling, like someone was inflating a balloon inside his skull.

Kayla needed to get inside him. To slip in through the bars of his mind and speak without words. He knew he'd be vulnerable. Opening himself up to possession—or worse, if this whole thing was some elaborate illusion. Or he could push her away and press on without whatever it was she wanted him to see.

It wasn't even a debate. He knew what he had to do.

"Show me," he said.

The silent battle faded around him, like a curtain being

drawn across a stage, as fingers of cold gelatin pressed through his skull and into his brain. The moonlight faded and everything went black.

Then, a spotlight.

Lionel floated, disembodied, around Kayla and Maddie. They stood in a puddle of light, pouring down from...nowhere. Maddie was holding her, Kayla's face buried against Maddie's chest as she poured out her grief. Her sobs echoed into the infinite black, bouncing back distorted and tinged with a static hiss.

Maddie held her, stone still and stoic, staring into the distance. A single pinpoint of blood welled at the corner of her left eye, glinting like a garnet.

The image shifted, blurring as their bodies parted. They stood in front of a particleboard counter, hanging disembodied in the gloom. Lionel recognized the pattern of the faux-wood grain: it was from Kayla's trailer, the spot where he'd found the three-card tarot spread. Maddie was drawing delicate brushstrokes along the white clay flask. She paused to dip her brush into an earthenware pot, scooping up another daub of scarlet paint.

"Aegean clay," Maddie told her, "taken from a very particular, very sacred site. I had to barter for it, but it'll help with the potency of the spell. What really makes the cunning-call work is the emotional link. Do you have it?"

Kayla brandished a wedding band, simple and plain gold, a match to the one Lionel had found on her bedside table.

"It's all I have left of him. They cremated his body in Athens. They didn't ask my permission. They just *did* it."

Maddie took the ring. It vanished into the mouth of the flask.

"Most likely didn't want anyone stateside taking a close look at his wounds," she murmured, focused on the paint job. "That means we'll only get one shot at this. Remember, you have to be *close*. And if you can get him to commit an act of hubris before you crack the seal, even better. Nothing draws the Furies like hubris."

"And Tisiphone will come?" Kayla asked. "She'll really come?"

"She's not a dog, and this isn't a whistle. The cunning-call is designed to snare her attention, and the wedding band will make your case. She'll hear it, and she'll decide. If she decides to come, you'll know it. *He'll* know it. She'll pass judgment and do what a Fury does."

Kayla tilted her head, staring at the flask. Maddie added another spiral of rust-red paint, mouthing a silent incantation as she drew.

"Can she, though? You know what he is."

"There are rules. A divine order of things. You can skirt around them, break them, even thrive and prosper...for a while." Maddie gave her a sidelong glance. "But there are no exceptions. Everyone faces judgment in the end. Even heroes."

"I wish you could be there. I'm not sure I can do this alone."

"You can," Maddie said. "And I'm sorry I have to leave this on your shoulders, but my business is west. I have to get back to my friends before they leave without me."

Beneath the spotlight, the world shifted once more. He felt Maddie sliding away. She went translucent, turning to glass. He reached for her, lunging into the light, desperate not to lose her again.

His hand closed around the white clay flask. Fingers

of ice—Kayla's fingers, as she stood face-to-face with him—clamped down over his.

"Please," she said. Her lips, pursed and pale, didn't move.

She wanted him to finish the job. To fulfill the mission that left her dead on a museum gallery floor. Lionel hadn't been sure, until now, if there was anything to avenge; Cordell Spears could have been an innocent man.

But Maddie believed her, he thought. *And I believe in Maddie. That's all there is to it. Besides, this thing is some kind of beacon, not a weapon. If I open it in front of Cordell and the man's done nothing to be judged for, he'll be safe and sound.*

He needed to go west, to catch up with the convoy and reunite with Madison. But she hadn't turned Kayla down, and neither would he. He'd been there when she died, and wasn't fast enough to save her; honoring her last request was the least he could do.

"I'll finish the job," he said. "Just...one question. Why did he do it? Your husband worked for Cordell. Why kill him?"

Kayla's face remained a frozen mask. A man's voice echoed from the inky void all around them.

"I'm in Athens. Listen, I can't talk long. I don't trust the phones here and I think someone's following me."

"Athens?" Kayla replied, her mouth unmoving as she stared, unblinking, into Lionel's eyes. "I thought you were in Skiathos—"

"I'm not with the team. I left in the middle of the night. I'm trying to charter passage back to the States, but I can't use my company card. Nothing he can trace. Love, listen, this is important. If anything happens to me, stay away from Cordell Spears. Don't trust him. He isn't who you think he is. He isn't *what* you think he is."

"Jurgen, slow down. You're not making any sense."

"We found something out there," His voice dropped to a church whisper. "Something impossible. I took a piece of it with me. Just have to figure out how to get it past Customs. The world has to see this. The world has to—"

Silence.

"Jurgen?"

"I have to move," he said. "I love you."

The rattle of the receiver, the final *click* of the line going dead, echoed like a gunshot.

CHAPTER FIFTEEN

Lionel's eyes snapped open. The stool wobbled under him, teetering, starting to capsize—and he caught his balance at the last second. He took a slow, aching breath, his bruised ribs flexing, the hempen noose squeezing his throat.

The hungry-jawed apparitions, and the shades who had come to defend him, were gone. There was nothing but moonlight now, seeping down through the tangled boughs. Crickets trilled in the dark. Lionel adjusted his balance, the scratchy rope chafing his raw wrists. He was still bound, still one wrong lean from death by slow strangulation.

Still standing, though, he thought. *That's something.* And now he had even more reasons to survive the night. Along with a promise to keep.

The bushes rustled. Something big was moving in the dark. *Please be a deer, and not a wolf. A paramedic with a first-aid kit would be even better. Or a tow-truck driver who randomly happened to be passing by, that'd be fine too. Just not a wolf.*

The tip of a gnarled wooden walking stick whipped at the underbrush, beating a crude path. The grizzled figure who emerged into the moonlight, his hooked nose shadowed by his wide-brimmed hat, made Lionel think of an Old West prospector. He had skin like beef jerky and a short, scraggly white beard, his lopsided frame draped in a battered leather duster. He might have been a backwoodsman or a hermit, living off the forest's bounty.

Then he lifted his chin, just high enough for Lionel to get a good look at his eyes. They caught the moonlight and glittered like opals.

"You must have really spooked those girls," he said, shuffling closer and peering up at Lionel. "I've been following 'em for three weeks now, and you're the first beau they left breathing. 'Course, you're also the first witch they laid hands on. Mostly they've been playing with long-haul truckers and traveling salesmen. Lousy diets, those folks. Does awful things to their insides. All pickled livers and sour bellies. Still, I'm not choosy. A free meal is a free meal."

Ghouls. Great. The Keres had warned him, but Lionel figured he should have guessed anyway. Ghouls lived beneath human cities—under the radar, literally underground, or both—and feasted on what the mortal world threw away. Including corpses. The fresher, the better, and the renegade death-spirits had been dropping bodies at every stop along their nightmare road trip. Only natural that they'd pick up a supernatural entourage.

"Where's the rest of your pack?" Lionel asked, looking over his shoulder. "Hiding in the bushes?"

The ghoul flashed a maw of jagged, curving teeth, his lips spreading inhumanly wide. He offered a graceful bow.

"Just me. Call me Morticore. You find wisdom yet, Odin?"

"Pardon?"

"Odin. Hung from a tree for nine days and nine nights to attain mystic wisdom, the story goes. Just wondering if you had any luck."

"If I had any luck," Lionel said, "I wouldn't be here."

"See? That's wisdom."

"I don't feel particularly enlightened right now."

"Well, Odin also just had the one eye." Morticore nodded up at him. "I could pop one of those suckers out for you, see if it changes your perspective any."

"How does a ghoul end up without a pack?" Lionel asked.

"How does a witch end up in a tree?"

"Questionable life choices."

"Same answer to both riddles," the ghoul replied. "My pack is on the move. More than just mine. We've been hearing strange rumblings underground. Concrete whispers, and prophecies in spray paint. I'm old enough to remember the last few times this happened, and it always goes down the same way: big trouble, and a big feast. Sometimes for weeks after. Sometimes for months."

"You're talking about...what, a natural disaster?"

He scratched under his armpit. "Or an unnatural one. Same outcome. What you call a tragedy, we call a banquet. But I can read the writing on the wall, and I caught wind of those Keres a couple of states back. My pack can starve while they chase whispers. Me, I'm going to bed with a full belly every night."

The writing on the wall. Literally. *He must have found the directions their boss has been leaving for them*, Lionel thought. *So he knows where they're going to be every night, and where to find a fresh corpse.*

And that meant he knew where they'd stop next.

"Where's the final destination? They said they're heading to meet with the man behind it all."

Morticore's opal eyes glittered. He looked Lionel up and down, sizing him up.

"Don't see how that information would benefit you any."

"Because I have to stop them."

"I don't think we're communicating here," the ghoul said.

He reached under his duster and drew out a long arc of razor-honed steel, gleaming like mercury as it captured a sliver of moonlight. A hunter's knife, built for skinning deer.

"I go to bed with a full belly *every* night," he said. "And not much tastes better than a true-blue witch. Your bone marrow is marinated in secrets. Now don't worry, I'm not like those gals who strung you up: you hold still and I'll make it nice and quick, ear to ear. Can't promise it's painless, but it's really the best death you could have had out here."

Lionel's thoughts raced as the blade loomed. He had crossed paths with ghouls before. They were amoral scavengers, bottom-feeders who would break their word at the drop of a hat. Maddie had warned Lionel never to bargain with a ghoul. Then again, they'd done it once, recruiting the aid of Manhattan's pack—a gamble that turned the tide in their favor. He just needed to dangle something in front of Morticore's gemstone eyes, something juicier than his own flesh and blood.

"Ever eaten the flesh of a Ker?" he asked.

The tip of the stainless-steel blade—inching

dangerously close to Lionel's neck—quivered as Morticore let out a wet, rasping chuckle.

"You going to serve 'em up for me? They bushwhacked you, strung you up, and left you to die. I don't see a rematch going any better, sad to say."

"I'll have surprise on my side," Lionel said. "Cut me down, show me where they're headed, and watch. Best-case scenario: you dine on death-spirits tonight. Worst case, they kill me, and you get my body—same outcome as right now. You can't lose."

"Mm, see, that sounds like extra work. I'm not a big fan of work in general. I'd rather just stay on the ladies' trail and enjoy a sure thing."

Lionel tried to shake his head. The noose squeezed his windpipe like a fist.

"They didn't just come here by random chance. They were *called*. And like I said, they're on their way to meet with the person who called them, to find out what he wants and what he has to offer. Whether they say yes or no, the road trip—and the gravy train—is over. Starting tomorrow you go back to hunting your own dinner. So why not end things with a chance at a *really* special meal? The Keres aren't going to give you any more free corpses. Might as well have them on the plate instead."

Morticore pulled the blade back. He didn't sheath it, not yet, but he tapped his fingertip against the business end as he contemplated his options.

"One flaw in that notion," he said. "You're right, I've never eaten a Ker. Not sure anybody has. Which means I'm not sure anybody *can*. Could be tainted, toxic. Could be a drop of their blood would kill me stone dead. Right here and now, you're a sure and yummy thing. I set you loose and you win, I might wind up with nothing but three bodies I can't eat. That doesn't do me any favors at all."

The possibility had occurred to Lionel. He just hoped it wouldn't occur to the ghoul, too. Still, Morticore was staying his hand—for now—and they were still negotiating. Lionel just needed to toss in one more thing. A little bit of sweetener to seal the deal. He considered what he had left to bargain with.

Just one thing.

"Ghouls live longer than humans, right?"

"We are inclined toward longevity and disinclined toward taking foolish chances." His hand drew an invisible line between the blade and the noose around Lionel's throat. "A situation drawn perfectly vis-à-vis our current positions. What of it?"

"Cut me loose and I can offer you a solid, one-hundred-percent guarantee of an edible corpse, no matter whether I win or lose tonight."

The ghoul craned his neck, taking a long, exaggerated look to his left and right.

"I don't see anybody else out here. Who have you got to offer?"

"Me," Lionel said.

CHAPTER SIXTEEN

Morticore tipped the broad brim of his hat, pulling it down over his eyes as he studied Lionel. Hunting for a trick in his words, or maybe a trap.

"You're gonna put yourself on my dinner plate, even if you beat the Keres? You don't look suicidal to me. I mean, if you were, you wouldn't have stopped me from slitting your throat in the first place and we wouldn't be having this conversation."

"I'll land on your plate," Lionel said, "but not now, and not tonight. Here's my offer: help me out, and you get exclusive rights to my corpse—whenever, wherever, and however I die. Twenty years from now, or tomorrow. All you have to do is collect."

Morticore's eyes narrowed, shrewd now.

"You'd be willing to swear an oath, make it binding?"

"In Hekate's name," Lionel said.

"And you don't have any loved ones or significant others who might have a problem with that? Dead is dead, but most mortals have a strange issue with seeing their family members turned into cold cuts."

"You ever hear of a witch who goes by the name Madison Hannah?"

"Might have," he said, "here or there, around the way."

"She's my significant other. She honors her debts. And she'll make sure mine are honored, too."

Morticore contemplated his hunting knife.

It caught flashing moonlight, rising high in the ghoul's clenched fist, then whipped through the air. The stool went out from under Lionel's feet, capsizing—and throwing him with it, down to the muddy forest loam. He landed hard on his knees, gasping for breath with the frayed end of the noose dangling like a necktie.

"Hold still. Let me get these off you." The ghoul stepped around him and crouched down. "Ugh. Purple. Ropes cut your circulation off. Shouldn't be any long-term damage, but brace yourself, this is gonna sting like a mother."

That was an understatement. Lionel hissed between his teeth as the knife sliced through his bonds, hot blood flooding strangled veins and leaving a trail of pins and needles and fire. He brought his hands to his chest and gently rubbed them, shrugging the last shreds of rope from his raw and bloody wrists.

"My truck's just down the road," Morticore told him.

"Truck?"

"Sure. Until I see how your reunion with the Keres goes down, I'm not letting you out of my sight. I'll deliver you straight to wherever they're holed up, just because I'm so nice."

"Fine. Have to find my car first. I wrecked it...not far from here, I don't think. I need my luggage."

Lionel rose. He tugged the knot at his throat, loosening it, and pulled the coil of rope over his head. He tossed the severed noose to the mud at his feet. Then he turned to face Morticore.

A Time for Witches

"And I need to borrow that knife."

~~

Morticore's truck looked older than he did. It was more rust than steel, a Frankenstein's monster of welded parts and mismatched tires, and a string of cardboard air fresheners lined the windshield like a Christmas garland. The vinyl seat crinkled under Lionel as he got in. The musty air overpowered him with a nauseating blend of chemical pine and something sickly underneath, like the odor of rotten chicken bones.

"I'll be honest," Morticore told him, "I don't know where we're headed exactly. But I will. Real quick."

"Real quick" was twenty minutes down the road, at a Shell station on a lonely country lane. They were the only customers. Maybe the only customers all night. The door jingled as they walked inside, and the long-faced man behind the counter gave Lionel a silent nod of greeting. His sleepy gaze slid over the ghoul like he wasn't even there.

Morticore caught Lionel's look. His opal eyes shone under the hard electric lights as he shambled down the snack aisle.

"I'm a trapper from the old school," he said. "Old-school tricks of the trade. Hey, watch this."

He gave a big wave to the clerk.

"Hey, friendo. Point us to your facilities? Me and my companion need to snort some cocaine. We might shoot up the place when we're finished."

The counterman's expression didn't change. He didn't even look up. He just pointed toward a door in the rear of the store, then went back to staring at the cigarette rack.

"People look, but they don't see," the ghoul murmured

to Lionel. "They listen, but they only hear what they want to hear. You can use that, if you learn the trick. Speaking of, let's get ourselves a little road knowledge."

The bathroom was a cramped cesspit. One stall, one urinal with a jagged lightning-bolt crack running down the yellowed porcelain. The light bar over the cloudy mirror hummed and made spitting sounds. Lionel stood at Morticore's shoulder, just outside the yawning door of the stall, and stared at the wall of graffiti inside. A maze of knife scratches and black marker doodles, layer upon layer like the strata of an archaeological dig.

"Mind the ghosts," Morticore told him, not looking back.

Lionel saw it. A shadow in the corner of his eye, a reflection in the dirty mirror. He turned slowly, like a hunter creeping up on a rabbit.

Bill was with them. He stood in the corner, cheeks caked in rust-red tears, his eyeless face fixed on the restroom wall. He raised one hand and pointed his finger. Not at the graffiti Morticore was studying, but at the dirty eggshell wall just above the urinal.

There was tiny, crabbed writing there, a mix of smudged ballpoint and Sharpie, in a half dozen hands. *GARY SUX* jostled for space with *This is the Limerick that Never Ends—*

Bill was behind him now, the dead man standing at Lionel's shoulder.

"I'm sorry," Lionel whispered. "For what happened to you. I tried to...I tried."

Morticore's voice drifted over the wall of the bathroom stall. "Don't talk to ghosts, son. Attention whores, every last one of 'em. You talk to them, they'll follow you forever."

Bill's voice was a gust of clammy breath. It washed across the nape of Lionel's neck, curled up and into his ear, and slithered into his brain.

This knowledge took everything from me. I didn't realize it, until I had already paid the price.

"It happens," Lionel said. "People...step sideways sometimes, by accident. Out of the ordinary world. It wasn't your fault. Nothing that happened was your fault."

I tried to find my way home. But I couldn't live there anymore. The people there—my girlfriend, my family—they couldn't understand me, and I couldn't understand them. Magic changes everything.

"I know," Lionel said.

I am the language of the road, the thing that was Bill whispered.

And Lionel knew he'd see him again. And again, in road stops, and restrooms, and standing beside back-alley walls. In death, all that remained of the man was his obsession. He had given himself over to it, and it had devoured him long before the Keres tore him apart. There was only one thing left for Lionel to say.

"Teach me."

~~

The man in charge, the Keres' beckoner, had left his final message on the dirty eggshell wall. What looked like a doodle of a dangling prick became a road map. The letter tips and curls of a ribald rhyme turned into code, and Lionel had translated it with a ghost's fingers buried in the meat of his brain. It all made sense now.

Wait for me at this address, he'd written. *I may be delayed.*

A family lives here. They will keep you fed until I arrive.

The engine of Morticore's truck died with a sputter and a cough, rumbling to a stop at the edge of a cornfield. A dirt road wound its way past a barn and an old, slumbering tractor, up to a farmhouse that slouched on rotten bones.

"This here's as far as I go," the ghoul said. "Your girlfriends are waiting just up the road. Figure I'll hang back and come in to scoop up whoever loses. My money's on them, just so you know."

"On them winning or losing?"

Morticore stared at him.

Lionel's luggage was in the bed of the pickup. The Samsonite had taken a beating in the car crash, but the contents—everything important, anyway—had stayed unbroken. He took what he needed, along with Morticore's hunting knife, slipping the blade into his belt and pulling his windbreaker over it.

From there he moved alone. On foot, crouched low, a loping shadow at the edge of the rippling corn. The dusty earth was barren under his feet, hard as a tombstone. A dry wind ruffled his hair and set an old weather vane, perched atop the barn, to turning; it rattled and let out a rusty squeal.

The Keres' Jeep sat parked in front of the farmhouse, not far from a box van with Indiana plates. If the van belonged to the family, the man pulling the strings hadn't shown his face yet.

Or he'd already come and gone, and the Keres were just finishing their meal.

CHAPTER SEVENTEEN

Lionel circled the farmhouse. No lights burned inside, the windows dark. He hopped a fence with a Beware of Dog sign, and the soles of his shoes landed in something wet. Ten feet away he found the dog. The Keres had taken care of it on their way inside.

Around back, a kitchen door hung open a crack. No sign of a forced entry; someone had let the invaders in. Lionel could only hope they were still breathing. He could save them. If he was smart, if he was fast, if he wasn't too late...

The hope was all he had. He was about to do battle with a trio of death-spirits, maybe about to die, and the fear turned his bladder to a fist of ice—but it also kept his feet in motion. Light steps, faster, forward, as he thought about the family that lived here. If they were still alive, they were counting on him. They needed him to keep moving, to fight the fear, to get this right. Maddie's words drifted back to him: *Sometimes the best way to push through the darkness and keep fighting is to be strong for someone else.*

The kitchen door groaned under his fingertips. He stood on the threshold, ears perked. No one came to check out the noise. He pressed on, the tip of his shoe touching down on a faded linoleum floor.

He heard new sounds now. Footsteps on creaking wood, just above his head, pacing on the second floor.

He slid a butcher knife slid from a block at the edge of the kitchen counter. Lionel already had Morticore's knife in his belt, but he felt better with an extra weapon in his hand.

Light reflections shone, flickering, off a wall of photographs in the hallway. The glow of a muted television set washed over a mother, a father, a little boy, smiling faces framed and frozen in time. Lionel's heart pounded faster as he crept along the thin olive runner. He peered around the corner, through the open arch of the living room.

They were still alive.

The kid was older than he was in the pictures—maybe twelve or thirteen now—but he sat with his parents lined up on the rug in front of the big-screen TV. All three of them with their wrists bound, mouths gagged with strips of torn linen. They'd tried to put up a fight: the woman had a black lump over one eye and a patch of dried blood on her scalp where a fistful of hair had been torn out. Her husband, dressed in his undershirt and boxers, looked like he'd been worked over like a punching bag.

But they were alive. The woman's good eye opened wide and she started to squeal through her gag. Lionel quickly put his finger to his lips, hushing her.

More footsteps from the second floor. He looked back over his shoulder, past the archway, to the staircase. A shock of fight-or-flight adrenaline surged up from his stomach, roaring down his arms and legs.

Easy choice. Fight. He wasn't leaving these people behind.

He crossed the room with three quick, light steps, crouched behind the woman, and sawed at her bonds with the butcher knife. The rope frayed and snapped. She pulled the gag from her mouth but didn't say a word, helping to untie her son while Lionel freed her husband.

He put his finger to his lips once more, making sure they all got the message, then gestured for them to follow him. He led them around the corner and back through the kitchen, waving them past him and through the open back door.

The father was the last one out. Lionel grabbed his arm, leaned close, and whispered in his ear.

"Take your family and *run*." He thought about Morticore, out there in the dark. His deal didn't cover these people's safety, and ghouls were known for breaking their truces on a whim. "Do you have a neighbor? Someone you can rely on?"

The father nodded. "Up the road a ways."

"Go there. Have them drive you into town. Don't come back here. And if you see an old, beat-up truck near the main road, stay away from it. Don't trust the driver. He's not your friend."

He'd thought the glazed look in the man's eyes was from the beating he took. Now Lionel caught something else there. *Haunted*, he thought. The floorboards above let out another long groan, and a muffled peal of laughter drifted down.

"Go." Lionel gave his arm a shove, sending him out with the rest of his family. He watched from the open doorway until the three of them vanished, swallowed by the silent cornfield.

He was alone now, in the den of wolves.

He held the butcher knife in front of him, close and ready, as he took the stairs one slow step at a time. He had a plan. Sort of. The knife wasn't part of it—he had never been in a knife fight in his life, and he didn't know if a Ker could even bleed—but it made him feel a little better.

Either this will work or it won't, he thought. *My fate was sealed the second I walked through the door, and the dice have already been rolled. I'm just waiting to see what number comes up.*

At the top of the stairs, a landing wrapped around the bend of a narrow hallway. At the end of an L-shaped corner, a crack of electric light streamed from an open doorway. He heard another giggle and low, whispering voices. He checked his pockets, the blade on his belt, touched his fingertips to his pounding heart. Then he willed himself into motion, creeping toward the light.

He didn't know he'd been hit until he was falling. There was a thunderclap of pain along his spine—the heel of a shoe, he realized half a second later—and then he was pitching toward the floorboards in a stomach-churning dive. He landed hard, scraping one arm raw on the grainy planks. The butcher knife went flying from his grip; it spun across the wood, blade flashing, clattering to a stop at the end of the hall.

Lionel had a plan. Sort of. Before he could put it into action, Beth's hands clamped onto his wrists, wrenching his arms behind his back as she hauled him to his feet. The doorway ahead of him was already opening wide, the other two Keres coming out to eye their catch. Mindy was silent, her lips pursed, no lollipop this time. Nikki put her hands on her hips and glared.

"I'm starting to think you're not really a witch," the short blonde said, staring up at him. "Witches are supposed to be fonts of knowledge, and it looks to me like you're not capable of learning a damn thing."

"I told you not to follow us," Mindy said, her voice soft.

"Fine, this is fine. No idea how long we're going to be stuck here waiting. More food is—" Nikki's eyes narrowed with fresh suspicion. "You better not have fucked with our food supply. Mindy? Check it out."

She scurried down the stairs. A second later, her voice drifted up from the living room.

"They're gone!"

Beth's hands turned into crushing bands of iron, squeezing Lionel's wrists hard enough to make his eyes water. Nikki got in his face, close enough for him to smell the blood on her breath.

"You *asshole*."

"I've been called that once or twice," Lionel said. "I mean, it's fair."

He needed his left hand free. His left hand, and two seconds. Beth wasn't giving him either one.

"We *live* on death energy," Beth hissed in his ear. "Now what the hell are we supposed to do?"

Nikki smiled. He liked it better when she was frowning.

"Well, we've got one victim right here."

"So we're good for tonight," Beth shot back. "What about tomorrow? Or the day after? We have no idea when this guy is even going to show, *if* he shows."

Nikki answered her, but she kept her eyes locked on

Lionel, her fingernail tracing a slow and winding road from his collarbone to his belly.

"We'll just have to make this one last. You know, Lionel, usually we have to work quickly. The night is only so long, and we like to be on the road before our victims go cold, but this? This is a special situation."

"I don't think we should—" Mindy started to say.

Nikki silenced her with a wave of her hand.

"No. Not this time. I listened to you back in the woods, we strung him up, and this asshole *still* got loose and came after us again. You want to talk about signs and portents? That's a sign, right there." She looked back to Lionel. "It's a sign that you're going to die. Slowly. We're going to take our time and savor every second of it. You're going to keep our bellies full. For days. The only question now is...where, oh where, do we begin?"

"Let's skin him," Beth growled.

"In good time," Nikki said, studying Lionel from his head to his toes. "I want to build up to the *serious* mutilations. It'd suck if his heart gave out on us. Hey, I know."

Her gaze flicked to Beth. She flashed a hungry smile.

"He makes me think of a puppy. So let's drown him."

They wrestled him into the bathroom at the end of the hall. It was a cramped closet painted in pea-soup green, with a claw-footed tub and exposed piping that snaked into the bare rafters. The pipes rattled as Nikki wrenched both of the handles over the spigot, conjuring a waterfall.

Mindy's hunger apparently won out over her reservations. While Beth gripped his wrists, she patted Lionel down. The ghoul's hunting knife slithered free from his belt loop, and she laid it carefully on the edge of the sink. Then she reached into the pocket of his windbreaker and tugged out the white clay flask.

"What's this?" she said, frowning at the wax seal before setting it next to the knife.

"Keeping it safe for a friend," he said. "I promised to handle something for her."

Nikki reached into the tub, fixing a stopper in place as the water crashed down. She snorted.

"Won't be keeping that promise. Or...y'know, any others you might have made. Sorry, not sorry."

He needed one hand free. One hand, and two seconds.

CHAPTER EIGHTEEN

Beth kicked the back of his knee, buckling his leg and shoving him down on the fuzzy green bathmat. Then they tortured him for a while.

He wasn't sure how long. Time stopped the second Nikki forced his face under the water. He held his breath until he couldn't anymore, until the blood roared in his ears and his face was frozen, and then his lungs inhaled on its own and icy well water went pouring down his windpipe.

His body wasn't his anymore. His chest spasmed, and he was breathing air again, but it felt like he was inhaling and exhaling at the same time, signals crashing behind his blurry vision, and he puked on the bathmat before Nikki grabbed a fistful of his hair and pushed his head back into the tub.

At some point he thought he was watching himself, floating outside his own body. He could still feel the burning, the limb-racking convulsions, could feel the ice water surging down his nose and throat and spurting back up again. But it was muffled, and it almost wasn't him there, going limp like a pale doll as his body slapped against a wet puddle on the floor. There were wisps in the air, purple vapor. The Keres sucked them down.

Nikki's fists hammered his back. He was in his skin again. He didn't want to be. She was shouting something in his waterlogged ear.

"*Breathe.* You don't get to die all the way yet. We're not done with you, not by a long shot."

He choked, coughed, vomited again. Then she hauled him up onto his knees, pulling him by his hair, and shoved his face back under the water.

He was back on the sodden bathmat. He couldn't remember how he got there. Beth wasn't bothering to hold his wrists anymore; he was too weak to move on his own. His arms hung limp at his sides, his shirt and slacks soaked, his legs bent at odd angles. They were arguing over him.

"—fourth time you've pulled him back from the brink," Beth was saying. "This is getting too dangerous."

"*Taste* that." Nikki made a suckling sound, pulling air and a wisp of purple mist between her teeth. "We're getting what we need out of him. Don't tell me that isn't delicious."

"I'm not. I'm saying we can death-edge him for a week if we need to, but we have to change up our methods or you're going to push it too far."

"Electricity?" Mindy suggested.

"Electricity could be fun," Nikki conceded. "Then again, so could a few strategic amputations, if we make sure he doesn't lose too much blood."

She took hold of Lionel's shoulders and yanked him up onto his knees. He could barely keep upright, and the death-spirit was a watery blur as she crouched down in

A Time for Witches

front of him. A scarlet skin floated on the surface of the tub, choked-up blood turning the water to rust. His wet hands, smeared red, dangled at his sides.

Hands, he thought. He needed those for something. He had to focus. There was a plan, an idea, might or might not work—

"What do you think, sweetie?" Nikki asked him. "I don't want you to feel left out of the decision-making process here. Do we hook your testicles up to a car battery, or should we just cut 'em off? It's going to be one or the other, and now's your chance to vote."

He found his voice again, somewhere at the bottom of a watery grave. He tasted bile and sulfur on his tongue when he tried to speak.

"Had some time to…think, about what you said, after you left me in the forest."

Nikki shot a glance at Beth, along with a sarcastic smile. "And I thought he was just hanging around."

"About how you can go anywhere now," Lionel croaked. "It makes sense. But I still have a question."

"Always with the questions, this one."

"Why?" he asked. "Why are you doing this?"

"This?" Nikki waved her hand, taking in the cramped bathroom. "You know why. This is what we live on. It's how we eat."

"Not this. Coming here. Just because you *can* leave your battlefields doesn't mean you had a good reason."

"We've got two," Beth told him. "We were bored, and this is fun. That's all the reason we need to do anything."

"What about divine purpose?"

"Do you see anyone checking up on us?" Nikki asked. "Stopping us? Nobody cares, Lionel."

His vision cleared as he looked her in the eye.

"Aren't you afraid of being judged?" he asked.

She curled her lip in disdain. "We won't be judged. Not by you, not by anyone."

"What about the gods?"

Beth laughed, and Nikki joined her with a madcap grin. Behind them, in the doorway, Mindy wasn't smiling at all.

"Sweetie, honey. Listen very closely, okay?" Nikki squeezed his shoulder. "*Fuck* the gods. Fuck them, and fuck humanity too. You keep talking about 'purpose' and 'rules,' and the bottom line is, we *do not care*."

"Thank you," Lionel said.

She squinted at him. "For?"

"Going on the record. We both knew it, but I wanted her to hear you admit it."

He had been saving his strength. Getting it back, slowly, watching his breath and keeping his burning muscles ready. He was still weak as a kitten, but he didn't need much. Just two seconds to shove himself to his feet, lunge for the bathroom sink, and snatch up the white clay flask.

He hurled it to the floor. The flask hit the soaked gray wood and burst, blasting into a fistful of broken shards that scattered to every corner of the room.

Then he stood there, panting and frozen, listening to the sound of stunned silence.

"Uh," Nikki said, staring at the debris. "What the hell was that supposed to be?"

Mindy cleared her throat. "I think he was trying to do some magic."

"Wow." Nikki blinked at Lionel. "You...really suck at this. I'm genuinely impressed by how bad you are. Okay,

A Time for Witches

let's move this party downstairs for round two. I think I saw some jumper cables down in the hall closet—"

A bubble rose to the surface of the tub. It was the size of a billiard ball, and it broke the blood-tinged water with a head-turning *pop*.

"The hell?" Beth murmured, standing behind Lionel.

More bubbles followed. Tiny, rippling, rising as the bloody water started to simmer like a pot on a stove.

Then it began to boil.

"What is this?" Nikki asked the water. She turned, locking eyes with Lionel. "What did you do?"

"Tisiphone," he replied. "The Fury who avenges murder. You know, like the ones you've been committing lately?"

Mindy took a step backward, shaking her head in horror.

"No," she breathed. "No, no, this...this can't happen. We're righteous. He said we were righteous."

"Who said?" Lionel asked.

Beth grabbed his shoulder and shook it, hard. "Send her *back*."

Lionel folded his arms and watched the water boil.

"Send her back? She's a goddess. I don't think she answers to me. All I did was grab her attention. You three gave her a reason to show up. Besides, you heard your sister." He shot a sidelong glance at Nikki. "I suck at this."

The brim of a peaked hat, wide and scarlet, slowly rose from the boiling water. A veil of silver chains hung from the brim, concealing the face beneath. Then a woman's slender shoulders, draped in bloody linen.

Mindy screamed. The house screamed with her.

As she turned to run, the building erupted in a cacophony. Every door in the house began to open and shut on its own, slamming in a mad drumbeat, old wood rattling on its hinges. Bulbs flashed, lamps igniting and dying and flaring again, painting the cornfields in long, jagged strobes of light from every window.

Nikki was right on her sister's heels. Beth wavered for a second, torn between Lionel—and one last murder—and the figure rising from the bloody broth. The woman's arms didn't stop where they should have. Lionel saw the bend of an elbow under the sleeve of her robe—and a second elbow, and a third, with no end in sight.

Beth ran. Lionel followed her. He snatched Morticore's hunting knife from the rim of the sink and darted over the threshold, out onto the second-floor landing.

Mindy was at the top of the stairs. Frozen, pale, staring down at something only she could see. A rush of air knocked Lionel off his feet and dropped him to his knees, like the breath-searing suction of a jetliner door blasting open at forty thousand feet. It took her and swept her down. The jackhammer rattle of slamming doors swallowed her short, shrill cry.

He didn't see Nikki. Beth raced for the door at the far end of the hall. It swung open, showing a bedroom beyond it and a window big enough to jump through. It slammed shut. Open, bedroom, window. Shut. She put her hand on the knob.

The door wrenched open a third time and there was nothing beyond it but an inky void. And red-gloved hands, eight of them, firing from the black and latching onto her arms and throat.

Gloved hands like the ones that fell over Lionel's face from behind him, clasping their velvet palms over his eyes and stealing his sight. More hands closed—gently now—around his elbows, his wrists, his hips, his knees.

Two mouths spoke, two warm puffs of breath against his earlobes, but they shared a single voice.

"This," Tisiphone said, "is not for your eyes, magician."

CHAPTER NINETEEN

Lionel was outside. He knelt in the hard-packed dirt in front of the farmhouse, at the edge of a vast and silent cornfield.

He couldn't remember how he got there. He'd had a sense of motion, or of standing still while the world rearranged itself around him. A searing pressure behind his eyes, a swell of nausea—and then it was over.

Crickets trilled in the night.

He looked to the farmhouse. All the windows were dark, the slouching timbers quiet now. No sign that anyone, or anything, had been there at all. He didn't go back inside. He would never go back inside.

The rumble of tires was coming his way, drifting down the backcountry road. He quickly hid Morticore's knife, slipping it back into his belt and pulling his windbreaker over it. If the escaped family had been quick enough or lucky enough to find one, they might have hailed a local sheriff. Or it was Morticore himself, coming to collect on his debt—and if there weren't any fresh corpses inside that house for him to dine on, the ghoul might not want to wait for Lionel's natural death.

The answer, as headlights bloomed and dazzled Lionel's

vision, was neither. He made out the shadow of a long and sleek SUV. Sport tires rumbled to a stop; the engine died, and then the headlights. It was a Lincoln Navigator, painted the color of gunmetal.

The driver's-side door swung open. Buttery-leather boots touched down on the arid soil.

"I wasn't lying, at the party," Cordell Spears called out to Lionel. He shut the Navigator's door and walked toward him with an easy and confident stride. "I really am a fan. All the same, couldn't believe *you* were the one to come and save me. Lionel Page, professional skeptic with some startling extracurricular activities. That's one hell of a double life you're leading."

"Save you?" Lionel echoed.

He asked the question, but a cold finger trailed down the nape of his neck, prickling his flesh, and he knew he already had the answer.

"C'mon," Cordell said. He stopped walking, five feet of distance between the two men. "I could spell it all out, but I wouldn't dream of denying you the pleasure. You've got all the pieces. Solve the puzzle."

"It was you. You were calling to the Keres. You lured them to the Midwest, away from their battlefields. You were the one leaving the coded messages and telling them where to drive. Do you know what those things are? Do you know what they *do*?"

"Well, they're death-spirits, so...not exactly tough to figure out."

"They've been murdering people. And you're responsible."

Cordell pointed to the silent farmhouse.

"They're not murdering anybody anymore. You just

took care of that. Besides, they were helping me out. And there's a moral balance to consider." He held out his open palms, adjusting them like a weighted scale. "Maybe they ate some hapless tourist yesterday. So? Just *one* of my hospitals—funded by my money and my tech—saved a dozen children's lives at the same time. More than a fair trade. Hey, not to be glib, but...think of the children."

"Why did you do it?"

"You know why," Cordell told him.

He did. Like the man said, he had all the pieces. He just didn't like the way they fit together, because seeing the pattern meant he had to accept his part in it.

"You used me," Lionel said.

Cordell nodded, amiable. He pointed again, up at the darkened eaves of the house.

"That cunning-call shouldn't have existed. I mean, you cannot imagine how hard I work to keep my hands clean, to distance myself from anything that could bring divine fury down on my head. It's a full-time job. Yes, I had to have Jurgen killed. Oops. My bad. I had his body cremated and every last sentimental belonging—anything that could forge a sympathetic link and fuel a revenge spell—sunk to the bottom of the Aegean Sea. If it wasn't for one morgue clerk who thought he was doing the right thing, sending his wedding ring home to his widow..."

Cordell dropped his hand to his side. He tilted his head back and let out a tired bark of a laugh.

"The one thing, the one thing on this *planet* that could actually hurt me was that flask. But I know your work, Lionel. And when I saw you scoop it up off the floor—meaning you and me were the only people in that museum who saw through Kayla Lambert's camouflage charm—I checked you out fast."

"What did you learn?"

"That you're for real, my friend. A true-blue crusader who can always be counted on to do the right thing. I already had the Keres in the palm of my hand; they had a different job ahead of them, one I'll have to find a replacement crew for. That's fine. See, I knew what kind of man you are. Which means I knew exactly what would happen if I sent them to crash at your motel. All I had to do was hand you the clues, and your righteous rage would do the rest of the job."

Lionel felt sick to his stomach. He thought about Kayla's last request. And about the flask, shattered now, powerless, in broken pieces in the upstairs bathroom.

"You knew I'd hunt them down," Lionel said. "You knew I didn't have any way to stop them, but I'd have to hunt them anyway."

"You had one way to stop them," Cordell said.

"That thing in your last message, telling them to hole up here and wait for you...you tricked them. You were never going to show your face here."

Cordell circled him, walking with a confident stride. "Not until you'd played your part. You had the weapon, and I knew you were both clever enough to figure it out and desperate enough to crack the seal. The cunning-call is a gun with a single bullet, and you fired it for me. The Keres, well, they were my sacrificial lambs, bless their vicious hearts. Everybody did their jobs tonight, and speaking as a captain of industry, that's always a pleasure to see."

Lionel's stomach boiled. Rage, simmering over, rising

like bile in the back of his throat. He thought about the knife on his belt, hidden under the fold of his windbreaker. He thought about how there was no question of guilt: Cordell had openly confessed to the murder of Kayla's husband. And he'd made a promise to her ghost.

He thought about how they were all alone out here, just him and Cordell, with no one around for miles.

"I can read your mind," Cordell said. "Well, not really. But tell me something: have you ever killed a man?"

"Once," Lionel said.

"Did you do it cold? Was he unarmed?" Cordell showed his open and empty hands. "Did you wrap your hands around his throat and just...squeeze until the lights went out? Can you, do you think?"

"You're not unarmed," Lionel said. "You came here to kill me. To tie up loose ends. It's going to be you or me."

Cordell offered up a schoolboy grin.

"Are you kidding me? I came here to *thank* you. You literally saved my life tonight. More than my life. I mean, the Furies don't *just* kill a man. That's the warm-up before the main event, down below. Not a party I care to be invited to. And what are you going to do, expose me? Tell the world the truth? Only if you change jobs and start writing for the tabloids. Here. Let me show you the only weapon I ever carry."

One of his hands slid beneath his tan sports jacket. Lionel tensed, his right hand opening, fingers curled and ready to go for the knife.

Cordell produced a fountain pen and a vinyl checkbook sleeve. He flipped it open with a flourish.

"What's your favorite charity, Lionel?"

Lionel stared at him. "Charity?"

"Like I said, I know you. I can't buy your silence. Others have tried, and failed, and you'd be offended if I offered you a stack of cash. So, name your favorite charity, and I will write one whopper of a donation, right here and now. A salve for the conscience. You can't *hurt* me, but I'd feel a lot better if you were on my team, or at least not trying to get in my way."

That was the second time he'd alluded to his invulnerability. Lionel was thinking about the knife again.

"You seem pretty convinced that you're untouchable," Lionel said. "Over the course of my career I've crossed paths with a few people who had that attitude. Most of them know better now."

"Ah, that. To clarify, I'm being literal. You physically cannot harm me. No one can. Do you know what a hero is?"

"A grossly overused word," Lionel said, "often applied to people who didn't earn it."

Cordell cocked a finger gun at him.

"You think you're insulting me, but you're actually one-hundred-percent correct. Because you can't earn it. A hero, in the historic, classic sense, is a figure of living myth. Most often the product of relations between a god and a mortal. Nine months later, what pops out is a baby hero. A human infused with divine energy, and thus uniquely entitled to a place in history."

"No one is entitled to a place in history," Lionel said.

"I am. See, my mom was trailer trash. I'm not being mean, honest. She was born in a trailer and she died in a trailer and never had the vision for a bigger life. But she was a looker, in her prime, and drew more than her share of would-be suitors at the diner where she worked. One of them, disguised as a long-haul trucker, wrecked her bed for about a week before revealing he was actually...oh, go for it. Guess. I'll give you three chances."

"I didn't think there was a god of assholes," Lionel said.

"Now you're just hurting my feelings." Cordell struck a dramatic pose and flexed a bicep. "Not just any god, but the ruler of them all."

Lionel's eyebrows lifted. "Zeus?"

"God of gods, king and judge of men, the thunderbolt! And...my dad. Not that he's been an active parent in my life. He took off and that was that, never even came back when Mom showed the first signs of a baby bump."

"Not to ruin your story," Lionel said, "but are you sure your mom didn't shack up with a mental patient?"

"She had physical evidence. That, and he appeared in a burst of blinding light when he revealed himself, and changed into a zoo's worth of animal shapes to prove he was who he said he was." Cordell's bright smile faded as he looked Lionel in the eye. "My mom wasn't crazy. And neither am I."

Lionel wasn't sure about that. But he knew the gods and goddesses of ancient Greece were real—he worked for one, technically—just like he knew Cordell might be only half-right.

It was entirely possible that Cordell Spears was the son of Zeus and a mortal woman. And it was entirely possible that he was also a dangerous madman.

"The comics got it all wrong," he told Lionel. "Being a hero isn't about fighting evil and saving the day. Sure, you can do those things, and heroes have and heroes will, but it's secondary to the real point. Have you ever heard the word *kleos*?"

Lionel shook his head.

"Roughly translated, it means 'glory.' A hero's purpose is to serve as a bridge between the world of gods and the world of men. To remind the mortals of their place, while encouraging their piety. To that end, a hero's sole drive, the only thing that matters, is to gather *kleos*. The more *kleos* you have, the stronger your myth will grow and the more powerful you become. The more powerful a hero becomes, the greater their deeds and the more *kleos* they gain."

"Hunting for glory," Lionel said. "Like...making a fortune in technology, founding a string of hospitals, slapping your name over everything, and working the talk-show circuit. Or throwing a massive party in Central Park."

"Have to keep up with modern times. I hope you'll come to my party, by the way. If you need VIP tickets, just say the word, I'm your hookup."

"I've got plans that night," Lionel said. "Like maybe taking down a corrupt billionaire who thinks he can get away with murder."

Cordell clicked his tongue and shook his head.

"You don't get it. Yet. You will, though. Look, buddy, I'm not a person. I'm a concept. I'm literally an incarnate myth. I'm a story coming to life right before your very eyes. We weren't costumed superheroes, back in the golden age, and we weren't role models either. We were divine, by right of our holy birth. We were *worshiped*. Heroes didn't have entourages; they had *cults*. All I want is my rightful due, and the plan to make it happen is already in motion. The world has been sleeping for too long. I'm going to wake it up with a bang."

"Your rightful due," Lionel said. "You seriously think

you deserve to be worshiped, just because of who your father was?"

"That's how the world works. Always has, and always will."

"Got news for you," Lionel said. "Your myth is ending tonight. Right here, right now."

Cordell peered at him, incredulous. He spread his arms wide.

"Why? Lionel, you're standing on the cusp of a brave new world. A new golden age, and you can be a front-row witness to it all. Why stand in my way, when you can't possibly win?"

Lionel thought about that. A dry wind whistled through the cornfield. A graveyard wind, blowing gray dust between the two men's shoes.

"Two reasons," he said. "First, I made a promise to Kayla Lambert. And I keep my word."

He knew the second reason, but it took him a minute to find the words. He knew why, too.

His journey to New York had opened his eyes to the real world. He was the Fool at first, stumbling blind, but he understood—then eventually accepted—that magic was real. That there were gods, and monsters, and mysteries beyond anything he'd ever believed possible.

What took longer was accepting his own place in that world. He had still felt that lingering hesitance, that stubborn refusal in his gut. But he was past that now.

"The second reason," Lionel said, "is because I'm a witch, in the service of Hekate, just like my mother was before me. And I'm standing in your way because that's my job."

CHAPTER TWENTY

Cordell's arms, once held open wide, now curled at his sides. Not a boxer's stance, not quite, but he was ready to throw a punch.

"Darn shame," he said.

Lionel squared his footing in the dirt.

"There are rules," he said, recalling Maddie's talk with Kayla, "and they apply to everyone. Even heroes."

"Who told you that? Sorry. They lied."

"You murdered an innocent man," Lionel said. "And you led the Keres here, knowing they'd butcher even more people—"

"A small handful of people, most of whom probably didn't even have families or anyone who will miss them. Be rational. Focus on the ends, not the means: a few eggs get broken when you need to bake a cake. But I *save* lives, every single day."

"I think your hospitals will carry on just fine without you," Lionel said.

Cordell took a deep breath. Then he clasped his hands in front of him, laced his fingers, and cracked his knuckles.

"Apparently 'you cannot physically harm me' wasn't clear enough for you. That's fine. You know, I understand.

It's a lot to take on faith. If you really need a demonstration, I'll see what I can do."

He was fast. Too fast. He closed the distance in a heartbeat and his hand locked around Lionel's throat.

Then Lionel's heels left the ground, toes dangling in the open air, as Cordell scooped him up. He held Lionel up by the throat as if he were weightless, fingers clenching to choke off his air.

"I'm stronger than I look," Cordell said through gritted teeth. "Comes from a healthy diet, regular exercise with a personal trainer, and—what was it? Oh, yeah. Being the *motherfucking son of Zeus*. Now do you believe me?"

Lionel's hand flailed under his windbreaker, fumbling, reaching for his belt.

"Not just yet," he croaked.

His fingers closed around the hilt of Morticore's hunting knife. He ripped it free and brought it plunging down. The blade punched through the meat of Cordell's forearm, impaling him.

Cordell shrieked. He let go, dropping Lionel to the dirt. The knife tore free, spattering a gout of hot blood across the soil. Lionel didn't give him a chance to recover. He barreled at Cordell, thrusting the knife out, and drove it straight into his belly.

Cordell doubled over, leaning against him, and his breath gusted out in a wheeze.

"The story," he hissed with the last of his air, "can't end this way."

"It just did," Lionel told him.

He twisted the knife and pulled, ripping the blade upward, tearing through Cordell's stomach. Pink foam frothed on Cordell's lips as his body bucked, convulsing in a death spasm.

Lionel laid him down on the hard-packed dirt at the edge of the cornfield. Blood soaked Cordell's dress shirt, trickled down his sides, and fed the earth beneath him. His eyes were glazed, staring up at the night sky. Body still breathing, but just barely.

And then not at all. Lionel crouched over him and put two fingers to his neck, checking for a pulse. Cordell Spears—billionaire philanthropist, medical pioneer, and alleged son of a god—was dead.

Lionel wasn't sure how he felt about that.

He had killed, once, before. But he hadn't been there for the aftermath of his battle with Jimmy Sloane. Sloane had beaten him half to death, and Lionel had to take his victory lap unconscious, on a hospital gurney. Recovery was slow and strange and he had a million things to think about, Maddie and magic and his own future, to block out the fact that he'd taken a man's life. He didn't really have to think about it.

Out here, at the edge of the cornfield in the dark, there was nothing but thoughts. Thoughts and the corpse at his feet.

Had to be done, he told himself. He caught the glitter of twin opals from the wavering curtain of cornstalks. Morticore was here after all. Watching their fight from a safe distance, waiting for a man to die, not particular about who.

Lionel patted Cordell's body down. He took his car keys and his wallet. Then he gestured to the remains.

"Bon appétit," he said.

He was answered with a wry snicker from the corn.

Lionel climbed into the leather seat of the luxury SUV. Then he shut the door, adjusted the rearview mirror, and fired up the engine.

~~

Morning found Lionel in another roadside motel, in another cheap bed with over-starched sheets, sunlight streaming around another pair of paper-thin curtains. He sat up and regretted it. He had pulled muscles he didn't know he had; his back was a clump of knots, his neck and shoulder burned every time he turned his head, and a line of fire ran down one battered leg, making his knee feel like it was going to explode if he put too much pressure on it.

He hobbled to the bathroom and brushed his teeth, trying not to look at himself in the mirror. Not until he got some clothes on, to hide the bruises. Looking would just make it hurt more.

For the twentieth time, he thought back over last night, walking through it step by step. He wasn't worried about Cordell Spears. He'd made sure the man was dead, and thanks to Morticore, there wouldn't be a corpse for the police to find. Maybe a few teeth and well-gnawed bones, and ghouls were good at covering their tracks: he would have made sure they were scattered far and wide or buried deep.

And it's not like Spears would have put this trip on his day planner, he thought. He couldn't exactly tell his administrative assistant that he was taking a jaunt to pull a lethal con job on a pack of death-spirits. Even if he'd given a bogus reason for sticking around after the museum show, nobody would be looking for him at the farmhouse when he turned up missing.

The Keres were gone, dragged off to face brutal

judgment. Cordell Spears was dead. Job done. Lionel had handled it.

So why didn't he feel like it was all over?

The only loose end was Spears's ride. Getting pulled over behind the wheel of an SUV he didn't own, registered to a famous celebrity who'd be on the missing-persons registry in another day or so, would be a disaster. On the other hand, his own car was totaled, lost on some backwoods forest road. No real alternative right now. He'd have to be careful. Drive the SUV safe—and watch the speed—until he caught up with Maddie.

At least I'll have one hell of a story to tell her, he thought.

He hobbled back out of the bathroom, leaning on his good leg, and turned on the TV just to break the silence.

Cordell Spears was on television. He lounged back in his chair, casual and smiling, on the set of *Good Morning America*.

"—so I said, my only problem is that I just can't stop winning. It's tragic, I know."

The studio audience laughed and made sympathetic noises as he mugged for the camera. Lionel's blood ran cold. Prerecorded. Had to be. *No*, he realized. *Live show. This is happening right now.*

The man he killed last night was sitting in a studio in Times Square, a thousand miles away, giving an interview. No sign of a stab wound. He was even wearing a short-sleeved polo shirt. No knife puncture on his forearm, no scar. It was like last night hadn't even happened.

Had it happened? Of course it had. Then why did the entire tail of the evening, everything after he smashed the clay flask, feel like an elaborate dream? Lionel fell backward, landing with a thump on the edge of the motel bed with his eyes locked on the screen.

"If you're just joining us," the hostess said, "we're here with Cordell Spears, the inventor and entrepreneur who some call 'the real-life Tony Stark.'"

Cordell grinned, batting the compliment aside with a wave of his hand.

"Oh, please. I'm nowhere near that cool. Though I will say that a certain couple of actors you might recognize from the Avengers movies are good friends of mine, and if you come to this little party I've got planned in Central Park, you *might* get a chance to meet them and take a selfie. No promises."

"You're talking about the upcoming 'Gala for the People.'"

Lionel jumped up and ran for the window, tearing aside the curtain. There was the proof he needed: Cordell's SUV, parked out front, right where he'd left it. He was still walking back through his memories. One thing stuck out. Maybe it should have before now, but he hadn't understood it. Cordell's last words.

The story can't end this way.

Lionel had taken it as a protest against an unfair fate. A desperate denial. But he was wrong. Cordell wasn't in denial; he was offering a simple statement of fact. It didn't matter that Lionel had stabbed him to death and fed him to a hungry ghoul: the story, his story, couldn't end like that.

So it didn't.

Look, buddy, I'm not a person. I'm a concept. I'm literally an incarnate myth.

"That's right," he said on the screen. "I'm throwing a party for the world, and I've got some surprises in store."

Cordell looked straight into the camera. His eyes bore into Lionel's. And though he was talking to the audience, Lionel knew Cordell's next words were a message for him alone.

"You will come and see me, won't you? It's going to be a night you'll never forget."

II: Queen of Swords

CHAPTER TWENTY-ONE

The last time Maddie carried a gun in Chicago, it was 1928.

She had carried a revolver then; automatics jammed, and she had watched a man die when his steel seized up at the wrong moment. She didn't take a chance on an automatic until the late '70s, when the winds of fortune carried her to the Italian coast and put an AMT Hardballer in her hand. That gun became her traveling companion for nearly a decade.

Now she was back in Chicago with a pair of mismatched pistols nestled in her purse. If she squinted, she could almost pretend it was the same city. Same woolly gray canyons, towers of stone that looked old on the day they were built. Same slick streets, dark and glistening under a cold sunset rain. The last dirty rays of sunlight were dying down in Chinatown, on the south side of the city, and the tourists were going home. Gusts of smoke from a sidewalk vent gave the darkening air a hazy tinge, carrying the scent of roasting duck.

Maddie stood under the shade of a travel umbrella, listening to faint droplets plink down against the black canvas, and savored the moment of calm before the storm.

There was a time, she recalled, when poison was her

weapon of choice. She'd dabbled with the spear but never really had the knack for it. She had taken lessons in fencing, but she was better with knives. Then came the birth of the modern gun, and everything changed.

She was good with guns. Then again, the benefit of immortality was that you could get good at anything, for a little while. Putting in your ten thousand hours of practice to attain mastery was just a matter of clearing room on your calendar. But there was only so much room in one person's brain, and memories and skills faded with time. Once, she could have been a champion racer on horseback. Once, she played piano like a virtuoso. But she hadn't saddled up in decades, and she wasn't entirely sure she remembered how to tap out a basic scale anymore.

Maddie had learned everything there was to know about the workings of steamboats for a single job, back in the summer of 1889. Over a century later, nothing of that time remained but the fond nostalgic glow of a night on the equator, breathing in steam off the water, brushing away mosquitoes and sharing cigars with Samuel Clemens at the starboard rail. She idly wondered if the engines and boilers she'd studied so hard to master even existed anymore.

At least she still knew the way of the gun. Those, she was confident, would be sticking around for a while.

Her new assignment found her riding west. Hunting, looking to settle a loose end that should have been severed a long, long time ago. She had a contact in Chicago: Trey, a hustler who made half his money slinging rock and the other half as a paid snitch. Regina Dunkle had saved his life once, and he would spend the rest of that life in her debt. He was accustomed to strange women showing up on his doorstep at two in the morning, wearing keys around their necks, and he knew to give them whatever they needed without asking questions.

"I found your guy," he told her. "You're looking for a fat cat named Liu Bingwen. He splits his business between here and Miami, but I happen to know he's in town this week, lining up a new score. Officially, his line is legal transpo. He's on the board of directors of Lucky Eight."

Lucky Eight Shipping was the thread she'd been following, from Montauk to Miami to the American heartland. "And unofficially?"

"Lots of shit winds up in those shipping containers, accidentally on purpose. Guns, blow, refugees, whatever and whoever you need moved. The man is intercontinental."

"How about this week?"

"Word is, firepower." Trey looked her up and down. "Which means you'd better bring some of your own, if you're going to have a chat with the man. You strapped? I can hook you up."

She bought a .32 revolver from him, handing over a hundred in cash. It was a janky, loose piece with a scratched-up serial number; the last owner had tried to forensics-proof it, but they had no idea what they were doing and gave up halfway. That was fine. She didn't plan on using it, and if she did, she'd only need to empty it once. It went into her purse alongside her real weapon of choice, a storm-gray Sig Sauer.

Trey pointed her to the Hope Pagoda on South Wentworth, down in the heart of Chinatown. One more restaurant in a sea of bright yellow signs, nestled between a bubble-tea parlor and a boutique offering imported housewares. She had been watching the place for two hours, noting everyone who came and went, counting heads as they pushed past the "Closed Today, Private Party" sign on the door.

It was dark now. Electric lights washed the slick street in a hazy glow, and the rain was starting to pour. The boutique cashiers scrambled to pull their displays in from the sidewalk, water guttering down blue vinyl awnings. Maddie took a deep breath.

She walked down a side alley, rain pelting her umbrella, puddles sloshing under her olive Reeboks. She'd dressed casually for this job—boot-cut jeans and an ivory blouse under her old battered cargo jacket, clothes she could move fast in. Hopefully she wouldn't have to. But "immortal" didn't mean "unkillable": Hekate's blessing protected her from old age, not bullets.

A pair of round aluminum garbage cans lined up next to the restaurant's kitchen door. The rain tap-danced on the battered lids, playing percussion. Maddie checked the back door. Then she checked the trash cans and reached into her purse for the palm-sized .32.

Back on the sidewalk out front, now one weapon lighter, the only thing barring her way was the sign on the door. Maddie ignored it. She breezed in, greeted by the aroma of fried seafood and the faint, lilting strains of Mandarin elevator music on a sound system. The big bruiser in the vestibule, planting himself between her and the party, was harder to slip past.

"Sorry," he said, not sounding sorry at all. "Private event."

She looked up at him. "I'm here to see Liu Bingwen."

"Private event," he said, over-enunciating his words like

she might be hard of hearing. "You are not on the guest list."

"Tell him I'm here to discuss the deal he made a year ago in Miami, with Cordell Spears. And if he won't talk to me, my next stop is the *Chicago Tribune*."

Empty bluff, but the pained look on his face told her it was a direct hit. He stepped back and waved a flunky over, the two of them whispering in rapid-fire back-and-forth. While they debated, Maddie leaned to one side and peered past the tea-stained folding-screen wall of the vestibule. Whoever decorated this place was into aquatic life. A lacquer wall mural depicted a giant octopus, glossy tentacles unfurling, while Chinese junks sailed across turbulent ocean waves. On the far side of the room, across a sea of clear blue carpet and empty tables dressed in white, a trophy swordfish hung over rows of bottles on teakwood shelves.

The bar was teak, too, a straight-razor slash adorned with intricate scalloped engravings. A lucky cat stood at the end, raising a porcelain paw in greeting. No one was drinking, but the bartender was working overtime, mixing up cocktails and setting them on a serving tray. More folding screens cordoned off a chunk of floor space at the back of the restaurant. Maddie craned her neck, and the bouncer moved to block her line of sight while his flunky ran off with her message.

"Don't move," he told her.

She wasn't waiting long. The errand boy came back, standing on his tiptoes to whisper into the bouncer's ear. He nodded and eyed Maddie.

"I have to search you first."

"There's a gun in my purse," she told him, handing it over by the strap.

He rummaged around, pulled out the Sig Sauer, and jammed it into his belt for safekeeping.

"You get this back when you leave."

"Sure," she said.

Then he patted her down. Brisk but professional—he'd actually had some training. That was fine; she didn't have anything else to hide. He was a bulky shadow at her shoulder, looming over her as he walked her across the restaurant.

The folding screens penned off a mahjong game in progress. She pegged the walrus in the red Hawaiian shirt, sweat glistening on his salt-and-pepper mustache, as Liu Bingwen. Two of the other players, like the men standing around them, cradling drinks and making soft small talk with bulges under their jackets, were clearly part of his business insurance policy. Maddie counted heads fast: nine men, plus Liu and the bouncer behind her, all armed.

The fourth man at the table wasn't part of Bingwen's regular posse. *The client*, she thought, looking from his acne-scarred face—*Russian, maybe*—to the heavy black plastic cases stacked to one side of his eight-hundred-dollar shoes.

Everything—from getting the answers she needed to her own survival—depended on her taking command of the situation. Bingwen was opening his mouth; she strode up to the table and spoke before he did.

"I'll keep this quick, so you can get back to your game. I don't want to waste your time, so I'll tell you what I already know. You're a ranking member of the 14K Triad. What they call a white paper fan: middle management, in charge of business administration, legitimate and otherwise. Specifically, you handle affairs for a shipping company. Lucky Eight. One year ago, you pulled a smuggling job for Cordell Spears, moving a shipment of contraband from Greece to Miami."

The new client gave Bingwen a hard-eyed look. He was in the middle of an unexpected situation here, and he didn't like it. Considering the smuggler had probably been talking up how great his security was, a stranger walking in and dropping intimate details didn't engender any confidence. Bingwen's lips parted again. Then closed. He forced a laugh, spreading his hand to encourage his men to join in.

"It...appears we have a very confused young lady here. I'm on the board of Lucky Eight, that's true, but it's a legitimate shipping company with a spotless record. We've never even been accused of a crime. As for Cordell Spears, I know *of* him—everyone does, I imagine—but I've never met the man."

She'd hoped this would be easy. It was never easy. Maddie put a hand on her hip.

"Now you're wasting *my* time. You should ask yourself what else I know. And how your superiors might feel if certain details of your operation were released to the press, along with supporting evidence."

He shifted in his chair, torn between nerves and bluster. He shot a glance to one of the standing men, who moved to a position near the edge of the folding screens. Another followed his lead and hovered close to the bouncer. It was a pincer formation, cutting off her only avenue of retreat.

"You know my name," Bingwen said, "but I don't know yours."

"Some people call me Madison. Madison Hannah. In New York City and in Moscow, I'm the *Nocnitsa*. In Serbia, some call me *Babaroga*."

One of the standing men took a slug from his whiskey glass and snorted at her. "What do they call you in China?"

"Good question," Maddie replied. "I've actually never been to China. It's on my bucket list. I suppose…"

She trailed off, doing the math. Distances, arm reach, all the weapons in the room, where they were and who could reach them the fastest. Which of the gangsters looked like followers, and which ones were leaders. Priority targets.

"I suppose," she said, "they'll know me as the woman who walked into a Triad hangout and murdered every single man in the room because they didn't give her what she wanted."

CHAPTER TWENTY-TWO

Time stopped. The room was frozen, every man looking to Liu Bingwen for guidance. The boss took a deep breath.

Then he laughed so hard his belly shook under his Hawaiian shirt. He slapped the edge of the table, making the mahjong tiles dance.

"Look at me." He held up his perfectly level hand. "I'm shaking. *Shaking* with terror. All right, all right, I think this hysterical little girl has been humored enough. Wei. Jiankang. Escort her outside. Take her out through the kitchen. I don't want her making a scene in front of the restaurant. Walk her down the block and call her a taxi."

One of the standing men grabbed Maddie's forearm, squeezing the sleeve of her cargo jacket. She let him.

"I'd like my weapon back." She pointed to the bouncer.

The Sig Sauer sat nestled snug in the bouncer's belt. He crossed his arms, leaving it there, and stared down at her like he was daring her to reach for it.

"We'll mail it to you," he said.

Another man—Jiankang, she figured—was sitting to Bingwen's left at the table. He pushed his chair back. Before he rose, Bingwen leaned over and hissed out a staccato command in Mandarin. He responded with a curt nod and eyes of stone.

Maddie had told the truth: she'd never been to China, but she hoped to visit someday. That didn't mean she didn't speak Chinese. She was rusty, but she got the gist of it, loud and clear.

"*Take her to the boat. Find out what she knows and who she talked to.*"

She played dumb and innocent, letting the two lanky men guide her away from the table—Bingwen giving her a mocking wave of his fingers—and toward the kitchen door. It was along the back wall, right next to the far end of the bar. The bartender shook his head at her, muttering under his breath, and went back to wiping down the lacquered teak.

The kitchen, a long and narrow aisle with stainless-steel fixtures running down the middle, was empty; the cooking staff had been sent home for the day, the burners cold, pots and pans dangling from hanging hooks. Maddie's big eyes took it all in as she measured distances and counted footsteps. The back door opened onto the alley, and a gust of cold, wet wind rolled in. The rain was still coming down, just on the edge of a storm, water rippling across the broken and muddy concrete in the dark.

"You don't need to call me a cab," she said. "I can take it from here."

Wei squeezed her arm tighter.

"We insist," he said.

"It's only polite," Jiankang added, giving his partner a pointed glance.

They marched her outside.

Mother of witches, Maddie thought, offering up a prayer in the cold rain, *guide my eye and guide my hand.*

Here we go.

She looked to Jiankang and asked, in conversational Mandarin: "So where's this boat you're taking me to?"

She felt Wei's hand loosen on her sleeve. Just enough for her to pivot on her heel, snatch up the lid from the trash can next to the kitchen door, and hurl it. The battered lid went sailing and hit Jiankang in the face. Not hard enough to hurt him, but he stumbled, off-balance. The .32 revolver was right where she left it, inside the trash can on a mound of rotting food and sodden cardboard.

She snatched it up, pressed the muzzle under Wei's chin, and pulled the trigger.

Thunder roared over the sound of the slug as it blasted through his mouth, his brain, and out the top of his skull, trailing a wet arc of powdered bone and glittering garnet. The dead man tumbled to the asphalt, bleeding out into a black puddle. Jiankang was fumbling for his weapon, blinded by the rain. She closed the gap between them with two quick steps and yanked him close, pulling him into a hug with the gun between them. She fired two shots into his heart and let his body drop.

Maddie looked to the alley door. Inside, they'd heard the gunshots or they hadn't; she had work to do either way. She swapped her weapon for Jiankang's, snaking it from his holster. He had a revolver, fat, adorned with chrome and an inscription in Hanzi etched into the grip. Six shots loaded and ready. She started a mental count and headed in.

The alley door swung shut behind her. On the move, she shrugged off her jacket and tossed it onto a counter.

Tempo was everything now. She reached out with her free hand and snatched a meat cleaver from a dangling rack, not breaking her stride.

She kicked the kitchen door open, emerged into the restaurant, already winding her arm back for a fastball throw. The business meeting was over; the Russian was on his way to the door, halfway across the restaurant, in the middle of Bingwen's posse. He'd left the bulky plastic cases behind. He turned at the sound, surprised—just in time to see the meat cleaver spinning through the air.

It hit him between the eyes, the blade chopping his nose in half and burying itself in his skull. He dropped to his knees. His eyes rolled back and his hands twitched in spasmodic jitters at his sides as blood guttered down his face.

Maddie fired off a shot. *One.* The bullet ripped a hole through Bingwen's Hawaiian shirt and buried itself in his gut. Not a kill shot, she just wanted him out of the fight. She hurdled the bar, swinging her legs up and over and landing on the other side. The bartender was reaching for a sawed-off shotgun, stashed beside the beer kegs. He was bringing it up to fire when she shot him in the head. *Two.*

Bingwen was down on the carpet, clutching his belly and howling, while the Russian was still in bewildered shutdown with the cleaver buried in his face. Bingwen's men answered with a hail of fire. Bullets peppered the bar, blowing out liquor bottles, showering Maddie in a rain of broken glass and alcohol. More slugs chewed through the antique wood, turning teak to splintered confetti. She loped in a crouch, snatching up the shotgun with her free hand. Then she rose from cover and fired blind on the move. *Three. Four. Five.*

One of the gangsters was smart enough to flip a table and hunker down behind it. One was slow. She shot him in the back as he dove for cover, the other two bullets leaving a tablecloth in tatters. She spent her last round forcing a thug to keep his head down, and she dropped the empty revolver as she danced across the room like a ballerina, making her way toward her real target. The bouncer was dead ahead, and her automatic was right where she left it, snug in his belt.

She put both barrels of the sawed-off shotgun to his chest and grabbed her pistol with the other hand, snatching it free just as she pulled the trigger. Two loads of buckshot turned his heart and lungs into ground beef and sent him staggering back on his heels. He crashed into a table and pulled it down with him. A tablecloth snared him in a burial shroud, the ivory linen seeping wine-stain red.

One of Bingwen's hitters darted out from behind the standing screen, a machine pistol braced in both hands. Maddie threw herself to the carpet as bullets chopped the air over her head and blasted the ocean mural on the wall into a spray of lacquered wood. She rolled, came up on one knee with the Sig Sauer, and fired three shots on the rise, peppering him from his groin to his face. The gun went wild in his hand as his arm flailed, finger still clenched on the trigger, and drew a line of shattered plaster along the ceiling until it clicked on empty.

She didn't see the one who had been hiding behind the table, not until he hit her in a full-on tackle, locking up her gun arm and hauling her to the ground. He had fifty pounds on her and gym-rat muscles, and he bore down on her with all his weight. Trying to get her weapon with one hand, wrenching her fingers loose, he rained down wild punches with the other. An elbow cracked across her cheek, hard enough to cut her open while she squirmed for a better position. He finally connected with his knuckles and split Maddie's lip, loosening one of her teeth while she struggled to keep control of the gun. She got her other arm out from underneath her, turning on her hip. Then she curled her fingers, stuck out her thumb, and drove it straight into his eye. She twisted her thumb and ground it in as he screeched, letting go of her hand and clutching his face on reflex.

She bent her other wrist and pulled the trigger until the screaming stopped. Then she brought up her knees, heaved, and shoved his corpse to the carpet at her side.

The echo of the last bullet faded, swallowed by the storm outside. Nothing remained but distant, rumbling thunder and the steady metallic pelting of rain on the restaurant roof. Maddie caught her breath. She pushed herself up, groaning, and stumbled toward the bar. She pressed a bar towel to the cut on her forehead while her tongue probed her loose tooth. Her spit tasted like copper pennies and her face stung.

A wet rattling sound turned her head. The Russian was still alive. Still kneeling at the heart of the carnage, surrounded by corpses, with his open hands twitching at his sides. The sounds were coming from his throat; he was trying to talk. Maddie stood over him.

"Are you kidding me?" she said. "There's tough, and then there's just *stubborn*."

More clicking. One of his eyes focused on her. The other, on the far side of the meat-cleaver divide, wandered in the wrong direction. Maddie sighed, took hold of the cleaver's handle, and wrenched it loose. A gout of hot blood came with it, spattering her gore-soaked blouse. She raised the weapon high and brought it down, hacking the blade halfway into his throat.

This time, he stopped moving. She ripped the cleaver free and took it with her.

She went to find Bingwen. A slug trail of dark carpet started at the place where she'd shot him in the gut, curling around the standing screens, back toward the mahjong table. The big man was in the far corner, propped up with his ankles spread and his hands pressed to his torn belly. Blood leaked between his clenched fingers. He whimpered, face slick with sweat.

Maddie held up her hands, casual, as if offering him a choice between the meat cleaver and the gun.

"We're going to try this conversation one more time," she said.

CHAPTER TWENTY-THREE

Bingwen was trying to negotiate.

"I...I can pay you," he gasped, wincing at the pain.

"I'm sure you can, but what I want is information." Maddie crouched down, meeting him at eye level. "Your deal with Cordell Spears. Tell me everything."

He nodded, squeezing his eyes shut as he offered his unconditional surrender.

"Greece. A year ago, give or take. He had an archaeological team out there, and they hit a mother lode on a dig."

"The relics that would eventually become the *Treasures of the Mycenaean World* exhibit, once they were cataloged and studied and vetted." Maddie shook her head. "That's not what you moved for him. I already checked: they were transported by his usual shipping company. The whole process was documented and clean. No reason not to be, he had a legal permit."

"Not...*all* of it. The expedition's leader, Jurgen...something, don't remember the name, he'd found something he kept from the rest of the team. He only told Spears."

"Then he dropped dead in Athens. Victim of a convenient mugging gone wrong," Maddie said.

Bingwen nodded. He was turning pale now, from blood loss or bad memories.

"Spears contacted me through a cutout. I never talked to him directly, but I knew who he was and what he was paying."

"More than your usual?"

The big man tried to laugh and regretted it. His face twisted in a grimace as his chuckle turned into a wet cough.

"A small fortune. He needed my best men, my best security, absolute secrecy. Top of the line all the way."

Maddie tapped his jaw, lightly, with the blunt side of the meat cleaver.

"Which brings us back to the question at hand," she said. "What, exactly, did you smuggle to Miami for him?"

"Don't know. And that's the truth. I wouldn't lie. Not…under these conditions. He had his people package it up for delivery. All I know is that it was a special container, a rush custom job, refrigerated with tanks of liquid nitrogen. Deep freeze. It was about the size of an industrial refrigerator."

"Anything else?"

"I told him—well, I told the man we were given to deal with, his intermediary—that I needed all the information he could give me, to ensure safe handling. He said that it was"—Bingwen winced—"biological material. His exact words. 'Biological material.' I asked if it was dangerous. I needed to know if my men needed to be warned of any unusual risk."

"What did he say?"

"'Only if it thaws out,' he said." Bingwen's lips twisted in a humorless smile. "And that if it did, my ship would never reach harbor. I raised the price on the spot. Double my asking cost. He didn't even blink. Looking back, I should have charged triple."

"From where I'm standing, looks like you should have turned him down flat. If you had, I'd be having this chat with somebody else right now."

He coughed again, hacking into the palm of his hand before clasping it back against his belly. His mustache glistened with sweat and scarlet flecks.

"I bow to your superior wisdom," he said.

"What happened when you got to Miami?"

"The intermediary was waiting for us, with a convoy to receive the delivery. He had a truck. Biggest truck I've ever seen."

"So you met him face-to-face," Maddie said.

"More than once. As I said, I knew I was working for Cordell Spears, but he kept his hands clean. Very careful man. The intermediary had a number of names. Names but no history. I like knowing who I'm doing business with, you see. I always vet. Too many undercover cops in this line of work. But he was a man with no past. A ghost. I even managed to get fingerprints, a DNA sample off a cocktail glass…no trace in any database, anywhere."

"Not surprised," Maddie said. "He was big though, right? Like his truck. Muscles on muscles, olive skin, black hair?"

Bingwen gave her a weak nod. "That's him. One of the information brokers I work through, he said all he could find was scraps and whispers. Smoke. One of the names they called him by, it stuck with me. Thought it was funny."

He looked up, meeting Maddie's patient gaze.

"They called him the Holy Roller," he said.

Maddie contemplated her gun.

"That was the last time I saw him," Bingwen said. "No contact after that. But as I said, if Spears is the man you're after—"

"Spears is being dealt with," Maddie said. "I'm after his henchman. That's why I'm here."

"You're hunting the man in the middle? Humor me. What's he to you?"

Maddie rose from her crouch, standing over the dying man.

"His name is Jason," she said. "And he's my ex-husband. We have some unfinished business."

"Your..." Bingwen laughed now, his face scrunched up, giggling through the pain. He couldn't help it. "You came in here, shot me, killed my client, and massacred my men, over a *marital dispute*?"

She could have explained. But time was short, and she'd gotten all she was going to get out of him. She put the muzzle of her gun to the side of his head, squeezed the trigger twice, and turned away.

She tossed the meat cleaver onto the mahjong table. Some cash lay scattered amid the game tiles, a colorful mix of American green and Chinese yuan. Not a lot, but she scooped it all up and bundled it into a messy wad. The hard plastic cases on the floor caught her eye. If Bingwen had been negotiating a firearms deal, there might be something she could use. The hasps flipped up under her fingertips and the top lid yawned open.

Not guns. Explosives. She gazed down at a neat row of bricks wrapped in black Mylar. The second box had foam cutouts for bundled spools of det-cord.

"You," she murmured, "are definitely coming with me."

She scooped up her jacket from the kitchen counter on the way out.

~~

In Australia, a rig like this was called a road train. Two forty-foot trailers riding behind a prime mover, twenty-two puncture-resistant long-haul tires holding up one hundred and twenty-five tons of dirty black steel.

Jason called it the *Argo 2*.

The road train screamed through the Midwest dark, riding the silver line of a moonless highway. The convoy followed: five cars, a snapshot of Detroit steel through the pages of history. A vintage Thunderbird, a '75 Dodge Charger, a refurbished Studebaker, a boat of a cloud-blue Caddy with shark fins, and a Country Squire station wagon. Rides as diverse as his steadfast crew. They'd been scavenged from the pages of history, too. Found and collected, one by one.

Tonight Baker was riding shotgun, sitting next to Jason in the mammoth front cab and coordinating the convoy over shortwave radio. Jason thought of him as his boatswain. Nobody knew motors like Baker did; he could identify an engine problem by ear and fix it with spit and duct tape. They had met in Laos in '69. Baker was a long-range recon specialist, and Jason was a deniable asset for the CIA's Phoenix Program. They hit it off on the spot, over the burning embers of what used to be a village.

Baker's seventy-third birthday was coming up in June. He didn't look a day over twenty-one. And he never would.

Faint flecks of pale scars marred the dark brown skin of his arms, flexing as he stretched and stifled a yawn behind his hand.

Jason yawned, too, putting a beefy fist to his mouth. "Contagious."

"Sorry, boss." Baker gave him a sidelong glance. "We need to talk."

"That sounds ominous."

"Yeah, well, it is what it is. I just keep an ear out, you know? I watch your back."

Jason watched the road, his steel eyes fixed on a distant curve. "Obliged."

"There's some discontent on the crew." Baker held up an open palm. "Nothing you need to worry about. I'm not talking mutiny. Just discontent. Thought you should know about it."

"And do you share in this...discontent?"

Baker shifted in the leather bucket seat. He turned to the road, too, both men talking to the windshield now.

"Little bit. It's the job."

"It's work," Jason said. "We're mercenaries. We start being picky about job offers, we'll be pushing this rig instead of driving it."

"Any war, anytime. I know. That's the policy, and it works for us. But we've never taken a job for...well, somebody like you."

"Cordell Spears," Jason said, "is nothing like me."

Baker seemed to catch the warning in his voice, the faintest hint of a growl.

"Never taken a contract like this one, either."

"What?" Jason glanced at him, reading his expression,

then looked back to the road. "You concerned about civilian casualties?"

Baker played it off with a laugh. "Never have been, no reason to start now. But this shit...it's going to be *gratuitous*, man."

"Check out the big vocabulary on Baker."

"You know what I mean. There's going to be fallout from something this big. Serious, long-term fallout. Do we even have an exit strategy? Because it didn't come up at the briefing, and we always—"

"Have an exit strategy," Jason said. "I know. I'm working on it."

The Thunderbird and the Charger shifted lanes, swooping around the truck and pouring on speed. Advance scouts, blazing into the darkness. Half an hour down the highway, they radioed back with directions to a truck stop.

More than their rides needed refueling. There was a honky-tonk a short hop down the road, offering country twang and late-night barbecue. They took over the back half of the parking lot and moved in on foot. Jason eyed his crew with fatherly pride. There was Saravia, who had earned the burn scars on his hands and left cheek during the Spanish Civil War. Tall Jonas, who had fought at Jason's side in the Congo. Dark-eyed Parrino—Father Parrino, dressed in the priestly collar he'd worn when they crossed paths in Sicily back in 1943. He had never been, to Jason's knowledge, an actual priest, but the tab on his shirt and a practiced, compassionate voice opened doors and roadblocks across Europe.

He had collected a Portuguese marine from a Mamluk slaver's ship and a Hungarian knight—now partial to shitkicker boots and denim jackets—during the Balkan campaign of 1529. Each man forged in the crucible of battle, tested and tempered by war. His Argonauts.

"Go on in and grab a table," he told them. "I'll be right behind you. Have to make a quick phone call."

"Beef brisket, heavy on the sauce?" Baker asked.

"You know me well. Don't forget the beer."

Baker snorted. "Like I'd ever forget the beer."

The door swung shut behind the last man, muffling the sound of a country ballad. Alone on the long porch outside, Jason tapped the screen of his phone. It felt tiny in his big hands. Most things did, nowadays. They kept making things smaller, more fragile, easier to break.

"Did you see me on TV this morning?" Cordell asked. "I think I nailed it. Nervous as hell, though. I hate public speaking."

"Live long enough, you get used to it."

"Anyway, thanks for calling me back. Everything smooth on your end?"

"We're on schedule." Jason frowned. He could hear the nervous tension at the edge of Cordell's voice. "What is it?"

"Tiny hiccup on this end. Nothing you need to worry about, but I wanted to let you know, just in case, you know—"

"In case we need to worry about it."

"Ever hear of a guy named Lionel Page? He's a reporter out of Chicago. Professional skeptic. He goes around debunking quacks and phony mystics, sort of like how Harry Houdini did, back in the day."

"Don't know him," Jason said. "Should I?"

"Before current events, I'd say no. I mean, his book's good, but you don't strike me as a big reader."

"I'm fluent in twelve languages," Jason said. "How about you?"

The line went silent for a moment.

"Anyway," Cordell said, "he stabbed me to death last night."

"Did he now?"

"It sucked."

"I'm sure it did. I was crushed to death by a ship's mast once."

"I'm not trying to turn this into a dick-measuring contest," Cordell told him.

"Just saying."

"Point is, somebody taught this guy some witchcraft. He's raw, but he has skills. And natural talent."

"The professional skeptic," Jason said. "Interesting sideline."

"Right? Here's the bit that's relevant to your interests: he said he works for Hekate."

Jason didn't answer right away. He pursed his lips, fighting the undertow of memory as it tried to drag him back in time. Nowhere he wanted to go.

"You don't know what my interests are," he said. "And people can say anything. Doesn't make it true."

"I've got a whole intel team that handles research for me. I sicced 'em on Page, trying to figure out what his deal is. Far as they can tell, he was exactly the die-hard non-believer-in-anything he pretends to be, until recently. He took a trip to New York."

The undertow was sucking at Jason's heels now. He

paced, back and forth on the wooden slats of the porch, trying to shake it off.

"You're saying he's Sisterhood?"

Cordell blurted out a laugh. "Damned if I know. Do they even let men join? I mean, the name sounds exclusive. I don't know anything about the Sisterhood of New Amsterdam beyond that they've staked a claim on the Big Apple. All I know is something happened to Page there, something that shuffled his brain and his life around. He's gone on indefinite leave from his old job, he's chasing mysteries across the country...whether he's legit or not, he's sure acting like somebody who answers to a higher power. And that just made me think about...you know. Her."

Her.

"Have there been any sightings?"

"No," Cordell said. "I mean, your ex has been underground for centuries, right? She could be dust and bones for all we know. But if Hekate's people are poking their noses into our business...your wife was a heavy hitter, once upon a time."

Jason took a deep breath.

"Call me if you hear anything," he said. Then he hung up the phone.

The warm aromas of barbecue sauce and draft beer washed over him just inside the doorway, along with the jangling twang of a bluegrass guitar. His crew had camped on picnic-style benches in the back of the restaurant, and a cold brew was waiting for him along with an open seat at the head of the table.

He took his place, raised his mug, and leaned to one side. He motioned Baker close.

"I need intel," he said.

"Name it."

"Guy named Lionel Page. Reporter. I need to know everything there is to know about him."

Baker's eyes narrowed. "Trouble?"

"Probably not. Not for us. But I don't want anything to blindside us. Spears is digging into him, but I don't trust his sources of information. I do trust yours."

"On it," Baker told him.

Jason knew it would be handled by morning. He could rest a little easier now. The last thing he wanted to do was jump at shadows; that kind of thinking, that paranoia, got good soldiers killed.

All the same, the undertow of memory was still sucking at his heels, trying to pull him back, and down. Down into an abyss of heartbreak. An abyss with a name.

Medea.

CHAPTER TWENTY-FOUR

The Pullman Hotel was a tomb. A five-story art deco slab of dirty white stone, with black wrought-iron bars at every window to keep grave robbers from getting in, or to keep the dead from getting out. It squatted at the corner of a downtown Chicago lot, flanked and shadowed by newer, taller, sleeker towers. Maddie stood on the corner across the street, wearing a fresh change of clothes—black seemed appropriate, a long flowing dress under her cargo jacket—with her rolling suitcase at her side. She suspected some real-estate developers were watching this spot like vultures. Hoping the doors would finally close for good so they could snap it up, knock it down, and make way for the modern age.

She doubted they ever would. Or that anyone who did manage to build on this cursed soil would be happy with the outcome. The Pullman's long-term residents weren't going anywhere.

The streetlight flashed hazard-yellow, and its reflection turned the puddles to pools of rattlesnake venom. She walked across the empty boulevard while a cold rain pelted her upturned face. The storm had mostly passed, leaving wet, glistening streets and a mud-smeared midnight sky behind.

Inside the tall double doors of the boutique hotel, the decor still said "tomb": white marble, black iron fixtures, cold. Museum cold. Piano music drifted from the lounge down the hall, free jazz, loose and more of a suggestion than a melody. Her suitcase wheels rumbled on the marble floor, then whispered across a long black runner embossed with the Pullman's silver seal.

Maddie didn't recognize the young, round-faced woman working the check-in desk; then again, it had been three or four years since she'd visited the city. Employees here tended to quit within weeks or stay forever, depending on their temperament. Maddie greeted her with a smile and a nod, fishing in her purse while she tried to remember which of her seven IDs she usually used here.

"Ms. Hirsig," the clerk said, glancing between Maddie's face and a Colorado driver's license. "Welcome, and thank you for choosing the Pullman. How long will you be staying with us?"

"One night," Maddie said.

It would have been zero if she could manage it, but she was tired to the bone and she knew better than to go off on a crusade half-cocked. A good night's sleep could bring fresh perspective. So could dreams.

The clerk glanced at her computer screen. "I see you've stayed with us before. One bed?"

"Please. And make sure it's a clean room, please."

She blinked. "Oh. I mean, all of our rooms are clean, ma'am. Our housekeeping staff is very diligent—"

Another woman, older, thin, with smoker's teeth, had been shuffling paperwork at the far end of the desk. She ambled over, leaned in, and whispered in the clerk's ear. Her eyes went wide.

"*Oh.* Yes, of course, ma'am. We can do that."

The older woman looked over her shoulder, studying the screen, and pointed.

"Room 315 is vacant. Give her that one."

Maddie nodded her approval. She'd stayed in 315 before.

The Pullman hadn't modernized its locks. She was given an actual key, sturdy and old, on a black plastic tag with *315* etched in silver. Maddie thought about sleep. She thought about a long, hot bath to soothe her aching muscles. She thought about a stiff drink. Glancing down the hall to the red-painted doors of the hotel lounge—one propped open, one closed—she decided to tackle that list in reverse order.

The lounge was dead, maybe sleeping. It was a kidney-shaped pool of black and scarlet, little round tables lit by votive candles in spun-glass bowls. The bar was a rounded semicircle in front of a mirrored wall, the glass artfully shot through with cracks of tarnished gilding. An emaciated man in a jacket with tails was playing the piano, head bowed and shoulders slumped. The music defied Maddie's attempts to catch it. Notes danced around her in the air, fading and changing on a whim, refusing to become a melody.

Hekate was sitting at the end of the bar.

She'd left her Regina Dunkle disguise at home. This was Hekate as Maddie knew her—as she had known her for what felt like forever. Flowing tresses of raven black, a scarlet torch singer's gown, an antique key at her throat. Her blood-red lips curled with feline pleasure, and she raised her cocktail glass—an amber drink, garnished with a twist of orange peel—in silent salute.

As Maddie approached, the goddess glanced down at her outfit, then at Maddie's funeral-black dress. "We match the decor."

"It's our kind of place." Maddie nodded to the empty stool beside her. "Is this seat taken?"

"I was saving it for you."

Maddie slid onto the barstool.

"What are you drinking?"

Hekate took a sip from her glass. "Bobby Burns."

Maddie raised a finger, catching the bartender's eye.

"I'll have the same." She looked to Hekate. "I didn't expect to find you here."

"Expect the unexpected." She turned her glass, catching candlelight in the amber. "I come by now and then, to play with the ghosts."

"Most haunted hotel in Chicago."

"A paradise for some, a prison for others. Madison, dear—wait, are you still Madison?"

She shrugged. "'Madison Hannah' is wanted on an outstanding warrant in Manhattan, so I'm going to have to give it up eventually. Still hate throwing away a name when I get attached to it. And my driver's license had a really good photo for once."

"There might be someone in the Sisterhood who could quietly quash that for you...oh, but that would mean you'd have to ask someone for help."

Here we go, Madison thought.

"I just came back to the coven, and to your service, after being gone for...well, the current generation never knew me at all. Outside of stories. Not good ones."

"The witch who ran away from home."

"I haven't given them a reason to do me any favors."

"So you'll fix that," Hekate said, "by avoiding them. That's a cunning plan. So cunning that even I can't figure out how it will possibly work."

The bartender brought Maddie a matching cocktail glass. She avoided answering by tasting her drink. Blended scotch, sweet vermouth, a hint of orange. The flavors kissed her lips with a swirl of wood smoke.

"So explain something to me," the goddess said.

Maddie braced herself.

"I found you a rather sweet young man and steered him right into your path. You certainly seem to complement one another."

"We do," Maddie said. Understatement. She'd been thinking about Lionel since she left Montauk. She swung between hating herself for slipping out of their bed in the middle of the night and knowing it was the right thing to do. And hating herself anyway.

"And yet here you are. Alone." She paused, as if remembering something. "Oh. By the way, he's about a day behind you."

"When I said I wanted to handle this assignment alone, you didn't stop me."

"Because I respect your free will," Hekate said.

"But you didn't stop him from following me."

"Because I respect his. When have I ever restricted my children's freedom? That's not my way. That's not a witch's way, either. You know better."

"He's not ready," Maddie said.

Hekate's voice was still light, but her eyes went stern.

"That's not why you left him behind. I don't approve of

my daughters lying to themselves, Medea. I strenuously dislike it. Deceive others as you desire and as you must, but never lie to yourself."

Maddie set her glass down. She stared into the amber pool. The flame of a votive candle danced in the corner of her eye.

"I don't know why he's back," she said.

Hekate held her silence, waiting for her daughter to find the words.

"Jason," Maddie said. "He *died*. He fell asleep, drunk on the rotting ruin of the *Argo*. A mast broke. Fell on him. End of story, and good riddance."

"And so goes the ruin of mortals who offend the gods with their impiety," Hekate said, "but Jason is no mortal. He's a hero, and heroes exist in a state of mythic reality."

Maddie's fingers strangled the stem of her cocktail glass.

"He broke his vows. He broke his vow to me, to you, to Hera—"

"A hero's myth must have a fitting ending," Hekate said. "The universe demands it. The story has to be a lesson, for mortals to learn by."

"I can't imagine a more fitting ending than the one he got."

"Someone does, apparently. Speaking of heroes, I have bad news and good news. Your assassin failed."

Maddie narrowed her eyes. "Kayla?"

"Dead."

"Damn. I knew I should have handled Spears myself. I just..."

The goddess sipped her drink. "Decided chasing after Jason was more important?"

Maddie didn't answer.

"The good news is, Lionel is acquitting himself quite well. He also stood against a pack of Keres and lived. You'd be proud of his progress. I certainly am."

"He's not ready."

"To battle your former husband," Hekate asked, "or to *meet* him? Medea, Lionel knows who you are. He knows your past, where you've been, what you've done. He didn't reject you when you told him the truth."

"I know."

"And yet."

Maddie didn't have anything to say to that. The goddess tossed back the last of her cocktail with a sudden, quick flip of her curls and set the empty glass on the bar.

"I'll tell you a secret," Hekate said. "The greatest power of necromancy can be attained by anyone. You don't need to be a witch to learn the trick. The greatest power is not conjuring the dead, or binding them, or commanding them. The pinnacle of art is to *listen* to the dead, and to learn their stories. And one doesn't need to be a divine hero to have a story worth sharing. The least of these mortals have that much, though they seldom realize their own value."

Maddie remembered something she was told once. "Everyone has value."

"Everyone. Spend the night, daughter. Listen to a few stories. You're never too old to learn something new."

She followed Hekate's gaze. On the far side of the lounge, a reedy man with a pencil-thin mustache and a sharp-shouldered suit was making eyes at her. He stood by the piano, tapping a wing-tipped shoe to the music.

A bleary-eyed tourist, returning an empty glass to the bar, walked right through him. He didn't seem bothered.

Hekate's pale fingers curled over Maddie's shoulder. She offered Maddie a faint, lopsided smile as she rose from her stool, and a reassuring squeeze.

"Oh," the goddess added, "and you of all people shouldn't need to be told, but don't die here. The Pullman keeps its dead."

CHAPTER TWENTY-FIVE

The road train slumbered under the electric glow of a truck-stop sign, surrounded by its entourage of vintage steel. Jason and his crew had made camp for the night. They were just north of Chicago, with three stops left on their route as they made their way west.

And then, back east, Jason thought. *Back to New York.*

He wasn't sleeping.

He rarely slept anymore. He was pretty sure he didn't need to, but he didn't know why. His own existence was something of a mystery. His story had ended and then...it hadn't. Intellectually, he knew he had died once. Maybe twice. But the details were hazy and at some point he'd found himself in a war zone, battling for pay, and the work suited him. So he just kept doing it, letting the years flutter by as he journeyed from battlefield to battlefield.

There was always a war somewhere. Always someone willing to pay for a seasoned crew of killers, and pay well. He'd had to change with the times, adapting, but he was good at that. His sturdy spear and *xiphos*-blade became a cannon, and then a musket, and then a Browning LMG, but they were just different tools for the same old job.

He stood on the second-floor landing of the budget

hotel next to the truck stop, taking in the cool night air, and shook a pack of Lucky Strikes against his beefy palm. He lit a cigarette, leaned his elbows against the railing, and took a long drag. Bad habit, but he was pretty sure he couldn't get cancer, either.

Boots strode along the bare walk. Baker nodded his way, taking the spot at the railing to his left.

"Got one for me?"

Jason handed him the pack.

"Found something," Baker said.

"That quick?"

"How long have I been handling your intel?"

"I'm not surprised," Jason said, "just impressed."

Baker shook out a cigarette. Jason flicked his lighter, a brass-plated antique. The tip of the cigarette sizzled and glowed.

"Don't be impressed just yet. What I've got is a solid maybe. And I'm not sure what kind of outcome you're hoping for."

"Neither am I," Jason said. "Let's find out."

"Your boy Page did, in fact, get in a little trouble up in New York very recently. He was brought in for questioning regarding a discharge of gunfire on a subway platform. Released without charges a few hours later. His lawyer's a local named Agnes Ashcroft."

Jason gave him the side-eye. "He's from Chicago, but he's got a New York lawyer?"

"A shady-as-hell one. The *criminal* kind of criminal attorney. And reading between the lines of her checkered history, what little I could dig up, she's old-school Sisterhood. But that's not the interesting part. Another woman, also repped by Ashcroft, was brought in with

A Time for Witches

Page. Calls herself Madison Hannah. Whatever Page was up to in NYC, him and Hannah were thick as thieves."

"What do we know about her?"

"That her entire background is bogus," Baker said. "Good counterfeits, she's got a legit SSN and solid credit, but it's built on a fake birth certificate and some carefully structured and entirely imaginary family history, all layered with false trails and double blinds. She uses some very familiar tricks."

Baker took a pull on his cigarette and blew smoke into the dark.

"Tricks like ours," he said, meeting Jason's gaze. "Same ones we use every few decades to keep our papers fresh. Madison Hannah's an immortal. Just not sure if she's *your* immortal."

"Can you get a photograph?"

"Step ahead of you." Baker took his phone out. Then he hesitated. "Permission to speak freely?"

"Always."

Baker took another pull and exhaled a thin gray plume of smoke while he weighed his words.

"You sure you want to know?" he asked.

Yes. No. *Fuck*, Jason thought, summing it up in a word. He wanted to be anywhere but here. Back on a battlefield somewhere. Life made sense on a battlefield.

"It's not about want," he decided. "Lionel Page is messing with our client's business. If someone put him up to it, if someone's pulling his strings, we need to know so we can brace for any trouble."

Baker nodded. He tapped his phone and the screen lit up, joining the glow of their cigarettes.

"Got my guy to pull her DMV file," he said.

A couple more taps, and a photograph sprang up on the screen. He turned the phone so Jason could take a look. He asked a question with his eyes.

"Put it away," Jason said.

"Is it—"

"Is it the woman who murdered my fucking children? Yes, Baker. Yes, it is, and I don't want to look at her fucking face. *Put it away.*"

He threw his cigarette down and stomped its glow dead under the heel of his boot.

"Sorry," Jason said. He looked away, out into the dark. "Sorry. You didn't do anything wrong. You did what I asked."

"Hey, man, it's okay."

"It's not remotely okay."

He sank into a sullen silence with his elbows on the railing. There was a storm in the distance, the clouds muddy, dirty from the hard electric glow of the distant city lights. Baker stood beside him and shared the quiet.

Jason didn't think about Medea, as a rule. He didn't think about that time, that part of his life. When he was war-fighting, focused on the battle, waging a campaign for the side with the biggest purse, he couldn't think about it.

Now all he had was thoughts and a pack of Luckies. And the looming sense that he needed to get ahead of this. *This isn't a coincidence. She's coming for me. We've got over two thousand years of unfinished business and I don't know why it's happening here and now, but she's coming for me.*

And that means I need to come for her, first.

"Is Parrino awake?"

Baker shrugged. "Probably. The Padre never sleeps,

usually just stays up reading all night. You want me to find out?"

"I'm going to have a job for him. Tell him to get battle-ready. I'll be back in about an hour."

"Where are you going?"

"Out. For a walk," Jason said. He turned and strode away. "Gotta do something I don't want to do."

~~

He had to walk farther than he expected to find a place with no cars, no lights, no signs of man's encroachment. His path took him down a long grassy embankment, where he marched until the sounds of the highway finally faded to stillness at his back. There was a time, he thought, when it was easy to find some quiet. Just unfurl the sail of his skiff, lean into the wind, and skim across the green-glass water. They would find a rocky island, nothing but warm white sand and—

They.

He stopped thinking after that. He just walked.

A copse of dying trees invited him in, the twisted branches like withered and beckoning arms. The air was sickly here, sweet, like toxic sap, and a web of tangled roots choked the gray soil. Appropriate, for the work at hand.

Jason was no witch, but you couldn't walk the earth for centuries and not learn a thing or two about magic. When Cordell Spears told him he needed the services of war spirits, Jason conjured a trio of Keres and set them to hunting. He didn't know what Cordell wanted them for and he didn't care: the bank deposit cleared, with a healthy bonus for his crew, and that was all that mattered.

Battlefields were steeped in blood magic, and calling the

Keres was a simple feat for a soldier with hands as red as his. They wanted to be close to him, like birds flocking to a man with a bag of seed. But he had something different in mind tonight. Harder. More dangerous.

Necessary, he thought. He found a fallen branch and rapped it against his palm. Then he dug the broken end into the dirt and walked, counterclockwise, drawing a rough oval. Deep in some places, shallow where it ran over the gnarled roots. Three times, he walked the loop, drawing it deeper. And he sang.

He sang an old mariner's song in the tongue of his homeland, thinking about his old crew, his first crew. Bold Melas, faithful Autolycus. A crew of heroes. All gone now. He remembered setting out on the *Argo*, their voices joined, singing loud and bold.

Should years or tides draw us apart,
I will not forget your face.
Never forget your sweet love vow,
And fly, your heart to me.

He tasted red wine on his lips, sweet as summer. And now he sang older words. The *voces mysticae*, crude and halting, barely under his command. He felt the words tug at his tongue like a wild horse fighting the saddle. But he held fast, making up for his lack of skill with raw authority and bluster. He tossed the stick aside and drew his boot knife.

He pulled up his sleeve and stuck out his arm. He was still chanting when the blade bit his skin, drawing a darkberry line across his forearm. Blood rained down, droplets pelting the dead soil, a stain starting to spread.

A cold wind rattled the boughs and seeped under his skin. He wasn't alone here.

The dead were always thirsty for blood. He saw them now, faceless shades wallowing like pigs at his feet, licking the wet dirt. They weren't the one he wanted, though. With the gates to Hades open, just a crack, he ended the chant in a shout. A single name, echoing across two worlds.

"*Creusa!*"

The echo faded, rumbling into the distance.

Shadows gathered themselves within the oval of soil. Weaving, becoming smoke and then ancient, rotten linens, layers of heavy veils. They took on color and tone: char, and ash, and the twisted pink of burn tissue. The glistening green of necrotic flesh. The shadows wove arms, crooked and long, draped in flame-seared sleeves. They wove legs with slippers, gnarled and scorched like the feet that wore them, mutilated toes dangling as she hovered in the air before him.

"From one torment to another," the apparition hissed. "Do you think this circle can trap me?"

Jason wasn't sure. Didn't matter. He knew what had to be done.

He took a step forward, crossing the line, and thrust out his bleeding arm.

She seized it, gripping him with fingers of ice and iron talons, and put her mouth to the open wound. Her tongue was a nub of scar tissue; he felt it greedily lapping, worming its way into the cut.

As she drank, she took on color. As she drank, she grew. Her charred and ashen dress turned cherry-red, her slippers becoming woven silver. A chill wind rippled her skirts and dangling bell sleeves, and her bowed head—bald a moment ago—now sported a mane of flossy golden hair.

"Enough," he said and wrestled his arm away. He stepped back across the oval's border.

She had taken on color, all right. Her glorious mane, her deep hazel eyes...and the rest of her, a wasteland of mutilation. Her burned skin was pink, marbled with melted fat, as if she'd just crawled out of a furnace. Her cracked lips spread in a mirthless rictus.

"My...betrothed," she said. "Am I not just as beautiful as I was on the day we met? Come. Tell me some sweet nothings. Whisper them in my ear while I bite into your neck."

He held his silence, stoic.

"Was I not worth all of your betrayals? Have you conjured me so that you can take me to bed one last time?" Her eyes narrowed, and she didn't even pretend to smile now. "Jason. How I loathe you."

"Princess Creusa. As you should. But there's someone you hate even more than me."

She floated, her arms rippling out to her sides like serpents. A low, deep rattle welled up from the seared ruin of her throat.

Jason held up an old, corroded bangle, caked with tarnish. It wore empty ovals where gemstones once sat, and one edge was a jagged slice of broken metal.

"This was hers," he said. "You can use this to track her down."

"You would have me take your revenge? I am no *servant*."

"No. I would have you take *your* revenge. It's a gift. A peace offering."

"There will be no peace between you and I. Never. Not until the death of time." Her claw drew an *X* in the air between them. "But...you are certain that Medea still lives?"

"Longer than anyone should, don't you think? Someone ought to do something about that."

CHAPTER TWENTY-SIX

Creusa floated to the oval's edge. Jason held out the bangle, careful, like a zookeeper offering a bloody haunch of meat to a lioness. She snatched it from his hand.

"So old," she murmured. "So very old. But she is not tarnished, is she? She is not withered, not ravaged by age."

"No," he said.

"Nor are you." Her hazel eyes studied him. "Still as young as the day we met. You're so...*pretty*, my betrothed."

"And you," he said, "were the most beautiful maiden in all of Corinth."

She gave him a pitiless smile. Her lips cracked and bled.

"Your existence is an obscenity," she said.

He didn't answer. He wasn't sure if she was wrong.

"You could have hunted her yourself," she said. "You've had centuries. Why didn't you?"

"She went underground. I didn't know if she was dead or alive."

"Why didn't she hunt you?"

"Same answer, I assume. I *was* dead, for a while. Ask her yourself if you care." He looked to the bangle. "Can you feel her?"

Creusa's flame-charred fingers trailed along its curve.

"Oh, yes. She's close. Closer than you think."

"And will you kill her?"

She floated in the oval of dirt. A gust of wind fluttered her dangling sleeves and made silky-gold streamers of her hair.

"This," the dead princess said, "is not peace between us."

"I understand."

He crouched, picked up the stick, and struck the circle. He drew a ragged *X* across the oval line, then rubbed the stick back and forth to obliterate it.

"You and I will meet again," Creusa told him. "Fear that day."

And then she was gone, lifted by the wind, soaring into the night sky with the skirts of her cherry-red gown trailing behind her.

Back at the motel, Parrino was waiting for his orders. He was fifty-one when Jason gave him the gift of immortality, and he'd been fifty-one since the fall of Mussolini, with his short-cropped charcoal hair flecked with streaks of white. He was a thin man: long thin nose, long thin fingers, a body like a stiletto blade. He wore a black raincoat over his black vestments, and a Catholic priest's ivory tab at the collar of his shirt.

Parrino had a way of getting people to open their doors for him. Often, the last mistake they ever made, though he didn't give them time to regret it.

"I need a favor," Jason said.

He nodded, curt. His voice still carried a faint Sicilian accent, though he hadn't been home in decades.

"Baker told me. Just say when, where, who, and how."

"Tonight. As soon as possible. As for the where, do you see that trail?"

Jason pointed to the night sky. Parrino looked high. His steel-blue eyes followed a line of rippling blue flame, like someone had poured a trail of gasoline across the clouds and set it ablaze.

"Back in the old country," he said, "*strega* left marks like those, when they flew to their sabbaths on broomsticks. That's what my grandmother told me."

"Probably," Jason said.

Jason knew that most mortal eyes couldn't see the trail of Princess Creusa's passing. But he also knew that no home she flew over would sleep soundly tonight. Even now, nightmares spread in her wake, billowing from house to house, from dreamer to restless dreamer.

Nothing like the nightmare she was planning to personally deliver, though.

"I'm sending you along as an insurance policy," Jason said. "Odds are you won't have to do anything at all. But just in case, if the princess fails, I need you to murder my ex-wife."

"I'll be back before sunrise," Parrino replied.

~~

The man with the pencil-thin mustache had lit up like a child on Christmas when he saw Maddie walking his way. He escorted her to a table for two by the piano, the slumped pianist still gamely noodling his way across the keys in a faint imitation of a melody.

His name was Herbert Wilby Woods, an "officially licensed field sales representative and duly-authorized field repairs technician" for the National Cash Register Company, and a proud native of Harrisburg, Ohio. He had been making his way across the heartland when his travels brought him to the Pullman Hotel, and he'd been a resident ever since.

"You have to grasp that there's a skill to selling something that's only a photograph in a brochure," he said, tapping a finger against his temple. "After all, can't be carrying sample cash registers in my hip pocket, those things weigh fifty, sixty pounds. No ma'am, and people are resistant to buy something they can't touch and try for themselves. To succeed in a line like that, you've got to have horse sense, a keen eye, and be a strong judge of character."

"I knew a traveling salesman once," Maddie said. "He was in typewriters."

"Ah, see? Any old Tom or Sam can sell a Selectric. You just set the customer down and let them type away. Doesn't cost you anything but a sheet of paper and a little ink, and the machine sells itself. They can buy it on the spot and keep it, too. Now instead of that, try giving 'em a typewriter brochure, and get 'em to hand over four hundred and forty-five dollars cash money in exchange for a promise that their machine will arrive in the post next month. I daresay most men would see a fraction of the success. They'd shy away from the very notion of such a challenge."

"But not you," she said.

"No ma'am. I relish it." He glanced to the table. "You haven't touched your drink."

No, she hadn't.

Herbert insisted on buying, leaving her at the table while he vanished behind a pillar by the bar. He came

A Time for Witches

back with cocktails, a matching pair of dirty martinis. He'd barely touched his either, too eager to chatter up a storm.

"You can't make a sale every time," Maddie said, edging around the subject.

"No, that's fair and true, and I say it with no shame. Not even Babe Ruth batted a thousand."

"So what do you do when you have a dry spell?"

"You make do and improvise," he said. "Why, I might pick up some spot work here and there on the road or diversify my portfolio. My loyalty is to the National Cash Register Company, don't get me wrong, but a salesman's skills are universal."

"You know, this hotel is famous in certain circles."

He peered at her, shrewd now. "Is that so?"

"It's had its share of famous occupants. The Axman of Marshfield Avenue, for instance."

Herbert wrinkled his nose. "I think you mean infamous."

"Or the Clover-Hitch Strangler, or Dr. Bari Kovacevic—also known as the Night Surgeon—"

"Now I *know* you mean infamous."

"—or Herbert Wilby Woods," she said.

He pursed his lips. Try as he might, though, he couldn't keep a tiny smile from rising up. Couldn't resist the bait.

"Do they give me a scary name, too?" he asked. "The breathers, I mean. You're the first one who could see me in…oh, has to have been a decade or thereabouts."

"No, but your death tally is still impressive. You killed, what, thirty-odd people?" She cast a pointed glance at her martini glass. "With poison, mostly."

"Can't blame a fella for trying. And I'd swear it was more like forty. Forty *before* I shuffled off this mortal coil. That's the funny thing about murder. You're right, I hit a dry spell on the road, couldn't afford shoe leather. Slipped a little rat poison in my landlady's drink and presto, free rent and all the cash in her purse. Well, I told myself it was a crime of necessity, and it was, but good golly does it become habit-forming."

"You made more money poisoning tourists than you did selling cash registers."

"And the same skills applied, my friend. A keen eye and horse sense. You can't kill somebody halfway, no ma'am. Too little of a dose in their drink and your ship is sunk. Too much and they'll taste the taint before they get their fill. Why, I daresay I was a maestro of the poison-selling art. A hustler of hemlock and a dealer of digitalis."

"And then you died here," Maddie said.

His ebullience froze on his face, then faded. He sagged back into his chair.

"And then I died here," he said.

A draft gusted through the room. At an empty table, a votive candle flickered and died. The ceiling groaned, as if heavy footsteps were lumbering just above their heads.

"He ruined this place," Herbert muttered, shooting a look at the rafters.

"Who did?"

"The 'Axman of Marshfield Avenue.' Oh, this place was grand before *he* came. The Pullman was a social whirlwind, the hottest place in town. Almost nobody could see me, or talk to me, but I could sit at their tables and pretend to join in the fun and it was almost…it was almost like human company. Then came that winter night in '77. I saw the shadows swirling around him when he checked in. I knew something bad was coming."

"He went on a rampage," Maddie said. "Murdered everyone on the penthouse floor."

Herbert nodded. "Don't go up there. Pretty thing like you. He hates pretty things. Anyway, the place stayed open after that, but it was branded with a bad reputation. *Cursed*. The social scene dried up, the tourists stopped coming, and now..."

He waved his hand, taking in the almost-empty lounge, the clean tablecloths and the lonely votive lights.

"I made a...terrible mistake," he said.

"You murdered over thirty people for kicks. I'd call that more than a mistake."

"Not *that*," he said. "No, it's life I didn't get. I saw myself as a lone wolf. You know, self-reliant, out on my own, able to tackle anything the world threw at me. Every time I had a chance to make a connection, and I had plenty, I turned it down flat. No lovers, no wife, no family, no friends. Anybody tried to get close to me, well, you know how they all ended up. I was an island unto myself. And then..."

He peered at his hand, squinting, like he was just noticing his own body for the first time. He curled his fingers.

"You know what's funny?" he said.

Maddie replied with a tilt of her head, her eyes curious.

"Every now and then, they'd die slow. Slow enough to figure out they were dying. And in the end, before the seizures took their voice, they'd almost always cry out for someone."

"Someone?"

"A husband, a wife. Sometimes a parent. They knew they were dying, and in that moment, what mattered most—more than living, more than anything in the entire world—was being with the one they loved. Not being alone." He lifted his martini glass, his gaze distant. "And I only figured it out after I died. Once I was trapped here, isolated. Once I wanted human contact, love, just someone who *understands* me—once I wanted it more than anything in the world, and *couldn't have it*—that's when I learned how much it's really worth."

He sipped his martini and winced.

"Can't even get drunk," he muttered. "The Pullman is a greedy bitch. Greedier than I ever was."

Maddie pushed her chair back. Her own glass sat right where he had placed it, untouched. He blinked flutter-fast as she rose to leave.

"Hey, wait. This is part of it, right?"

She paused. "Part of it?"

"You're...you're an angel, or a messenger from above, or *somebody*. You have to be. You can see me and hear me, and you've got a glow like nobody else. Like a...black halo."

"I'm not," she said, "but what if I was?"

"Well, I mean, this is how it works, right?" He shook his head as if it was obvious. "I learned my lesson and I made amends. So you can set me free now."

Maddie stared at him.

"Number one, I'm a witch," she said. "Number two, if I did send your soul to Hades, you would *not* be bound for any of the nicer parts, I can promise you that. The Pullman Hotel is the best deal you're ever going to get. Be thankful."

"But I heard you." He thrust a finger at the bar. "Talking to the other dame. 'Everyone has value.' You said that."

"Your *victims* had value," she said. "Make amends with them. As far as I'm concerned, you can rot here."

She turned and strode across the lounge. He called out behind her, his voice rising, tremulous and shaken.

"I'm not the worst!" he called out. "Don't you look down your nose at me! I'm not the worst. Not in this rogue's gallery. Oh no, ma'am, plenty worse than me around here."

The ceiling groaned above her head. She felt the sound, rattling down in the marrow of her bones. The hotel was waking up, drawn to her now, a maelstrom of hate and loss and regret. That was fine. Maddie walked with her head high. She was a witch and a servant of Hekate: she had no fear of the dead.

CHAPTER TWENTY-SEVEN

Not all of Liu Bingwen's crew had been in attendance at the Hope Pagoda that afternoon. The new client had a taste for a very particular, very expensive brand of imported vodka; Bingwen, always eager to make a good impression, had sent a flunky on a liquor-store run.

The first place he visited didn't carry the stuff. Which proved lucky for him, since it meant he was five minutes late for the massacre.

Just in time, though, to see the woman running down the back alley. Hair matted, her face turned upward to the storm, a jacket draped over her gore-soaked blouse. He snapped pictures on his phone and followed her as far as he dared, hiding behind a grungy stone pillar in the amber-lit bowels of a parking garage. She had pulled a quick change, swapped outfits from her luggage, and buried her sodden, bagged-up clothes at the bottom of a dumpster on her way out.

Calls were made. Deals negotiated in a back room, wreathed with cigar smoke, as up-and-comers jockeyed for position in the wake of Bingwen's murder. Nature abhors a vacuum. The new appointee, anointed by the powers above and below, had one job to prove himself: vengeance. He had one night to get it done.

Hard rain pelted the windows of a regional tech office. A middle manager in IT was working late tonight. Not by choice. He had a sweet tooth for the sports book; his bookie had him on a leash, the Triad had the bookie on a leash, and his debts were passed up the chain. He hunched over his screen and clicked fast, painfully aware of the two burly men breathing down the back of his neck—and the guns on their hips.

He found a photo. Magnified it as much as he could without turning it into a blurry smear. The woman in the cargo jacket was running across West Cermak, frozen in time by a red-light traffic camera.

"That her?" he asked.

They compared the screen-grab to the flunky's phone. That was her.

At that moment, other agents were following other threads, navigating the labyrinth of the underworld. As far as they knew, their organization had been attacked tonight without so much as a warning shot: finding out who sent the killer was almost as important as retribution.

"One word keeps coming up," a muffled voice said over a secure line. In the background, metal squealed on metal as an elevated train roared past. "*Nocnitsa*. She's freelance, but we know she's done work for Aleksandr Sokolov's crew up in Brooklyn."

Bingwen's replacement had an impossible math problem on his desk. Two plus two was adding up to five, no matter how he worked it.

"New York *Bratva*? We don't have any business with

them. And they have no reason to attack us. They gain nothing."

"We've sent word through an intermediary, trying to set up a meeting. In the meantime, Huang's people tracked the woman down."

"They have her?"

"Not yet. She's still in the city, though. Looks like she's holed up at an old hotel, the Pullman."

There was only one appropriate response. Only one that would ensure the respect of his overlords in the Triad and secure his new position.

"Tell them to wait. I'm on my way. We'll know everything there is to know before the sun rises. I'll get it out of her personally."

~~

Maddie's luggage wheels rumbled down a black hallway runner, embossed with the Pullman's silver seal. Her gaze took in the twists and turns of the hallway, kinking here and there for no apparent reason, and the almost imperceptible sigils carved over certain doorways.

The hotel had been built on condemned soil; knocking it down wouldn't remove the taint, and anything built on this spot would carry on the cursed hotel's legacy. The founder hadn't helped things, though. He'd drafted the plans personally, cleaving to principles of arcane architecture. He built it for his cancer-stricken wife, hoping to stay close to her for eternity. The man hadn't thought about the long-term consequences, how the Pullman would become a trap for the dead.

Good intentions, she thought.

The ghost of a doorway hung open on her left. Her immortal eyes saw two doors at once: solid wood, locked up tight, and an ethereal double that yawned open, looking in on the shimmering mirage of a guest room. A woman was hanging from the ceiling fan, her purple, broken neck trapped in a noose of knotted bedsheets. A man's bare and bloodless feet stuck out from behind the bed, the rest of him hidden from sight.

Bones made wet crackling sounds as the woman raised her head. She opened her eyes and stared at Maddie, her lips moving without sound. Maddie kept walking.

She always stayed at the Pullman when she was in Chicago. It was one of the only places where she could get a decent night's sleep. Ghosts didn't bother her: she knew how to deal with them, and she knew the regulars' trick of asking for a clean room at check-in, meaning one that hadn't been touched by the tragedies that this place drew like flies. And thanks to the veil being thin here, close enough to reach out and brush her hand against the netherworld, her dreams tended to be prophetic ones.

She needed guidance right now.

Another door was open on her right. Impulse made her look, like driving past a car wreck. A heavyset man with a frog mouth and sparse, thinning hair was setting out tools—scalpels, serrated spoons, a hand-cranked drill—on the nightstand. A sheet, spotted with scarlet blossoms, draped a body on the bed. Ropes bound pale, cold wrists and ankles to the bedposts.

He saw her staring and glared. "Do you mind? I am preparing for a very important operation."

She moved on.

Her room was at the end of the hall. It still carried its Depression-era charm, sparse but classy, with hints of art deco in the vintage wallpaper and the antique rotary phone on the bedside table. A sea chest sat at the foot of a queen bed, with a sunken mattress on a stout black iron frame.

She wasn't alone. A chambermaid was at work, tugging the end of a fitted sheet over one corner of the mattress. Fresh linens, crisp and white, sat in a neatly folded pile at the foot of the bed. The woman was young, maybe twenty, with freckles and the fading aftermath of a sunburn on her cheeks. She looked to Maddie with a surprised smile and hurried her pace.

"Pardon, miss," she said, her voice carrying the lilt of an Irish brogue. "I'll be out of your way in just a second."

"Take your time," Maddie said, rolling her suitcase over to the foot of the bed.

The maid reached for the folded sheets, flipping them with practiced hands.

"Where d'you call home?" she asked.

Good question. Maddie had to think about that. She'd been running, endlessly. Living out of her suitcase, hotel to hotel. She didn't expect that would end anytime soon, but all the same, she had an urge to sink a root into the soil. To have a reliable place she could come back to after her missions, a sanctuary to call her own.

"A little of everywhere," she said, "but lately, I think, New York."

"Ooh. I've always wanted to go. My Johnny shipped out from there, just last month, but I could only see him as far as Union Station. Kissed him on the train platform, and now I live for the postman's arrival. Johnny writes whenever he can."

"He's in the service?" Maddie asked.

"Infantry. He signed up the day after the attack. He

told me, Sally, there's a draft on, you know I'm going to have to go anyway. Better to march into the fight than be dragged into it. He wasn't the only one thinking it, either. He told me the line at the enlistment office went all the way around the block." She frowned down at the sheets. "He's right, I know that's the truth of it. Doesn't make it easier to take. I have family who died in the Great War. I don't know how long he'll be gone, or if…"

Her voice trailed off.

"You're waiting for him," Maddie said.

Sally nodded. Her eyes brightened a little.

"As long as I have to, miss. Because that's something he told me: that knowing he has me here, back home and waiting, is what keeps him strong. When he's afraid, or lonely, he thinks about me. I don't know what's going to happen or what next month or next year will bring, but I have to trust in him. I guess that's love, isn't it? It's all about trust."

"Even when you're afraid," Maddie murmured, reflective.

"Especially when you're afraid." Sally pulled the quilted blanket into place, squared it with an architect's eye, and gave it a pat. "There we go, all nice and tidy. I'll leave you be. Sleep tight, miss."

As she headed for the door, Maddie weighed her next words carefully. A certain level of caution was called for in cases like this. Delicate handling, to avoid doing more harm than good.

"Sally?"

The maid turned, smiling back over her shoulder. "Yes, miss? Something else you needed?"

"If you're...unhappy about being here, I might be able to help you."

"Oh, no, miss. I'm quite happy at the Pullman. I'm skilled at my trade, and I get to meet so many interesting people, even in passing, well...it's almost as if I get to travel the world myself, if only in my daydreams. It's a good job and a good life."

"But if you wanted to move on—"

Sally laughed and shook her head.

"And where would I go? I made a promise to my man. Don't you worry, miss, we're going to win this war. And when Johnny comes back on that train, he'll find me right here where he left me, waiting for him. Sweet dreams, miss."

Sally turned, humming a tune under her breath, and walked through the bedroom wall. She vanished into the wallpaper, leaving a single note hanging in the air until that, too, faded away.

CHAPTER TWENTY-EIGHT

The Bergmont Room was the Pullman's signature restaurant, offering French-American cuisine. It had closed up for the night, the staff gone home, the modest kitchen dark and smelling of lemon sanitizer.

The delivery door rattled softly as lockpicks rasped against the tumblers. Then it opened wide, the alarm already cut from an outside junction box. Six men with dead eyes and skilled hands entered from the side alley. They didn't speak a word. No need. They knew what they were here for.

Traditions kept the Triad strong. Some had faded over the years, but a few still hung on, usually those with a good reason behind them. For instance, Triad killers never brought weapons to a hit. They scavenged what they could find on arrival and left their implements of death behind when the job was done. The custom was sound: you didn't have to worry about being stopped and searched by the police if you weren't carrying anything illegal.

So one by one, they passed by the drawers of chef's tools—all scrubbed clean and ready for tomorrow's breakfast service—and took their pick. Cleavers, kitchen shears, a boning knife.

Triad kills tended to be messy. That, too, was considered a practical benefit of the custom. They'd been attacked tonight; what they were about to do to the woman responsible wouldn't be clean or quick. And the photographs would deliver a powerful message to whoever sent her.

~~

Father Parrino stood on the corner diagonal from the Pullman Hotel, black raincoat draped over his priestly habit, cold rain pattering down on an empty boulevard. He had followed the trail of fire in the sky. It ended here. Standing in the lamplight, he gazed up to the hotel's granite arches, looking from window to shaded window.

In all likelihood, the target was already dead, or about to be. He didn't mind making sure or getting some tangible proof of the kill to bring back to Jason. This was a job he'd performed for his commander many times over the decades, in the service of a debt—the eternal life he'd been given—that he could never truly repay. Most of the Argonauts were front-line warriors, all blood and thunder; his trade was subtler, just as he'd learned it under Mussolini's regime.

It helped that he enjoyed his work. And getting to murder a woman, especially if he could take his time, was a rare and exotic treat.

He patted his coat pocket, feeling the reassuring bulge of his wire garrote, its stout wooden handles flecked rust-red with old work and old memories. Tonight he'd make some new ones.

Parrino crossed the street with a confident stride. He took off his wide-brimmed hat as he stepped into the foyer of the hotel and made his way to the check-in desk. He made sure his coat was open enough to show the tab of his collar.

"I hope you can help me," he said to the night clerk, holding his hat to his chest. The same practiced words and practiced look of kindhearted worry that had opened countless doors for him. "I know you're not supposed to give out any information about your guests, but I'm very worried about one of my parishioners..."

~~

Maddie had forgotten more about witchcraft than most mortals would ever learn. Still, sometimes the simplest spells were the most effective.

She filled the stainless-steel ice bucket with water from the sink, setting it down upon a wooden floorboard near the foot of the bed, right next to an empty glass. She had a votive candle and a book of matches in her luggage, snug against the stolen black Mylar-wrapped bricks of plastic explosive. *Glad I pack light*, she thought. *Never know when you're going to find that special something you've just got to take home with you.*

She lit the candle. Then she poured the water from the ice bucket into the glass, letting it flow in a slow and steady stream. A waterfall of her will.

"Fair Aphrodite," Maddie whispered, "lady of *agape* and *eros*, of *philia* and *ludus*, of love in all names and all forms. Let love be my shield and desire drive my footsteps."

Home. The word kept echoing in her mind. She had never thought about it much. Her work kept her moving. She liked her work. Like Sally the chambermaid, she was skilled at her trade.

I can't do this to him.

That had become her latest justification for leaving

Lionel in Montauk. She couldn't inflict her lifestyle, her pace, her globe-trotting madness on anyone but herself. But even as she thought the words, she heard how hollow they rang.

Lionel was, apparently, hot on her heels. He hadn't just chased her; he'd thrown himself into the fire to do it. And survived, which meant her next argument—*he's not ready, he can't survive this*—collapsed in her mind like a house of cards.

She looked to the dark water, to the reflection of the candlelight. Of course she saw him. She knew that look in his eye. It was one particular night in Montauk.

She had been perched on the toilet lid like a bird, knees drawn up tight to her chest, head bowed and hair tangled from tossing and turning. It was two in the morning when the pressure forced her out of bed and forced her hand, sending her to find her bone-handled knife. The centuries had put on weight, memories turning visible, swirling around her like spirits. Conjuring up her bad decisions, her personal disasters. Mistakes and regrets formed a line outside the bathroom door, patiently waiting to rub her nose in her own filth.

One cut, a fresh scar to join the ones that lined her forearm, would make it go away for a little while. The flesh pain would flood in, and the heart pain would have to make room for it; she only had so much space inside her, after all. She couldn't decide to be healed, but she could set the terms of her own suffering. She felt more powerful that way. Maddie sat there, holding the knife, staring at her arm, debating as the pressure pinned her down.

But then he was there, standing in the doorway. No

A Time for Witches

judgment in his eyes. No disappointment. He moved toward her slowly, his hands open, his voice soft.

"I'm going to take this from you, okay?"

She let him pry the knife from her fingers. They went slack as they brushed against his. He set it on the sink. Then he lifted her, easing her to her feet, and guided her footsteps back to the bed they shared.

He held her. And his eyes were closed, but she knew the rhythm of Lionel's breath. *He's awake*, she thought. *He's not falling asleep until I do.*

"Does it scare you," she whispered, "that I might not ever get better? That I might always be like this?"

"I'm not going anywhere," he murmured into her shoulder.

"That's not what I asked."

He was silent then. Because they both knew what she was really asking. And he had given his answer. She slept after that.

Now, with miles between them, she gazed into his eyes and traced the sign of the dove upon the water in her glass.

Fly, your heart to me.

She was thinking about Sally. And trust. Even the poisoner in the lounge, lamenting his eternal loneliness, had given her something to chew over. Maddie was used to being a lone wolf, but that wasn't the same as *wanting* to be alone.

She wanted to be with Lionel. And if he wanted to be with her, and if he was willing to risk it...

"You might fall, out there on your own," she said to the water. "Guess I'd better come and catch you quick, huh?"

She blew out the candle.

Decided, then. She'd change course, come sunrise.

Tonight there was nothing to do but ease her aching muscles and restore her strength. She wasn't hungry for sleep just yet; the garden tub in the bathroom was calling to her. She left a trail of her clothes across the room, like she usually did, naked by the time she crossed the threshold. The porcelain felt cool against her bare skin as she sat on the edge of the tub and turned the old spigots, testing the water's heat under her fingertips until it was just right.

Maddie checked the toiletries while she waited for the tub to fill. She remembered the Pullman stocked a lavender-scented body wash she liked, and she was pleased to find it in a little ribbon-wrapped basket on the sink. She got her travel kit from her suitcase and set out her toothbrush, vaguely wishing she had some wine. Baths were always better with wine.

She twisted the spigots, the last of the water splashing down, and stepped into the tub. The water rose to meet her, steamy-hot and loosening the knots in her back, as she slid on down. And down, submerged in the dreamy warmth almost all the way to her chin.

This is nice, she thought. She closed her eyes and drifted for a while.

A drip rolled from the mouth of the tap, splashing into the tub. It sounded louder in the stillness. Maddie floated, breathed, serene.

Another drip. She felt it strike the skin of the water, rippling.

The third drip landed on her cheek, spattering her face.

Her eyes snapped open. She was bathing in bloody water. A line of scarlet trickled down her cheek. She looked up.

A skeletal horror in the shape of a woman, covered in twisted burn tissue and clad in a flowing red gown, clung to the bathroom ceiling. She let out a deafening screech and her gown ignited, billowing with flame. She hurtled down at Maddie like a living meteor. She hit the water in a steaming splash and the two women went tumbling through—into the water, beyond the tub, into another place as the world went black-and-white and flipped upside down—with fingers locked in a death grip around Maddie's throat.

CHAPTER TWENTY-NINE

Corinth, Maddie thought, *will be a good place to put down roots.*

It was time. Jason had given her children, two young and healthy boys, and they needed a place to grow and thrive. The sun was bright and the world was new, and her family had their entire lives ahead of them.

That was the day, standing out in the pasture behind the humble cottage they were slowly turning into a home, that Jason told her he was leaving.

She was so stunned he had to repeat it. The words couldn't penetrate the shock that enveloped her like a cocoon. So he said them again, sharper, until they cut their way through and buried themselves in the bloody meat of her heart. His face had changed; his eyes were different. He didn't look at her like his wife, or his lover, or his companion.

He looked at her like an inconvenience. And she wondered how long he'd felt that way. How long he'd been hiding it because he needed her help, time and time again. Her witchcraft had saved his doomed quest. He had won the Golden Fleece with her aid, when he would have been devoured by its guardians three times over. She'd saved him from the flames of fire-breathing beasts and taught him how to defeat an army of warriors grown from dragons' teeth. She'd risked her life to slay the mammoth golem Talos; he would have sent the *Argo* to the bottom of the sea if she hadn't been there to protect her lover and his crew.

She had opened her legs to him. She had borne his sons.

"The Princess Creusa accepted my proposal. She's not the king's first daughter, but she is his favorite. I may never take the throne of Thessaly, but Corinth is fine compensation."

"What about the children?"

"They'll be fine. They're too young to understand. I'll send for them once I've arranged for their care."

Her heart beat faster. She looked to the cottage windows. On the other side of the dusty glass, she could see the peasant woman they'd hired to tend the boys' cradles.

"You're not taking my sons."

"They're *my* sons," he said. "And they'll be raised as princes. They'll never need for anything. Never hunger, never suffer. If you were really a good mother, you'd want this for them."

"What about all I've done for you? You wouldn't be here if it wasn't for me. All of your success, all of your glory, came because I gave everything I had to support you. Don't you have any gratitude?"

Jason shrugged.

"I gave thanks. To Aphrodite. She's the one who made you fall in love with me. So if you're angry…blame her, not me."

Her mind was tilting, capsizing, her *this-can't-be-happening* horror at war with stark reality.

"You made a vow," she said. "We stood before the altar of Hekate and you promised—you *swore*—that you'd love me forever. That you'd be mine and mine alone."

He looked calmly into her eyes, so casual he might have been discussing the sunny weather, and delivered the words that shattered her into a thousand pieces.

"I said what I needed to say," he told her. "You wouldn't have helped me otherwise."

The weather turned sour that night, patchwork clouds and patchwork rain, an icy wind blowing in over the waters of the bay. Maddie set out alone. She wore a threadbare cloak, her hair ragged from her anguished pulling, her cheeks stained rusty with tears of blood. She carried a torch into the night and strode barefoot down into the wood, feeling the wet mud squelch under her callused soles.

"*Mother!*" she cried to the heavens. "I have been wronged. I have been used. Jason has spurned us both and trampled his sacred oath. Grant me the power to take vengeance."

She could flee. Take her children and go, run into the night. He'd never find them. Small comfort, but she'd still have her sons. She could deny him that one tiny victory.

No. She wasn't sure where the idea had come from, her own instincts or divine inspiration, but she rejected it. It wasn't enough. Not nearly enough.

Jason needed to pay for what he'd done to her. He needed to suffer. So did his bride-to-be, the puffed-up little popinjay who thought she could steal from a daughter of Hekate with impunity. *Take my husband? My CHILDREN? No. I'll see you burn first.*

Images filled her mind, and ideas. The words of a spell she'd contemplated but never had cause to weave. And a bolt of cherry-red linen she'd seen in the marketplace yesterday, which looked so fetching on display.

Yes, she thought. *I don't want to seem a graceless loser.*

I'll sew the princess a wedding dress. A one-of-a-kind gown, for her special day.

~~

Princess Creusa's banshee howl chased them downward, the two women grappling, tumbling end over end through a world drained of all but light and shadow. The only color in the chiaroscuro void came from the flames of the dead woman's burning gown. Maddie got her knees under her, twisted her body, and kicked as hard as she could.

Her vision blurred and suddenly the wet tile of the bathroom floor was racing to meet her. She landed on her forearm and hip, reeling from twin shocks of pain that lanced through her bones. No time to lie there and groan; she forced herself to her unsteady feet and ran. Through the bedroom, out the door, stark naked and trailing droplets of bloody bathwater down a black-and-white hallway. The light flickered with the cadence of an antique film projector. She heard Creusa howl again, a distant bellow. The princess was hunting her.

An elderly couple was making a late departure, coming out of their room and dragging a bulky suitcase. They didn't even look at Maddie, and as she ran, she billowed through them and out the other side, nothing but another pair of the hotel's resident ghosts. But they weren't the ghosts here, her intuition told her. They were living flesh and blood.

She was the ghost.

Maddie hadn't lived this long by surrendering to panic. She mastered herself, starting with her breath—breath that felt like it was passing through her body, leeching through her spectral lungs and out through her pale gray skin in gusts of billowing winter cold. Her mantra was simple: *focus, assess, plan, execute*. Her first priority was getting distance from that flaming horror before it could track her down again.

She scrambled down to the lobby and made a hard left, leaving wet and marshy footprints on the runner. She jolted to a stop. Streamers of black ink, like a giant spiderweb coated in dripping oil, hung draped across the hotel's front doors.

Dead-trap. The Pullman only let flesh-and-blood bodies go. Souls, it kept.

Another roar, like a distant Tyrannosaurus on a rampage, sounded from the floor above her head. Creusa was getting closer. Maddie had a handful of tricks and charms that could crack the Pullman's shell wide open, but she needed time to put them to work. *The kitchen*, she thought. *Delivery door. It'll take her longer to find me there.*

She drew a map in her mind as she turned on her heel. She could get there through the lounge. Maddie heard the music up ahead, but it was more discordant now, a mixture of a child's off-key piano toy and the sound of breaking glass.

"Well hello, beautiful. You came back in your birthday suit, just for me? I have to say, you looked fine in that dress, but you look even better out of it."

Herbert Wilby Woods was waiting for her, just where she'd left him. Vivid as life, the only source of color in the black-and-white room. The poisoner flashed his most charming smile.

His teeth were needles. They dripped with rattlesnake venom, drizzling down and sizzling on his corroded gums.

"You should run," Maddie told him.

"Oh?" He sauntered toward her, slowly closing the gap between them. "Why would I run, when this looks like my lucky night?"

Another strangled roar in the distance. The floor rumbled under Maddie's feet.

"Because *that*," she said, pointing toward the sound, "is going to level anything standing in its path. You don't want to be here."

"Sweetheart, I've spent decades 'not wanting to be here.' And if it's coming for you, well...that means I'll just have to gobble you up fast."

She didn't have time for this. She had a spell for destroying death energy—one so simple it was the first thing she'd taught Lionel—and it worked just fine on the restless dead. Maddie stomped one bare, wet foot down on the lounge floor and pulled her hands close to her chest, clasping her palms, gathering her focus and energy.

"*Akhas, Dromenei*," she shouted, thrusting out her palms, "*Keh!*"

Nothing happened.

"What's wrong?" he said, feigning dismay. "No gas in the tank? No pep in your step?"

She shifted me, Maddie thought. *Jarred me out of flesh-space. Need to get back to my own body. Or attune myself to this world, but I need time for that.*

Time Herbert wasn't going to give her. He lunged. Maddie swept up a chair and met his charge with a battering-ram swing. The wood broke, splintering over his shoulder, knocking him to his knees. That bought her the space of a breath. Eyes blazing, he sprang up and into her, driving her backward with his forearm braced against her collarbone. Maddie stumbled back until her shoulders hit the mirrored wall and the back of her skull cracked against the glass. She ignored the starburst of pain, fighting through it, grabbing the dead man's wrist as he speared it toward her face.

His fingers ended in needles. Venom welled up from beds of scarred-over flesh and along the stainless-steel points, dripping down. Maddie heard the droplets hiss as they spattered onto the floor, and smelled a foul electric tang, like smoke from a burning battery.

"Got something for you right here," he said, the needles coming closer to her cheek. "Fix you real quick, I promise you that."

She fired her knee up, driving it between his legs. Then she brought her leg down like a piston. Even barefoot, she drove her heel into his arches hard enough to feel tiny bones crack. He doubled over, letting out a wheezing grunt, and staggered away. Bracing himself against the bar, eyes wide with pain he hadn't felt in decades.

Maddie was deciding on her next move when Creusa found her.

Burned hands shot through the gold-laced mirror at her back. They clamped down on the sides of Maddie's skull, gripping tight, and hauled her through the glass.

CHAPTER THIRTY

Some might say, Medea knew, that she'd been cursed by Dionysus. There was a mania upon her as she packed her meager belongings, keeping one eye on her sons in their cradles. Her mood was a tempest, swinging from one wild extreme to another. Victory. Glee. Regret. She knew there was a very good chance her life was forfeit for what she'd just done. She'd fly, hide, try to survive. She had cast her lot; now it was in the hands of the Fates.

A pounding sounded at her cottage door. She braced herself for a fight. Instead, she found the peasant-maid, Alethea, her face pale and her patchwork gown drenched with sweat.

"I ran," Alethea said, gulping down air, "from the city gates. Soldiers, not far behind me—"

Maddie eased her into a chair and shut the door.

"Catch your breath," she said, "and leave. I don't want you in the middle of this. You've done nothing wrong."

"The children—"

"Will be fine. It's me they want."

"You don't understand," Alethea said.

The maid looked up at her, heartbreak in her eyes. They brimmed with tears.

"Medea, what have you *done*?"

"Don't weep for me, Alethea. I'll be fine. I always land on my feet. And like I said, the children will be fine. Jason won't let anything happen to them."

"Jason is gone."

Maddie blinked. "Gone?"

"Exiled. Banished. The dress you wove for Princess Creusa, it—"

"I know what it did."

"King Creon demanded answers as he wept over his daughter's corpse. Jason blamed you. The king blamed *him*, for bringing you here. He's been banished, told never to return on pain of death. Then Creon made his proclamation. You took his child. He wants yours. Both of them."

"Wants..." Maddie's gaze drifted to the cradles, to the sleeping infants swaddled in the blankets she'd woven for them. "He wouldn't."

"Nothing so easy as death," the maid said. "He wants to make an example. He wants them to suffer. He wants *you* to suffer, as only a mother can."

She hesitated, as if speaking the words would make them come true.

"Your sons are going to be sold into slavery. You'll be executed after. After you see them auctioned off. He said...there's a salt mine that likes to buy them young. Put them to work young enough, and they never know anything in their lives but toil and the lash."

Maddie's wild mania faded and fell, tumbling like a rock in the pit of her stomach. The world became a cold and heavy weight, pressing down on her, as blood roared in her ears. She couldn't move. Couldn't process.

She had expected Creon's retribution. She just never imagined his grief would drive him to vent his fury on her innocent children. *My grief became his grief became...*

Something monstrous.

Maddie was at the bottom of the sea. Crushed by unendurable pressure. But it was quiet at the bottom of the sea, and she could think. Draw the cold calculations. Creon's men were already on the way. She might escape alone, if she was quick. Taking the boys would slow her down, and if they were caught and captured...

"Alethea," she said, "thank you for your service."

Her voice was soft and terribly calm. The maid looked at her, fearful.

"Medea?"

"You should go now. Before they arrive."

"What...what are you going to do?"

The only thing she could do. There was no salvation here. No happy ending. Only a choice of monsters.

"I'm going to draw my sons a bath," she said.

~~

Maddie and the burning princess fought, entangled in a molecule of mirrored glass. They spun end over end, whirling, blazing through negative space like a Roman candle. It was a dance of ancient witchcraft. War magic and speed chess. Creusa thrust poisoned words into Maddie's heart; she transmuted them, changing a single syllable to render the toxin inert, then spat philosophy that wreathed the princess's mutilated face like a swarm of hornets. Creusa took hold of the swarm, twisted it in her hands until it became a razor-edged spear of rhetoric, and slashed at her.

Maddie kicked away. She followed a trail of boiling bubbles in the drowning dark, swimming upward until—

—water sprayed, blasting across the bathroom floor, as she sat bolt upright in the bathtub. She was back in her hotel room, back in her body, back in the world of color and flesh. Not safe. Not by a long shot. She jumped out of the tub, bare feet skidding on the slick tile, and made her battle plan on the move as she grabbed a towel.

Clothes, luggage, *out*. She had to get some distance, steal a little breathing room so she could turn the tables. She raced over the threshold into the bedroom. This was fine, she'd been in tighter spots than this, this was manageable.

The door burst open under the heel of a steel-toed boot. A pack of men flooded in from the hallway, gripping the cleavers and knives they'd taken from the kitchen below.

"Fuck," Maddie said.

She turned back the way she came, chanting under her breath, and threw herself into the bathtub. She dove like a champion swimmer and vanished under the frothing water. The Triad killers were right behind her—standing, staring and dumbfounded, around the rim of an empty tub.

~~

Father Parrino had followed the pack of killers upstairs. Curious. This wasn't Jason's pet monster. Apparently his ex-wife had accumulated an entire list of enemies.

As long as the job gets done, he thought. Though he did want to kill her himself.

He hung back. Then he shivered. He had felt something—an ice-cold gust of wind. It moved *through* his body, away from the shattered door and back toward the stairwell. He turned, squinting, and caught the faint scent of lilacs in the still and silent hallway.

His grandmother had taught him things, as a boy in the old country. Special ways of seeing. He thought back to those days in her kitchen, recalling her lessons. Bits of the world were wrong here. Spots on the ivory paint that had turned to sepia ink, little specks of black-and-white glitter that hung in the open air.

A trail.

Feeling the reassuring weight of the garrote wire in his pocket, Parrino followed it.

~~

Maddie fled down chiaroscuro halls as Creusa's frenzied roar shook the floor beneath her spectral feet.

A T-shaped junction was just ahead. Intuition held her back. The dead princess boiled past, trailing fire in the wake of her billowing gown.

Too close. If she doubles back and spots me—

A mirror hung on the wall at the hallway's other end. The world on the other side was a window of shimmering light. Maddie broke into a run, leaped, and hurled herself at the glass.

She barreled through, bursting into living color. She hit the carpet on her naked shoulder and rolled, thumping to a stop. Maddie had barely gotten back on her feet when a shout in Mandarin split the air.

"*She's over here!*"

She spun, sprinting back the way she came, leaping toward the mirror. Her outstretched fingers hit the surface and the glass became liquid mercury, splashing around her as she passed through to the other side. Back to the world of gray shadows, back into the belly of the beast.

~~

Herbert Wilby Woods strutted the halls, putting a little kick in his step as he hammered on doorways. One after another, calling out with a voice that only the dead could hear.

"Wake up! Wake up, my good worthies, my gentles, my morning, noon, and nighttime clientele. You hear that sound? Those aren't my knuckles pounding your door, friends. That's opportunity. And it comes this way but once in a great long time."

One door swung open before he could knock. The brutish man on the other side wore a bloodstained surgeon's mask and clutched a hand-crank drill in his hairy hands.

"Get out of here, Woods. I am conducting a very delicate operation."

"Doctor, you've been cutting up that same unfortunate stiff since 1947. Now I am here to offer you something unique, unprecedented, and unmissable."

"I doubt that," he growled behind his mask.

"How about the cure to your perpetual doldrums?"

"Snake oil. And what doldrums? I am quite content in my work." He gestured behind him. Intestine hung, wet and glistening, strung from bedpost to bedpost. "I am unraveling the mysteries of life itself."

"Now who's selling snake oil? Doc, you and I both know one thing perfectly well."

Herbert leaned against the open doorway, crossed his polished shoes at the ankles, and folded his arms.

"You only enjoy your work if the patient is alive and wide awake for the procedure. We both know this. Now are

A Time for Witches

you really happy with the same old, same old, or are you in the market for something fresh?"

One bushy eyebrow went up. "Fresh?"

"C'mon down to the lounge."

One by one, he gathered them all. The piano lounge became a den of shades. Upturned gray faces, broken necks and slit throats, dusty dry veins and clutching fingers that yearned to feel again. To feel anything at all, beyond the endless tedium and the record-skip hours of their own deaths.

Herbert stood on the piano bench and trilled his fingers like he was warming up. Finally, after so many years, he was back in his element.

"People! Either you have been misled as to what's happening under your very noses, or you're simply not paying attention."

The surgeon tugged his mask down, shoving to the front of the pack. "Start talking, Woods."

"Very well, I'll jump straight to the point. We have some special guests tonight. We've got a witch, right here in the Pullman Hotel. A living breathing bounty of delicious power, and she is—at this very moment—jumping in and out of our homes as she attempts to elude not one, not two, but...well, quite a few troublemakers intent on causing her grave bodily distress."

He flashed a needle-toothed smile.

"And none of them will be missed. Friends, I propose we give them a down-home welcome and have ourselves a feast."

CHAPTER THIRTY-ONE

Maddie had a plan in the making. What she didn't have was her gun, or her clothes. Going back to the room wasn't an option with a pack of Triad hitters on her tail; she needed to take them off the table first. She had found another mirror, made her way back to the world of living color, and now she was racing up the Pullman's back stairwell. Concrete steps smacked against the soles of her feet and she heard shouts and running footsteps boiling up from two flights below.

Good. She wanted them to chase her. All the way up to the fifth floor, the penthouse suites. As she barreled through a door and into a long, art deco hallway with vintage striped wallpaper and a zigzag carpet, silver on black, she felt pressure on her sinuses. It was a warning. She already knew that the ghosts here could hurt her, and that Woods was roaming the lounge. But like he'd told her, he was far from the worst of the Pullman's permanent guests.

This labyrinth came with its own Minotaur. And he lived on the penthouse floor.

A necessary risk, for what she had in mind. She only hoped Creusa hadn't made her way up here yet. She followed the lightning-bolt trail of the carpet around a corner, down a tall, wide gallery lined with penthouse doors and brass light sconces, their soft, small bulbs shrouded under domes of frosted glass. And mirrors, spaced out as copper-framed decorations from one end to the other.

She held her breath and jumped, crossing to the other side.

The shadow world of the fifth floor hadn't changed since one dark winter night in 1977. The carpet here was a murky, sticky river that stank of dirty copper. Maddie's bare feet sank into it, coming away coated in blood that would never dry. It felt like walking barefoot through a marsh. Doors firmly shut in the flesh world hung open here, some of them kicked open, others chopped to kindling. And beyond the doors...

Maddie was normally immune to revulsion. She'd learned the necromancer's trade as a girl and could bury her hands in a dead man's guts just to dig for a speck of knowledge. She had seen the circle of life play itself out in more ways and more times than she could possibly count and had come to appreciate the beauty of the human body from its first spark to its final moments of rot and decay. It was all part of the Earth's grand cycle. But this...this was overkill. Pure animal rage given form and a weapon and set loose upon innocent flesh.

The snort of a bull turned her head.

The Axman of Marshfield Avenue had, in life, been consumed by his own inner darkness. In death it turned literal. He was a living blot of black smoke, seven feet tall at the shoulder, with eyes of yellow flame. The hulking figure stood at the hallway's end, clutching the same ax he'd brandished when the police gunned him down over forty years ago.

Maddie turned and curled her fingers, beckoning. Her timing would have to be perfect.

"You're a big one," she said. "Come on, then. Let's play."

~~

The pack of killers moved slow now, footsteps soft on the silver and black carpet, spacing out as they made their way along the penthouse floor.

They'd chased their quarry up the stairs, all the way to the top. The elevator banks sat still and silent, and the glowing amber numbers showed that both cars were down in the lobby.

Meaning she was still on this floor. Cornered at last.

Jeong, the man destined to replace Liu Bingwen—if he proved himself capable tonight and delivered his bosses some vital answers along with the killer's head on a platter—took the lead. He squeezed the cleaver in his hand until his knuckles turned white, but he kept a stoic face and a slow, steady stride, putting on a show of bravery for his men.

Bravery he didn't feel. He'd expected a tough fight from the assassin who butchered Bingwen and his crew. He didn't expect her to jump into a bathtub and vanish, only to reappear, dripping wet and stark naked, out in the hallway a moment later. Or for her to turn a corner, disappear again, and suddenly be running up the stairs.

The magic act wasn't what worried him the most. There had to be a rational explanation, and he'd figure it out after the killing was done. Illusions, mirrors—for all he knew, she'd rigged this entire hotel with tricks and traps for a situation just like this one. What worried him was his growing suspicion that she could have escaped by now if she really wanted to.

We didn't chase her up here, he thought. *She LED us up here. But why?*

Something moved in the corner of his eye. He turned to the mirror on the wall, framed between a pair of frosted glass sconces.

It wasn't his reflection. The mirrored glass was a silver screen and the woman, looking like a vision from a black-and-white movie with her wet hair matted to her bare shoulders—Aphrodite, rising from the sea—stared back at him.

Then her hand fired from the mirror, clamped down on his throat, and hauled him through to the other side.

The world flipped and spun around him. Disoriented, stumbling, he twirled in place in a swamp of blood-soaked carpet. He had just enough time to catch the flash of burning yellow eyes and hear the roar of a bull before the ax swooped down.

~~

The pack of killers fell back, shouting over one another, pointing to the mirror. They could see their boss in the shadow world on the other side, falling to his knees with an ax blade buried halfway into his skull. A raspberry geyser erupted as the grunting behemoth ripped it free. The last man in the pack was so fixated on the impossible sight in front of them that he didn't think to look back.

Maddie lurched from a different mirror, hooked her arm around his throat, and dragged him through. She spun him around and shoved him in the path of the rampaging juggernaut. He tripped and stumbled, his knees hitting the sodden carpet, and threw up a desperate arm to protect his face as the ax hissed through the air.

The blade lopped it off at the elbow, leaving him a stump of torn flesh and jutting, splintered bone. His howl of agony faded at Maddie's back as she propelled herself through another pane of glass, clutching the meat cleaver she'd pried from Jeong's dead hand. She fell to the carpet, tucked and rolled, and came up swinging right in the middle of the chaos. The cleaver hacked into the back of a hit man's neck; then she ripped it loose and spun to block a filleting knife as it thrust toward her eye. Their blades clashed. The hitter with the knife was a knife *fighter*, trained by professionals, and she hadn't even recovered before he was coming at her again. She danced back as he punched with the blade again and again, herding her up the hallway and trying to pin her in a corner.

Then she heard the rumbling freight-train howl. Princess Creusa had picked up her trail.

She feinted with her clenched fist, throwing a punch. The knife man thought he saw an opportunity and slashed at her wrist. She yanked her hand back, anticipating his move, and hurled the cleaver. It spun like a saw blade and caught him in the throat.

She scouted for threats, assessing her position—and a switchblade gleamed in her eye before it carved across her collarbone, drawing a line of torn skin and bloody fire.

Father Parrino inclined his head, brandishing the blade with an artful flourish of his wrist. He eyed her naked body like it was a canvas waiting for the brush.

"Your husband sends his regards," he said.

"Ex-husband," she said.

One of the Triad hitters, half-mad with panic, had gone

into full berserker mode. He came barreling up the hallway, howling a battle cry with a carving knife raised high in his trembling fist. Maddie sidestepped, caught him around the waist, and used his momentum, keeping him running, moving, stumbling until the two of them tumbled headfirst through the closest mirror. She landed on top of him with both knees and drove her curled knuckles straight into his neck.

He dropped the knife and clutched his throat, wide-eyed and convulsing. Maddie heard the axman's bull snort of breath behind her. And Creusa's howls, closer now, just under her feet. She got up and ran, leaving the Triad killer as a sacrificial offering on the gore-soaked carpet.

She rounded the corner, trapped in the black-and-white world, windows of colored light streaming from the mirrors along the wall. That would just take her back to where Jason's assassin was waiting. One crisis at a time. She turned the other way—and found Parrino casually strolling toward her. He was a living sketch here, protected by some unfamiliar magic and drawn in lines of faded sepia ink.

"I'm pleased to find you still alive," he said, "and impressed. But mostly pleased. As you can see, there is nowhere you can go that I cannot follow."

"I'm a little occupied at the moment," she told him. "Could you come back later? Or take a number, maybe? I've got a lot on my plate."

"Alas. Death is so rarely convenient."

The man in the priestly collar had to be an insurance policy. Now there was no question who had conjured Princess Creusa up from the depths of Hades and sent her on a mission of revenge. But Jason was thorough. He'd want to make sure the job got done, because he knew what would happen if Maddie escaped and came gunning for him. She couldn't keep a tiny smile from her lips.

If she lived through the next fifteen minutes, Jason's insurance policy would be the best thing to happen to her all night. He eyed her and tilted his head to one side.

"Something funny?" he asked.

She pointed. "Check your six, chief."

He turned—and dodged, throwing himself to the carpet as the axman swooped in with a thunderous bellow. The spectral ax cleaved into the wall just above his head, ripping wallpaper and shattering the plaster beneath. Parrino was fast. He slithered back and leaped to his feet like an acrobat.

Maddie ran, but not *too* fast.

CHAPTER THIRTY-TWO

Maddie sprinted down two flights of black and white stairs, silver light drifting down from the penthouse floor like a streetlamp in a film noir. She waited on the landing, crouched, listening for the sound of Creusa's howls. She tried to ignore the burning sting of the cut on her collarbone while blood drooled down her chest in trickling, syrupy rivulets. It was deep enough to give her a scar to remember this night by, but not bleeding badly enough to threaten her life. She'd fight through the pain. No choice.

There was the distant, mad-dinosaur roar. One floor up. Good. She darted along a hallway, jumped through a mirror, and her feet touched down in the land of the living. From there she doubled back, watching for any stragglers from the Triad kill team, and navigating back to her room. She didn't know what Parrino was using to track her, but she figured he'd find his way to her quickly, faster than the burning princess at least. She was counting on it. She flicked off the lights, checking the ambiance. Pitch black. Good. She turned them on again.

She scooped up the metal trash can from under the room's writing desk and set it on the sea chest at the foot of the bed. She angled it so she could see its reflection in the hanging mirror. Then she grabbed her book of matches. A struck head sizzled and flared, and she used it to ignite the entire matchbook before dropping it into the can. She flicked off the electric lamp. Now the only light was the crackling orange glow of the flames, shimmering up from the metal can like an aurora.

Then one last passage through the mercury glass, passing from the real room to its faded ghost. She pressed her back to the wall, eyes on the mirror, and waited.

The priest didn't disappoint her. He turned to a sepia-ink illustration as he clambered over the mirror frame, dapper shoes dropping down on her side of the glass. His hand dipped into his raincoat pocket. He didn't reach for his switchblade. Instead, he brandished a garrote, with razored piano wire strung between a pair of worn, scarlet-flecked grips. He drew the wire taut between his hands.

"Nowhere left to run," he said. "Now...the garrote is a unique tool. It can kill very quickly, or very slowly indeed. Are you going to fight me?"

She pressed her palms to the wall at her back, chin tucked down, cowed.

"No," she said. "I won't fight you."

He took a triumphant step closer. Behind him, on the other side of the glass, the orange glow was fading fast. Maddie pushed herself away from the wall and raised her head high.

"The word 'fight' implies I'd give you any chance of winning," she said.

He paused in mid-stride, bringing the wooden handles closer to his chest.

"What...is this?" he said, squinting at her.

"A trap."

On the other side of the mirror, the burning matchbook guttered and died. And with the last light gone, the world on their side of the glass became an inky, empty void.

~~

Parrino let the wooden handles fall from his fingers. He whipped out his switchblade. He heard it click open, felt the familiar kick against his curled fingers, but he couldn't see it in front of his face. He stepped out of his shoes, fast. His cashmere socks whispered against the floorboards as he sidestepped, getting clear. He couldn't see the woman, but she couldn't see him. Or the mirror, now that all light was gone, meaning she was still trapped in here with him.

"You're thinking you'll track me by sound," Maddie's voice said at his shoulder.

He spun, whipping his hand toward the sound of her voice, and sliced at nothing.

In response, her laugh boiled from the far side of the room.

"I noticed how this side of the glass drew light from the living world. Not much. Filtered, drained of color, struggling to get through...which meant if I knocked out all the light on that side of the glass, and we were on this side..."

He had been moving, tracking her as she spoke, circling the furniture by memory as he closed in. There she was, right in front of him. He could feel her breath, smell the floral soap on her skin.

He lunged, thrust out his blade, and skewered empty air.

Now her laughter came from behind him. "Jason really didn't prepare you for this, did he? Not surprised. Planning was never his strong suit."

"Show yourself!"

Silence greeted him. A silence so deep it was like a physical weight, driving him down to the center of the earth. She shattered it with a whisper.

"Are you sure you want that?"

His mouth was dry. The handle of the switchblade slick, damp in his clammy hand. He squeezed it like a life preserver. This wasn't happening. He couldn't be harmed. Jason had told him that he was immortal, unstoppable. *Promised* him.

"This is a trap in two parts," Maddie said, "and I don't have much time, so let me level with you. I need to know where Jason is right now and where he's headed. So I'm going to take that information from you now."

"I'll tell you *nothing*," he spat. He swung, wild, slashing at sounds in the void. Sounds like the fast patter of light feet. Something gossamer-soft brushed his face. He slapped his cheek and staggered backward, tears of panic welling in his eyes.

A hand clamped down on his shoulder. Not the young woman's. It was withered, old, *centuries* old, with yellow talon nails and a grip of cold iron.

"You'll tell me everything and more," Maddie whispered in his ear.

~~

Creusa billowed through the halls, her flaming gown trailing burning embers in her wake. She could *smell* the hated witch, so close, her trail lost in this hellish maze. Now she smelled something new. Fear. Pain. The aroma of a man's soul being torn out, one bite at a time. She changed course and followed the scent.

A mind-scream shook the shadow hotel and tinted the

edges of her vision in spiderwebs of frost. As it faded, a voice echoed along the corridor.

"Princess Creusa," Medea called in a singsong lilt. "Come to me. Come to me here. Come to me now."

The burning princess was a meteor with claws and teeth, blazing toward the sound.

~~

Maddie held her breath and waited. Listening. She heard the crackle of undying flames and smelled the stench of charred pork. Then she saw the glow of dawn from the hallway, a false sun coming to burn her alive.

Creusa floated into the room, triumphant. The princess hesitated. The figure laid out on the bed wasn't Maddie. It was Parrino, eyes wide and glassy, his emaciated body a road map of wormy black veins. His bloodless lips moved in an unending litany, an unanswered prayer to someone, somewhere.

Maddie was off to the side, pressed against the wall, right next to the mirror. A mirror that now, thanks to the eternal bonfire she'd made of her enemy, had light for her to see by. And light to capture, bridging the worlds on either side.

She grabbed onto the frame, hoisted herself up and over, and tumbled into the world of the living. She raced to the bed, snatched up the metal trash can she had used to set the trap, and spun on her heel. On the other side of the glass, she saw them both: Parrino, soul-shattered and catatonic, and Creusa as she whirled to track her prey.

Maddie hurled the can. The mirror burst. It erupted in a storm of glass shards, the silver world on the other side flickering in a broken waterfall. The pieces hit the floorboards, bouncing, shattering, spinning across the room. Creusa's bonfire became a scattering of embers in a dying firepit.

One by one, they guttered out, leaving only darkness behind.

It was one hour to sunrise. Maddie turned toward the bathroom door. She needed a towel, she needed her clothes, she needed her stolen explosives, and she needed her gun.

~~

Maddie left a generous tip for housekeeping on the bedside table and shut the door to her room behind her. She wheeled her luggage along an empty hallway gone quiet, tranquil now.

Almost. It was still dark, and the Pullman was still awake, still hungry. Always hungry. She felt the ebb of winter cold coming from the lobby. She knew what she'd find before she arrived. The night clerk sat with her head down and noise-canceling headphones on, blocking out the world as she stared intently at her phone. Her hands were shaking.

She was the only living soul in the room. The hotel's dead had gathered here, a broken and crooked mob, ringing the marble floor and barring the way out. There was only a single sympathetic face: Sally, the chambermaid, penned in one corner of the room and looking miserable. She locked eyes with Maddie and whispered, "*Run.*"

Maddie stood her ground. She rested her luggage at her side and squared her footing.

"All right," she said. "Try me."

She saw the poisoner in the crowd; she wasn't surprised that he hung back, waiting for someone else to take the risk. He didn't have to wait long. The energy of the crowd shifted, tensing, taut as a rubber band—then it snapped.

A wraith with blue-white skin, his eyes and mouth hollow pits of darkness, let out a nails-on-chalkboard screech as he came for her. Maddie was already moving, drawing her hands together, harnessing her will. She spat the words of the *voces mysticae* and fired her shot. A lance of gray steam hissed through the air, a spear wrapped in graveyard mist. It hit the wraith in the chest and the dead man shattered: flash-frozen, hollow inside, he hit the marble floor and broke like a porcelain statue smashed by a hammer.

The room fell silent. Maddie lifted her index finger to her pursed lips and blew. A puff of smoke wafted across the lobby.

"You can't stop us all," Woods called out, though he kept himself safe behind a wall of grim-faced followers.

"Only one way to find out," she said. "If you want to step up, we can roll those dice. Or we could parley."

"Parley?" croaked a broken-necked woman, her noose still dangling around her bloated and purple throat.

"Parley," Maddie said. "I won't grant you freedom, but I will grant you parole. From this dark moon to the next, on my authority as a daughter of Hekate. If you want to remember what the wind feels like on your skin, if you want to remember what open sky and sunlight looks like...bend your knee."

"What's the catch?" Woods asked.

"Not a catch. A cost. I require a service. One service, and the rest of your time—before you must return to this place—is yours to do with as you please. But time is short. The sun is about to rise and I'm about to leave. I won't be back for a good long while, I don't think. Make your choice."

She raised one hand high, fingers spread, a benediction hanging in the wintry air.

"Either clear my path or join my company. All you have to do is promise your obedience for a single task, and I'll grant you a taste of freedom." She swept her gaze over the ghostly congregation. "Bend. Your. Knee."

CHAPTER THIRTY-THREE

Sunrise came. Father Parrino's motel room was empty.

"What do you think?" Baker asked. The Argonauts were packing up, loading their vintage cars, breaking camp. They had a schedule to keep. Jason looked to the horizon.

He didn't want to say what he thought.

"We can't fall behind," he said. "I'm sure he got caught in traffic or something."

Baker gave him an *or something* look. Jason shrugged.

"He knows the route. He'll catch up with us."

The engines of the *Argo 2* roared like a hungry lion. The road train pulled onto the highway, its entourage trailing behind. The convoy drove west through the long, dry day, past farmland and table-flat plains, carving a trail through the heartland of America. Sunset found them off the beaten path, following a country road barely wide enough for the massive truck's tires. A necessary detour, to get them to their next stop on Cordell Spears's to-do list.

Almost done, Jason thought as the steering wheel thrummed under his steady grip. *And then...*

He'd never been good at planning ahead. He liked to think of himself as a man of action.

The sky turned a shimmering, radiant turquoise, then

faded to lapis lazuli. The last bands of light shone on the horizon as the sun fell. They were far enough into the country for the stars to come out, a scattered handful of diamond pinpoints glimmering in the deep blue void. In the copilot seat, Baker craned his neck.

"They say there's more places where you can't see the stars now than places you can. All around the world. Light pollution blots 'em out."

"Huh," Jason grunted.

"You remember Medina Ridge?"

"Basra."

"Those were some good stars," Baker said.

"Good war."

"Kept us afloat." Baker leaned back in his seat. "The padre should have called by now."

Jason didn't answer. He felt the heat of the man's stare in his peripheral vision.

A bloody glow erupted in the distance. Baker's sudden murmur echoed his thoughts.

"The fuck is that?"

As they drove closer, he realized what he was looking at. His mouth went dry and he reached for the radio transmitter.

"Convoy, full stop. Repeat, full stop. Stay behind me."

Burning flares filled the road ahead, forming the points and ring of a pentacle in eye-searing scarlet light and smoke. Maddie stood at the heart of the five-pointed star. Waiting for him.

Jason stepped on the air brakes, slowing the truck down. Baker shook his head and waved at the dashboard.

"What are you doing, man?"

"Stopping."

A Time for Witches

"Run the bitch down," Baker said. "Hell, use the countermeasures. That's why we built 'em in. This truck is *made* to handle freaky shit."

The brakes squealed as the *Argo 2* slowly ground to a halt. The pursuit cars formed a V-shaped line behind the truck, headlights bright, engines revving and ready. The pentagram of flares was fifty feet ahead, nothing but black asphalt between them and long, fallow fields on either side.

"It's made to handle witches," Jason said, his eyes fixed on the silent, staring woman in the road. "It's not made to handle *her*. If there was any chance I could run her over, she wouldn't put herself in that position in the first place. Which means there's a trap here. Something we can't see."

"Or she just wants you to think that," Baker said. "Mind games, man."

Jason threw the truck into park, but he left it running. He shoved his door open.

"Stay here," he said.

"What are you gonna do?"

"Talk to her." Jason climbed down from the truck cab, sturdy boot-heels hitting the asphalt. "Toss me my gun. It's behind the seat."

A hand-tooled belt trailed down from the open door like a snake. Jason caught it and strapped it tight, a holster riding his hip with a long-barreled .357 nestled inside. He checked the Magnum's load, force of habit, then holstered it again. He glanced up the road. Then he started walking.

In the glow of the road flares, Maddie bathed in blood-red light. Chemical smoke wreathed her, swirling and bending in unnatural ways. The night air was still.

"Is he dead?" Jason asked.

"Your man with the priest's collar? I left him trapped inside a broken mirror. There wasn't much left of him anyway."

"I've got more," Jason said.

Steel shone in the dark as heavy doors swung wide. The Argonauts got out of the chase cars, becoming a pack on foot as they moved up and around the road train. Jason's crew formed a ragged, silent line, faceless shadows silhouetted in the truck's headlights.

"Ambrosia," Maddie said. "You've been feeding ambrosia to mortals."

"Only once in a while. Now and then, over the years. Sometimes I meet a soldier who's too good for the war he's fighting. So I bring him onto my crew."

"Lonely?" she asked.

"Maybe I just wanted some sons who you couldn't kill."

Her cheek twitched, just under her left eye.

"I know you're working for Spears," she said. "What's he planning?"

"Don't get involved."

"Too late. Hekate wants him dealt with. You remember Hekate, right? We stood at her altar when you swore your undying love to me."

"You're still sore about that?" he asked. "Clingy."

"Oh, I'm pretty much over you. I'm just wondering how the mighty Jason ends up an errand boy for the new kid on the block."

"Spears is a kid, sure, but he's a smart kid. He's going to turn the clock back."

Maddie shook her head. "Not possible. The only way is forward, like it or not."

"You remember the good old days? People like me were

worshiped. We were more than celebrities, more than something for the bards to write songs about. We were living gods."

"So you're social-climbing again," Maddie said. "Your entire life has been nothing but social climbing. You used me. You tried to use Creusa. You use everyone because nothing matters but your own glory. And no matter how many times it blows up in your face—"

His fist thumped against his chest. "I'm a hero. *Kleos* is all I have. My myth, my glory. This is what I'm *supposed* to do."

"You have free will," she said. "You have choices. Make better ones."

"Don't stand in my way. Or in Cordell's."

"He's hurting innocent people," she said.

He stared at her, not following.

"It goes like this." He held out the flat of his hand, drawing horizontal lines. "Mortals, then heroes, then gods. I have a call to greatness. If some mortals forget their place and get hurt in the process, that's on them, not me."

"Mortals can do great things, too," she said.

"They're not *supposed* to," he snapped, bringing his hand down in a curled fist at his side. "They're supposed to sit on their asses in front of the television, or pack the movie house and watch *us*. And look up to us. And revere us. When you put grand ideas into mortals' heads and make them believe that they can actually change the world, do you know what you get? Chaos."

Maddie nodded past him, over his shoulder, toward the line of shadow-faced men in the distance.

"Your followers are mortal, too. Ambrosia renders a human ageless. Ageless doesn't mean unkillable."

"Same goes for you. You're not bulletproof, last I checked. And my crew's been battle-hardened in most every war that's ever been fought. You like those odds?"

Maddie tilted her head, contemplating.

"No," she said. "Though I didn't come here to fight you. I was reminded, just last night in fact, that my priorities have been misplaced. I need to get back to what really matters. I came here to give you a chance to see reason and stand down."

"And if I don't?" he asked.

"I figured I'd slow you down long enough to buy a little time, and come back with reinforcements later."

"How do you see yourself managing that?" He wore a lazy smirk. "You weren't specifically on our list of possible threats, but my men are trained for all forms of warfare. And the *Argo 2*? That's a custom rig from the wheels up. Designed the specs myself. We came prepared for trouble."

"Oh, Jason."

Her smile was a small and terrible thing.

"You have never," she said, "been prepared for me."

She turned her hand. He reached for his gun. But he realized, just before she pushed the button, that she wasn't carrying a weapon.

It was a detonator.

Two high-pitched beeps sounded from the box, and ten pounds of plastic explosive—carefully shaped and buried in the grass on both sides of the road—erupted. The long span of highway between them and the truck became a firestorm of whirling flame and shattered asphalt, the road torn to smoking rubble. Jason was staggering, ears ringing from the blast, feeling furnace heat wash across his sweat-soaked back when Maddie's short, shrill whistle signaled the second part of her plan.

A host of spirits, the bound captives of the Pullman Hotel, fell upon the convoy. They swooped and howled, barreling through the darkness and trailing silver smoke. Jason cupped his hands to his mouth and screamed: "Fire countermeasures! *Now!*"

Inside the truck's cab, Baker flipped half the switches on the dashboard with a sweep of his hand. Flares, diamond-white and burning like phosphorus, launched from tubes nestled behind the cab. They turned the night sky into high noon, firing starbursts of light that drifted down over the battlefield while the Argonauts rallied. Hoses mounted beneath the *Argo 2*'s trailers, fed by hidden tanks, blasted the roadway with a torrent of wet, foamy crimson. Pools of pig blood spread across the black asphalt. Some of the murderous spirits—always parched, craving blood like a man in the desert thirsts for water—had already broken off from the fight, throwing themselves down to wallow and lick the puddles.

Maddie whispered words of magic as she ran. The scarlet flares on the road burned brighter, hotter, leaving bloody smears in Jason's vision. He snapped off a couple of rounds, firing at her shadow as he strafed sideways and made himself a moving target. The flares spat gouts of smoke. He barreled through the clouds, eyes stinging, keeping low.

He saw two distant silhouettes on the other side of the pentagram of flares, each running in a different direction from the roadway and fading fast. One might be real. Maybe neither was. He could try to chase her down or he could double back and support his men as they fought off the conjured dead, but not both.

He roared out his rage and emptied his gun into the dark. It didn't make him feel any better. Medea was gone, but he still knew her, after all these years.

He knew she'd be back.

III: The Chariot

CHAPTER THIRTY-FOUR

Lionel had been leaving messages.

He drove west in Cordell's stolen SUV. Careful, with one eye on the rearview mirror. At every highway-side fast-food restaurant and gas station, he slipped into the restroom with a Sharpie in his pocket. He was slow to pick up the road tongue, but each stop taught him new vocabulary. He didn't see Bill's ghost, though he felt the dead man's presence. Heard him once or twice, he thought, whispering in Lionel's ear as he etched careful code on a toilet-stall wall.

At a fried-chicken joint in Dixon, Illinois, about a hundred miles outside of Chicago, he finally found a reply. It was in the shape of someone's half-finished game of hangman. The angles of the filled-in letters—M_RTU_RY—were modified by the direction and thickness of the dangling stick-figure victim. Blank lines were participles. The message gave him the address of a campground outside of town and a date to be there by or he'd be left behind. He was right on time.

Finding the camp was easy. From there, he was adrift. He parked in a secluded, shady spot—to keep the SUV out of sight from any curious cops—and started walking. The

Fairview was a spacious campground on the edge of an artificial lake, warm and green. RVs and campers filled a generous lot, while the lawns were taken up by cookout pavilions, hikers, and the occasional pup tent.

He decided to wander. To make himself visible and hope the hangman found him.

He was walking past a high-end RV, big and sleek and painted the silver of a full moon, when he heard a door swing open behind him. He started to turn back—and the muzzle of a gun jammed against the base of his spine.

"You make a sound, you die," a woman said. "Nod if you understand."

He nodded.

Then the world vanished as a black cloth hood dropped down over his head. A drawstring yanked it tight around his throat. He could still breathe—mostly—but the hood blotted out every trace of light. Rough hands spun him around. The woman didn't speak again until she'd marched him a few paces back the way he'd come.

"Stairs. Two of them."

He lifted his feet carefully, climbing into the big RV.

The hands guided him again, turning him, then gave him a shove. He fell, stomach lurching for one heart-pounding second, and tumbled into a padded chair. The slick leather seat swiveled under him.

Then silence. He held his, too, thinking about the gun. They made him stew for a while. Eventually, another voice spoke. Huskier, sultry, with tones that made Lionel think of syrup and smoke.

"'Man creates myths not to explain the unexplainable, but to light torches in the dark. Their false light is reassuring because it allows us to pretend that the darkness—the darkness of fear, of uncertainty, of chaos—can no longer hurt us. We create myths because we fear chaos.'"

He heard the sound of a paperback slapping shut.

"From the introduction to *Crackpots, Quacks and Messiahs: Tales from the Fringes of Journalism*, by Lionel Page. Tell me, Mr. Page: do you fear chaos?"

"Not anymore," he said.

"Fair enough."

The hood ripped away. He squinted at the sudden flood of light. When he could see again, he was staring at a kitchen nook in the back of the RV and a pair of strangers. One stood at casual attention off to the side, dressed in workout clothes with her strawberry-blond ponytail drooping out the back of a baseball cap. She could have come straight from a volleyball court, if it wasn't for the machine pistol she was cradling.

The other, with Lionel's book resting closed on one curled knee, was...striking. Perfectly androgynous and sleek, dark skin and steely-calm eyes, crescent-moon manicured fingernails and a tailored suit.

"Dakota," the speaker said. A graceful hand uncoiled, catlike, to gesture to one side. "This is Berlin. The lady behind your chair, who escorted you into my office, is Montreal."

"Pleasure," Lionel said.

"Is it?" Dakota's head tilted.

"Is that a rhetorical question?"

"I don't ask rhetorical questions. And I don't, as a general rule, entertain the presence of reporters."

"I'm not here as a reporter," Lionel said.

"Why, then?"

"I'm a witch," Lionel said, "and I'm here to parley."

Dakota flashed a curious smile. "Now you're speaking my language."

"Madison Hannah. She rode with you for a while. I'm looking for her."

"Reason?"

"I'm her apprentice," he said.

"She ghosted you?" Montreal said, standing just out of sight behind his back.

"That's one way to put it."

"And you think she *wants* you to find her? That's a lot of faith."

"I never had much faith," Lionel said. "Guess I'm making up for lost time."

"Could be a friend. Could be a foe." Dakota studied him. "Tell me something about Madison Hannah. Tell me something only a friend would know."

He had to think about it. He wouldn't betray Maddie's confidence, and he had no idea what these people knew about her. He couldn't tell them her true name, couldn't talk about her past. He thought about Maddie. About the quieter moments they'd shared together. The things that made her...her.

"She hates shoes," he said.

"Hates shoes," Dakota echoed.

"Absolutely hates them. We shared a houseboat for a while, and she was barefoot for two weeks straight. She told me once that she grudgingly tolerates clothes because fashion is fun, but shoes were a mistake. Also, the inventor of the high heel is suffering for eternity in Tartarus alongside the man who decided dresses shouldn't have pockets. I...*think* she was joking about that? But

A Time for Witches

when I asked if she was serious, she just tapped the side of her nose and winked at me."

"She does hate shoes," Dakota said. "All right. That's good enough for me."

Berlin flicked a sidelong glance. Despite the name, her accent was pure Kentucky twang.

"A spy could have found any of that out."

"It wasn't what he said," Dakota replied. "It was the look on his face when he said it."

"So do you know where Maddie is?" Lionel asked.

"We parted ways a few days ago. She had some business to take care of, but we're supposed to regroup farther on down the road. You got a set of wheels?"

"Sure."

"You can follow us for a day or two."

"But you're not *with* us," Montreal warned him. "You fall behind, you get left behind."

"I think I can keep up," Lionel said.

"We'll find out what you're capable of." Dakota rose and beckoned with a slow, graceful hand. "Take a walk with me, witch. I feel like getting some fresh air while the sun's still high."

CHAPTER THIRTY-FIVE

The campground had come to life during Lionel's hooded interrogation—or maybe because of it. Someone had sounded an all clear, and lanes between RVs that had been empty on his arrival now bustled with life. Clothes hung on lines stretched between campers, drying in the sun, and women with toolboxes and clipboards moved from engine to engine, keeping the convoy tuned and ready. A pair of young girls in white dresses squealed, chasing each other along the grass at the edge of the lot, under the watchful eye of an elderly woman as she cleaned her hunting rifle.

Dakota wasn't just walking for the fresh air. Lionel noticed how the nomads' leader saw everything, taking in the fine details, offering direction here and there. A young woman ran up, breathless, and rapped her knuckles on the olive metal lid of a cashbox.

"Collections are complete," she said with a chipper British accent. She flicked a suspicious look at Lionel. "Who's this?"

"A friend of Madison's," Dakota replied. "Part of the New York crowd, signed and sealed."

The newcomer didn't look mollified, but she let it slide.

"The brakes on Posadas's rig are in a bad way," she said. "Aberdeen gives them two, three thousand miles, at the absolute most, and says we really ought to have them replaced in five hundred or less."

Dakota nodded. "What else is priority?"

"I just ran inventory on all three of our backup pantries. Nonperishables are fine and we've got plenty of bottled water, but if we're heading into real trouble and might not be able to resupply for a while..."

The woman trailed off, flicking another pointed glare at Lionel.

"Speak freely," Dakota said.

"I want to get us on a war footing. Mesa's already checked grocery stores on the road ahead for sales, and she says we can get the pantries filled for two hundred bucks, tops."

"Do it. And I'm authorizing the brake replacement, too. Tell Aberdeen to make it happen."

"On it, chief."

She scurried off, darting between a pair of parked RVs.

"It's a commune," Lionel said.

"It's a community." Dakota moved with a slow and easy stride. "We pool our resources here. We've got people who can make money—or get what we need to keep moving, one way or another—people who can build things, fix things, make things. Everyone contributes, doing what they're best at, and everyone gets their needs met. We fight together or we fall together."

"It's all women here?" he asked, walking at Dakota's side.

"All women. Most in body, some in spirit." Words

punctuated with a sidelong glance. "That a problem for you?"

"Not at all. When I was a kid, me and my mom...we stayed for a while at this place in Michigan, up by Lake Huron, called the Emerald Ranch. It was sort of a new-age hippie thing, but they took in a lot of women who needed shelter. Women who needed a safe place to heal."

Dakota's nod was almost imperceptible.

"Then you understand why many of *these* women are going to be very slow to extend any trust in your general direction. I'm sure you're a nice guy when people get to know you and all that jive, but a few of my foundlings, they've been hurt too many times to risk it. I hope you don't take that personally."

"I don't," Lionel said. "I get it. And I'm not looking to cause anyone any trouble. If you need me to leave and come back when you break camp—"

"Nah. Just understand that there are places in this camp where you can walk freely, and places that aren't for you. You respect that, we'll be just fine."

"No problem. But how do I know where I can go..."

He thought about the route Dakota had been leading him on, a very deliberate circuit around the outer edges of the lot. The innermost vehicles, circled like a wagon train, concealed their secrets.

"...because you've been showing me," he finished.

Dakota flashed a breezy smile. "I multitask. Kind of a necessary leadership skill around here."

"Can I ask a few questions?"

"Are you writing another book?"

"I think my agent fired me because I stopped returning her phone calls," he said. "I guess that happens when you go underground on secret missions for ancient Greek goddesses."

"Shame. I liked your first one. Ask what you want to ask."

"The woman back there called you 'chief.' Is that your formal title?"

Dakota laughed. "Oh, no, Bristol calls *everybody* chief. And I'm not in charge. We have a council of five to make the big decisions—it's more democratic that way—and I'm the baby on the council. Just appointed last year when one of the old-timers went to serve Artemis, in her hunting grounds on Olympus."

"I'm assuming that's a metaphor."

Dakota shrugged. "Nothing metaphorical about it. She died. What do you think is going to happen when *you* die? Unless you got a one-of-a-kind deal, your contract with Hekate doesn't have an expiration date."

He changed the subject.

"I'm noticing an unusual number of people with place names."

"One of our customs. When someone joins our fold, they leave their old life behind and become someone new. They take a new name to mark the occasion. For some, they pick a place they came from or a place they love. Some choose a place they've never been. Somewhere far away and aspirational. Our Paris has never been to Paris, but she had a poster on her wall and a dream. That dream got her through some very bad nights before we found her at a bus station with nothing but a black eye and the clothes on her back. What else?"

"Are you really Amazons?"

"Are you really a witch?"

A Time for Witches

"Last I checked," Lionel said.

Dakota shrugged. Same answer.

He tried again. "I mean, historically. Is there a line of continuity?"

"All the way back to Herodotus and Strabo? Your guess is as good as mine. I know we've got photographs dating back to the horse-and-wagon days, and this band was rolling long before that. Maybe yes, maybe no. Maybe somebody dreamed a big dream and suddenly there we were, born from nothing but myth, roaming the wildlands. My people and your people, though, we've always held common cause."

"How so?"

"Well, back in the day," Dakota said, "we scared the living shit out of the powers that be. See, the Greek elite put forward a world of order and structure. A world where everybody knew their proper place in the status quo, nobody rocked the boat or asked questions, and everybody followed the rules. Amazons, witches, the occasional mad gadfly of a philosopher...we don't fit. We're not a part of the equation."

"Chaos," Lionel said.

"Options," Dakota said. "Look at it this way: authoritarian structures depend on never, ever being questioned. You start asking questions, the whole thing falls apart because they're not built on anything solid in the first place. So people are given a script: do as you're told, live how everyone else lives, go with the flow, and hopefully—if the gods smile and it doesn't rain—you'll be happy. It's so ingrained that folks don't even realize they *can* question it."

"Herd mentality?"

Dakota waved a hand. "I don't like words like 'herd' when it comes to people. Human beings are more complicated than anyone wants to give 'em credit for. Authoritarians, they want to keep everything *simple*. Spoon-fed answers you don't have to think about. And then we come along. Our very lives are a question that challenges the status quo. We're over here waving our arms saying, hey, there are other ways to be. And you have the right to choose your own path. Here, look at this."

The Amazon led him around a parked camper, to the lush, dew-damp lawns surrounding the pond on the other side of the grounds. A warm breeze rippled on the glassy water.

"You see the woman in the tank top and jeans, sitting on the lawn over there, teaching the little ones?"

Lionel nodded. "Sure."

"That's Tampa. Tampa was getting her medical degree. Not even halfway done, she had so much student debt it would take her thirty years to pay it off. Not that she had a chance to think about that, splitting her time between school and two minimum-wage jobs that *combined* wouldn't cover her rent, her train fare, her health insurance, and groceries. And sharing an apartment with two roommates, all of 'em in the same boat."

Dakota watched her from a distance, lips pursed.

"Now she rides with us. And there are a *lot* of Tampas out there. Young folks realizing they've been sold a lie their entire lives and there isn't any pot of gold at the end of the rainbow, no matter how hard they work or how many hours they put in. You know what I think?"

"The system's fucked?" Lionel asked.

Dakota chuckled. "That too. But on a more

metaphysical plane. See, the elites at the top are greedy shits. They could keep their golden thrones forever if they'd just share a little, but they've got to squeeze and squeeze and squeeze."

"Pretty sure that's how we got the French Revolution."

"You aren't wrong. But this—you, me, all of it—maybe it's a natural consequence. I don't know her name yet, but I know for a fact there's a woman out there who's going to cross our path next week, maybe next month, and she'll join our band. Because she was *born* an Amazon. She just needs to find us, and find herself. There's another trying to make her way in the big city. Maybe she's young, heartbroken, feeling lost and alone...and she has no idea that Hekate is coming right up behind her, getting ready to tap her on the shoulder and turn her around. Just like she doesn't know she's already a witch. But she will."

"Hekate does have a way of reaching out and shaking your world like a can of soda," Lionel said. "I know this from personal experience."

"I bet you do, riding with Madison. She's a good teacher." Dakota eyed him, contemplative. "More than a teacher to you though, isn't she?"

He considered a glib reply, then tossed it aside. The question demanded honesty.

"She was once. As for now...I guess we're going to have to have that conversation."

"You'll know," Dakota told him. "When you look her in the eye, you'll know."

~~

Night brought a cool breeze, cookouts, celebrations. Charcoal grill smoke and the aroma of hot dogs and hamburgers wafted across the campsite lawns. The

Amazons broke into knots of conversation, feasting, laughing. A playful drumbeat echoed across the parking lot and a fire dancer drew an appreciative audience as she practiced her trade, spinning a pair of blazing pots at the ends of metal chains. The firepots drew lines of light, circles and spirals, leaving comet trails in Lionel's eyes.

He kept his distance. He didn't feel unwelcome, exactly, but he knew he was an outsider; the boundaries here were polite but firm, and he was still an unknown factor. He had broached the question of their plans with Dakota, recalling Bristol's mention of getting "on a war footing," but she gently brushed him off.

"When we meet up with Madison," Dakota said. He got the message. The Amazons believed his story, believed it enough to let him tag along with them for now, but they were waiting on proof. That was fair.

So he made camp alone at a picnic table on the far edge of the campground and watched fireflies flare and dance in the dark. And waited. Lonely sentries were on patrol, here and there, keeping an outward watch. They toted rugged, scoped rifles on their shoulders, a modern bow for a modern warrior of Artemis. One gave him a long, steady stare. Then a respectful nod. He returned the gesture. She turned and continued her patrol.

Lionel's eyes grew heavy and he started thinking about turning in. *No motel bed for me,* he thought. He'd have to sack out in the back of the stolen SUV. *Cordell Spears might be a psycho, but at least he's not a cheapskate. Glad he shelled out for the model with the comfy reclining seats.*

A semi chugged along the arrow-straight highway, hauling a refrigerated trailer for a local grocery chain. Lionel watched, curious, as it squealed to a stop on the shoulder. The passenger-side door swung open, and a grateful hitchhiker dropped down to the roadside.

Maddie.

She saw him across the distance. He rose from the picnic table. He wasn't sure if he should meet her halfway or not. He started walking, but Dakota was already ahead of him. Dakota and Maddie clasped hands, then hauled each other in for a tight hug.

"Saw Spears on TV yesterday," Dakota said.

"The plan failed. He got away."

Lionel felt a lump in his throat, thinking about Kayla's flask and how Cordell had manipulated him into wasting it on the Keres. *The plan failed, and I'm the reason why.*

"How about his henchmen?"

"I slowed them down, but not for long."

"Damn," Dakota said. "You bring any *good* news with you?"

"We're still here and still fighting," Maddie said.

"That'll do."

Now Maddie looked to Lionel. Neither one of them spoke. The air between them was too fragile to risk it.

Dakota held up a key ring and pressed it into Maddie's hand.

"Keys to my RV. I think you two need a little privacy right now."

CHAPTER THIRTY-SIX

They left the lights off. Electric light from the parking lot's lampposts streamed between the venetian slats of the RV's window blinds. Muffled drumming reverberated through the walls and up from the floor, a steady but distant heartbeat. Lionel sat in a padded swivel chair in the conversation nook in back. Maddie took the couch on the other side of a foldout coffee table.

"I don't—" Lionel began.

"Let me—"

They both started at once. Both stopped at once. They both stared at the empty table between them.

"I'm sorry," Maddie said.

Now they met each other's eyes.

Lionel wrestled with himself, his thoughts all tangled up in his guts. He wanted to tell her how much it hurt when he woke up alone in Montauk. He wanted to tell her he understood why she did it. He wanted to tell her a thousand things at once, but all the words kept jumbling together. He wanted to avoid the one question he knew he had to ask.

Fine. Time to rip the bandage off. Moment of truth.

"I'm going to make this easy for both of us," he said.

Maddie nodded, waiting.

"I'm not...I'm not a stalker," he said.

"I know that."

"But you left, and I didn't know why. I thought you wanted to be with me—"

"Lionel—"

He held up a hand. "Please. Just...let me do this. If you changed your mind, that's your right, but after all we've been through together I think you owe me the courtesy of saying it to my face instead of disappearing in the middle of the night."

His hand fell to his lap.

"So if you want me to leave," he said, "tell me so, and I'm gone. I won't argue, I won't yell, I'll just leave. You'll never see me again. But let's respect each other enough to make this a clean breakup."

She looked away. A pinpoint of ruby shone in the corner of her eye. She slid to one side. Her hand patted the vinyl cushion beside her.

"Come here? Please?"

Lionel rose. He circled the table and sat down gingerly, like the cushion might break as he sank into it.

Maddie took his hand.

"Back when we first got together," she said, "I told you."

"That you always leave. I know. You warned me. But I thought..."

He kicked himself. Thought what? That he was different? That he was special? That he was going to fix her, mend her wings, save her? Ego. His ego got in the way, blinding him just like it always did—

"Hey," she said, breaking his train of thought, the parade of self-recrimination.

She squeezed his hand.

"I shouldn't have started with an apology," she said. "I should have started with an explanation. It's just...not a great one."

"I'm listening," he said.

"I got scared. I wasn't going to leave, but then I got the call in the middle of the night—"

"I would have gone with you."

"I know. It wasn't the job. It was the target. I told you everything, in Manhattan. You know my name, you know who I am and what I've done."

"I never judged you," Lionel said. "If I made you feel like I did, I'm sorry."

"No."

Maddie let go of his hand. She reached up. Her fingertips traced the curve of his cheek.

"You made me feel...seen, and accepted, and *okay*. You made me feel *okay* for the first time in I can't remember how long. And I knew that I was going to have to deal with Jason again, and if you were there, I thought...well, what if something changes? What if Lionel hears something or sees something and then when I look in his eyes, that acceptance, that *okay* isn't there anymore? What if I fuck it all up, like I always do? I'm not—I'm not good at relationships."

"Hey," he said, "you're talking to Chicago's reigning breakup king."

"I wasn't thinking when I left. I did everything I could not to think about it. I told myself I'd come right back, that I'd call you on the road. I told myself you'd be fine. Then I came up with all the reasons to make you stay behind. That you weren't ready, that it was too dangerous."

"You're not...*totally* wrong," Lionel said.

"They weren't reasons, though. They were excuses. I learned some things on the road these last few days. It all comes down to trust. And I'm so used to being alone, so used to not trusting anyone, I just..."

She bit her bottom lip. Coming to some quiet resolution.

"That's what I'm apologizing for. Because I didn't trust you, and I didn't trust myself. And I need to learn how to do that."

Lionel took that in. It brought him back to the question.

"So," he said, "do you still want to be with me?"

"Do you want to be with me?" she asked.

"Yeah. I really do."

She gave him a trembling smile. "Me too."

He opened his arms to her, and they came together and held on tight. Quiet, for a while, just feeling each other's warmth, sharing breath and a heartbeat in time with the distant, muffled drums.

"Do something for me?" she whispered.

"Name it."

"Just...say you forgive me? I need to hear you say it."

"I forgive you," Lionel said. "Maddie...if you ever vanish on me again, I'm going to assume you mean it this time. And I won't come after you."

"That's fair," she said.

He felt it was important to say it. To set a boundary, for both of them. All the same, he didn't think it was anything to worry about. It felt like they'd both grown a little lately. He took a deep breath, steeling himself for what he needed to say next.

"And now I have to ask you to forgive me. Because I really fucked up."

She pulled back, just far enough so she could look him in the eye. She kept her hands on his arms, holding him. The corners of her eyes glistened with wet pinpricks of blood, the tears she was barely keeping in check.

Lionel told her where he'd been since leaving Montauk. What he'd seen, what he'd done. She slowly shook her head.

"Lover, no. You didn't do anything wrong."

"I wasted Kayla's flask—"

"To save your own life, and it would have been just as lost if the Keres killed you. It's not like *they* were going to use it for its intended purpose."

"But I got caught in the first place." He squirmed a little, sheepish. "Twice."

"And you saved a family from being murdered by death-spirits. Along with who knows how many more victims they would have taken by now if you hadn't routed them. That's not a weakness, and neither is being manipulated by someone like Cordell Spears."

"He says he's the son of Zeus, by the way."

"He's *a* son of Zeus." Maddie wrinkled her nose.

"So, explain that to me? Why would the king of the gods disguise himself as a long-haul trucker and shack up with a waitress for a week?"

"Was she hot?" Maddie asked. "I mean, that's the criteria."

"That's it?"

"A nice smile, good hair, and perky boobs."

"So this wasn't some sort of divine master plan," he said.

"That...is harder to pin down. Something big is going on, plans in motion, just not sure *whose* plans. It would help if we knew what Spears was trying to accomplish, beyond vague talk about 'bringing back the age of heroes.'"

"Guy's got a serious messiah complex," Lionel said. "Except he didn't wait three days to come back from the dead after I stabbed him."

"Welcome to mythic reality. A hero's ending has to be..."

"Heroic?"

"Yes, but not 'heroic' like the comics. It has to be mythically resonant. Tell a story. Teach a moral."

"We have to *morally* kill him." Lionel sighed. "I don't suppose Hekate could just give us a straight answer and tell us exactly what's going on?"

Maddie's answer was a deadpan stare.

"I'll take that as a no," he said.

"Welcome to my life. No. Figuring it out ourselves, and handling it ourselves, is part of the process. That's part of *her* lesson. Her design. She'll give us the tools and nudge us in the right direction if we really need it—and we won't necessarily know she's the one giving the nudge. The rest is up to us."

"Well, we had a great tool. I broke it."

"And that's on me," she said. "If I had taken care of Spears myself, instead of trusting Kayla with the job so I could go charging after my ex-husband, none of this would have happened."

Lionel shook his head. "Considering your history with the guy, nobody could blame you for that. I would have done the same thing. And whatever this cross-country errand Jason's running is, stopping it dead would probably throw a big spanner into the works. We should focus on that: if we can track the convoy, maybe we can get eyes on it from a distance and figure out the master plan."

"Agreed." She sighed. "You're smarter than my ex. I like that about you."

"So am I better-looking, too?"

Maddie turned on the vinyl cushion, bending her knees, and kicked off her shoes. She pulled Lionel against her, so that he was resting with the back of his head against her shoulder. She put her arms around him, holding him there.

"You're pretty cute," she said.

"Am I...more muscular than Jason?" he asked.

She ran her fingers through his curls.

"You have great hair," she said.

He snuggled against her.

"Am I...better-endowed than Jason?"

"Lover?" Maddie said. "You need to remember an important tenet of witchcraft."

"What's that?"

"Don't ask questions if you aren't prepared for the burden of the truth."

"Ouch," he said, bristling with mock offense. "You could lie to me."

Maddie leaned her head back, smiling up at the ceiling.

"No," she said. "Not to you."

Her arms curled tighter around him. Keeping him like a treasure.

"Can we just...be like this for a while?" she asked. "Is that okay?"

That was okay.

CHAPTER THIRTY-SEVEN

Maddie's stamp of approval came with perks. The Amazons treated her like a visiting diplomat or maybe a B-list celebrity, and Lionel felt the air around him starting to thaw just by association.

"It's not me, it's who I'm repping," Maddie murmured in his ear as they strolled through the parking lot, crossing a puddle of electric light. "Apparently, while I was on the run and avoiding the Sisterhood of New Amsterdam, they got tight with these folks. A lot of mutual respect and back-and-forth favors over the years. So now that I'm back in the Sisterhood, I'm on the Amazons' cool-person list. I'm told that the last time this war band passed through New York, our coven threw the mother of all welcome-back parties. I'm kinda sad I missed it."

"That reminds me, I've been meaning to ask. Am I actually a member?"

"Of the Sisterhood? Well, your mom was, so you're a legacy, but nothing's official until it's official. I think they're waiting for you to ask. Why? Do you want to be?"

Lionel glanced up to the lamplight as they passed, and to the sliver of moon beyond, hanging in a midnight-blue sky.

"Well, this is the world I live in now. I was thinking it might be nice to have a...a feeling of community, I guess. And I know how much the Sisterhood meant to my mom. It'd be a way of honoring her memory."

Maddie gave him a sidelong glance. "How do you feel about New York?"

"It's the place where my entire world got flipped upside down and inside out."

"I mean in general. Compared to Chicago. Do you think you'd like it there?"

He nodded, ambling along at her side. "I mean, sure. Yeah. When we're not dealing with murderous rogue witches and angry ghosts, it's a pretty cool city."

"I was thinking, the other night. Thinking it might be nice to put down roots somewhere. Tiny ones. Just to have a place where I can rest my head between missions, instead of living out of hotels."

"Yeah?" he said. "Were you...thinking it might be nice to have somebody waiting for you when you come home?"

She took his hand and gave it a squeeze.

"We should talk. After the job. Let's get this done first. Priorities."

"Priorities," Lionel said.

"Oh," she added, "if you do decide to join the Sisterhood, the process of cleansing for a new member involves a ritual swim in the Hudson, in the middle of winter."

"Say what now?"

She nodded, absolutely earnest. "It's part of the standard initiation. Also, there's the ceremonial butt-paddling."

"You are definitely making that up," he said.

She couldn't hide a tiny smirk.

"Maybe," she said. "But you won't know for sure until the night of your initiation, will you? You'll just have to wait and wonder."

"*Someone's* going to get a ceremonial butt-paddling."

"There you go," she said, "threatening me with a good time."

Maddie's presence opened the Amazons' supply cache. A tent was found—small, but much better than the prospect of dozing off in the back seat of Lionel's stolen SUV—and a pair of sleeping bags. Lionel gamely wrestled with the tent poles, calling on every skill his month in the Boy Scouts had taught him. Once he was satisfied that it wouldn't collapse in the middle of the night, they crawled inside and laid out the bags.

Crouched beside him, snug under the triangle of bright yellow canvas, Maddie looked at the side-by-side bags. She rubbed her eyes and muffled a yawn behind her hand.

"I feel like..." she said, looking from the bags to Lionel.

"Like for an appropriate reunion, we should be humping like bunnies until the break of dawn?"

"That," she said. "But also..."

"We are both ridiculously tired and about to keel over."

"You *get* me," she said.

They settled for a kiss. Then they lay down and drifted off into separate dreams, but with their hands touching, bridging the divide.

~~

They struck camp at first light. Lionel was bleary-eyed and craving coffee—or just another four hours of sleep—as he tore down the tent and Maddie ran to get the scoop on their next destination. She came back with a map on her phone, showing a short scarlet line running roughly southwest.

"We're just getting some distance," she said. "Thirty miles, then we dig in again."

He slung a canvas tent-sack over one shoulder. The poles clanked against his hip.

"What's in thirty miles?"

"Another campsite, smaller, private. They rented the whole place out, so we don't have to share it with anyone and we can work freely. We've got no time for masks and charades, not now."

He wasn't sure what that meant until he pulled onto a long, serpentine dirt road beside a stone sign reading "Winter Springs Campground." The faster nomads, driving SUVs and pickups instead of lumbering RVs, had arrived before dawn to set things up. A covered pavilion for cookouts became a tactical center, with tablet PCs, satellite phones, and battery-powered printers at the ready. Down a grassy slope, beside a tranquil pond, white silken streamers caught the wind and rippled in the air; they ringed a stone cairn, a shrine to Artemis, and a woman in a flowing white dress was adorning it with wildflowers.

The *crack* of a rifle made Lionel's hands tense around the steering wheel. Maddie pointed into the distance, a line of women shouldering their weapons near a copse of trees.

"Training drills," she said.

"They're ready to mess somebody up."

"They're Amazons," Maddie said. "They're *always* ready to mess somebody up. Park up here. Let's go find Dakota and roll up our sleeves. We've got a lot of work to do today."

Dakota was down at the covered pavilion. Bristol was with her, the young Brit overseeing a small team of specialists. They huddled over their tablets, pulling up data, firing files back and forth as they discussed a battle plan.

"Okay," Dakota said, "now it's a party. We ready to put our heads together?"

"Absolutely," Maddie said.

Lionel pointed to the end of one of the picnic tables, where a carafe sat beside a stack of paper cups. "Is that coffee?"

"It is," Dakota said. "Fuel up. My goal is to be out of here by sunset. To do that, we have to have a destination. Preferably one that has either Cordell Spears or his lackey at the end of the road."

"I know where Jason *was*," Maddie said. "And after the mess I made of the highway, it probably took him most of the night to get his truck out of there, but I'd like a more definite map."

"Same."

Lionel zeroed in on the carafe and cups. Before he could reach for them, Bristol got in his way. She blocked him with an outstretched hand and a click of her tongue.

"Miss Hannah?" Bristol chirped. "Is your apprentice allowed to have coffee?"

"He can have coffee," she said, not looking over.

Really? he mouthed at Bristol, incredulous. She went back to her table without another word.

"Good news is," Dakota said, "our info team's plugged-in and ready. If there's a data source that can be pulled, they can pull it."

Maddie nodded her approval. "Impressive."

"Cyber-warfare isn't the future of conflict; it's the here and now. And Artemis wants us battle-ready on all possible fronts."

Lionel poured three cups. Ripples of coiling vapor carried the scent of rich, dark-roasted beans.

"Have to pick our target," he said. "Jason is driving west, but Cordell is going east. Maddie, two sugars?"

"Yes, please."

He ripped open a tiny paper packet. "Whatever Jason's up to, it's got to be tied to Cordell's big party in Central Park. His 'Gala for the People.' Dakota, how do you take yours?"

"Black's fine, thank you. What do we know about Jason's cargo?"

"I confirmed that he hired a shipping company backed by the 14K Triad to move it from Greece to Miami," Maddie said. "All of the artifacts that ended up in the touring exhibition were sent by normal secured couriers, so it was something he couldn't risk exposing to a customs inspection. The witness I interrogated said it was some sort of 'biological material'—his words—kept in a secured refrigeration unit. And it was implied that turning the fridge off would be very, very bad for everyone on the smuggler's boat."

Dakota's brow furrowed. "Some kind of virus sample? A bioweapon?"

"That would track, but it's not something Cordell bought from a shady lab. The head of his archaeological team found it on their dig."

"So it's at least as old as..."

"Me," Maddie replied. "You can say it."

Lionel carefully braced the three cups, nestling them together and walking them back across the pavilion. Dakota and Maddie reached for theirs, and Dakota offered a salute of thanks before taking a sip.

"Mm. That's the stuff. Lionel, Madison tells me that you jabbed a knife into the rich boy?"

"It didn't stick," he said. "I mean, the *knife* stuck. It stuck just fine. The death didn't."

"The world bends the rules for heroes," Maddie said. "We can't get rid of Cordell, not permanently, until his myth comes to an appropriate end."

"I thought your ex had one of those, and the Fates brought him back anyway," Dakota said.

"True. I thought 'drunk, destitute, and crushed by a rotten ship mast' was perfectly apropos, but then again, I'm a little biased."

"What counts as a proper ending?" Lionel asked.

"It usually hinges on the hero. Some are meant to serve as an example of the rewards of piety and virtue. Great deeds, great *kleos*, immortal reverence and glory."

"That sounds like what Cordell is going for," he said.

"And some, afflicted with a critical flaw, are consumed and vanquished by that flaw. It's nearly impossible for a mortal human to destroy a hero, but a hero can destroy himself."

"Like Jason," Dakota said.

"I thought he had. Imagine my surprise."

"There's our in," Lionel said. "We need to engineer an ending to this story. The ending *we* want. We know that there's one thing Cordell is afraid of: the Furies. He bent over backward to trick me into using Tisiphone's calling charm against the Keres, and he made damn sure he was nowhere near the scene until it was all over. Can we try that again?"

Maddie thought about it. Briefly. She shook her head.

"Two problems. One, the flask itself has to be made from a very particular type of Aegean clay, harvested from one specific ritual site. Not something you can usually get on short notice. Might be doable, though. Maybe. I'll have to make some calls."

"And problem two?" Dakota asked.

"If you're conjuring Tisiphone to avenge a murder, you need something of the victim's, preferably something very intimate, something they carried for a long time, and ideally—best-case scenario—something they were carrying when they died."

"Which is why Cordell pulled strings to have Jurgen Lambert cremated before his body could be shipped home from Greece," Lionel said.

"And stole everything on him. Everything but his wedding ring. It was a lucky fluke that it made its way back to Jurgen's widow. But that's all there was. We fired our only bullet, and we missed."

"Maybe," Lionel mused. "Maybe not. We're working on a bad assumption here."

Maddie tilted her head. "Which is?"

"Jurgen's murder was sloppy. He was on the run, trying to make his way back to the States, and Cordell panicked. He had to wing it."

"He still got away with it," Dakota pointed out. "Legally. *We* know he killed the man, but he's as squeaky-clean as ever."

He tapped his finger against his lips, pacing.

"That's my thought. Exactly. He's always been Mr. Clean. We also know he thinks he's naturally superior to us mere mortals. He can do what he wants and nobody can touch him because he was born a hero." Lionel stopped pacing. He turned to face them. "What are the odds that Jurgen Lambert is his *only* victim?"

"He fulfilling the destiny that he believes that he's entitled to," Maddie said. "Sure. He'd kill any mortal who stood in the way of his *kleos*, if there was no other option."

"He went from the son of a diner waitress, barely a penny to his name, to a biotech billionaire. There had to be a lot of people standing in his way over the years. And I'd bet more than a few of them ended up in shallow graves."

"All we need is one," Maddie said. "One, and the right object to fuel the charm."

Dakota looked dubious. "With a life as sanitized as his? Good luck finding it."

Lionel smiled. Dakota's people brought the firepower; Maddie brought the witchcraft. Now he had something to contribute, too.

"We don't need luck," he said. "We need an investigative journalist who spent his entire career digging into big shots like Cordell Spears and exposing their darkest secrets."

Maddie tapped her coffee cup against his. "Found one."

CHAPTER THIRTY-EIGHT

Dakota called the brain trust to attention. Bristol and her foursome of data technicians—hackers, by a politer name—and five tablets fired up and ready.

"Listen up. Lionel's going to pass down your assignments. Treat a request from him like a request from me."

Bristol didn't say a word, but she had a look on her face like she'd just drunk curdled milk. Her team, twenty-somethings with a Skittles rainbow of hair colors, followed her lead. After all, until a minute ago this had been their job alone, and now a stranger was taking over. Lionel knew they'd fall in line because of Dakota, but he didn't need their obedience; he needed their cooperation. He held up his open hands.

"I can't do what you can do," he said. "Back in Chicago, when I did deep dives like this I had my boss, Brianna, and her team—we called 'em the Technical Twins—handling the digital intel. I know it takes a lot of skills and training and hard work to do your job. I respect that, and I respect you. Now, me? My job is to take all the reams of data you can get your hands on and to assemble it into a picture.

Separating the signal from the noise and digging out the truth. So, can we work together on this?"

That was better. Silent, nodding heads, a lot of affirmative glances shooting back and forth across the picnic table. Even Bristol seemed mollified. Lionel clasped his hands around his cup of coffee and got on track. He knew exactly where to start.

"Almost all of the puff pieces about Cordell focus on the here and now. But his rise to money and power was meteoric, and if he was young when he learned what he really was...well, young people do stupid shit. He's learned to cover up his crimes by now, but a teenage Cordell Spears might not have had the same know-how or the same level of impulse control."

"You want everything we can get on his childhood," Bristol said. "We can do that."

"Official records and media pieces," Lionel said. "Any interviews where he talks about his upbringing, TV profiles, feel-good press releases from Spears Biomedical, all of it."

Bristol's brow furrowed. "Why bother? It's just going to be PR nonsense."

"Carefully curated nonsense. We'll build two pictures—the real man, and the image he wants the world to see—and look at the places where they overlap. The way a person presents their past tells a story in and of itself. The things they focus on are just as important as the things they never talk about."

Maddie's fingers curled over his shoulder. She gave him an affectionate squeeze.

"And with that," she said, "I'll leave you to it. I need to make a phone call."

~~

Maddie took a walk.

She needed distance. Didn't want anyone to overhear the conversation she was about to have, and she needed to build herself up for it. There were times in life, she reflected, when it was necessary to do something both healthy and deeply unpleasant. Like a trip to the dentist.

She would have taken a cavity over this. She decided she'd put it off long enough, though. She took her phone out and tapped the screen.

"Wen Xiulang," said the curt voice on the other end.

"Xiulang. It's Maddie."

"Hn. Haven't seen you since the dustup at the Parthenon Theatre. You just went and vanished on all of us. Back to your old habits, I suppose."

"No," Maddie said. Then again, more firmly, to herself as much as to the woman on the line. She felt it now. "No. I'm not. I'm making some changes in my life."

"You'll forgive my skepticism."

"I will," she said, "if you'll do something for me. I need your help."

This part was harder.

"Not just your help," Maddie said. "I need the Sisterhood."

The hard edge of Xiulang's voice faded, turning to curiosity.

"Is this a personal affair, or...?"

"In service to the Queen."

"Then you hardly need to ask." Xiulang paused. "So how long did you stand there with your phone in your hand, wrestling with yourself over whether you'd make the call?"

"How long have we known each other?"

"Feels like a thousand years. Probably more like eleven or twelve hundred."

Maddie heard beeping in the background. "What are you doing?"

"Patching in Agnes."

"Wait," Maddie said, her stomach twisting in a knot. "You don't need to do that."

Too late. A perky voice answered the phone. "Ashcroft and Associates, Attorneys at Law. How may I direct your call?"

"Kayleigh? This is Wen Xiulang, and I've got the prodigal daughter on the line with me."

"The prodigal—*oh*. Hello, Ms. Hannah. Ms. Wen."

"We need Agnes," Xiulang said. "You stay on the line, too. This is Sisterhood business. Do you know if Jillian is in town?"

"She's over at city hall today. Would you like me to add her to the call?"

"No—" Maddie started to say.

"Yes," Xiulang said. "Maddie, while we're waiting for Agnes, give me a hint."

"Cordell Spears," she said.

That prompted yet another addition to the call, coming from a crowded room with ringing desk phones and overlapping voices in the background. "Speak," said a gruff voice.

"Detective Mathers," Xiulang said. "I've got the Prodigal on the line."

Mathers grunted. That was her only reply.

"She's on the Queen's business, regarding Cordell Spears."

"Finally some answers," Mathers said. "Hopefully. Is she still on the phone, or did she already hang up and run away again?"

"I'm here," Maddie said, cringing. She stood in a patch of grass, digging the toe of her sneaker into the wet dirt, feeling like a kid in the principal's office.

"Sorry, sorry," Agnes said, joining the call. "I was in conference with a client—"

Another chime, another new addition. "Linda Jackson Fine Arts."

"Linda," Xiulang said. "The Prodigal is on the line."

The deep voice was noncommittal at best. "Is she."

That was it. Maddie's discomfort and apprehension and anxiety boiled over and she gritted her teeth to keep her anger in check. She took a deep breath.

"I know that none of you owe me anything," she said. "And I wouldn't make this call if I didn't have to. But I'm on a mission, and it's important, and I can't..."

She fell silent. So did the conference line. They were waiting for her to say the words.

"I can't do this by myself," Maddie said.

"Now why would you think," Agnes asked her, "that you had to?"

Maddie slipped one foot out of its sneaker. She bent her knee, reaching behind her to peel her sock off. She needed contact with the ground. A tiny comfort as she searched for an answer that would make sense.

"I spent a long time on my own. I had to learn to be self-reliant. Always. Not being able to handle a problem myself was...weakness. Worse than weakness." Her bare toes curled in the dewy grass. "Look, I know you don't like me, and that's fine. But I'm not asking for myself. I hope you'd help me in the name of the Queen."

"I think," Agnes said, "you're misunderstanding some things. Let me clarify the matter on record. We don't dislike you, Madison. Most of us don't *know* you. Xiulang is blessed with an immortal lifespan. For the rest of us, you're a myth who vanished centuries before we were even born. 'The witch who ran away from home.' You were a cautionary tale, not a flesh-and-blood woman."

"Till you showed up out of nowhere," Mathers said.

"All we know is this. You have our lady's favor, and you're still, as far as we're concerned, a member of our coven. But you went silent again after we dealt with Sloane. Think about it from our perspective: most of us assumed you'd vanished again. Maybe you neither needed nor wanted our company."

"I didn't—I didn't mean for it to come across that way," Maddie said. "I thought you wouldn't want *me* around."

"I think we'd all like a chance to get to know you," Agnes said.

"It's called the Sisterhood of New Amsterdam," Linda pointed out. "Not the Socially Distant Absentees of New Amsterdam. And we've got a cookout scheduled next month. Nothing heavy, just a little get-together. You gonna be there?"

Maddie peeled her other sock off. A warm wind rustled through the grass. The morning sun shone down, dazzling her eyes as she tilted her head back to drink it in.

"Yeah," she said. "I think I'd like that."

"Bring Lionel with you," Detective Mathers said. "So let's get down to it: what's the scoop on Spears? Because I've got my people keeping an eye on this whole 'Gala for the People' thing. Nothing shady about it, on the surface, but my gut's not happy."

"Your gut's right," Maddie said.

"Usually is."

She gave them the short version. Which turned into the long version as the voices on the line peppered her with questions, homing in on details.

"So we don't actually know what Spears's plan is," Mathers said.

"Not yet. We just know it's going to culminate at the gala. Is there any way we can shut down the event? Pull his permits?"

"Not on my end," the detective said. "He's got serious pull at the NYPD. A generous contributor to the brass's favorite charitable causes. Jillian?"

A latecomer to the call spoke up. "It's a big ask. Let's just say the mayor has a photo of Spears on his office credenza. I can go through the paperwork with a magnifying glass and see if there's a technicality we could nail him on, some reason to hold up the permits. But if his plans are that elaborate, I have to assume he's triple-checked every last detail."

"Do it anyway," Xiulang said. "If the show does go on, what's our backup plan?"

"The only thing he seems to be afraid of, really afraid of, is Tisiphone," Maddie said. "I'm working on another cunning-call. But even if we find a sympathetic link that can fuel the spell, we need a proper flask for it."

"I'll make some inquiries," Xiulang said.

"Same," Agnes added. "I know some antiquities dealers overseas who might have a line on one, and they have a good reputation for authenticity. Do we need to deliver it to you in the field?"

"Hang on to it," Maddie said. "I think Spears is in New York right now. We'll get the rest of the ingredients and meet you there."

"We'll have a ritual space ready for you on arrival," Xiulang said.

Another voice joined the call. No one had heard the telltale beep of a new connection, and there was no telling how long she'd been there. But they all knew her voice.

"Ladies," Hekate said.

The call fell silent.

"My expectations for you are high," she said. "Higher than usual. As are the stakes, but I know that each and every one of you is more than equal to the challenge at hand. Make me proud."

Then came a soft click and nothing more.

"Was...was that—" asked Agnes's receptionist.

"Yes," Maddie said. "And we all heard her. Let's get the job done."

CHAPTER THIRTY-NINE

Bristol's team worked in perfect coordination, tossing angles and ideas back and forth across the picnic table like a basketball team running a passing drill. Dakota sent a messenger to bring back a standing corkboard; reams of printouts went up, tacked to the cork, slowly drawing a picture made of raw data. Lionel studied it all, from public-relations puff pieces to a stolen dump of Cordell's earliest known income-tax filings.

It was a picture of a man who had worked hard to bury his youth. No school records, no vaccinations on file, and every whisper of his life before he turned twenty-one had been burned or buried deep. Not out of shame, though. Cordell never lost a chance to talk about how he'd bootstrapped his way up from poverty. He was proud of his humble origins.

No, Lionel thought, digging into the clues. *He's proud of his version.* Lionel had been doing this his entire professional life. He knew where to look, and more importantly, he knew how to see. How to pick out the tiny details that gave the truth away. Sometimes what was missing was more important than what was there.

"He's not from New York," Lionel said out loud.

He felt eyes on him. He looked to the table.

"Any of you from NYC?"

One young woman, with hair like lime sherbet, raised a hand. "Queens."

"There any trailer parks in Brooklyn?"

She squinted at him. "It's not exactly a big, open place. The only parks are...parks."

Lionel kept coming back to what Cordell had told him, bragging about his origins. What he'd said about his mother: *She was born in a trailer and she died in a trailer and never had the vision for a bigger life.*

"When he talks about his past," Lionel said, "he always reps Brooklyn. 'Just a poor Brooklyn boy, scraping change together to afford secondhand shoes.' That kind of thing. But when we faced off in Indiana, he told me he grew up in a trailer park. Now let's look at his charities and who he donates money to."

Lionel crossed to the far side of the corkboard, running a finger along the white and green bars of a spreadsheet. The page, freshly printed, was still warm to the touch.

"He gives generously to youth causes. Scouts, Boys and Girls Clubs of America, a lot of individual donations to inner-city schools and programs to fight childhood hunger. Notice what's not on this list?"

Bristol did. "Nothing for Brooklyn."

"No love, in cash, for the borough he loves to represent. No hometown hero moments where he goes back to the old hood. He owns a condo in the city...in Manhattan. He doesn't set foot in Brooklyn. Everybody's different, but you do enough investigations on guys like Spears and certain patterns emerge. One thing billionaires love is milking the 'small-town boy makes good' thing. Lets them pretend to be humble. It's good optics."

"He does that," Dakota said.

"In interviews. But not a single bio or publicity piece has a quote from anyone who knew him as a kid. No classmates, no teachers. PR people normally can't get enough of that stuff. He never shows his face in the neighborhood, never goes back to raise money for his old school or the YMCA he went to as a kid..."

"Because he didn't," Bristol said.

"Exactly," Lionel said. "He doesn't go back because he can't. He's young enough that there should be a ton of old-timers who knew him as a kid. They don't exist. At least not in Brooklyn. When I'm following a subject's trail, I start with the very first data point that can be positively verified. Where'd he go to college?"

"University of Central Florida, in Orlando," one of the analysts said, "but his transcripts are buried along with his admission paperwork. I tried getting his high school records, but that's a dead end."

"Okay, so either he's a Florida boy or he relocated. Lots of college students travel far from home, so it's even odds, but...keep Orlando in mind." Papers ruffled on the board. Lionel pulled a few pins, consolidating printouts and making room for more. "Let's look at his early money. He graduated with honors, a biomedical company snapped him up on graduation day—"

Bristol glanced at her screen. "And he climbed his way into a position on the board of directors with considerable haste. Then he racked up honorary board positions at other companies, high-dollar 'advisory' posts...it's the kind of career you normally have to be plugged into the old-boy influence network to get. Those are 'who you know' jobs, not 'what you know' jobs."

"And you don't make those kinds of connections at the University of Central Florida," Lionel said. "It's not the bottom of the academic heap by any means, but it's a long way from Harvard and Yale."

"Don't discount his nature," Dakota pointed out. "He's a hero. The world greases the wheels for heroes. And there's always the chance some keen-eyed god, wanting to curry favor with Cordell's father, pulled strings to make his climb to the top even easier."

Lionel's gaze slid along the board and the skeletal history of Cordell Spears. He landed in Cordell's mid-twenties. His first million, which became five, then ten, almost overnight.

"Here," he said. "This is what I'm interested in. He came from nothing, had nothing, then all of a sudden he's wallowing in cash. Absolute freedom, on a level most people never experience in their lives. So what did he do with it?"

"Invested, mostly," Bristol said. "And almost every gamble he made was a winner."

"Almost. But even if he had the God of Good Investments standing at his shoulder, telling him which bets to place, nobody gets that much money after a childhood of poverty and doesn't treat themselves a little. Skip the smart investments: tell me about the *bad* ones."

The team went hunting. It didn't take long to find a candidate.

"Here's one," Bristol said. "And it's Floridian."

"Even better. Orlando?"

A Time for Witches

She tapped the print-screen key. The printer began to whir.

"No," she said. "North Florida. A town called Holyoake, with an *e* on the end. He sank a lot of capital into the Summer Smile Ice Cream plant, never made a penny back. Summer Smile's a regional brand with a small distribution chain. It's never been a serious contender in the market."

"This is what I'm talking about," Lionel said. "That distribution chain—does it stretch as far as Orlando? Any chance he found himself with a craving for Summer Smile while he was cramming for exams?"

Lionel waited while the team dug in, each woman taking one chunk of the map and splitting up the legwork. Bristol delivered the verdict. "No. Doesn't look like any store in the area carries them. Orlando is inside the distribution radius, but the big brands have a lock on that market."

"If the investment was an obviously bad bet, we're seeing sentiment in action. Cordell *likes* that kind of ice cream. He wanted to see it survive. And if he didn't pick up the sweet tooth in college..."

"It was before," Dakota said. "When he was a kid, living in the trailer park."

"When did the company shut down?" he asked.

Bristol frowned at her screen. "It didn't. In his thirties, he actually bought the company outright from the family that founded it, and pumped it full of cash just in time to keep it from going under."

"And did he turn it around?"

"Not even close," said the analyst with the lime-sherbet hair. "I'm showing a solid profit...four years out of the last twenty. It's not hemorrhaging cash or anything, but if he didn't feed the kitty out of his own pocket it'd be a memory by now."

"Like I said, sentiment. He knows that company is never going to turn around. He keeps it alive because it means something to him. Something personal."

"That gives us a search area," Dakota said. "He had to have grown up somewhere in Summer Smile's distribution range. Bristol?"

"The farthest store they deliver to is four hundred and eighty-three miles away, chief. Lot of ground to cover."

Still, they'd narrowed it down. Lionel contemplated the list of investments. Spears was good at covering his trail, but this was a slip they could use. A crack in the door.

"Check for large expenditures in that distribution region, between one and three years ago."

Dakota gave him the side eye. "Why that time range?"

"Whatever he's trying to accomplish, he's been planning it for a while. One year ago, his team in Greece discovered something. Something dangerous. He had the Triad smuggle that discovery into Miami, where Jason and his team picked it up." Lionel pointed to the corkboard. "But we know it has to be carefully stored and refrigerated. Then nothing happened for an entire year until recently, when Spears was ready to put the rest of his plan in motion. So where were the goods in the meantime? He would have kept his discovery somewhere off the grid, somewhere secure. And if he's still carrying a torch for his hometown and his favorite childhood ice cream—"

"Sneaky bugger," Bristol murmured. "Looky here. I've been exploring Spears Biomedical's HR database, hunting for blips. And now that I know what to look for, it's clear as day. Eleven months ago, they went on a hiring stampede.

Fifteen new top-level staff hired in one week, vetted personally by the big man. Degrees in applied chemistry, biochemistry, pharmacology..."

"Doesn't sound too unusual," Lionel said.

"Also, three mechanical engineers specializing in cryogenics. But the real interesting thing isn't their CVs or their salaries. Officially, they all work out of Spears's New York office."

"Officially?"

"Every single one of them has been filing steady expense reports, attributed to 'fieldwork-related duties.' Check the receipts."

She turned her tablet so he could read the screen. She'd pulled up an email to HR, with a digitized bill attached: $476.32 for a one-week hotel stay.

"The Jessup Hotel," Lionel read aloud. "In Holyoake, Florida. Of course. He's got biological material that needs to be monitored and maintained in a freezing environment..."

"So use the ice cream factory," Dakota said. "Place full of sterile food-grade vats and freezers. Who's going to notice if one of them gets repurposed?"

Lionel looked to Bristol. "Is Cordell's team still on-site?"

"Last receipt is dated two days ago and there's no requisition for plane tickets home, so it looks like they're sticking around for the time being."

Lionel was craning his neck, looking for Maddie, about to ask for a lift to the airport. Dakota cut him off.

"Get me a route."

Bristol's fingers danced across her tablet's screen. "Already on it, chief. Full pace?"

"Full pace. We stop for nothing but fuel."

"If we break camp now, on the road in twenty, we can reach Holyoake in sixteen hours."

Dakota looked at Lionel. "Can you drive fast?"

"Sure, but my ride is kind of stolen. I pushed my luck just getting it this far."

"Bristol, update the driving order: we put Maddie and Lionel in the middle of the convoy. Vans ahead and behind at all times, tight ranks, so no cops get a chance to look too close at their plates."

Maddie made her way across the lawn, shoes and socks dangling from the curl of her fingers. "Where are we headed?"

"Florida," Lionel said. "Cordell's team has the answers we need. We just have to get one of them to talk to us."

Maddie and Dakota shared a smile, like they were appreciating some secret joke. Bristol powered down her tablet.

"Oh," Bristol said, "they'll talk. All right, team, carry the word. We're packing up and we're rolling out."

CHAPTER FORTY

When Lionel thought of Florida, he thought of bright, sunny beaches. Disney World. Tropical drinks. When the convoy rolled across the outskirts of Holyoake, not far from the Alabama border, the state had a different face to show him.

Scraggly pine trees became a forest of charred stumps, the remnants of a clearing nobody ever bothered to finish. The streets of Holyoake were broken lines drawn between patches of mud and overgrown vacant lots. A pickup at the side of the road rested on two flat tires, a lifetime collection of tickets pinned under the windshield wiper and slowly turning to rain-drenched mulch. A clump of loose scrub bounced past, rolling on a humid breeze, looking like a tangle of barbed wire.

There was no "welcome to town" sign at the end of Gadsden Street, where the convoy slowed to a cautious crawl; this wasn't the kind of town anybody came to. The only people who ended up living in Holyoake, Florida, were the people who were born here. And either spent their lives dreaming of escape, Lionel imagined, or gave up dreaming altogether.

They pulled over a safe distance from the main drag, the

entire procession sliding to the curbside in a serpentine conga line that wrapped around two sides of an empty, weed-choked playground. A single swing dangled from a broken chain. Lionel didn't see any kids around.

The air outside the SUV was muggy and thick with a strange chemical smell, like a fistful of sugar drizzled with sour milk. In the distance he saw plumes of frozen white vapor curling into the overcast sky, billowing from the tall stacks of the Summer Smile Ice Cream plant. The stacks might have been a bright sky-blue once; now most of the paint had faded away, leaving blue flecks clinging to gray, chipped concrete.

Maddie circled the SUV and gravitated to his side. He felt pulled her way, too, like a pair of magnets that had been apart for too long. Her hand found his, fingers twining.

Dakota met them at the front of the convoy. All around them, the nomads were hopping out, taking stock of the scene, messengers running from RV to RV with instructions from the top. Dakota jerked a thumb over one shoulder, pointing to the plant.

"I'm tasking my people with recon. We know Cordell's team is staying at the only hotel in town, but I want a look at whatever they're keeping in that factory, too."

"Quietly," Maddie cautioned. "Best-case scenario, we get the answers we need and leave without Cordell ever finding out we were here. We need every advantage right now."

"Hence the recon. I figure we go into the plant after quitting time, scope the place out, see if we can get the intel we're looking for. In and out, nice and quiet, and we don't leave a trace. If that doesn't work, we raid the hotel and grab a geek or two. They'll tell us what we want to know."

"And then?" Lionel asked.

"Depends," Dakota said. "Could be they don't know what they're mixed up in and their motives are pure. In which case we just sit on them until this is all over, then we let 'em go. If not...we don't. Either way, we'll make it look like they took off on their own. We'll get into their email accounts and send Cordell an 'I quit' letter."

Maddie looked to Lionel. "It's a little after three. We have a couple of hours to kill."

"Cordell didn't necessarily grow up here," he said. "Could have been any town that Summer Smile delivered to, but..."

"Reporter's intuition?"

"I want to talk to some old-timers and see if his name rings any bells."

"Where are you going to look?" Dakota asked.

"I'm feeling a little scruffy." Lionel ran his fingers through his curly hair. "If you want to know the scoop in a small town, you go to the barbershop."

"I'll start with the library," Maddie said, gazing up the street. "Goddess, I hope there's a library."

Dakota's watch was a sturdy diver's model, built to stand up to anything short of a bullet. The Amazon showed them the time.

"We meet back here at eighteen hundred, got it? On the dot. Be safe out there."

~~

A boxy TV sat on leaning metal brackets, high in the corner of the town's only barbershop. There was a line of seats up front, somebody's salvaged coffee table, and a scattering of *Sports Illustrated* magazines. Three barber's chairs but only one barber, with liver-spotted skin and hair like fine tufts of snow. He was snipping away, turning a tundra of wild dirty-blond hair into a manicured lawn. His customer filled out the chair, half fat and half muscle, with a long scar slicing his bottom lip.

Both of them gave Lionel a look as he walked through the door. Neither one friendly.

"Just have a seat," the barber told him. "I'll get to you."

Lionel took a chair and grabbed a magazine, pretending to read while he listened. A reality show played on the TV; a surfer type with a shark-tooth necklace was delivering his philosophy of life to the camera, talking about how he didn't come here to make friends, how the only way to win was to look out for yourself.

"He's got the right idea," the man in the chair grunted. "You know they're talking about another round of layoffs?"

"I heard," said the barber. "You worried?"

"Hell yeah I'm worried. What'm I supposed to do if I don't make the cut? Plant's the only steady work in town. I'm underwater on the mortgage. Ain't like anybody's going to buy my house either. Can't make a dollar in this town, can't leave. What are my choices?"

"Hope for the best, I suppose."

The barber's scissors snipped away, locks falling to the green-and-white checkered floor.

Lionel felt eyes on him. In his peripheral vision, he saw the man in the chair watching him in the mirror's reflection.

"Company's got plenty of cash to hire eggheads," he grumbled. "One of their salaries probably covers ten of

A Time for Witches

ours. 'Researching improvements to the product,' they say. Bullcrap. The formulas haven't changed since my old man was pulling shifts."

Lionel set his magazine down.

"Talking about the ice-cream plant?" he asked.

Now both men were looking his way.

"The hell do you think?" said the one in the chair. "You know anybody else hiring around here? Hey, here's an idea. Go back to San Francisco or New York or wherever the hell you're from, and stop taking money out of our pockets. We actually work for a living in this town."

Lionel kept a few odds and ends in his wallet, kicking around as keepsakes. Very rarely, they came in handy. Like his first business card, from his first job important enough to give him one. He rose from the chair, digging it out as he crossed the hair-littered floor.

The man in the chair read it, brow furrowed. "'*The Chicago Worker*'?"

"We cover workplace issues," he said. "Labor disputes, union activity—we try to show the world from a blue-collar perspective. A tipster told us that there's been some mismanagement at the Summer Smile plant, and it might be worth checking into."

The man snorted, dubious, but the suspicion in his eyes had faded to curious interest.

"Yeah, 'some.' Over a year ago they brought in a whole crew of techs from out of state. Ivory tower assholes, they're too good to eat in the cafeteria with us mere plebes. They get their own section of the plant, their food's catered in, won't even give you the time of day if you ask. Look, Holyoake is what it is, nobody's going to mistake this place for Beverly Hills, but we've got pride in our town. We don't need people coming in here, acting like they're better than us because they've got letters after their name. Besides, they're not doing any real work."

"How do you figure?" Lionel asked.

"Like I said, they came in to 'modernize our process' and shit. Know what's changed since they got here a year ago? Nothing. Not one damn thing."

Because they're not here for you, Lionel thought. He kept his reporter hat in place.

"Does upper management ever come to the plant?" he asked, angling to see if they knew who wrote their paychecks. "Do you have any means of voicing your concerns?"

"Yeah, right. 'Upper management' is just another company that owns another company. Bunch of Wall Street guys pushing money around. They don't care about us. Keel over on the production line, they'll have a replacement covering your shift by breakfast tomorrow."

Lionel asked a few more questions after that, about OSHA violations, his union reps, gently digging around the edges. He came up empty. The barber whisked a brush across the back of the man's neck, scattering stray hairs.

"One last question," Lionel said. "This might be a long shot, but do you know a man named Cordell Spears?"

"The guy on TV? He's a doctor or something, right? Beyond that, couldn't tell you a thing."

The barber could, though.

He'd been holding his silence, letting them talk. He was still quiet, but the look in his eyes said he had something to get off his chest.

The customer left. Lionel waited. The barber gestured to the chair.

"Just a trim," Lionel said.

"I can do that." The barber dipped his scissors in a bottle of murky disinfectant, eyeing Lionel's reflection in the glass. "Now why would you come asking about Cordell Spears?"

"Part of my background research."

"That so," the barber said. It didn't sound like he believed him.

"He hides the money trail, but I've found evidence that Spears owns the Summer Smile plant."

The barber's wintry eyebrows lifted. "*That* so."

"But that's not where you know him from," Lionel said. "Not from the TV, either."

Shears whisked just above Lionel's ear. Quick whispery snips.

"I'm old enough to remember some things," he said.

Lionel met his eyes in the glass.

"He grew up here, didn't he?"

"He did." The barber broke his gaze, looking down at his work. "When he comes on the TV, I change the channel."

More whispering snips. A chestnut curl fluttered to the floor.

"What did he do?"

The barber was quiet for a while. Deciding. Lionel gave him time.

"Some people," he finally said, "are just born rotten. You the kind of reporter who takes things, what do you call it, off the record?"

"We never had this conversation," Lionel promised.

"If you're looking for proof, I ain't got it. If anybody had *proof*, someone would have done something back in the day. Tell you this, though: everybody in this town past a certain age knows the name of Cordell Spears. And we all know what he did."

~~

The town had a library. One room, high windows along the walls above rows of dusty shelves, clinging to life with whatever donations and dignity it could muster. Shafts of light from the slowly fading sun streamed across shabby carrot-orange carpet. Maddie drifted through the aisles like a ghost, her fingertips trailing along a row of decades-old hardcovers jacketed in glossy plastic.

She was the only patron here. The librarian, an elderly woman pushing a cart with a stiff, squeaky wheel, reshelved books here and there as she made her way through the section for home repairs and how-to guides. She gave a start as Maddie came into sight, as if she was surprised to see anyone at all. Then she gave her a second look.

"Don't see many out-of-towners here," she said.

"How do you know I'm an out-of-towner?" Maddie whispered.

The woman's paper-thin cheeks crinkled in a smile.

"Oh, honey, this is Holyoake. Everybody knows everybody. Just passing through?"

"I'm on a road trip. Tracing my family, trying to get in touch with my roots."

"You've got family in town?" she asked.

"Had," Maddie said. "My grandfather, Lou. I didn't really get to know him before he died. Mom said he worked as a short-order cook at a diner in town. Not sure what it was called. I just know they had a lot of long-haul truckers coming through."

"Oh, that would have to be Norma Jean's. It's over on 85,

just a stone's throw from the on-ramp." She lowered her voice, conspiratorial. "But unless you're really aching to see the place your granddad worked, I'd steer clear. Food's not what it used to be, and that's putting it gently. You'd be better off driving ten minutes south, to the Big Wheel. Food, grocery, and gas, no complaints about any of it."

"This might sound weird," Maddie said, "but I've got to ask."

The librarian chuckled. "Ask away. You're distracting me from...not much of anything at all, to be honest."

"Well, when I was setting up this trip, I asked my mom for any memories she had about Lou. And she said that—well, you know who Cordell Spears is?"

A light switch flicked off behind the old woman's eyes. She was still smiling, still focused, but something inside her just...left.

"I know him," she said.

"Well, my mom said that my grandfather worked with a woman who was Cordell's mother. Which is weird, because I thought Cordell grew up in New York, but he swore to his grave that it was true."

"Oh, I knew her. Leticia Spears. More than knew her. She was a friend of mine."

Maddie's pulse quickened. "So it's true? Cordell grew up here?"

"He lived here. Don't know where he lived after that."

"After...?"

"The incident," the librarian said.

Her gaze went distant, drifting to some other time, some other place. She waved, vaguely, and leaned against her squeaky-wheeled cart as she shoved it back to the circulation desk. Maddie followed her.

"I always figured him for being ashamed of his roots." The librarian gave Maddie a look as she circled the desk. "Some folks don't respect where they came from."

Maddie changed her angle of attack, seeing an opening there.

"That's why I'm here," she said. "Can you tell me about Leticia? I mean, it sounds like she was a close friend of my grandfather's, and I'd like to know anything you feel like sharing."

"Think I got—hold on," she said, stooping over to rummage under the counter.

She opened a square metal tin, digging through a stack of photographs. Faded Polaroids mostly.

"Used to take a picture of every one of my regulars and put it up on a board," she explained. "Board's been gone ten years now, but I keep the photographs. Lot of memories in this old tin. Ah, here we go."

She flipped a photograph around, showing it to Maddie.

"That's Leticia."

Sun and time had faded the picture to drab shades of sepia ink. A sun flare blotted out half the scene, turning bookshelves to a cigarette-burn corona. But the two people in the shot were still visible, still frozen in time and smiling for the camera. Leticia was a looker in a crop top and Daisy Dukes; Maddie could see why Zeus had picked her. Her gaze was drawn to the toddler on her lap, fat and cherub-cheeked, swaddled in a Big-Bird-yellow blanket.

Her lips parted. Her breath was frozen in her throat. The librarian squinted at her over her bifocals. "You okay?"

Maddie's fingernail rapped the photograph. "This blanket."

"Oh, I remember that, yeah. Cordell's security blanket.

They were inseparable when he was a toddler, never saw one without the other. Leticia was proud of that ratty old thing, I think she sewed it herself. I remember her being concerned, though, said she couldn't get him to put it down. Must have weaned him off it at some point. That boy got big, fast. He came by now and then, over the years. Until he left."

The librarian paused, glancing to one side, tripping over a bad memory.

"You said something about an...incident?" Maddie asked.

"Mm-hmm." She pursed her lips. "Small towns, you have to understand...everything's all rumors and whispers, and when people make up their minds, that's that. But I knew that family, and Leticia was my friend. She raised him up right, best she could while holding down a job, no husband around. I know there's no chance he did what they said he did. No chance. And I mean, just look at him on TV. Shame he's got no pride in where he comes from, but he does good for people. A whole lot of good. Somebody who does that much good would never..."

She fell silent.

"Would never what?" Maddie asked.

The librarian looked up, meeting Maddie's gaze.

"Kill his own mother," she said.

CHAPTER FORTY-ONE

Holyoake's police station sat in the middle of a half-empty strip mall. Lionel was walking up to the plate-glass door, shadowed by an overhang where fat spiders wove away in the muggy heat, when he saw Maddie coming from the other direction.

"I just had a long and very interesting conversation with the town barber," Lionel said.

"We were right about Cordell," she said. "When he was a teenager, his mother was his first victim."

"That was my take, yeah. Barber said the cops treated it as a home invasion, and Cordell was conveniently out with friends when it happened. But none of his 'friends' had the same alibi. They let him walk anyway. He couldn't remember what happened to Cordell after that, only that he was gone by the next day, and people said an 'uncle from up north' whisked him off."

"There's something else," Maddie said. "I think I know how he got my ex-husband to help him out."

"I figured it was money."

"It was a bribe. Not money." She gestured to the door. "We're here for the same reason?"

"Same," he said and held the door for her.

The cop shop might have been a travel agency once. Desks up front, a single glass-walled office in back, and one secure door tucked down the stub of a hallway. They had room for two cells, maybe three. The chief, a burly warhorse named Whistler, was eating an early dinner; marinara sauce from a three-meatball sub drizzled onto a brown paper wrapper on his desk, next to a Styrofoam bucket of Mountain Dew.

"And you are," he said two minutes after Lionel had already made his introduction, "who exactly?"

"We're writing a piece about Cordell Spears," Maddie said. "About his early history."

"Shouldn't you be up in New York, then?"

"We know he lived here," Lionel said. "Just like we know he owns the only factory in town."

Whistler's response was an eloquent "Huh." He chewed his sandwich.

"And we know about his mother," Maddie said.

The chief put his sandwich down. He rubbed his fingers on a sauce-stained paper napkin.

"We have a nice, quiet little town here," he said. "Real quiet. Saturday night, maybe me and my deputy have to answer a drunk-and-disorderly at Norma Jean's. Maybe a domestic-violence call. Once in a great while, somebody breaks a window. People don't get murdered in Holyoake."

"Leticia Spears was," Maddie said.

"Leticia Spears," he said, "was murdered by a vagrant. I know. I caught that call. It was my first week on duty and the worst damn thing I've seen in my life, before or after."

"A vagrant," Lionel echoed.

"Uh-huh. Cops in the next county over caught him red-handed. Literally. He had dried blood on his fingers and

Leticia's jewelry in his backpack. He was trying to pawn it."

"What about his clothes?" Lionel asked.

"Huh?"

"Leticia Spears," he said, "was beaten to death."

Whistler's eyes narrowed. "Where are you getting your information?"

"Am I wrong?"

He didn't answer that.

"You don't beat somebody to death and get blood on your fingers and nowhere else," Lionel said. "But if you happened to see an open door and find a dead body in an empty trailer with no witnesses around, and if you were desperate and hungry and saw a jewelry box, you might just help yourself and run."

"Like you said. No witnesses."

"What about her son?" Maddie asked.

"He had an alibi."

"Did it check out?"

Whistler put his hands on the edge of his desk. He lowered his head and stared them down, like a bull who was thinking about charging.

"The case is closed. The boy was a victim, not a killer. Do you people not get it? You come out here, raking up mud, and for what? You're not going to help anybody. You're just going to stir up controversy. Cordell Spears disowned this town because of what happened to his mother. If it was me, I'd want to put the past behind me, too. We respect that, which is why you never see any of us calling him out on that 'Brooklyn boy' act. We honor his wishes. Why can't you?"

"One last question," Maddie said. "Then we'll go."

"I hope you'll go straight to your car and get the hell out of my town. I better not hear about you two harassing my citizens."

Maddie held up the Polaroid.

"This blanket," she said. "Was it found at the crime scene?"

He stared at her. "Lady, do you have any idea how long ago this was? Do you honestly think I'd remember a *blanket*? We were a little more focused on the woman's valuables. Which, I say again, were found in the hands of a man with a history of violence, petty crime, and mental instability. Case closed."

"Thank you for your time," she said.

As they walked toward the door, Lionel saw the cop up front, a kid in a too-big uniform shirt, watch them go in silence. They were out on the sidewalk when he came after them.

"Hey," he said.

They stopped and turned. The cop looked back over his shoulder.

"I gotta make this quick. Don't need Whistler on my ass today. Do me a favor, okay? Take a hint."

"Meaning?" Lionel said.

"Office door was open. I heard y'all talking. Know why people around here don't make a big deal about Cordell Spears?"

"Because he doesn't want you to," Maddie said.

"Yeah, but it's not a damn thing to do with respect. It's an open secret that he bought the Summer Smile plant. Know who pays the bills for ninety percent of the able-bodied citizens of Holyoake? Summer Smile. If anything happens to that plant, this town *dies*. We do not rock that boat. So take my advice and get out of town before sunset."

"That sounds like a threat," Lionel said.

The cop held up his hands, exasperated.

"Look, this isn't some mafia shit. I'm not saying anybody's going to make you disappear. But you will suddenly get pulled over for a whole lot of speeding violations, smashed taillights—whether or not they were smashed when you got pulled over—and that kind of nonsense. So save yourself some cash and trouble, okay?" He took a second glance over his shoulder. "I have to get back before he starts screamin'. Welcome to Holyoake, thanks for visiting, hope I don't ever see you again."

The glass door, bearing a scratched-up decal of the town seal, swung shut in his wake. Lionel looked to Maddie.

"I've had worse interviews. What was that you were saying earlier? About the world bending the rules for heroes?"

"He's benefited from more than his share of lucky breaks," she said.

"But we're agreed, I assume, that he's guilty as sin."

Maddie nodded, grim. Her fingers clutched the faded photograph.

"He murdered his own mother," she said. "One of the worst crimes against divine law you can possibly commit. No wonder he's so afraid of Tisiphone. And no wonder he got so good at covering his trail. He knows that if he ever faces the Furies' judgment, that's the end for him."

"Mythically appropriate?" Lionel asked.

"Despite all he's built and all his mighty deeds, a hero is dragged into Tartarus for the crime of murdering the woman who bore him? Oh, yeah. Highly. That's a moral lesson for the ages. Here, look at this."

She showed him the picture. Lionel shook his head, not following.

"He was a chubby little kid. And?"

"The blanket."

He met her gaze. This was the second time she'd brought up the blanket. He couldn't see anything unusual about it. It was just frumpy yellow cotton, the kind you could buy off the rack at a discount store.

"Look the way I taught you," Maddie said. "See with your heart, not with your eyes."

It wasn't a blanket.

The Polaroid shifted in Lionel's vision. She was holding *two* photographs, one laid on top of the other. In one, the blanket was drab yellow. In the other, brighter, bursting with color, it was...*a pelt?* Like a fur throw, expertly crafted from the skinned hide of some rare and exotic beast. Instead of yellow dye, it shone like burnished gold.

"Zeus doesn't linger when he takes a mortal lover, but he is known to be generous with his gifts. That's what he gave Leticia Spears, and she turned it into a baby blanket."

"What am I looking at?" he murmured.

"That," she said, "is the Golden Fleece."

He tore his gaze from the photograph.

"Are you sure?"

Maddie gestured at herself. "Hello. I do have some authority on this subject. Let me float a theory here. It's just a theory. The librarian said Cordell had a fixation on his 'security blanket' and Leticia was going to try and break his habit."

"How'd that work out?"

"It wasn't a security blanket. Even as a toddler he knew, on some instinctive level, what the fleece really was. And I think, years later, when he was finally old enough to understand, he and his mother had a long talk one night. She told him the truth about his father."

"Tracks with what he told me," Lionel said.

"Maybe he tried to take the fleece back, and she wouldn't hand it over. Maybe he said he was leaving to find his destiny and she tried to stop him. We'll probably never know, but..."

"But at the end of the night, she was dead. So that's why you asked if the blanket was found in her trailer."

"I'd been asking myself...Jason's acting like Cordell's lackey. Why? What would make him lower himself like that?" She waved the photograph. "This would."

"You're going to have to help me out here," Lionel said. "I'm a little mythologically challenged. I mean, I watched the Harryhausen flick with the stop-motion animation when I was a kid—"

"I saw it on opening night. Not impressed, but they tried. I'll make a very long story short. Jason was the rightful king of Thessaly. Pelias, the squatter on the throne, said, 'Sure thing, guy, I'll give you the crown. Just go on a quest for the Golden Fleece to prove you've got the right stuff.'"

"That sounds like a setup," Lionel said.

"Oh, it was. He wasn't supposed to make it back alive."

"So...what is the Golden Fleece, exactly?"

"The wool of a very special, one-of-a-kind ram who was sacrificed to Poseidon after—you know what? We don't have anywhere near enough time to get into that right now. Suffice to say it represents royal authority. Power.

If you're strong enough to win the fleece, you're strong enough to rule."

"So Jason went and found it."

"Oh, sure," Maddie said. "Big heroic quest, lots of trials. He had to face down a fire-breathing ox, which would have killed him if I hadn't brewed an ointment to protect his skin. Then he had to deal with a small army of magic warriors. He was going to try and fight them in a head-on charge, until I told him how to trick them instead and, you know, not die. Then he had to battle a dragon, and by 'battle' I mean I gave him a potion to make it fall asleep."

"Did he do any of the actual work?"

"He worked hard at taking all the credit," Maddie said.

"So how does the Golden Fleece end up passing from Jason to Zeus to Leticia Spears?"

Maddie held up her open palm, snatching at the air as they walked.

"Relics like the fleece have a way of...drifting in and out of the world. It's probably been the heart of a hundred lost myths and stories since the days of Jason's quest. The point is, Cordell's out to forge new glory. Jason wants his *old* glory. He's done his best to recreate the past, in his own way: he built a new *Argo*, he gathered a new crew of Argonauts. He's stuck back in time, back when he was legendary. He can't see a way forward."

"You know who he sounds like?" Lionel said. "That guy who was great at high school football, and now he's in his forties, still talking about that one homecoming where he made the game-winning touchdown."

"An apt comparison. Now what do you think would make Jason bend the knee to Cordell Spears? What's the one bribe that would get him to go along with whatever madness he's planning?"

It clicked. "His football trophy."

"It's not just a memory of the past. It's validation."

"The right to rule," Lionel said.

Maddie nodded. "Cordell's got enough confidence that he might want the fleece, but he doesn't *need* it. It's only symbolic, and as far as he's concerned, he was born with the right to rule. And he's smart enough to swap it for Jason's loyalty."

"So here's the million-dollar question: if we get our hands on the Golden Fleece, can you use that to make a new calling charm?"

Maddie stared into the distance, grim.

"The fleece was passed from mother to son. It was in the trailer, the night he murdered her. There's a good chance it was the reason he beat her to death. You couldn't ask for a better link. We take the fleece, we enchant the cunning-call...and Tisiphone will come, I can promise you that."

CHAPTER FORTY-TWO

A ring of tall fence topped with spools of concertina wire turned the Summer Smile Ice Cream plant into a prison camp. The sun had gone down an hour ago. Electric light flickered across the football-field span of the parking lot; half of the lampposts were dead, some flickering, buzzing in the dark. The air had gone from humid to wet. Lionel's shirt clung to his back, matted with sweat, and he could feel the swampy air in his lungs.

He slapped at a mosquito while he crouched in the shadows at the south edge of the parking lot. One of the Amazons was working on the fence, carving a slow and careful hole with a pair of long-handled wire cutters.

"Guard post over there," Dakota whispered, pointing to the other end of the lot. The last few employees lined up in their cars, waiting to leave through a swinging gate. "We got eyes inside the plant, did a little digging. There's a second security shift, twenty-four seven coverage. Cordell doesn't want anyone stealing his ice cream."

Down in the huddle, Maddie's gaze flicked from the guard post to the gray concrete and barred windows of the factory. Dakota had brought four Amazons for backup; another team had been posted on the opposite side of the lot, on watch. A third was handling surveillance in town, keeping an eye on the police station, ready to intercept if they had to.

"Armed?" Maddie asked.

"And no easy way to slip past them. The interior has camera coverage just about everywhere."

"What about Cordell's team?"

"They apparently work late," Dakota said. "Still on-site, and not on the main plant floor. Our infiltrator spotted a security door that might lead to their lab. Emphasis on 'might.'"

"Can we get it open?"

Bristol nodded, clutching her tablet to her chest. "I can. Fast if we can get access to the security room, slow otherwise, but I can."

"What if we wait?" Lionel suggested. "Cordell's team has to leave sometime. We know they're staying at the hotel down the street."

"Situation's hinky," Dakota said. "Armed guards in the lobby in plainclothes, and they don't work for the hotel. Bristol? Show 'em what you found."

Bristol's fingers danced across her tablet, the oblong window lighting up the dark. It cast blue shadows beneath their huddled faces.

"On reconnaissance, I was picking up strange transmissions from inside the hotel. I managed to tap into one."

The screen flickered to a bird's-eye view of a hotel room, with a neatly made bed and an empty, open suitcase sitting out on a chair.

"Cordell is spying on his own people. He has cameras inside their rooms. I assume they aren't aware."

Maddie pointed to the tablet. "So no matter how we do this, Cordell is probably going to know we were here."

"Quick and quiet is our best bet," Dakota said.

"Then we hit the factory," Maddie said. "We take his team and whatever they're working on, all in one swoop."

"Things are going to move fast after this," Dakota warned her. "Real fast. I assume you're coming in with us?"

"Wouldn't miss it."

"And Lionel?"

Dakota was asking Maddie, not him. Maddie's hand found his in the dark. Her fingers curled and squeezed tight.

"Lionel goes where I go," she said.

They faded back to the convoy to gear up. The chrome bulb of an Airstream travel trailer served as the Amazons' mobile armory. Wall racks bristled with firepower, all of it meticulously cleaned and oiled. Dakota's team moved with trained precision, picking out the right tools for the job.

"Maddie? You strapped?" Dakota asked.

"Always, but I'm low on ammunition."

Dakota gestured to a standing cabinet. "Help yourself. We've got a little of everything. Lionel?"

He stared at the wall of weapons, feeling faintly out of his depth.

"I'm not really a gun guy," he said.

"You are tonight. Artemis would have my ass if I brought an unarmed man into a firefight. I'm hoping we can get in and out without firing a shot, but hopes aren't plans."

Dakota took a sleek, snub-nosed machine pistol from

the rack, a twin to the one swinging on a shoulder strap at the Amazon's side.

"You ever shoot one of these?"

"Can't say I have," Lionel said.

Dakota's fingertip pointed to a toggle switch on the side of the weapon. "Safety on."

Click.

"Safety off. You have thirty rounds in the magazine, and it fires three-round bursts. It'll kick when you squeeze the trigger, so aim low. Never point it at anything you don't intend to destroy, and never fire warning shots. Lesson complete. Everybody ready? Let's go. Moonlight's burning."

~~

The crack of a bat against a baseball echoed over a phone's tinny speaker, then the static-hiss wash of a roaring crowd. The guard on booth detail had been glued to his chair for six hours and it felt like sixty. He set his phone down, still keeping an eye on the highlights reel, and picked up his walkie-talkie.

"Central? My rotation isn't here yet. Kinda need to take a leak."

Static answered him. He waited, then clicked the side of the handset again.

"Central?"

No answer. *Comm's on the fritz again, great.* He looked out his Plexiglas window, eyeing the almost-empty parking lot.

"Well," he said, shoving his chair back, "if the guard can't go to the bathroom, the bathroom will come to the guard."

He wandered out into the muggy night air, circling the

booth. There was a patch of weeds around back in need of watering. He picked his spot, spread his feet, and reached for his belt buckle.

A hand clamped over his mouth as a heel drove into the back of his leg, buckling his knee. The cold slick loop of a zip tie leashed his wrists and pulled tight.

"Don't *make* us kill you," hissed a voice in his ear. "You sit still, you keep your mouth shut, and you get to go home to your family tonight. Understood?"

He understood.

~~

A flashlight beam swept across empty concrete floors and glinted off the stainless-steel hulls of tall industrial vats. Another guard was making the rounds. The ice-cream mixers were sleeping giants in the dark, monoliths beneath the slanted skylights. He couldn't see anything through the glass but murky clouds. *Storm comin'*, he thought.

He crossed the alley between a pair of steel vats. Hands shot from the darkness, grabbed onto his arm, and hauled him out of sight before he had a chance to scream. His flashlight clattered to the concrete, spinning, strobing its beam in all directions until it slowly wheeled to a stop.

~~

"You see something just now?"

Two guards manned the security station, a long and narrow booth up on the factory's second floor. By day, the most exciting thing that ever happened was catching somebody sneaking a pint of ice cream into their backpack. By night there wasn't anything to watch at all. But one man leaned forward in his chair, neck craned, staring at the bank of monitors above a window overlooking the factory floor.

His partner kicked his boot heel against the floor, sending his chair gliding on wheeled casters. He scuttled to a stop at his side. "What's that?"

The first man frowned. "Nothing, now. I just thought..."

A knock sounded at the door.

"Who's there?"

"Hey, uh, it's Walter," said the muffled voice on the other side. "Can you let me in?"

The guards gave each other a look. One spun his chair around.

"I'm sorry, who?"

"Walter. Walter Winchell. It's my first night. Anyway, I cut myself on one of the mixer blades. Can you help me out?"

"*How the hell...*" the guard muttered. The other was already on his phone, calling a supervisor. "Go down to the break room. There should be a first aid kit under the sink."

"It's...it's really bad, man, like I can see the bone and I'm feeling really shaky. I think I need an ambulance."

The guard propelled himself out of his chair and steamed toward the door, cursing under his breath. Behind him, the other had just gotten the boss out of bed. "Yeah, confirming a new hire? Says his name is Winchell?"

The lock clicked under his partner's fingertips.

The door blasted open, knocking him flat, and the room filled with guns. Lionel strode in, swift. He framed the other guard in the iron sights of his machine pistol. Then he shook his head, slowly, and mouthed a silent warning.

Behind him, a pair of Amazons jumped on the fallen man and zip-tied his wrists behind his back.

"Uh, no, he's not inside. He's outside the front gate," the guard said, blood draining from his face. "Probably a vagrant or something. I'll, uh, send him away. Nothing to worry about, sir. Everything's good here."

Lionel took his phone.

~~

Money never slept. Neither did Cordell Spears.

He didn't like sleeping. When he slept, he dreamed, and dreams were the only place he wasn't in absolute control.

He liked his windows, though, a twenty-million-dollar view of Central Park from a high-rise condo. He liked his designer furniture, his imported art on the walls. And he liked the square bank of monitors, set up by his staff, that showed him a constantly shifting view of his empire. Stock-market feeds on one screen, racing lines of colored neon. A black-and-white camera feed from a fish market in Beijing on another, next to a crisp but motionless stream from the silent lobby of his office in Los Angeles. They flickered, changing every thirty seconds or so. He had hundreds of cameras and only twelve screens to watch them on. They lit the dark chasm of his condo, casting him in a radiation glow.

Down on the bottom left, the feed shifted to the bedroom of a city administrator Cordell had vaguely planned to blackmail at some point. The hidden camera captured two men engaged in intense, acrobatic, and extremely painful-looking intercourse. Eyebrows lifting, Cordell tapped one button to lock that screen in place, and a second to start recording.

"Here we go," he murmured. "Now that's

entertainment. I was going to rent a movie tonight, but hey, you two keep going and I'll make popcorn."

The screen next to that one shifted. He caught movement in the corner of his eye, glanced out of idle curiosity...and stared into the eyes of Lionel Page. He wasn't alone, a long shadow striding across the floor of his factory in Holyoake with a wolf pack of women, all of them bristling with firepower.

He changed cameras manually. An electronic eye overlooked the door to the high-security wing. The keypad dangled from a broken screw, its wire guts leaking out. Another woman crouched beside the steel-plated door, concentrating on a tablet; she'd spliced some kind of a bypass, a ribbon cable snaking from her tablet to the mutilated wiring.

"Aw, Lionel," he sighed. "Why'd you go and do that? We could have been buds."

He took out his phone.

"Now I have to kill you."

~~

The lab in the high-security wing looked like a shrunk-down version of NASA's mission control. Console banks lined the sterile floor in slanted *Vs*, all facing the master screen on the far wall. The main feed kept a running update on Project Caduceus, monitoring temperature and containment status. The smaller stations ran simulations, crunched numbers, projected possibilities. Three members of Cordell's team were on duty tonight, pulling a late shift while the others were back—under armed guard and watched by cameras that documented their every move—at the hotel in town.

The guard here, keeping a silent watch over the trio

of lab-suited engineers, was a man named Pugh. Pugh wasn't an employee of Summer Smile. Like everyone on the project, he reported directly to Cordell Spears. He was thankful for this job. Most people wouldn't take a chance on a man who had just done a fifteen-year stretch in maximum security, but Cordell had seen his potential.

His phone buzzed. He took it out, checked the screen, and answered the call.

"Sir?"

Cordell gave him his orders.

"Yes, sir. No, that won't be a problem. You told me it was a possibility when you hired—yes, sir. Right away. I'll report back when it's done."

Pugh looked to the team. They were spread across the room, silently moving from console to console, intent on their work. He popped the snap on his holster.

Damn shame, he thought. *I really liked this gig.*

He put the barrel of his gun to the back of an engineer's head and said, "Sorry, doc," before squeezing the trigger. The round blew out through his forehead, the crumpled slug cracking the glass of his monitor and washing it in a gout of raspberry jam.

~~

The strike team huddled around the security door, waiting for Bristol to get it open.

"Sorry," Bristol muttered, fingers fluttering against her tablet screen. "The encryption's more sophisticated than I thought. They really spent some money on this."

"Don't apologize," Dakota said, standing over her. "Just get it done."

Lionel felt the current of urgency in her voice. He looked back, to the silent bowels of the factory. They had taken out the security force one by one, but that didn't mean they'd gotten all of them. There was no accounting for someone being late to work or coming back from a break, or just a passerby spotting odd lights or movement from the windows and calling it in. Speed was the difference between getting out clean and finding a police cordon waiting in the parking lot.

Dakota handed out the marching orders. "Soon as that door's open, I want full momentum. You two, cover the exit. You two are stationed right here. Phoenix, I want you trailing the main team. I'll take point."

Lights strobed green on Bristol's tablet. The door, coated in a sheet of stainless steel, let out a trio of hollow clicks. Dakota hauled it open to reveal a long, sterile hallway, hospital white under hard fluorescent overheads, running deeper into the plant.

The sound of a bullet echoed up the corridor, rippling like thunder. Then a second.

Dakota didn't need to say a word. She led the charge, sprinting toward the gunfire.

CHAPTER FORTY-THREE

The secure wing was a maze of storage closets and darkened rooms. Reinforced windows looked in on rows of steel-hulled tanks. Other rooms were empty, gathering dust. Lionel heard two more shots as he ran with the pack, his weapon heavy in his grip. Then another sound, metal crunching against metal.

They passed through some kind of control center. A man in a lab coat, shot through the head, lay slumped against a blood-spattered console. A woman's body sprawled in the center aisle, arm outstretched like she had tried to crawl for safety. She'd been shot in the back.

Another metallic crunch. Back out in the hallway, around the next corner, a man in a security guard's uniform brandished a fire ax. He swung it at a reinforced door. The battered metal caved in another half inch.

"Come on, doc," he called out, "knock this shit off. Let's just get it over with—"

He caught movement and spun. The ax fell from his hands, hitting the floor at his feet, and his empty hand slapped his holster.

Dakota's machine pistol spat fire. Three rounds, stitching from his belly to his face as the gun kicked. He crumpled in a bloody, broken heap. Maddie glided up the hallway, her footsteps silent. She knocked at the door.

"Hey," she said. "It's okay. He's gone. You're safe. You can come out now."

They waited while the person on the other side made up his mind. The door opened, just a crack. A sweaty, ruddy face peered out, fat cheeks and worried eyes framed with crow's-feet, under a balding ring of gray hair.

"Who—who are you?" he said.

"Friends," Maddie lied.

She put her hands on his shoulders and gently walked him back to the control room. He saw the corpses and started to cry.

"Lionel, Phoenix," Dakota murmured, "get those bodies out of here. Drag 'em to the hallway or something. He doesn't need to look at that right now. Bristol, whatever—whatever *this* is, crack into it. I want every file, every last scrap of data."

Phoenix was built like a weightlifter. She hoisted the head-shot engineer by his shoulders like he was a sack of laundry, not even reacting when his broken skull lolled back and smeared her jacket with a crescent of red. Lionel took the dead man's ankles. They hauled him out into the hallway and dumped him in the storage room where the scientist had been hiding.

By the time they moved the second body and came back, Maddie had the survivor sitting down and talking, clutching a wad of wet tissue in his hand.

"I don't—I don't know what happened. Pugh just went crazy. I ran. He, he shot and he missed and I ran—"

Maddie looked over her shoulder to Dakota. "He knows we're here."

Dakota nodded. "Shutdown protocol. We must have tripped an alarm on our way in. Damn."

Lionel put it together. Cordell didn't want anyone learning his secrets. The guard was probably supposed to kill the scientists, then wipe the servers clean. If they'd been any slower, or if the third target hadn't gotten lucky, there wouldn't have been anything here to find.

Maddie turned back to the scientist. "He didn't go crazy. He was acting on Cordell Spears's orders."

"He..." A wash of emotions flickered across the man's face, his tear-slick cheeks contorting. His expression settled somewhere around quiet acceptance. "I knew something like this might happen. We all volunteered for this team—anyone would have jumped at the chance—but I knew he wasn't telling us the whole story. A couple of months ago, one of us got cold feet and wanted to leave. Pugh 'escorted' her to the train station. Right after that, they took our phones. No social media, no outside contact, for the security of the project."

"Or so you wouldn't find out that your friend never made it home," Maddie said.

"I knew. I didn't know, but I *knew*, you understand?" He pressed the wadded tissue to his heart. "I hoped that if we just did what we were told and kept our heads down, he'd let us all go when it was finished."

"When what was finished?" Lionel gestured to the wall screen, where a glowing line fluttered like a heartbeat next to a steady temperature reading. "What is all this?"

"We called it Project Caduceus. We were going to change the world. Revolutionize medical technology. Spears had an archeology project working out in Greece. They found something. A lost temple, buried under the sea. Divers came up with stone coffers, still hermetically sealed after all these centuries. An incredible find. One in a million."

"That was Jurgen Lambert's team," Lionel said.

"That's right. Jurgen found something else. He—he thought it was a broken statue at first, until he got it to the surface. It wasn't stone, it was just…hibernating, in a form of stasis. I think it was Jurgen who figured out how it reacted to extreme cold. He kept it in a meat locker until Spears delivered an industrial freezer for transporting the thing back to America. We were recruited to study it, to learn how it worked and the practical applications. The applications—"

"What was it?" Maddie said. "What did he find?"

He waved them over to a console and rattled off a string of commands. His hands were shaking but his eyes, still wet, shone with the memory of his greater purpose.

"It was extraordinary," he murmured, unlocking secure files. "A living organism capable of indefinite hibernation and endless cellular replenishment through transdifferentiation—like a jellyfish, but on a scale never before seen in nature. Biological immortality."

A grainy video clip played on the wall screen. A tiny, squiggling worm writhed in a dish.

"Imagine the applications, if we mastered the process," the scientist said. "We could conceivably repair severed spines. Regenerate lost limbs. It would be the greatest breakthrough in medical history."

On the screen, a gloved hand tentatively extended a pair of tweezers toward the worm.

The worm reared up, three petals of flesh splitting open to bare a maw lined with tiny diamond-point teeth. It struck at the tweezers hard enough to rip them from the researcher's hand. The metal crumpled under its sudden, furious onslaught.

"It was also…very aggressive," he said, his voice going soft. "This was a tiny piece that we broke off, to see if severed parts would repair themselves and grow on their own. They do. Each severed piece eventually becomes its own independent organism. Parthenogenesis."

He brought up a second clip. Tentacles, bilious green, slapped against a reinforced window. Beyond them, a semblance of a great and roiling bulk, reptilian scales, teeth.

"Aiko"—he looked to the center aisle, where all that remained of his coworker was a rust-red smear—"Aiko was a mythology buff. She said this was more than a breakthrough. It was proof of a myth. The truth behind the story."

Lionel had his gaze fixed on the screen. He thought he caught a flash of something deep in the tank, a cluster of baleful yellow eyes. A massive head, slipping past on a serpentine neck. Then another.

"Doctor? What are we looking at here?"

The scientist's hands rested, faintly trembling, on the console.

"The Lernaean Hydra," he said. "From the legend of Heracles. That's what Cordell's researchers found. We have the hydra in a containment tank."

The overhead lights shifted from white to hazard amber. The floor rumbled under their feet. Metallic rattling echoed through the halls, like steel shutters sliding down.

The prerecorded clip on the wall changed to a camera feed. Cordell was on the screen. He raised a martini glass in a wry salute. The lights of New York gleamed through a wall of glass at his back.

"Dr. Wolcott," he said, "are you breaking your nondisclosure agreement? There are severe legal penalties for that sort of behavior. Nah, I kid, I kid. Where's Pugh?"

"Dead." Lionel took a step toward the wall screen.

"He murdered my friends," Wolcott said, his bottom lip quivering.

"Well, don't blame me." Cordell waved a hand at the screen. "Blame them. If they hadn't tried to break in and expose my research, I wouldn't have been forced to sanitize the facility. I tried to be nice. Lionel, you in particular. You disappointed me. I gave you every opportunity to walk away, and you just kept coming at me."

"Yeah. I've been known to do that from time to time."

Cordell leaned back, eyeing the feed, sipping his drink.

"Have to say, though, I didn't know you were such a player. You're apparently a magnet for the babes. Hello, ladies."

Dakota stood at Lionel's shoulder, chin high, eyes made of cold steel.

"I speak for the Amazons," Dakota said. "In the interest of justice, I offer you one and only one chance. Surrender. Now. You won't be given a second opportunity."

"Wait, you're actually—hold on. Hold on. This is awesome. I have to call somebody."

Cordell whipped out his phone and held it to his ear.

"Hey, pal—no, listen, I'm watching the surveillance camera at the facility down in Florida, and guess who just invaded the place. Amazons. Actual freaking real-life Amazons. Is that not—" Cordell paused, listening. Then he looked to the screen. "Jason wants to know if his wife is in the room."

"Ex-wife," Maddie said.

"Yeah, she's here. You want me to pass on a message or—no, no, I gotcha. No, I'm about to kill 'em all. Hold on a second."

He clicked a mouse. The floor shuddered a second time, and a klaxon split the air. Cordell put the phone to his shoulder.

"Guys, I really have to take this call, so I'm going to let you go now. I mean, not *let you go*. Obviously."

The screen went dark. Wolcott was hammering at his keyboard, head shaking wildly, like he could will this all away if he wished hard enough. Before Lionel could ask what he was doing, a second sound, louder than the alarm, roared in the distance. It was a grating, metal-edged screech, like an echo from a room filled with running buzz-saws.

"It's loose," Wolcott whispered. Beads of sweat ran down his wrinkled forehead. "I didn't know he had remote access. He shouldn't have—there are fail-safes—he shouldn't have been able to open the containment grid—"

A second roar got them up and moving, Dakota taking the lead as they fled the control room and rounded the bend, heading for the exit. They jolted to a stop. Emergency shutters had rolled down, blocking the hallway with a wall of steel.

"Bristol," Dakota said.

She fumbled with her tablet and shook her head. "No good, chief. I'm locked out."

"It's worse than it looks," Wolcott said.

Lionel arched an eyebrow. "Worse than being trapped

with a rampaging hydra? Because that thing sounds pissed."

"There's a fail-safe," he said. "Early on, as soon as we discovered how aggressive the organism was, we focused on developing an emergency protocol in the event of a containment breach. We finally developed a gas-based solution: Athena-18. We made cuttings, creating new hydras to use for testing, and refined the gas until it guaranteed one-hundred-percent lethality."

"That sounds like good news," Lionel said. "Why is that not good news?"

Wolcott pointed up to the fat pipes snaking their way along the corridor wall.

"Because it's also lethal to humans. It attacks the respiratory system like chlorine gas. And unless Cordell overrode the fail-safes, we have ten minutes before the entire facility floods with it."

CHAPTER FORTY-FOUR

Something about Cordell's order to "sanitize" the facility didn't sit right with Lionel. He thought fast, working through the problem, looking for the missing piece.

He poked his head around the bend in the corridor. Pugh lay crumpled in a heap on the hospital-white floor, his bloodless face turned upward. The amber emergency lights strobed in his glassy eyes.

"What was his exit strategy?" Lionel asked.

The scientist squinted at him, not following. Maddie understood.

"He was supposed to kill your team and wipe the servers," she said. "And then what? He couldn't risk being taken alive, and I strongly doubt he was willing to kill himself for Cordell Spears. And means he wasn't going to leave in this direction, because he would have run straight into us if he tried. There has to be another way out of the labs."

Wolcott rubbed his temples, concentrating. Another chainsaw roar thundered in the distance, and a hail of sledgehammer tails pounded into the corridor walls.

"This place wasn't purpose-built," he said. "No time for that, Spears needed a team and a facility up and running immediately. He just sealed off the old R&D wing to keep the plant's employees in the dark, and we made do with the space we had."

Maddie nodded to the steel shutters. "We passed some empty rooms on our way in."

"We had more storage space than we could use. Not enough space for other needs. He literally just plopped us down here and told us to make the floor plan work."

"What about the guards?" she asked. "Did they go anywhere that was off-limits for you and the other scientists?"

"I don't know about 'off-limits.' There are some utility closets and such, for maintenance. We were never told we couldn't access them, but there wasn't any need to either."

Phoenix, the weightlifter, had her rifle slung over one shoulder. She crouched and patted the dead guard down. A heavy ring of keys jangled in her hand.

"Utility closets." Maddie grabbed Wolcott's arm and turned him around. "Show us."

"They're over that way," he said pointing a quivering finger toward the distant roars.

She pulled him down the hall, pausing just long enough to scoop the fallen fire ax off the floor. Phoenix tossed Bristol the keys and unslung her rifle, taking point, sweeping the muzzle of her weapon across the hallway as they rounded the next bend. Locked doors and dark windows lined both sides of the corridor, no signs of movement behind the reinforced glass. About fifty feet ahead, the hallway split into a four-way junction.

"We need to go right, up here," Wolcott said. "It isn't far."

"Stay behind me," Phoenix growled. She crossed the intersection.

She swept her rifle right, then turned the other way. She shouted a sudden warning and opened fire, muzzle blazing, leaving streaks of light in Lionel's vision as a tidal wave of bile-green tentacles spilled from the mouth of the corridor. It was a wall of blubbery flesh driven by hunger and madness. A tentacle snared her arm, yanking it upward with her finger still on the trigger, her rifle blowing out the overhead lights in a shower of shattered glass. Another took her ankle and a third, thicker than an elephant's trunk, wrapped around her waist. More tentacles whipped the air, seeking prey, sniffing them out.

Maddie ran in, rearing the fire ax high in a two-hand grip.

A tentacle snapped in her face, driving her back, getting between them as the creature hauled Phoenix step by struggling step down the hallway. Maddie swung the ax. It buried itself in the blubber and the wound spat a gout of black ichor. The goo spattered the wall, hissing, giving off a smell like rotten eggs as it ate away at the paint. While Bristol ran up the hall in the other direction, keys tight in her grip as she hunted for the utility closet, Dakota charged into the fight. She dropped to a crouch, squinted, and took careful aim, drawing a line on the tentacle wrapped around Phoenix's waist.

A three-round burst punched into the blubber. The creature screamed. The sound was earsplitting, louder than the gunfire, and venomous bile rained from the bullet-riddled tentacle. The blood steamed with clouds of gray smoke, sizzling into the floor. Lionel ran behind Phoenix, grabbing on to the tentacle at her arm, struggling to pry it loose while he ducked under a whip of greedy flesh.

Down the hall was a vision of hell. The hydra filled the corridor, and Lionel's eyes refused to focus on it. There was nothing to latch on to, just an endless slithering mass of reptile scales and fat, pulsing suckers, wrapping around itself and firing out another half dozen tendrils to try to capture more prey.

The mass parted, and a head began to emerge. It was draconic, massive, with burning three-lobed eyes and a maw that dripped black, toxic blood from its corroded gums. The tentacles yanked Phoenix another two steps toward the eager and waiting teeth, and she dug her heels into the floor, roaring back at it, pulling with all of her strength.

Cold, Lionel thought. They'd kept it refrigerated for transport from the dig site, even warned the smugglers to keep it frozen at all costs. He turned on his heel and sprinted back up the hallway, to the emergency firebox mounted on the wall. Next to the red enameled case where the ax had hung was the heavy canister of a fire extinguisher. *Please be carbon dioxide*, he thought, snatching it up and charging back into the fight. *Please be carbon dioxide—*

A torrent of freezing gas blasted from the nozzle, filling the air with icy mist. The hydra shrieked. A tentacle, caught in the cloud, fell to the floor like a dead slug and lethargically twitched.

"It's working," Dakota shouted. "Keep hitting it!"

Lionel focused on the tendrils grappling at Phoenix. The one around her ankle fell away, limp and leaden after a blast of cold. Its bile-green scales took on the bluish sheen of rotten meat. He raised the nozzle, taking aim at the fat tentacle snaring her waist—then the creature focused on the source of its sudden pain. Maddie grabbed him and yanked him backward as a tree-trunk slab of blubber came crashing down, pulverizing the tiles where he'd just been standing.

Fresh tendrils lashed from the endlessly shifting serpentine bulk. They leashed around Phoenix's legs. Lionel raced back into the fight, ducking a whipping tentacle, jumping a fallen one as it began to shake off the icy torpor...and the world wrenched to a slow-motion heartbeat as the Amazon lost her footing. Lionel fired a last, desperate blast from the extinguisher, too little, too late. He watched the tentacles haul her down the hallway, a twisting, bucking shadow in the frozen mist.

She roared her defiance until the end. The hydra's dragon head silenced Phoenix with a single bite, cutting her in half. It chewed, wet and greedy, while the tentacles waved the severed chunks of the Amazon's corpse in the air and painted the walls red.

Bristol had been fighting with the ring of keys. She finally found the one that fit, jiggling it until the tumblers turned, shoving open the windowless steel door. She gave a shout, waving. Lionel covered the retreat; he walked backward, facing the armada of tentacles, firing bursts of winter cold to stave it off while the others raced for the doorway. The hydra reached for him, groping blind through the fog like a monstrous hand with a hundred fingers.

His heel hit the doorframe as the nozzle spat one final, tepid cloud of mist. He threw the empty canister and jumped inside. Maddie slammed the reinforced door shut and flipped the lock. The room beyond was the size of a walk-in closet, with a circuit breaker on one bare concrete wall and pipes running along the ceiling. A steel hatch, painted hazard-orange, was set into the floor, and Dakota was already throwing the latches and heaving it open.

"How big is that thing?" Lionel asked. The tentacles began hammering on the door, a demanding hailstorm thrum.

Wolcott was pale, his face glistening with terror sweat. "That's the original subject. The way it replenishes its own cellular structure…it's consistently grown to fill whatever containment we place it into. We haven't quite reached a theoretical limit."

Maddie shot him a look. "Original subject?"

"Time?" Dakota shouted, clambering into the hatch.

Bristol was right behind her, hustling down a ladder made of iron brackets stapled into the concrete shaft. "Four minutes thirty-seven seconds, chief."

Four minutes and change until the facility flooded with poison gas. Lionel was the last one down the shaft, climbing blind. He dropped down into an underground tunnel. The air had a chemical tang, the smell of diesel vapors mingling with something sickly sweet.

"Utility tunnels," Bristol said, drawing a line with her finger in two directions. "Sewage, water, cabling, which means…this way."

The pack ran behind her, feet pounding the water-stained concrete. The tunnel was a web of darkness interspersed with faint emergency lights, casting wedges of glowing amber every twenty feet or so.

"Are you sure?" Dakota called out. Bristol nodded, panting for breath, keeping the pace.

"This is municipal, not part of the plant. Has to be a way for town workers to access it for maintenance and repairs. We're heading south, closest way to the outlying streets."

Her gamble paid off. A second shaft rose to meet the closed lid of a manhole cover. "Let me," Dakota said, taking point.

The lid rattled against Dakota's shoulder. It moved aside, inch by inch, and moonlight streamed down to flood the shaft.

Dakota waved down, giving the all-clear. One by one they emerged into the muggy night air, gathering on the road outside the factory gate. Lionel was out of breath, but he didn't stop. Couldn't stop. He ran for the gate and the parking lot.

"The hell is he doing?" Dakota said.

Bristol gave her a sidelong glance. "Eighty-six seconds, chief."

Dakota and Maddie chased him down. They caught Lionel halfway across the desolate lot, grabbing his arms, pulling him back.

"The guards," he said, trying to yank himself free, "the ones we left tied up in there—"

Dakota shoved a heel against the back of his leg, buckling his knee, and wrestled him down to the concrete.

"It's too late. You'd never make it in time. Stop fighting me, goddamn it! Maddie, tell him—"

Maddie took his chin in her hands, turning his desperate eyes from the factory to her gentle face.

"No," she said. "Lionel, no."

"There's still *time*." He bucked against Dakota's steel grip. "We can't just let them die in there. We *can't*."

"Hey," she said. "Listen to me."

A silence fell over the parking lot. Lionel met Maddie's gaze. He stopped struggling.

"We can't save everybody," she said.

There was no dramatic moment. No explosions, and the plant didn't cave in and collapse into the earth. Just a distant watery hiss, like someone opening a fire hydrant down the block. Wisps of luminous vapor, the color of glistening wet jade, kissed the factory skylights.

CHAPTER FORTY-FIVE

The Amazons fell back, regrouping at the parked convoy on the edge of town. Word spread that Phoenix had died in battle. Lionel and Maddie gave them time to grieve, what little time they could afford to spare.

Lionel was grieving, too. He leaned against the bumper of their stolen SUV, arms crossed, staring at a patch of wet dirt. Not really sure what he was thinking or feeling, beyond ache and hurt. Maddie walked over. She leaned right next to him, sharing his silence for a while.

"Put the blame where it belongs," she told him.

"Oh, I'm doing that," he said. "I know. Cordell set the hydra loose. He set off the fail-safe, but—"

"There's no 'but,'" she said.

"We ambushed those guards. We tied them up. We left them to die in there."

"And if we had any way of knowing that factory was a literal death trap, we would have done something different," she said. "But we couldn't have known that. We made our choices based on the information we had. That's life, hon. You make the best choices you can, and you roll the dice. Tell me something. When you were a reporter, did you ever have a story go wrong? Consequences you didn't see coming?"

He didn't have to think hard. A face and a name boiled up from his memory, an old wound that never quite healed.

"I busted this...phony medium, back in Chicago. She went the whole nine yards, latching on to grieving families, stringing them along for months, even years with fake séances and messages from the dearly departed. Anyway, I went undercover, exposed her techniques and the tricks she used, blew open the whole racket."

Maddie listened, silent. A mosquito buzzed past.

"This guy, his daughter had died in an accident. He couldn't handle finding out that he hadn't been talking to her at all, that he'd been forking over his retirement savings to a fraud." Lionel raised a hand. Then dropped it limply to his side. "So he went to join his little girl. He thanked me, in the note he left behind. Said I showed him the light."

She took his hand.

"Now be honest," she said. "If you could go back and do it all over again, would you still write the story?"

He thought about it. Fought past the knee-jerk responses, past what he thought he should say—the words that would make him noble and bright—to the truth beneath.

"Yes," he said. "I would. I don't regret putting a grifter behind bars and stopping her from conning people out of their life savings. I regret that one of her victims couldn't pick up the pieces after. But I couldn't control that."

"Exactly. When we take action and intervene in the world, sometimes there's collateral damage. Sometimes

A Time for Witches

we can't save everyone. That's the price of action. You know...some people spend their entire lives terrified of change. They'd rather be consistently, dependably miserable than face the unknown. So they keep their heads down. They never rock the boat. And maybe nothing gets worse, but nothing ever gets better, either."

"I'm a habitual boat-rocker," he said.

"To be a witch," Maddie said, "is to court change. We walk with chaos because we know the only way to improve the world is to change it. Sometimes our plans work out. Sometimes they don't. Sometimes there's fallout, and innocent people get hurt."

He caught the look in her eye. Distant, fixed somewhere on another crescent moon, centuries away. She wasn't talking about tonight.

"And you'll carry those wounds," she said, "and you'll carry the guilt, and you'll keep walking. Because you're strong enough to do it."

They fell back into an intimate silence, hand in hand, listening to the night.

Bristol walked up. She nodded back over her shoulder, to the lights behind the blind-shrouded windows of Dakota's RV.

"The doc is talking," she said. "And you're going to want to hear this."

~~

Wolcott sat in the same chair they'd put Lionel in when he first met Dakota. Dakota sat across from him, on the padded bench at the back of the RV, flanked by a pair of stone-faced Amazons. Lionel read their eyes, and how their hands never strayed too far from the holsters on their hips. They'd lost a battle sister tonight, and they wanted to hold someone responsible.

Dakota nodded to Lionel and Maddie, then looked back to the scientist. "Tell them what you told me. About why you called that the *original* hydra."

"Cordell contacted us and said he was opening additional lab sites. Each site would be studying the hydra, working independently."

"And did that make sense to you?" Maddie asked. Her tone made the answer clear.

He stared down at his hands.

"No," he said. "Multiple teams studying the same phenomenon without sharing data is counterproductive, to say the least. And we told him so. But we didn't have a choice. In anything. You understand that, don't you?"

"Go on," Dakota told him.

"He shipped us seven large containment units. Reinforced freezer systems with multiple redundant battery backups. An improved version of the original. We were told to make cuttings, as we'd done before for studies. But we'd always *destroyed* the cuttings before they could grow into full-fledged hydras."

"But you did it anyway. Made the cuttings. Boxed 'em up for delivery."

"Large ones. Not tadpoles, these were nearly mature, and frozen just before an expected burst of cellular growth. The first was picked up by a shipping company, Lucky Eight." Wolcott wrung his hands. "It was bound for one of Cordell's storage facilities in Manhattan."

Dakota flicked a glance at Maddie. "Lucky Eight. Those your Triad boys?"

"The same," Maddie said. "And the other six freezers?"

"He said he was sending a special courier to take them to the new laboratory sites. Some 'courier,' the man was a brute. Drove the biggest truck I've seen in my life."

"That would be the *Argo*," Maddie said. "Jason. Bristol, do you still have the dossier on Cordell Spears? All that data your team gathered?"

Bristol held up her tablet. "All two thousand-odd pages of it."

"Pull up all of his acquisitions in the last year, after he got his hands on the hydra and set up shop here. Real estate."

"Look for bad investments," Lionel suggested. "Same deal as Summer Smile. He won't be looking to make his money back if what he really wants is secure lab space. And the purchases will probably be clustered together."

Bristol found what they were looking for. She looked up from the screen, somewhere between grave and perplexed.

"I found a batch of same-week purchases, five months ago," she said. "Six in all. He paid too much, and it would take him years to recoup the cost, but—"

"Six sites, six freezers," Lionel said. "That has to be it."

"But they aren't industrial sites," she said. "They're homes."

They gathered around her as she flicked through real estate listings. There was a half-completed suburban tract in Houston, a tenement slated for demolition in Philadelphia. A housing project recently handed over to private investors, on the south side of Chicago, and a condominium in East LA.

Lionel's blood ran cold. The locations were jigsaw pieces, snapping together, drawing a bigger picture.

"San Antonio and San Diego," he murmured, finishing

out the list. He looked to Wolcott. "I know why he didn't want you sharing data with the other teams."

The scientist's brow furrowed. "Why?"

This is a time to celebrate, the Ker had told Lionel. *The age of heroes is returning to this world.*

And then Cordell, the night he revealed his true nature. *All I want is my rightful due, and the plan to make it happen is already in motion. The world has been sleeping for too long. I'm going to wake it up with a bang.*

"Because there aren't any other teams." Lionel pointed to the tablet. "These aren't laboratories. They're population centers in some of the nation's biggest cities. And New York makes seven."

He looked to Maddie.

"He wants his *kleos*."

"Goddess," she breathed. "The 'surprises' he's planning for his party in Central Park. He's going to set them loose."

"He wants to bring the past back to life," Lionel said. "And what better way than to reveal himself as the son of Zeus and slay a hydra in front of the entire world?"

"That's one," Dakota said. "What about the other six? He's just going to let them rampage?"

Lionel thought it through. He nodded, grim.

"Of course he is. Step one, he wakes the world up and single-handedly defeats a mythic beast. Step two is terror. He'll let the other six run wild, destroying everything in their path, and people will beg him to step in and save the day. He'll get everything he ever wanted, by ending the crisis that he created in the first place."

"That poison you developed," Maddie said to Wolcott. "Athena-18. Can you brew another batch?"

"Theoretically. The ingredients aren't hard to source,

but I'd need lab space, equipment to produce an aerosol gas—"

"Assume you'll be provided with anything and everything you need," Dakota said. Bristol was already jotting down notes. "How fast can you get the job done?"

"If I was able to start in the morning—"

"You'll start work *tonight*," Dakota said.

"Two days?"

Maddie glanced at Lionel. "Cordell's party is two days away."

"Do it anyway," he said. "It won't be ready in time, but we might need a backup plan."

"Bristol, I want volunteers." Dakota's fist clenched. "We know exactly where those containers are. Worst-case scenario, I want someone at each site to help evacuate the civilians. And, if they have to, hold the hydras off as long as possible. Make sure they know what happened to Phoenix. I want them to understand exactly what they're volunteering for."

"Meanwhile, my people in New York are working on getting another flask for a cunning-call," Maddie said. "We need the Golden Fleece."

"You still think Jason has it?" Lionel asked.

"He has it. I would bet...well, I *am* betting everything on it, aren't I? He'll be heading back across the country once his final delivery is done. He wouldn't want to miss the big event. So we know he started from Florida. Moved east to west. What's the westernmost address on the list?"

"Los Angeles," Bristol said.

Maddie's thumb tapped her fingertips as she counted under her breath.

"So that's...twenty-seven hundred miles, give or take,

two days on the road minimum, and that's only if you stop for nothing but fuel. He has to have already finished the last delivery, so he's either already in New York or he's headed there now. We can narrow down his possible routes. He can't take just any highway, and I don't think that road train he's driving is anywhere near street-legal."

"I'll put my team on task," Bristol said. "If we can cut the possibilities down to a handful, they can start combing speed-camera and traffic-copter surveillance footage. A road train isn't exactly inconspicuous."

"A road train followed by a pack of vintage muscle cars. They'll stick out like a sore thumb."

"Any idea about how we're going to handle Jason once we catch him?" Lionel asked.

"I was thinking about shooting him," Maddie said. "More than I usually think about it."

"Will that work? I mean, mythic reality, heroes, appropriate endings..."

"It won't *keep* him down," Maddie said. "But it's like when you stabbed Cordell. Didn't stop him, but it got him out of your hair for the night while the universe figured out how to rewrite his story. All we have to do is get our hands on the Golden Fleece and deliver it to my sisters in New York. I can deal with Jason—on a more permanent basis—once Cordell's been fed to the Furies."

She leaned back against the wall of the RV.

"Besides," she said, "I just really want to shoot him."

Bristol had been typing away, firing off messages and marching orders. She looked to Dakota.

"Chief, we're going to be stretching ourselves dangerously thin here. Too many jobs and not enough hands."

"I'm putting you in charge of the fallback plan," Dakota said. "Take the supply trailers, take the doctor here, and get us that poison gas. Task your team with finding Jason's truck. I only need a small battle group: ten warriors, a few sets of wheels."

"Where will you go?"

"North. We're seventeen hours away from New York, no reason not to get a head start. The drivers can sleep in shifts and change out when they get tired. Let us know as soon as your team spots anything. Maddie, Lionel, you ready for this?"

Lionel saw something when he looked into Maddie's eyes. Maybe it was a decision she'd made, maybe it was a reassurance just for him. Either way, the message was clear.

"We're ready," she said.

Together. Because *together* was the way things were going to be, all the way to the end of the line.

CHAPTER FORTY-SIX

The convoy split up on the road out of Holyoake. Dakota led the strike team, not that anyone spotting them on the highway would think they were anything but vacationers on a road trip. The long and loaded RV took point, faster than it looked; it wasn't nimble, but it made good time. Then came a pair of shorter, fatter motor homes—a white and blue Chateau and a Fleetwood painted in swirling stripes of silver and black. Lionel and Maddie filled out the rear of the pack in their SUV, alongside a platinum F-150 pickup truck. Heavy plastic crates lined the bed of the pickup, supplies for the road, mostly gathered from the munitions trailer.

Lionel drove while Maddie slept in the seat beside him, slumped back, softly snoring through the small hours before dawn. They changed places when she woke, pulling over just long enough to swap seats at the edge of the road. Then Maddie hit the gas to catch up with the others. Lionel leaned the seat back and drifted away.

They were both wide awake by early afternoon, and neither one felt like resting. They changed places when it came time to fuel up, and Maddie walked ahead to check in with Dakota while Lionel filled up the tank.

She came back running.

"Bristol radioed in," she said. "Her team spotted Jason's convoy on a traffic cam. They're an hour ahead of us."

The pump clicked. Lionel holstered the nozzle and screwed the gas cap on. "We're going to have to move fast."

"Dakota knows a shortcut. You drive, I'll navigate."

Even with the shortcut they were chasing a fast-moving target, and one hour stretched into three. The sun shimmered down, becoming a long topaz line on the dark horizon. The highway curved east and put the light in the rearview, nothing but stark headlights and billowing clouds of road dust ahead.

And somewhere, not far now, a whale to hunt.

~~

Jason drove through the big wide empty. Six lanes of highway carved through the countryside, drawing a line between dirty scrub and open fields of barren soil. The diamond-hot lights of the *Argo 2* swept over a farmhouse, a leaning windmill, a concrete factory in the distance with smokestacks spitting white smoke long after sunset. This nation was a broken machine still trying to work, cogs jerking and spinning, aching to make connections across the gulf of distance. Little pockets of life, here and there, electric lights struggling to push back the murky void in between.

"They're so small," he murmured.

Baker was riding shotgun tonight. He gave Jason a sidelong glance. "Hmm?"

"Was just thinking. The mortals. They're so small. But they fight so hard."

"Hell yeah, they do." Baker leaned back in his seat. It

thrummed, the vibrations of the wheels carrying up through the road train's cab. "Remember that scrap out in Kandahar? Partisans with duct-taped guns, looked like they hadn't eaten in a week, and they damn near took us out. We earned that paycheck."

Jason's big hands clenched the wheel. He frowned.

"Not the kind of fighting I meant."

Baker gave him a longer look now.

"You having second thoughts? We don't have to do this, man. We can tell Spears to pound sand."

"You having second thoughts?" Jason asked.

Baker held up an open hand. "Hey. You're the captain, we're the crew. You lead, we follow, and that's how it's going to be. But it's like I told you, back in Chicago: nobody's thrilled about the overkill. It's one thing to take on an armed force. You pay me, I'll gun down any man in any uniform, no questions asked and no fucks given."

He fell silent for a moment, letting the rest hang in the air between them.

"But Spears's plan..." Baker shook his head. "A whole lot of civvies are going to die."

"It's a wake-up call."

"Sure. The 'new age of heroes.' Just saying, you sure this'll be worth it in the end?"

The plan had sounded better when it came from Cordell's lips. He had it all together: poise, confidence, a verbal stride that never missed a step.

"Not going to lie," he had told Jason, walking him through the air-conditioned utopia of his Fifth Avenue condo. "I wanted Heracles."

Jason had squinted at him. "Heracles has been gone for centuries. It wasn't a gentle death."

"Yeah, well, I know that now, after throwing a few million dollars at the problem."

"You could have tried reading a book," Jason said.

"The same books that say *you* died? You know that's not how it works for men like us."

Fair point.

"Anyway," Cordell said, "you never got a Disney cartoon, but 'Jason and the Argonauts' still has name-brand recognition. That's what it's all about. Marketing."

"Marketing?"

"Sure. Look, I don't have a myth like you. I'm writing my myth, here and now. When I slay a hydra in the middle of Central Park and reveal myself as the son of Zeus, I'll get some big pop, no doubt. But having a real living icon of the ancient world at my side? Even better."

"*A* hydra. What about the other six you created?" Jason had asked.

"I take three, you take three. Cameras rolling every step of the way. Titanic, earth-shaking battles! *Kleos*, baby."

"I'm not sure you understand what the Lernaean Hydra really is," Jason said. "It exists to grow and devour and kill. It has no other purpose, no place in any natural food chain. Once you wake these things up, they will not stop, period. There's going to be a catastrophe."

Cordell patted his shoulder, easing him over to the bar. Bottles of top-shelf liquor lined rows of glass shelving, under-lit in sapphire blue.

"Why do you think I'm having you plant the freezers in major population centers? The carnage is the point, my new friend. The fear is the point. These mortals have to wake up. They have to be made to understand and accept that we're the only ones who can save them. Besides...they want this."

Jason's thick eyebrows lifted. "How do you figure that?"

"Look at their media, the stories they tell. Hollywood's become a superhero factory. It's all these people consume. What you're seeing is sublimated desire. It's not about the tights and the special effects. They really do remember, in the backs of their animal brains. They remember the glories of the old world, and they remember *us*. That's what they really want. They want their heroes back. To idolize, and worship, and rule over them like kings. So that's what we're going to give them. Don't turn your back on your true purpose, Jason. Don't refuse your birthright."

It all made sense when Cordell was talking.

That was weeks and miles ago, a cross-country trip and almost back again, and motives got hazy out on the open, empty road. Jason asked himself questions that just led to more questions, and he didn't *like* questions, he didn't like not being certain and sure and brave, so he shut it all down.

His fingers drummed the steering wheel.

"Everything's going to be fine," he told Baker. "How are we on time?"

Baker glanced at his phone. "There's a truck stop twenty miles ahead. If we refuel and drive through the night, we'll hit the outskirts of New York by sunup. Then we can catch a few hours' shut-eye and be rested and ready for the big show tomorrow night."

~~

A small crew of Amazons were getting locked and loaded in the belly of Dakota's RV. Dakota was on the phone with Maddie.

"We've got 'em spotted about a mile ahead. The road train and a posse of cars spread out behind it. Question about the Golden Fleece. Is it indestructible?"

"Hasn't been put to the test, to my knowledge," Maddie said.

Behind Dakota, one of the women held up the burnished olive tube of a grenade launcher, a question in her eyes. Dakota replied with a headshake.

"So we need to *stop* the truck, not destroy it. What about Jason's entourage?"

Maddie didn't take long to think about it.

"If they surrender," she said, "they can walk away."

Dakota nodded and hung up, then looked back to the gathered warriors.

"She says we're going to have to kill them all."

"Orders?" one asked.

"Speed and precision. We get in, we get this done, we get out. If we're here long enough to draw the police, we'll be knee-deep in shit all night. Careful with the truck, the cargo might be delicate. We take the escorts out first, then we go for the tires. Pass me that launcher."

~~

"Don't like that," Baker muttered.

Jason gave him a look. "Hmm?"

He nodded at the side mirror. The glass glowed soft and white.

"We've been the only people on this highway for the last hour."

"Welcome to the middle of nowhere," Jason said.

"So what's with the whole convoy of campers rolling up behind us?"

A whistle split the air. Jason saw a flash of silver in the corner of his eye, like a sparrow with steel wings.

The sparrow crash-landed into the left lane, a hundred yards up, and detonated in a fireball.

Chunks of shattered asphalt hit the cab's windshield. Jason wrenched the wheel hard, the pack on the *Argo 2*'s heels swerving to escape the blast. He snatched up the radio handset.

"Jonas! Saravia! Buy us some breathing room and scatter that formation. Everybody else, stick close." He looked to Baker. "Where'd you say that truck stop was?"

"Eighteen miles ahead now, give or take. Why?"

Jason gritted his teeth and glared at the rearview. He reached for the row of switches and buttons on the dashboard, controls for the *Argo 2*'s custom arsenal.

"Because that's my fucking *wife* back there. Last time I trust Cordell to get the job done."

"She made friends, looks like."

"Friends who won't want to fight an army of cops. That's why they hit us in the middle of nowhere. We reach civilization, they'll back off. Of course, that's plan B."

"What's plan A?"

"They want a battle," Jason said.

He flipped a rocker switch. The trailers hummed, onboard generators whirring to deadly life.

"So we can battle," he said. "I don't mind. I don't mind at all."

CHAPTER FORTY-SEVEN

Five cars sped in the road train's wake. The cloud-blue Cadillac, the Country Squire, and the Studebaker moved tight, swerving around the ruptured asphalt and forming a protective shield.

The Thunderbird and its partner, a midnight-black '75 Dodge Charger, pulled a bootlegger reverse. Tires screamed as they spun out, whipping around to make a 180-degree turn, pointing the wrong way on the six-lane highway and facing the oncoming convoy.

Like jousters at a medieval tournament they lurched into battle, charging the Amazons head-on.

Burning flares erupted from the fore-trailer of the *Argo 2*, sizzling into the sky. Lionel threw a hand over his eyes as they burst like white-phosphorus bombs, turning night to blinding day. Ribbons of raw twisting sunlight drifted down, sparking fires where they hit the scrub alongside the highway.

"That truck is huge," Lionel said. "Any idea how we're going to stop that thing?"

"We don't need to stop the truck," Maddie said.

She slid a fresh magazine into her semiautomatic and racked the slide.

"We just need to stop the driver."

~~

Saravia first tasted death in 1937 Guadalajara, blown from his sniper perch by a stray shell from a Republican bomber. Jason's silhouette blocked the sun from his smoke-burned eyes, like an angel of the battlefield. He gave Saravia something sweet to drink, a taste of honey and apples and spring mornings, and took him by the hand to haul him back onto his feet.

Over eighty years of endless battle followed, one brushfire war to another across a globe that never knew the meaning of peace. Saravia would die for Jason. Without hesitation. He hadn't had to, yet. He was very good at killing.

The engine of his Thunderbird screamed as he stomped on the gas, heading straight for the oncoming convoy. One hand, blistered with pink burn scars, clutched the shaking steering wheel and held his course. The other reached to the passenger seat and scooped up a long-barreled revolver.

He picked his target: a blue-and-white motor home, muzzle flash popping from a window as the passengers opened fire. He curled his hand and his weapon around the windshield, feeling the rush of the hot breeze, and began squeezing off shots. Aiming, careful, going for the spot along the black windshield where he knew the driver was sitting. They closed the distance in the left lane, both vehicles rocketing toward each other, neither flinching. Close enough now to see the cracks, the motor home's windshield fracturing into a spiderweb of broken glass. A hundred meters and closing. Saravia was calculating range like he was staring through his sniper scope. Plenty of room left, plenty of room to swerve once he'd disabled the lead car—

Close enough now to see the shadow of the motor home's driver in his high beams. He saw his last bullet strike home, saw her slump against the steering wheel and drag it with her sagging corpse. The motor home spun out, wheels smoking as it turned sideways on the highway, and what had been a missile became a wall of thundering steel.

The Thunderbird swerved, angling for the shoulder. Too late. Saravia plowed into his target at ninety miles per hour, his body launching through the windshield a second before his engine erupted.

~~

Lionel wrenched the wheel and the SUV went veering, gliding across lanes to escape the sudden fireball. The burning wreckage of the motor home, vintage steel Thunderbird buried halfway into its belly like a torpedo, fired past on the left. Lionel's ears rang, his vision imprinted with the corona of the blast. On his right, the oncoming Charger jousted with the silver-and-black Fleetwood. Both drivers swerved at the last second, their sides scraping, paint and steel shearing away.

The Charger spun, pulling another spinout and reverse. It poured on the gas, coming up behind the convoy fast.

Dakota's RV accelerated, advancing on the speeding road train. It became a gunship, ports and windows open along one side and steel barrels bristling. As one they began to spit fire. Bullets pelted the *Argo 2* in a flashing storm, clanging off bulletproof glass and reinforced steel. Doubled-up tires, built for military use in the harshest landscapes, sucked up bullets and kept rolling as the hubcaps sparked. The Country Squire, a station wagon from the seventies with a souped-up engine out of a modern garage, swung out of formation and roared up between the road train and Dakota's RV. Windows hissed down and a pair of long guns opened up, stitching pitted bullet holes along the RV like moon craters.

Another metal-winged sparrow screeched through the air, fired from the passenger side of the silver-and-black motor home. The rocket-propelled grenade shattered the back window of the Studebaker, landing between the passenger and the driver seat.

Then it erupted. Roiling flames and gouts of black smoke swallowed the vintage sedan as the air took on the stench of a gasoline fire. The Cadillac, right behind it, veered away from the wreckage. The Argonaut behind the wheel oversteered, lost control, propelling the Caddy's nose toward the scrub-littered embankment at the side of the road. It hit the incline, flipped off its wheels, and went into a roll, Detroit steel crumpling like tin foil in a giant's fist.

The driver of the black Charger shifted lanes, focused on his target.

~~

Loose munitions rolled across the belly of the silver-and-black Fleetwood, jarred loose by their joust with the Charger. It was barely controlled chaos, as the motor home's crew scrambled to stay in the fight. Dakota's voice crackled over the dashboard radio, handing down instructions, changing the order of battle on the fly.

"—shift fire, take out that damn station wagon. Does anyone see where the Charger went? Rear guard, watch yourselves. He has to be coming back around for another pass."

Saratoga was focused on the fight ahead. She'd been recruited straight out of the military and she ran her crew with single-minded efficiency. She swayed on bent knees to keep her balance, clutching a hot firing tube as her driver swerved to avoid the wreckage of the Studebaker, and called for a reload.

"We're out," called the woman behind her, scooping up loose magazines from the mouth of an overturned ammo bin.

"How can we be—forget it, give me a pineapple. I'm going topside." Saratoga snatched a grenade from her outstretched hand and looked to a hatch in the motor home's roof. "Paris, get us closer. Radio Dakota, tell the driver to get ahead of the station wagon and force it back our way. Once they do, get right alongside it. I'm going to rain some hell the old-fashioned way."

She pulled the grenade's pin, keeping the firing lever tight in the grip of her tactical glove, and reached for the ladder with her free hand.

The black Charger boiled from the darkness with its headlights off, a phantom on the highway. Its grille crumpled as it rammed into the back of the motor home at full speed.

The live grenade went flying from Saratoga's jolted hand, hitting the debris-littered floor, bouncing and spinning away. She lunged after it, throwing herself in a tackle with arms outstretched as she shouted a warning.

~~

Maddie cursed under her breath as the Fleetwood erupted. Windows blasted out in gouts of flame and the side door rocketed off its hinges, a severed arm still clutching the handle. The Charger shot around it and clicked its high beams on, dazzling Lionel's eyes in the rearview mirror.

He swerved left and stomped the brakes. The Charger blazed past on the right, brake lights flaring as the driver tried to compensate. Maddie anticipated Lionel's move, already taking aim through the open passenger window as hot wind gusted into the cab. Her first two shots sparked off the up-armored steel door, leaving nothing behind but silver claw marks across matte-black paint. The Charger peeled away, killing its headlights again, a shark diving back into deep water.

"Get us closer," Maddie said.

"To the Charger?"

"No." She nodded up the road. "To the *Argo*."

She put her phone to her ear, reaching for her seatbelt with the other hand, the strap unbuckling and flying free.

"Dakota. Is the ammo truck still in the fight?"

"Fifty yards behind you, why?"

"Radio to cover us," Maddie said. "I'm boarding the road train. I'll open up an opportunity for you. Get ready to use it."

~~

Machine-pistol fire rattled like hail from a gunport and the Country Squire's side wheels detonated. The station wagon fishtailed wildly as it rode on its rims, bare steel grinding the highway in a shower of sparks.

Dakota reloaded on the go, marching to the front of the RV, and snatched up the radio handset.

"All hands, Madison is boarding. Protect the SUV at all costs until she gets onto that truck. Repeat, *protect that SUV*."

One of Dakota's fighters fell back from an open window,

sliding a fresh round into a bolt-action rifle. She'd taken fire from the station wagon, one sleeve of her blouse sodden and scarlet and blood trickling down her hand as she worked the bolt. Her face was sweat-slick and pale.

"That thing," she said. "I don't know what kind of Frankenstein tech they built it with, but nothing that heavily armored should be able to move that fast. We can't crack it."

"Keep shooting, keep them distracted." Dakota moved back through the RV, eyes on a long, bulky rifle case, strapped down and double-locked. "I'm grabbing the fifty. I only need one perfect shot."

~~

Lionel leaned into the wheel, the *Argo 2* in his sights. Fresh flares erupted from the fore-trailer, igniting the night sky. Maddie holstered her pistol and grabbed the open window at her side with both hands.

"You sure this is a good idea?" he said.

"Remember what I said about not asking scary questions if you don't want an honest answer?"

She lifted herself up, bracing one sneaker on the passenger seat. Then she paused.

"Hey," she said. "I love you."

"Love you too," he said.

"Get close and hold it steady."

Then she was up and out, hoisting herself onto the SUV's roof and carefully rising to her feet. Lionel was gentle on the accelerator, wheel clenched in his grip as he closed the distance between them and the back of the *Argo*'s rear trailer. Fifty feet now and shrinking. He'd have to get just close enough to nudge bumpers, but not close enough to collide and throw Maddie off her perch, and hold perfectly steady long enough for her to jump across.

One mistake, and she was dead. She was counting on him now. Lionel's jaw ached and he forced himself to unclench it, forced himself to focus on the flickering white line of the highway.

High beams flashed in the rearview. The midnight-black Charger blazed from the darkness, firing across two lanes on a collision course. Lionel sped up as much as he dared, trying to seal the gap in time, stomach knotting as the Charger roared in.

A savior swooped in from the other direction. The platinum F-150, bed laden with supply crates, sideswiped the Charger and sent it off course. The Charger's tires screeched, rear fishtailing, the Argonaut behind the wheel struggling to keep the muscle car under control. He straightened out and slid behind Lionel, angling for another attack.

The back of the road train filled Lionel's windshield. He inched forward as far as he dared, breath held, bumpers a fraction of an inch from kissing as they barreled down the highway at eighty miles an hour.

A shadow flitted overhead, graceful as an acrobat. Maddie scampered onto the hood and launched herself toward the trailer, grabbing the dangling chain for opening the back doors and pulling herself up, hand over hand, as the chain rattled. She mounted the lip and clambered onto the *Argo*'s back.

CHAPTER FORTY-EIGHT

Jason was focused on the RV riding alongside his rig and keeping pace, muzzle flash blaring from a string of open windows and gunports. The damage display on the cab's console was in the green: two ruptured tires but they were still rolling strong, fuel lines stable, nothing but pockmarks and lost paint.

"Time till we hit that truck stop?" he said.

Baker gave a nervous look at the passenger-side window. A stray round struck home in front of his face. The high-caliber slug left a tiny chip in the glass.

"Five minutes. They're not backing off."

"They will. We just—" Jason paused, eyes on the console. The cargo-weight meter was flickering. Fluttering off, on, off, on, green to amber, matching the cadence of light footsteps running along the trailers. "Need you to do something for me."

"Name it."

Jason's side window rolled down. He shot a glance to the roof of the cab.

"Take the wheel," he said.

~~

The F-150 dueled with the Charger, side-slamming it

again and sending the muscle car reeling. It came back just as hard. The pickup's side door crumpled, mirror dangling on a twisted cable, while the Charger looked like a chewed wad of bubblegum.

The Charger veered in. The F-150 braked, falling back, then poured on steam. The Amazon behind the wheel hooked a fast curve, turning her nose toward the Charger's left back side, and then hit the gas.

They collided with a scream of tortured metal, and one of the Charger's back tires blew in a storm of shredded rubber. It became a moving roadblock, both vehicles locked together in a clinch, jolting to a shuddering stop in the middle of the highway as the chase left them both behind.

The Argonaut in the Charger didn't hesitate. His gun, a .357 with a pearl-handled grip, sat nestled on the vinyl seat at his side. He snatched it up and kicked his door open. He had just enough time to register two things: the shadow standing on the steaming asphalt, at the edge of a fractured headlight beam, and the rifle cradled in her grip.

She squeezed the trigger. Bullets riddled his chest, cratering his ribs and spitting gouts of blood, turning the crumpled muscle car into a coffin.

~~

Maddie moved in a low and graceful crouch, the night wind billowing against her face and whipping her hair as she crept along the top of the speeding fore-trailer. She was halfway there when a hulking figure pulled itself up from the roof of the cab.

Jason stared her down, half of his face glowing under the bone-white moon.

"Told you I'd be back with reinforcements," she said.

"It's over, Jason. We know about Cordell's plan, about the hydras. We even know the exact addresses where you hid the freezer units."

He rose up to his full height and spread his boots apart, getting his footing as the rig swayed dangerously beneath them.

"Doesn't matter," he said. "You'd never get to them all in time."

"Tomorrow night, right? The 'Gala for the People.' That's when Cordell is going to set them all loose."

"His plan. Not mine."

"You went along with it," Maddie said.

He didn't have an answer for that. Just a narrow-eyed glare and a sullen pout.

"I came for the Golden Fleece," she said.

He cast his gaze downward. Just for a second, a flicker so fast she almost missed it. But there was the tell. *It's here. On the truck.*

"It's mine," he said. "You know what the fleece stands for? The right to rule. The right to be a king. I earned it."

"I held your hand every step of the way. *I* earned it. I could have gotten the damn thing myself."

"You *supported* me," he said. "That's not the same thing as earning it."

Maddie rolled her eyes. "I'm not having this argument. Hand over the fleece and you and whatever's left of your crew can walk away."

"And if I don't?"

Maddie's eyes became pits of shadow. They caught the moonlight, tiny opal pinpricks glowing in the night.

"I'm here on Hekate's business, Jason. Don't stand in her way. *Never* stand in her way."

He cracked his knuckles.

"Think I'll take my chances," he said.

He came at her like a juggernaut. Her hand slapped her hip, drew her pistol, and he was already on top of her, knocking her hand aside with a blow hard enough to break her grip. The pistol fell, spinning across the speeding trailer, tumbling over the side and into the dark. She ducked under a wild punch and drew breath, conjuring a curse to her lips. The first syllable crackled free, kissing the wind-whipped air with static electricity, as he snapped out a kick. The heel of his boot fired into Maddie's belly, driving the air from her lungs, shattering the spell.

She fell backward, rolling, falling along the trailer's roof. She dug her toes in, frantic to stop her slide as she careened toward the edge.

~~

Lionel pulled alongside the road train, advancing on the left while Dakota's RV pelted it with fire from the right. He craned his neck, watching Jason advance on Maddie. Then he watched her fall.

The SUV surged up alongside the truck, running parallel with the cab, then passing it. Lionel tugged the wheel and swerved out in front. His brake lights flared.

He slammed against the seatbelt, his spine jolting, as the *Argo 2* rammed him from behind. He tugged the wheel, holding fast, keeping himself on course, and tried again, using the SUV's weight to slow the monster down. Another impact threw him against the harness and knocked the SUV's bumper loose, crumpled metal rolling free and chewed up beneath the road train's tires.

No good. The SUV just wasn't heavy enough. Even if he put both feet on the brakes and pressed down for all he was worth, the massive engine under the cab's long hood could push him along until its fuel ran dry. He had to try something different. And a hell of a lot riskier.

Lionel slowed more carefully now, letting the nose of the truck bump against the SUV and shove him along. He hit the cruise control button, matching the truck's speed. He looked at the steering wheel, trembling in his clammy grip, and worked the math. They were barreling down a straight stretch of highway—for now—but if he let go for more than a few seconds any change in momentum would send the SUV rocketing off in one direction or another.

He'd have to be fast. Faster than he'd ever been in his life. Driven by equal parts courage and terror, he made his move.

~~

Perched behind the wheel, Baker stared in disbelief at the SUV trying to bar the behemoth's path. He sped up to give it another bone-rattling *bump*. It still wouldn't clear the road.

"Gotta be kidding me. What've you got under that hood? Eight cylinders? You got two and a half tons of weight? Three, tops? Might as well be driving a ten-speed bike." Baker punctuated his words by hitting the heel of his hand against the middle of the wheel, air horns blasting. "Get. Out. Of. The. Way."

The driver's-side door of the SUV swung wide. Baker blinked.

"Oh, you're not gonna—"

In one smooth motion Lionel pulled himself onto the roof of the SUV. Uncontrolled, it instantly started to veer, pushed off-center by the truck's momentum. He rose from a crouch, ran, and jumped.

The SUV spun out, driverless and wild. Lionel flew and landed on the nose of the truck, clinging to the hot metal. The two men stared at each other from opposite sides of the bulletproof windshield.

~~

Maddie was crouched, a spider at the back lip of the trailer. She ran her curled knuckles across her lip. It came away bloody. She gave Jason a scarlet, feral smile.

They'd been dancing, trading punches at the edge of oblivion with the asphalt roaring beneath them and the night wind howling. He came at her, hands sweeping down like a pile driver, and she twirled out from under the shadow of his fists. She shot a punch at his belly. He twisted, tried to catch her wrist. She feinted and went for his eyes. He dodged back, teetering close to the trailer's edge. Then he dropped low, deceptively fast for his bulk, and kicked out a steel-toed boot.

She jumped as the trailer suddenly lurched to one side. Then the other, the truck veering drunkenly from lane to lane. A giant trying to shake a flea from its back. *Not us*, Maddie realized. *Whoever's driving wouldn't put Jason in danger like this. Unless—*

She saw the SUV in the ditch at the side of the road, headlights pointed down at the barren scrub. *Lionel.*

The truck careened left again, nearly throwing them both. Maddie dropped to one knee, pressing a palm to the thrumming steel beneath her, and leaned as the truck veered right. The driver was trying to throw Lionel off. One problem. He was predictable. Same hard turn, same three seconds before he wrenched the wheel in the other direction. The width of the road, and the RV still peppering the bulletproof cab with small-arms fire, limited how far he could go.

She could work with that.

~~

Lionel's legs kicked at empty air. He clung to the truck's hood, nothing but his weakening grip between him and the *Argo*'s deadly tires. In the driver's seat Baker was cursing, yanking the wheel back and forth, a brutal and reckless hell-ride as he tried to knock his boarder loose.

Lionel caught a glimpse of the RV, running parallel to the truck. A side door hung open, electric light burning out from within. Dakota stood in the doorway, legs spread in a shooter's stance, bracing a monster of a rifle. Lionel wasn't a gun guy, but he knew the incarnation of overkill when he saw it. It was a fifty-caliber, an anti-material rifle designed to shoot engine blocks and stop military machines in their tracks. Maybe it would work against the *Argo*, maybe it wouldn't, but one look from Dakota and he knew what was expected of him.

Maddie couldn't deliver the distraction the Amazons needed, not while she was battling Jason on the trailer. It was all on him now.

He took a deep breath, waited for the pendulum of the swinging truck to hit its peak—the one sweet second before it veered back in the other direction—and scrambled up the hood. He kicked off, one dizzying heartbeat in free fall, and grabbed with one hand onto the cab's side mirror. His foot flailed out, reaching for purchase on the rungs beneath the driver's-side door. His fingers curled around the handle.

~~

Maddie rocked on her hips. Jason's fist snapped in the

air, his jacket whipping back, knuckles falling an inch short of her nose. He didn't let up. She turned her shoulders, twirling on one foot as the trailer veered left and he threw another wide punch. She counted under her breath. Now that she knew the rhythm of the truck, how it would sway, moving with it was as easy as dancing.

"Think you're going to tire me out?" he said, laughing. His boot lashed out at her. She dodged—too slow. It caught her on the hip and sent her flying. Maddie curled her legs under her, slowing her skid, gritting her teeth against the explosion of pain lancing up her side. She pushed herself up to a panther crouch.

"No," she said. "I needed to keep you busy while I moved you closer to this side of the trailer. Then I just needed to wait."

He squinted at her. "Wait for what?"

The cab reached the apex of its swing, the driver still wildly trying to shake Lionel loose. He spun the wheel in the other direction. The trailer careened to the right, momentum pushing Jason backward, making him wobble at the trailer's edge. Maddie lurched forward, rolled onto her back, and kicked out with both feet.

Her heels drove into Jason's kneecap. She heard a satisfying *snap* as he teetered backward, arms pinwheeling—then plunged over the side of the trailer. He hit the highway, bouncing, tumbling into the darkness.

~~

The driver's-side door of the cab swung open. Lionel clung to it, the road whipping by under his dangling feet, while Baker held the wheel with one hand and grappled for the inside handle with the other. Lionel bucked his hips, swinging one foot around the door, kicking at Baker's fingers.

"Don't know who you are, but you picked the wrong fight, asshole." Baker grunted, flailing at him while he struggled to hold the truck steady.

"Who, me?" Lionel said. "I'm the distraction."

He flicked his gaze back over Baker's shoulder. Baker turned.

The RV had pulled perfectly parallel to the cab, lining up the open doorway with the impenetrable glass. Dakota had the bulky rifle shouldered, the shot zeroed in with absolute precision.

Blue flame erupted from the weapon's boxy muzzle. A single bullet, long and sharp and lethal like the brass head of a huntress's spear, plowed through the passenger-side window and trailed a volcanic blast of shards in its wake. Then it punched through Baker's skull, in one side and out the other, on a wet-ruby geyser of blood and shattered bone.

Lionel grabbed Baker's sleeve and pulled. The corpse sagged from the driver's seat, then fell free. It hit the highway and the truck swayed as its tires pulverized the dead man's body. Lionel's muscles were on fire, but he dug deep and found one last burst of strength. He swung himself around the door, shoes grabbing a precarious perch on the outside rungs of the cab. Then he climbed up and inside.

The *Argo* was already off course, careening straight for the side of the road. He hauled on the wheel, bringing it back under control as he hit the brakes—slowly, more slowly than his pounding heart wanted him to—and brought the road train to a shuddering, squealing stop.

CHAPTER FORTY-NINE

The back door of the conquered truck rattled upward. Overhead LEDs clicked on in unison, casting pale blue light down across a cavernous bay long swept clean.

"No surprise to find it empty," Dakota said, giving Maddie a sidelong glance. "He finished his deliveries. No fleece, either. You think he stashed it somewhere?"

Maddie leaned into Lionel. His arm curled around her waist, keeping her steady. She'd survived, but not without a quilt of fresh bruises and reopened cuts. That was fine. She could keep moving. One foot in front of the other.

"No," she said. "He'd keep it close. Once he had it in his hands again, after all this time, he wouldn't want to let it out of his sight."

She led them around the twin trailers, to the cab. Steel rungs led up to the open driver's-side door. She climbed up, careful of her footing, and studied the scene. She could smell Jason here. His musk, that huntsman's cologne he always wore. Or maybe it was just the ghost of a memory. Her nose wrinkled.

She slid the driver's seat forward. A fat vinyl pouch nestled behind it, like a stash for an emergency poncho.

She brought it down with her, knowing what she'd find when she peeled the zipper back.

It looked the same as it always did, untouched by time. The Golden Fleece was as vibrant as the day it was crafted, the curly wool glistening. Even in the dark of night, it seemed to capture sunlight, and the warmth of a summer day radiated from the pouch.

"It's...beautiful," Lionel breathed.

Maddie glanced up at him. The fleece glowed softly, casting their faces in shifting tones of molten gold.

"Do you want to touch it?"

"Is it safe?" he asked.

"Nothing's safe, but life isn't a museum. Want to touch it?"

Lionel's fingers trailed across the shimmering wool. His shoulders shivered.

"Whoa."

"Uh-huh." She looked to Dakota. "You?"

"I'll pass." Dakota's eyes were made of ice-flecked steel. "Will it work? To bring the Furies?"

Maddie took one last, long look at the fleece. She tugged the zipper back into place, sealing it away.

"Cordell Spears murdered his own mother. The fleece bore witness. Two or three plucked strands should be enough to fuel the charm." Maddie's palm pressed against the pouch, feeling the warmth beneath the slick vinyl. "It'll work. And I'm sorry."

Dakota glanced over her shoulder, back to the RV. The survivors were regrouping, taking stock of what they had and what they'd lost. Mostly what they'd lost.

"We're the daughters of Artemis. That means we hunt. We fight. Sometimes it means we don't come home again.

Considering what's at stake here, the price of *not* fighting is steeper."

The Amazon locked eyes with Maddie.

"But my sisters died in your service tonight. Which means you owe us a blood price."

Maddie held up the vinyl pouch. Dakota nodded.

"That'll do," Dakota said. "We'll get you to New York. You put Cordell in the ground, the kind of underground he can never come back from, and all debts are paid."

~~

So this is Tartarus, Jason thought.

A dusty wind blew across his tear-stained face, stinging his eyes in the darkness. He limped through rough scrub, dragging his left leg in the dirt, every step a percussive explosion of pain.

It wasn't enough for me to die, drunk and alone, everything taken from me. No. They had to bring me back one more time, shame me one more time, humiliate me one more time before casting me into the outer darkness. Who decreed it? Hera? Hekate? Doesn't even matter. Nothing matters.

He stumbled to a stop. He took a deep breath, wind dust caking the back of his raw throat, and bellowed at the starless void.

"*I did nothing wrong!*"

His defiance echoed back at him, ebbing, fading to silence. Useless.

And a lie.

Jason walked.

In the distance, a white corona glowed against the darkness. Olympus? Jason tortured himself with hope. He limped faster, praying to any god who would still listen, praying that this was his redemption.

He crested a rise and gazed down upon the electric lights of the truck stop. Plastic glowing signs offered gas, car washes, a twenty-four-hour diner.

Down at the pumps, a young man with two days of blond stubble was fueling up his Honda. The back was stuffed with dorm-room furniture, every inch of space packed tight. His bloodshot eyes focused on the big man hobbling toward him, and the revolver swaying in his hand.

"Give me your keys," Jason said.

"Okay, okay!" He held up his hands. "I'll give you my wallet, okay? I only have twenty bucks, but you can take the credit card—"

"I don't want your fucking money. I'm not a—" Jason shoved his gun in the kid's face. His teeth gritted until his jaw started to shake. "Give me the keys. *Now*."

Jason was two miles away, cramped in a too-small seat and his hands strangling a trembling steering wheel while the speedometer kissed ninety-five, when he started to scream.

~~

The first time Lionel came to New York, his eyes were wide but he couldn't see a thing.

He had only ever seen the teeming concrete sprawl, the mountain spires of granite and glass, on movie and television screens. When he caught his first glimpse of an ambulance in FDNY livery, he wondered what show they were shooting, then realized he was actually here. The entire world knew New York from stories, a place that existed in fiction as much as it did in reality. The streets ran thick with mythology.

Then Lionel learned the wall between fiction and reality was nothing but the border between the pages of a book.

He stepped across, out of his rational world and into a fairy tale. He had been there ever since.

He found a world of wonders, and terrors. And responsibilities. Seeing the truth meant you could never stand on the sidelines again. And when that world needed help, he had to stand up and do his part.

The convoy, what was left of it, rolled into Brooklyn at dawn.

They snaked through streets already awake with traffic and backing up fast. Delivery trucks and taxicabs jostled with standing-room-only buses for position along the old, angled streets of Red Hook. The sunrise glinted gold off the icy waters of the Hudson River, and the air smelled like hickory smoke.

Their destination wasn't far from the waterfront. Maddie had gotten a text on the way, pointing them to an auto-body shop ringed by a rusted fence. A woman in grease-flecked overalls and a short-chopped haircut was waiting, waving them around the crumbling brick garage and into the lot. The mechanic opened the back door for them.

The regular employees had been sent home for the day, and the big shutter doors stayed down and locked. Electric light flooded the vehicle bay. The delegation from the Sisterhood of New Amsterdam, six women and two men, stood gathered around a folding card table. They turned as one as the Amazon crew—still armed to the teeth—fanned out along the cinder-block wall.

Agnes Ashcroft met Dakota halfway across the oil-stained concrete floor. The elderly lawyer, her steel-gray hair pinned in a bun with lacquered chopsticks, flashed a string of hand signs. Dakota responded in kind, a silent exchange of ancient custom, dark fingers fluttering with military precision. They nodded, as one, and clasped each other's forearms.

"Glad to have you working with us," Agnes said.

"Somebody has to teach you people how it's done."

"Our turn now." She nodded back over her shoulder. "Madison. Will this do?"

One of the witches brandished a long, thin flask of white clay, a twin to the cunning-call Maddie had crafted for Kayla Lambert. Maddie's palm hovered over the flask, an inch away, feeling the power sleeping there. She nodded.

"Exactly right. And we have the fleece. All I need is a few solid hours, uninterrupted, in a room equipped for ritual."

The back door whistled shut. The mechanic leaned against it and folded her arms.

"Basement. My shop's a Sisterhood outpost. I keep an emergency shelter down there, with all the fixings." She looked Maddie up and down. "You're her, huh?"

The prodigal. *The witch who ran away from home.* Maddie took the flask and cradled it in her pale fingers, feeling the weight of an expectant silence. She turned, put one foot forward and lifted her chin, her posture offering a challenge.

"I'm her," Maddie said. "And I'm here to help."

"You sticking around, after?"

"If the Queen wills it."

The mechanic nodded, nonchalant. "Cool. All right, then. My shop is your shop. You use any tools, put 'em back where you found them."

A woman in a smart pantsuit and kitten heels, from the Sisterhood's side of the room, bustled forward. She took Maddie's free hand in a firm, dry grip.

"We haven't been introduced yet. Jillian Shay, liaison to the mayor's office."

"Jillian makes things go away for us," Agnes observed.

Lionel knew what she meant. His first visit to New York, he'd seen the evidence of a subway-tunnel ghoul attack—including multiple dead bodies, none of them human—vanish into thin air. They'd implied it wasn't an uncommon incident.

"Not *this* particular thing." Jillian curled her lip. "I've explored every loophole, pulled every possible legal string, anything I could do to cancel or just delay Spears's gala. He outmaneuvered me at every point. As we speak, the main stage is being constructed and fencing is going up around Central Park. Gates open at two p.m., every ticket's been sold, and they're expecting a capacity crowd."

"So we can't even get in?" Lionel asked.

Over by the table, Mathers let out a derisive snort. The police detective wore a loose, spring-weight blazer over the bulge of her shoulder holster. She fanned out a handful of bright yellow tickets like they were a winning poker hand.

"I can get us in," she said. "And NYPD's handling crowd control, traffic, and security all around the park tonight. Slipping somebody past a cordon's not a problem for me, tickets or not. But first things first. We need to have a talk."

Lionel remembered his stint in a police interrogation room. "Last time we 'talked,' I was pretty sure you were going to beat the hell out of me."

"Had to see what you were made of. You passed the test. And Hekate put her mark on you—we can all see it, plain as the moon. But that doesn't mean you need to be in on this."

"Sure it does," Lionel said.

"You aren't one of us."

"My mother was."

"*She* was," Mathers said. "You've got free will, and nobody's making you do a damn thing. You can walk away, right now."

He understood what she was asking. Commitment. How far was he willing to go? He had already decided that, hundreds of miles ago. Now he just had to give it voice and make it real.

"If you'll have me," he said, "I'd like to join the Sisterhood."

"For your mother?"

"For me," he said, then cast a glance skyward. "And for her."

"Good answer. Agnes?"

"We had…extensive discussions about you, during the Jimmy Sloane affair," the lawyer said, approaching Lionel with a brisk stride. "Largely contingent on how you proved yourself—which you did, with aplomb. It was generally agreed that we'd hold the door open and wait for you to ask. Now then. No time for a formal initiation in the heart of a crisis. Ceremony will keep until tomorrow, if there is a tomorrow. Raise your left hand."

He did. She fixed him with her gaze.

"Lionel, born of Sheila, do you—acting of your own free will, unencumbered by promise or pact—offer your oath to the Sisterhood of New Amsterdam? Will you stand in defense of our coven and our people, and devote yourself to Hekate's design? Offering even your life, should it be necessary?"

Easy answer. "I will."

"Will you keep our secrets, and guard them well?"

"I will," he said.

"By your oath, let our bargain be sealed."

Lionel recognized the skeleton key in Mathers's hand. He had found it, six inches of old brass with an elaborate and scalloped fleur-de-lis design, gathering dust in a hack reporter's attic. Hidden away, and waiting for him. It had gone missing after his battle with Jimmy Sloane, while he recovered in a hospital bed. He thought it had been lost forever.

"My mother's key," he whispered.

"Yours now," Mathers said and pressed it into his palm. "Welcome to the Sisterhood."

"Now let's get to work," Agnes said.

CHAPTER FIFTY

A council formed around the makeshift strategy table. A paper map of the city, held down at the corners by an ashtray and a half-empty cup of ice-cold coffee, marked the impending battleground. Mathers pointed the tip of a red marker to the long rectangle of Central Park, dominating the heart of Manhattan. Then she drew a quartet of tiny circles.

"Four ways in. This side, they'll be taking tickets at West Eighty-First and Eighty-Sixth. Other side of the park, East Seventy-Ninth and Eighty-Fifth. Gates open at two and the kickoff is at six." She drew another bigger circle. "All the action's happening on the Great Lawn, but Spears's permits extend to the entire park. Whole place is on lockdown."

"By the NYPD?" Lionel asked.

She shook her head. "His own technical and security staff. Which we have to assume includes his hydra wranglers. They'll need the beast in place and ready before the show starts."

"Lots of ways to disguise a refrigeration unit," Dakota said. "Judging from the size of Jason's truck, and the number of units he was hauling...they're big, but not *that* big."

"I've been thinking about that," Maddie said.

All eyes turned her way.

"I thought it was odd at first. What we learned in Florida—that he had Jason carrying the six other refrigerators west, while his Triad smugglers brought one straight to New York ahead of schedule. But it makes sense. What does Cordell Spears want more than anything tonight?"

"Spectacle," Lionel said. "He's going to shake the entire world awake. It's got to be big and flashy and unforgettable."

"Exactly. He wants everyone to see him battling a monster. Not a small, sleepy one, either. That's fine for the other six. They can take their time, growing and rampaging, before Spears gets around to dealing with them—solving the problem he created, and getting applauded for it. But tonight has to be explosive, right from the start."

"Dr. Wolcott said the hydra grew to fill any containment unit they placed it into," Lionel said.

"Hence the early direct delivery," Maddie said. "He moved it into a bigger container and probably let it grow for a while before refreezing it for tonight's show. We're looking for something big, but still concealable. A semi trailer, a production van. It'll have to be close to the Great Lawn, so that when it busts free, it'll see a big crowd full of yummy people."

"And so he can slay it for the cameras and save them all," Mathers said. "Or at least most of them. We know he's fine with civilian casualties as long as he comes off looking like a hero. What options do *we* have if this thing gets loose?"

"Wolcott's in a lab, synthesizing a batch of Athena-18," Dakota said. "Says it kills these things stone dead."

"But we won't have it here tonight, when we need it."

"Tomorrow night at the earliest."

Agnes looked to Maddie and Lionel. "*Can* Spears defeat the hydra if it gets loose?"

"He's arrogant," Maddie said, "but he's not stupid. This is supposed to be the defining moment of his life, tonight. Safe to say he hasn't left any detail to chance."

Mathers's clenched fist rested on the map.

"I wanted to plant a sniper," she said. "Take him out as a just-in-case. I know he'd come right back to life tomorrow, but at least it'd ruin his big night. That said…if the hydra escapes, we might *need* his evil ass to help put it down. He gets everything he wants, but at least there'll be fewer casualties."

"So we don't let it escape," Lionel said. "We can be there at two when the gates open. We get in, we scour the park, and we find the containment unit. All we have to do is keep it offline until Maddie has the new flask ready."

Maddie held up a hand. "Speaking of, I need to get to work right now. We'll only get one shot at this and I can't rush the operation. It has to be perfect, first try."

"How long do you think it'll take?" Dakota asked.

"Optimistically?"

"Be pessimistic. Tends to be more accurate."

"I'll need most of the day," Maddie said. "I should have it ready by five or six."

"In that case," Agnes mused, "we'll need to task ourselves with some very difficult magic. Namely, finding a way to deliver that flask from Brooklyn to Manhattan, at high speed, in the middle of rush hour."

~~

Maddie and Lionel stood at the top of the basement stairs, stripped concrete descending into musty darkness. They held close, apart from the crowd at the table, sharing one last moment of calm before the storm.

"Welcome to the front lines," she said.

"No regrets. I was already here. We just made it official."

"Guess so." She reached up. Her fingers caressed his cheek. "I'd keep you here with me, but this isn't exactly a good teaching moment. More of a 'several unbroken hours of intense chanting and concentration' thing."

"I can do more good in the park, helping the scouting party. We'll find the containment unit before the show starts." He took a deep breath. "And hopefully—if we're very lucky—figure out a way to jam it until you get there with the flask."

"Watch yourself. Cordell knows your face."

Lionel had to smile. "I think this is one case where his ego might help us out. He doesn't think I'm any kind of a threat, and he wants to gloat. If he spots me in the crowd, he'll probably give me a front-row seat."

"And if Jason makes his way to the party, he'll be looking to screw your head off like a bottle cap. So be careful." Her hand drifted down to her hip. "You'd better be alive and in one piece when I get there tonight. Don't do anything crazy."

He tilted his head.

"Maddie? Last night I jumped onto the hood of a speeding truck."

"Don't do anything crazy by *my* standards."

"My threshold for reckless behavior was already pretty high before we met," he said. "I was a little notorious for it, but you're encouraging me to up my game."

"I'm a terrible influence, I know."

He pulled her close. Their lips met as his hand curled around the small of her back, and he kissed her like he wanted to steal her breath. They parted—eventually—and her cheeks were flushed. She gave him a sly smile.

"Talk about reckless."

"You're a terrible influence," he said. "But now I'm ready for battle."

"No battles. Just reconnaissance. Absolutely no battles until I get there."

He didn't say a word. He didn't want to make any promises he wasn't sure he could keep.

~~

After a lifetime of seeing it on television, Lionel still couldn't appreciate the size of Central Park until he stood there in person. Almost eight hundred and fifty acres of cultivated parkland, at the heart of one of the biggest cities in the world. Condos ringed the rectangular border, throwing up walls of granite and glass, every window a ten-million-dollar view of the lush rolling green.

Lionel was out on Fifth Avenue, standing in an endless line. The scouting party had split up, every explorer on their own and tasked with covering a different quadrant of the park. They'd have four hours, at most—and given how slowly the ticket holders were being let past the gate, he figured he'd lose at least an hour before he could begin his search. The park, beyond a line of temporary fencing, was on his left. He could see thick, bountiful trees from here, and an empty bicycle path, snaking down a man-made canyon. On his right, the avenue was choked solid and a chorus of angry horns drifted down from the traffic light at the end of the block. Traffic was rough at the best of times, and bringing a few thousand extra people to the island for a massive event was having a predictable effect.

Cordell, already flexing his muscles, Lionel thought. *The money and the influence to grind New York to a standstill, just because he wants to throw a party. And that's before he reveals his true nature to the world.*

The smell of falafel made his stomach grumble. A street vendor was cleaning up, tempting partygoers to abandon their space in line and join the growing queue in front of his cart. He wasn't the only one: more carts had taken up space on the gray octagonal paving stones, from halal to hot dogs, spice-laden steam kissing the hot city air and wafting down the sidewalk.

It was a quarter to four by the time he reached the gate. Private security guards, under the casual eye of a couple of uniformed cops, were hand-wanding new arrivals and checking bags for contraband. He didn't have anything for them to find. He showed them his ticket and they moved him along with a disinterested wave.

Lionel put his reporter hat on and got to work.

Chunks of Central Park had been closed off—at least, as much as it was possible to "close off" a vast open-air park with a hundred winding paths. The barricades were more like guidelines, people hopping them freely, and security was spread too thin to offer much resistance. All the same, the crowds moved down the funnel to the vast open green of the Great Lawn. The soundstage was already up and waiting, with a full lighting rig and flanked by amplifiers that would fit in at any top-quality concert hall. Lionel watched the roadies scurrying, plastic passes dangling from lanyards around their necks as they set up the sound equipment.

East of the stage, the technical camp ate up a chunk of pasture. Parked RVs and minibuses jostled for space with equipment trailers, all of it dedicated to making the show run smooth as silk—and making sure that Cordell's message was broadcast to the world in real time. Lionel stepped over a fat orange cable, snaking its way through the grass, and went to get a closer look. The camp was an anthill of activity but he was watching doors, seeing which ones were in active use and which were locked up tight, hunting for any trailer that might be a hydra containment unit in disguise.

Perfect place to launch the attack, he thought. *Or is it? No. Everyone in the crowd, if they're not running in terror, is going to be whipping out their phones and filming the action. Cordell's counting on that. Last thing he needs is some eagle-eyed detective to look at the footage after the fact and ask why the hydra burst out of one of his own trailers.*

Close, then, but not one of the tech trailers. That said, he wanted a closer look. Cordell's hydra wranglers were on site, and he might be able to dig up a clue—

A hand, thrust toward his chest but not quite touching, jolted him from his thoughts. A roadie looked to Lionel's neck, hunting for a pass that wasn't there.

"Authorized personnel only," he said. "Party's behind you, pal."

Lionel didn't argue. All the same, he needed more access than this. He fell back and took a long, slow walk around the perimeter, hunting for a way in.

Then he saw his opportunity, walking through the tech

village with an entourage of roadies and bodyguards, jotting his signature on a clipboard. Cordell Spears.

Intuition gave him a plan. He wasn't sure if it was a good plan, but it was the only one he had. Lionel ducked out of sight, just for a moment, and took his phone out. "Agnes? I might have an opportunity here. It's risky—for me, I mean—but I need a little backup."

CHAPTER FIFTY-ONE

Cordell saw Lionel coming. He stopped in his tracks. Still wearing his easy smile, but his eyes shifted, uncertain, giving Lionel a visual pat-down. His bodyguards, enduring the afternoon heat in suits and dark glasses, sensed their master's energy and bristled.

"Lionel Page," he said. "Now this is a surprise. I mean, considering."

Considering you tried to murder me, Lionel thought. Cordell's hangers-on clearly weren't in on tonight's master plan. Cordell wouldn't want to say anything that might shock them. That was fine. Lionel could play along. He was about to risk his life on a gamble and a bluff, and he needed Cordell to be open to it.

"I thought I might be stuck down in Florida and miss the party," he said, "but I made it out at the last minute. Do you have a second? I won't take too much of your time."

"Sure thing. Guys? Just give us a few."

Cordell put his arm around Lionel's shoulder, tighter than he needed to, and walked him a little bit downwind. Just far enough that his voice, pitched low, didn't drift back to his followers.

"You do understand," he said, still smiling, "that I could

walk you around behind that trailer over there, punch a hole through your chest, rip out your heart, and show it to you before you died, right?"

He was perfectly aware. Cordell's arm was a yoke made of concrete. It squeezed against his neck.

"I know what you're planning," Lionel said, careful now.

"So you came to...what, take another shot? Come on, man. I can let the 'stabbing me to death' thing drop. I tried to kill you with poison gas, so I figure we're even on that score. But coming back for another round? When you know how this works? You know that old saying about the definition of insanity, right?"

"Doing the same thing over and over," Lionel said, "and expecting a different result."

"That's the one."

"I'm not here for a fight," Lionel said. "I'm here for the party."

Cordell let go of him. He turned, standing face-to-face, considering Lionel with fresh eyes.

"You mean..."

"Come on," Lionel said. "Don't make me say it. I've got my pride."

Cordell nodded, slow. Lionel's stomach clenched while he put on a contrite face. Pulling his shoulders in, his body language selling a lie. If Cordell didn't buy it—

"You've seen the light," Cordell said.

"I don't believe in fighting for lost causes."

"That's not the Lionel I met in Indiana."

"I've seen a hell of a lot of death between there and here. Too much of it. It's easy to be an idealist when blood isn't spilling. I thought I was above it all, that it couldn't change me, but..."

"But it does," Cordell said. "And now you know there's only one way forward for this world. The only way forward is *back*. And you know who needs to be calling the shots."

Lionel spread his hands. "Don't make me grovel, Cordell. Like I said, I've got my pride."

"Nah. Never." Cordell grabbed him, almost yanking him off his feet as he pulled Lionel into a bear hug. His meaty palm hammered his back. "We're good, bro. We're good."

He pushed him back, holding Lionel's shoulders.

"Like I said, I want you on my team. There are going to be opportunities opening up, in my new media division. I need the right people telling the right stories about me. Have to make sure the people get my message, the way I want it told."

"I'm interested," Lionel said.

"We'll talk after...well, you know." Cordell mimicked locking his lips with a key, shooting a glance at the waiting technicians behind him. "So, on the subject, I do have to ask..."

Here it comes, Lionel thought. He had anticipated a test of loyalty, if his bluff even got this far.

"I can't have interruptions or any weird emergencies tonight. Any of your buddies see the light too, or...?"

"We parted ways," Lionel said. "But I know what they're up to."

He led Cordell—and his security crew—to the edge of the Great Lawn. Agnes was making her way across the crowded field, peering over her bifocals, an NPR tote bag dangling off one shoulder. Lionel pointed her out. Then, as a pair of security guards swooped in to discreetly take her by the arms, he put the finger on a pair of Sisterhood scouts on the nearest hiking trail.

He didn't point out the other, more inconspicuous scouts who were watching from a distance, ready to swoop in if Cordell's men did anything rougher than kick them out of the park. Agnes had already made the arrangements: Detective Mathers was waiting out on West Fifty-Ninth Street with a couple of loyal uniforms, standing ready to hustle the "evicted" spies under a cordon and right back inside.

"I'm going to need protection," Lionel said. "These aren't forgiving people."

"Consider it covered. In the meantime, I've got a million things I've still gotta do before showtime, so—wait, how did you get in, anyway?"

Lionel shrugged. "Tickets were sold out, but slipping a twenty to the guy at the gate worked just fine."

"Sneaky." Cordell flashed a toothy grin. "But you need an upgrade. Petey, get my man here a VIP pass. Lionel, enjoy the show. We'll talk after. And when next we meet, it's going to be a very different world."

~~

Maddie sat cross-legged in a ring of red candles, their points shimmering, shifting in the humid, still darkness of the garage's basement. Smoke from kyphi resin, burning on a disk of glowing charcoal, touched the air with desert spice and wreathed around her head. She didn't feel the hard concrete beneath her anymore, or the sweat trickling down her spine. She'd left her body and become one with the work.

The brush in her hand painted sigils, scarlet pigment over warm white clay. The sigils were words she'd learned centuries ago and never forgotten, memories of ancient pacts, of obligations and reciprocity. She breathed them as she painted, and her breath turned the air to a mirage.

She reached to her side and took hold of a single curly strand from the Golden Fleece. The pelt rebelled against her touch. It was a piece of myth and stuck in time, meant to remain unchanging, inviolate.

"For justice," she whispered.

The curl pulled free. She put it to the mouth of the Aegean clay flask and dropped it inside.

~~

The laminated VIP pass around Lionel's neck was an all-access key to the kingdom. More access than Cordell probably realized. Lionel made his way through the tech village unimpeded, the roadies spotting the lanyard and glossy sheath and not bothering to challenge him. Or more likely, not wanting to be the person to ask one of Cordell Spears's personal friends to leave. Nobody wanted that kind of friction with the boss. Lionel had years of experience going places where he didn't belong—he put on a don't-mess-with-me face and a fast stride.

A quick circuit confirmed his suspicion: wherever the hydra was being kept, it wasn't here. He poked his head into one of the bigger trailers, curiosity guiding his footsteps. It sounded like static and smelled like weed. A tech with a shaggy beard and a mullet, suspenders over the shoulders of his crew shirt, was tuning up a soundboard. He gave Lionel the faintest nod of acknowledgment, focused on the job at hand.

Lionel took a second to admire the setup. It brought his days with Channel Seven back, nostalgia for a life left behind. Cordell had spared no expense: everything here was top-of-the-line gear, better than he ever had. He studied a rack of body mics, slender nozzles on lapel clips leashed to thin, square battery packs.

"These the new Woodhills?" he asked.

The tech looked at him like he was a caveman. "Woodhills suck, dude."

"I always liked mine."

"Where'd you work, public access?"

"Network TV, local market," Lionel said.

"So basically public access." He rolled his eyes and turned in his swivel chair. "Those, my friend, are Cosmo 98s. Perfect sound fidelity, six hours of battery life, and they never lose connection."

"Never?" Lionel asked.

"Well, if you get out of range you're screwed, but we're pumping out so much power you could cart one of those to the far end of the park and keep broadcasting, loud and clear."

"Goes up to eleven, huh?"

The tech gave him a blank stare.

"Never mind." He pointed to the gear rack. "I need to borrow one of these."

~~

Impending darkness brought electric lights, flooding down from the gantry over the stage. Thousands of voices, cheering as one, packed shoulder to shoulder on the Great Lawn. Thousands of people standing inches from a meticulously planned disaster. The air was electric, concert and crowd energy rising, a feedback loop that fueled itself with the rising excitement.

Cordell Spears took the stage. He beamed, cameras capturing his triumphant face and streaming it to television and computer screens across the globe, and waited for the fervor to die down.

"Now tell the truth. Was that for me, or for Maroon 5?" He cupped his hand to one side of his mouth. The body mic broadcast his voice crystal-clear over the stacked speakers even as he dropped it to a conspiratorial whisper. "Because Maroon 5's warming up right now, and they're going to come out and play a set for you in a minute. Maybe I should have kept that a surprise."

He surfed another crescendo of cheers, laughing like a kid at a birthday party.

"I'm just so glad you could all come. We've got a hell of a night lined up: three bands, some celebrity friends of mine, and surprises galore. And it's all for charity. How often can you have this much fun doing something good? You know, once upon a time, nobody knew my name. I was a local boy, playing stickball, so broke I couldn't even pay attention. But I had a dream. A dream of a better world..."

Cordell's voice chased Lionel across the park. He dipped into a gully along a biking path, staying low, evading security guards' flashlights as he made his way south. He'd already tried north of the field, looking under every rock that might be big enough to hide a hydra. No good, and none of the other scouts had found a clue.

Time was running out.

~~

Maddie emerged from the basement. Hollow-eyed, her copper ringlets touched by static frizz, her skin paler than usual. She held the fruit of her labor: the flask was sealed, cork held in place with a blob of red candle wax. The clay glinted as if it was shot through with flecks of white quartz.

"Time?" she asked. Finding her voice again, finding the concept of time again. She'd been Outside.

Dakota had left a warrior behind. She strode across the oil-stained floor, brandishing a folded piece of paper.

"Late," she said. "Show's already started."

Maddie was already off-balance. She felt the ground slide out from under her. The Amazon pressed the paper into her free hand.

"Not *too* late. Not yet. Everyone's ready and waiting. That's your route."

She pointed to the back door.

"*Run.*"

CHAPTER FIFTY-TWO

Maddie hustled down the subway platform steps, expertly darting around the commuter crowds, making her way to the turnstile. She recognized the woman standing close, raising a walkie-talkie to her lips, from the Sisterhood delegation. She was already swiping a MetroCard through the turnstile reader as Maddie rushed up. It pinged green just in time for her to pass on through without missing a step.

"Take the number-four train, board the third car from the front," she called out, then clicked the walkie-talkie. "She's on the move. Get everyone in position."

The next train rumbled into the station, standing room only, packed to the doors. Maddie was right where she'd been told to wait. A man inside the doorway, in the closest seat on the left, nodded to her. He quickly rose as she approached, gave her the seat, and stepped off the train before the doors whistled shut.

Her phone buzzed. A text message came in: *Congestion up the line. Don't ride all the way to East 86th, you won't make it in time. Get off at Grand Central. Solution will be waiting.*

She cradled the flask under her cargo jacket like a

marathon runner in a baton race. Except the baton was made of clay, fragile, and packed with deadly magic.

~~

Lionel prowled through the park. The first band took the stage. Drums thundered through the dark, riding on a guitar lick, and quickened his footsteps.

He knew the criteria. The containment unit had to be out of sight, but close to the Great Lawn. Close enough that when the hydra woke, it would make a beeline for the crowds, eager to devour and kill. He'd ruled out the tech village, checked behind the stage, hunted for displaced dirt and signs of a buried vault.

He looked up instead.

South of the lawns, at the edge of Turtle Pond, Gothic stone rose upon a promontory. A gray and slumbering castle perched there, with slate-roofed pavilions and a turret overlooking a stony cliff and the water below. Lionel grabbed his phone.

"Agnes? Any word from Maddie?"

"On her way. We have eyes on Cordell. If he leaves the stage, we may have to consider other measures."

Other measures meaning a bullet or a knife. It wouldn't stop the hero from coming back as if nothing had happened—again—but it would foil his plans tonight. An easy choice, if not for the fact that Cordell was their best hope if the hydra got loose. And if the cage was on some kind of a timer, poised to release the beast whether he was here or not...

"I'm looking at a...tiny castle," Lionel said, closing in. "Tell me about that."

"Belvedere Castle? It's a folly."

"Pardon?"

"Architectural term," Agnes said. "A folly is a grand structure that serves no useful purpose. It's there to be pretty. Well, used to be. Now I think there's a nature conservancy and a gift shop inside."

And a perfect view.

A flashlight beam swept his way. Lionel scampered behind a clump of reeds at the edge of the artificial pond, keeping low, waiting for footsteps to pass him by. Security was thick here, thicker than the rest of the park. Another tell.

He held his breath, knees starting to ache as he kept perfectly still, crouching down. The music was his ally: muffled here, but still pumping strong from the massive speakers and covering his moves. He waited until the light swayed in the other direction, the guard patrol moving on. Then he sprinted up the ramp to Belvedere Castle.

~~

Grand Central Terminal at rush hour was an explosion of barely controlled chaos, even without a massive event just fourteen blocks north. This was New York; fourteen blocks could be a breeze, or it could be an eternity. Maddie got off her train just as they were announcing backups down the line and warning about a twenty-minute wait at the next stop.

She didn't have twenty minutes. She wasn't even sure if she had ten.

A fresh text pinged in: *Leave through the 45th St exit.*

She dodged through the crowds, evading clumps of commuters, darting past tourists with their phones raised to capture the vast marble vault of Grand Central's great hall. She burst out onto the street. The sidewalk was almost as congested as the train station. She looked left, right, hunting for a sign.

She found it fifty feet down the sidewalk. A woman was holding a cab, leaning into the open doorway as if she was about to get in, talking to the driver. She spotted Maddie and gave her the high sign. As Maddie ran over, she passed a folded wad of cash to the cabbie. Then she stepped back, waved Maddie into the back seat, and shut the door behind her.

"Central Park," Maddie said, breathless.

She wasn't sure how this was going to help; Midtown traffic was a nightmare on a good day. All the same, the cabbie threw the old sedan's stick into drive and waited for a chance to pull into the bottleneck.

"Traffic's shut down at Fifty-Ninth," the driver told her. "I can get you close, though. That all right?"

"That's fine," she said, craning her neck to watch the sluggish stream of cars inching by. She wondered if she'd be better off getting out and running. It was what, a mile? She could run a mile. Her fingers trilled over the precious cargo under her jacket.

Sudden flashing lights snared her gaze. An ambulance with private livery had been parked at the curb just ahead. Now it was moving, siren starting to wail, responding to an emergency call...and perfectly poised to cut a hole in the wall of traffic. Cars jostled aside, making way. Someone in the passenger seat casually held one arm out the window, fingers twisting in a sign Maddie recognized. She smiled for the first time all night.

"Follow that ambulance," she said. "I have a feeling they're going our way."

~~

"I need some backup," Lionel breathed.

"Did you find it?" asked the voice on the phone.

His fingers brushed across a slab of cold gray steel. Behind the slate stone walls of Belvedere Castle, beneath the Victorian battlements, Cordell had hidden his big surprise. The refrigeration unit, the size of a delivery truck, hummed in the dark. It made mechanical chugging sounds, a compressor working overtime to keep the contents stable and sleeping.

"I found it," he said. "And Maddie was right. No way this would have fit on Jason's truck. Cordell must have given the hydra time to grow, and moved it into a bigger fridge."

His fingertips rested on a control panel at the edge of the unit, beside a pair of tall smooth double doors with no obvious lock or handle. Almost like it was designed to open from the inside. The panel offered a keypad and a softly strobing display, outputting a neon-green line that pinged upward every few seconds. Nothing more.

"Problem is," he said, "I've got no idea how this thing works."

At first he didn't recognize the mechanic from the Brooklyn safe house out of her grease-stained overalls. She had changed into ripped jeans and a dark flannel hoodie, her coal-black hair in a punky pompadour wave. She darted up the castle walk, dodging flashlights, and gave him a perfunctory nod before setting a small toolbox down on the octagonal paving stones. It rattled when she opened the lid, and her fingers hunted tools by muscle memory while she studied the machine. Lionel stood guard while she worked.

"He's good," she said, delivering her verdict. "And that's bad."

Lionel looked back over his shoulder. The mechanic had a side panel open, dangling from a single screw, the compressor's guts exposed and chugging away.

"Meaning?"

She put her tools away and flicked the clamps on the box, shaking her head.

"Meaning Cordell built fail-safes, and I'd need more time than I've got to bypass 'em. Try to mess with the temperature, it releases the hydra. Enter the wrong code on the control pad, it releases the hydra. Try to access the refrigerated compartment—so, for instance, we could try to kill this thing in its sleep..."

"It releases the hydra," Lionel said. "Great. Any sign of a timer?"

"No way to tell. I dug as deep as I could, and that wasn't far. Cordell really doesn't want anyone messing with his baby."

Lionel felt himself twisting on the tines of a fork. If the container had to be manually opened, taking Cordell down by any means necessary—temporarily, with a bullet, or by unleashing the Furies on him—was the best plan, and they needed to do it *now*. If the hydra was set to wake at a certain moment, timed to the crescendo of the show...well, the poison wouldn't be ready until tomorrow and their best hope of killing it lay with Cordell Spears, the man with the master plan. If Cordell was already dead when it burst loose, there was no telling how much carnage the monster could inflict.

They had to stop him, and they couldn't stop him.

Maddie was coming with the flask. One way or another, she'd be in position within minutes. Lionel's thoughts raced. There had to be something he could do, some way he could help.

The thought came to him on a thunderbolt. It was crazy. But maybe crazy was what the situation called for. He sprinted down the castle ramp, sights on the Great Lawn and the rainbow flares of the stage lights. He put his phone to his ear while he ran.

"Do we have eyes on Cordell?"

"No," Agnes said. "He slipped out of sight after the second band went onstage. I have scouts hunting for him as we speak."

"I've got an idea. Can we get control of the audio-video trailer? Commandeer the speakers and lights?"

"Should be easy enough."

"I also need someone to carve me a path to the stage. Clear any security in the way. And if somebody could grab me a bottle of water from one of the concession stands, that'd be great."

Agnes didn't answer right away. "What exactly are you planning, young man?"

"You know, I built half my reputation on rock-solid investigative journalism."

"Mm-hmm," she said, suspicious.

"The other half was mostly reckless and risky stunts that occasionally landed me in the hospital."

"And this would be…"

"The second thing," he said.

He had to buy time for Maddie, so she could corner Cordell, get the truth about the hydra's cage, and deal with him once and for all. Time, he could manage. Maybe he couldn't stop a hero's rise to glory, but he could sure as hell slow it down.

~~

Maddie ran the last block. Their ambulance escort had carved a path all the way up to Fifty-Eighth Street, shoving traffic out of the way; she jumped out at the curb and ran. Detective Mathers was waiting for her, hustling her past a cordon.

"Situation?" Maddie said, ducking under a low tree branch.

"Unstable. We can't make a move on Cordell until the hydra is definitely contained, and it isn't. The only one who can tell us for certain is the man himself."

"I'll get the truth out of him," she said.

"Also, your apprentice is doing...something."

"Something dangerous and possibly leading to personal bodily harm?"

"How'd you know?"

"Because he's mine," Maddie said.

They sprinted along a jogging path, winding deep through the park. Maddie heard the music up ahead, and saw the lights of the stage glowing like an aurora against the starless night sky.

Then a hulking shadow stepped into their path.

Maddie jolted to a stop. The detective slung her blazer back, hand slapping her calfskin holster.

"Don't," Maddie said. "We're too close to the lawn. This crowd hears gunshots, they'll stampede. People will get trampled."

"Wouldn't keep me down anyway," Jason said.

Mathers sidestepped, slowly circling him, hand still on her gun.

"Go and help the others," Maddie told her.

She looked to Jason. One of her sneakers inched

sideways on the path. She rolled her shoulders and squared her footing.

"I'll catch up."

CHAPTER FIFTY-THREE

White steam hissed from the containment unit. The internal lock let out a mechanical *clunk* as it rolled over on command.

The band onstage had finished their set. The park went silent. Just for a moment.

Now, Cordell thought.

The trailer doors whistled open. Vapor billowed, spilling down the steps of the park overlook, flooding the castle walls and dripping from the battlements. And deep within the frozen fog, a shaggy dragon's head roused itself from slumber. And another. And a third, its three-lobed eyes glowing in the mist.

The hydra was awake. And loose.

A massive foot slammed down on the paving stones, crushing them to powder. Three heads lifted to the night sky and screamed in unison.

~~

The energy changed. No one on the lawn could see what was coming—yet—but they could see the mist pouring from the castle's ramparts. And they could hear the hydra's roar, three chainsaw voices screeching their unearthly rage. People shifted, anxious, pointing, the teeming crowd falling into uncertain murmurs. The tech crew were scattered, running, confused—where was Cordell? Where had half of the security team vanished to? And why was the door to the AV trailer locked from the inside? The show was going further off the rails by the second and no one was in charge.

Lionel leaped onto the stage, taking the steps two at a time. The last musical act was still onstage, instruments silent, staring at him with naked confusion. He snatched the singer's microphone. His heart was pounding, breath short from the run. He didn't even know if this would work. But he had to try.

Fair Aphrodite, he thought, feeling the heat of thousands of eyes, the entire crowd watching him now. It was enough to throw him off, to break what little focus he could muster. He took a deep breath and tried again.

Fair Aphrodite, lady of agape and eros, of philia and ludus, of love in all names and all forms. Let love be my shield and desire drive my footsteps.

"I need you all to do something for me," he said. His voice carried over the speakers.

The hydra let out another scream. Now they could see its shadow, silhouetted on the rising torrents of white fog. A slithering, serpentine bulk, like a dozen giant snakes joined in a flailing, fleshy knot. Lionel held up his open hand.

"It's okay. Listen. Someone once told me that when things are dark and you're feeling afraid, sometimes the best way to push through it is to be strong for someone else. So…do something for me, okay? I need you all, every one of you, to think about someone you love. It could be someone standing right next to you or someone a thousand miles away. A lover, a friend, a parent, a child. Think about someone you love, okay? Picture their face. Imagine their voice."

People were holding hands. Whispering. Touching. He felt the crowd energy shifting, like a change in the wind. And rising fast.

"If you're watching on TV right now," Lionel said, "or on the internet. Wherever you are, whoever you are—we need you too. Please. Join in. It might not make sense right now, but just...trust me. I need you to focus. Think about the person you love more than anyone in the world."

Agnes was at the side of the stage. Lionel ran over and traded the microphone for the bottle of water in her hand.

"Take over," he said. "Keep them focused."

He sprinted across the park, muscles burning, every breath like fire in his lungs, until he reached the ramp of Belvedere Castle. A draconic roar tore through the air. The stones trembled as the monster shook off the last of its slumber, ready to hunt and devour and kill.

"Not today," Lionel said. He dropped to his knees in the dirt.

His mother's key—his key—became a trenching tool. He dug a quick furrow, a tiny pit, stabbing at the soil. Then he uncorked the bottle and poured it in, turning the pit into a reflecting pool.

No candle. That was fine. Like Maddie taught him, witches could work dirty. And improvise. He still had her lighter, the cheap pink plastic Bic from some forgotten gas station. He flicked the wheel, sparked a flame, and held it high in the air. The flame glimmered off the makeshift pool of water.

Lionel didn't have any weapons to battle the hydra. All he had was a bottle of water and a cheap lighter.

And love. The love of thousands of hearts, all standing together.

The energy crashed across his back, washing over him, spreading through the park, as he pictured Maddie's face and drew the sign of the dove upon the water. He looked up to the battlements and sealed the spell with a whisper.

"Fly, your heart to me."

~~

Cordell was ready for his moment. Everything, his entire life, had led to this. He was waiting in the wings, hiding at the edge of the park. The plan was simple: let the hydra wake up, let it rampage a bit, maybe stomp and gobble up a few hundred people to show it meant business, then swoop in to save the day while the whole world watched.

Which should have happened two minutes ago, he thought. He checked his diamond-encrusted Rolex. He could hear the hydra's rusted-metal howls. He knew it was loose...so why was it still thrashing around the battlements of Belvedere Castle when it should have been making a beeline for the human buffet?

"Where the *fuck*," he snarled, storming across the twilit green, "is my rampage?"

~~

Jason nodded at the starless sky as the hydra's roar shook the air.

"You're too late," he said.

Maddie shook her head. "Not by a long shot."

"Even if you had a way to kill that thing—which you don't, that's a hero's trial and me and Cordell are the only men for the job—there are six others waiting."

"Released?" she asked.

"Not yet. It's a time-release system. One a couple of days from now, then the others, slowly. The idea is to keep the mortals terrified, wondering when and where the hydras will strike, or if there's a whole army of them out there. By the time we take out the last one, they'll be begging us to rule them. And we can always make new ones if they need a reminder. Cordell's idea."

"This whole thing was Cordell's idea," Maddie said. "You're a good little soldier."

"Don't start that again. This is my purpose. Heroes are meant to win *kleos*. It's what we do."

"To win it," she said. "To *earn* it. Is that what you think this is? It's a con job. There's nothing real about any of this. Nothing honest. What kind of myths do you think will be written about tonight, Jason? What stories will the bards tell about you?"

"They'll write what we tell them to write. I don't understand why you're even standing in my way. Don't you want the old world back?"

"I prefer the world we've got right now," Maddie said. "It's a long way from ideal, but we're working on it."

"Why?" He flung up a frustrated hand. "These mortals can't rule themselves. They need us."

"This isn't about them. This is about you and your ego. At least have the honesty to admit—"

She fell silent. The air shifted around them.

At first, it was the temperature. The night grew warmer. The wind, soft through the trees, carried the faint scent of incense. Then came the sound.

Singing.

The people were singing. Thousands of voices, as one, filling Central Park and rising up to the night sky.

Jason squinted. "What...what is this?"

"You know what this is."

She raised her open palms, basking in the wave of energy as it washed over her like warm water on a white sand beach. She had to smile.

"These mortals," she said, "they're *strong*. So beautiful, and so strong. Stronger than they know. And when they stand together, your monsters are powerless. They don't need heroes, Jason. They don't need masters. They just need each other."

"No," he said. A stubborn, last-ditch denial.

"Your time in this world is ending."

"*No.*"

"You were almost right about something once. Like you told me: when you put grand ideas into mortals' heads, and make them believe that they can actually change things, do you know what you get?"

"Chaos," he said.

"No," she replied. "You get witches."

She reached under her cargo jacket and pulled out the white clay flask.

"You know what this is, too," she said.

He nodded, frozen where he stood.

"I can use it on Cordell," she said, "or I can use it on you, right here, right now. Make your choice."

Jason gave her an incredulous look. "You're bluffing."

"Am I?"

"Tisiphone," he said. "The Fury who avenges murders."

"You've got plenty of blood on your hands."

"And so do you," he said. "It's suicide. She'll destroy us both, and you know it."

"Sure will," she said.

Not the answer he expected. He blinked.

"You'll *die*."

"And you'll be gone, and these mortals will be safe. One problem down, one to go. As for Cordell, I'm pretty sure my coven has this handled. I trust them."

"When did you join a coven? And since when do you trust anyone but yourself?"

"I'm learning," she said. "Slowly, but I'm getting there. Now you need to ask yourself a very important question. Am I bluffing...or am I willing to die if it means saving thousands of innocent lives?"

They locked eyes.

"Well?" Maddie said. "Am I?"

He took a halting step backward.

"Looks like you know me after all," she told him.

Jason looked away. He seemed to be fumbling for something in the dark, something beyond his own angry defiance and denials. When he spoke again, his voice was softer. Distant.

"I didn't want any of this," he said.

"I believe you."

"I just spent so long, drifting from war to war with...no purpose, no reason. I didn't want to come back. I didn't know why the gods *sent* me back. Then Cordell found me, and he just...he's got a way of planting ideas in your head."

Maddie put the flask away.

"For what it's worth, from where I'm standing," she said, "I think there's a possibility you haven't considered."

He asked a question with his eyes.

"Like you said. They brought you back. Your story was over, the first time around, but here you are."

"Sure," he said. "To suffer. To be humiliated. My first death wasn't enough for them. You were right, Medea. About everything. I broke my vows, I used people, used you. All in the name of my glory. I got what I deserved. But I guess it wasn't enough. Hera or Hekate, one of the goddesses I scorned—they must have decided I needed more punishment. So here I am."

"Maybe. But did you consider that maybe, just maybe, they wanted something *better* for you?"

He looked her way again, head tilted.

"Better?"

"This story needs an ending," she said. "A proper ending, to satisfy the Muses. And if you're ready, and if you're brave…you can help us write it."

CHAPTER FIFTY-FOUR

The hydra slammed an elephantine foot down on the ramp of the castle. The stones quaked, icy mist spilling from the turret windows. But it went no farther. Its teeth gnashed, biting at the air, boneless necks yanking as though invisible leashes held them back.

Lionel knelt before his makeshift pool, holding Maddie's lighter high. A single tiny flame to hold back the darkness. He felt the shared energy of the crowd washing over him, the voices raised in song. The power flowed through him, to the reflection, to the flame, feeding the spell.

He held the line.

"You've got to be kidding me," Cordell snapped, striding toward him with his fists clenched. "This is what's holding up my show? A parlor trick? How are you even doing this?"

Lionel didn't move. He held the flame high.

"I'm not," he said. He nodded back over his shoulder, to the chorus of voices. "They are."

"Not possible. These people don't know any magic. They're weak."

"Stronger than you," Lionel said.

Cordell's foot swung like a sledgehammer. Lionel caught it on the jaw. The kick split his skin open and filled his mouth with blood as he hit the grass. The lighter fell from his hand. The flame flickered and died. Cordell bore down on him, his mask of civility gone, seething with rage.

"All you did was slow me down. And for what? You could have had everything, you stupid fuck."

He punctuated the last word with another kick, driving his heel into Lionel's gut. Lionel doubled over, rolling along the grass as the hydra screamed. It took its first trembling step onto the green, the barrier shattered.

Jason charged from the shadows. He ran in a marathon sprint, arms pumping, head down, a missile locked on target. Steel glinted in his hands: a pair of fighting knives, sharpened for battle.

"Good, at least you showed up," Cordell said. "And we're back on schedule, so get ready. Lure the thing down to the lawns, let it chomp on the stage a little—"

Jason crouched as he ran, back bending, knees ready—and leaped.

He sailed through the air, bellowing a battle cry, and landed on one of the hydra's necks. He drove a knife through its bilious scales, clinging on tight as it screeched and tried to buck him off.

"What are you *doing*?" Cordell screamed.

Jason's knives plunged in. He pulled himself up along the twisting, writhing neck one stab at a time, making a ladder. Gouts of black ichor splashed across the hero's arms, his flesh sizzling and running like wax under the beast's acidic blood. He gritted his teeth and kept fighting, kicking away a second head as it snapped at his heels.

"What I should have done from the beginning," Jason grunted. "I'm changing the ending. Changing *my* ending."

Down on the ground at Cordell's feet, Lionel struggled to catch his breath. He had just enough for a shaky laugh.

"Guess your big day's canceled, huh?"

Cordell whirled around, teeth bared, lips contorted in a mad grimace.

"That's right. My day. Not his. Not yours. Mine."

His shoe came down, stomping Lionel's stomach, his ribs, each word echoed by a bone-fracturing explosion of pain.

"Mine. Mine. *Mine.*" Cordell stood over him, pulling back his foot for another kick. "Who the hell do you think you are, trying to stand in my way? You're nothing. You're just like the clueless sheep out there on the lawn. Stupid. Worthless."

"I'm the sheep who knows what you did," Lionel wheezed. He crawled back on his elbows, trying to steal a few feet of breathing room. "I know you killed your own mother."

Cordell fell silent. Reflective. On the castle ramp, one of Jason's blades plunged into the hydra's eye. It burst. His other knife had broken at the hilt, a useless nub of melted slag, and he threw it aside. A third head fired at him from the icy mists, jaw wide to swallow him whole. He grabbed onto its teeth, twisted and tore, ripping them from the gums. He flipped the monstrous teeth in his hands, turning them into fresh weapons.

"Why did you do it?" Lionel said. "She couldn't have stopped you. She wasn't any kind of a threat. So why did you do it?"

"You really want to know?" Cordell asked.

Lionel nodded, swallowing a burning lump in his throat. His ribs were on fire as he inched back on the grass.

"Because she was just like everyone else," Cordell said. "Small. Weak. Like I told you, my mother was trailer trash. Not a judgment, a simple fact. Spreading her legs for my father was the only valuable thing she did in her entire pathetic life. Then, once I learned who I was, my destiny, my birthright...she denied me."

"Denied you," Lionel echoed.

"I needed the fleece. I needed money. She wouldn't give me what I wanted, so I took it. There's a lesson in this, Lionel. One you should have learned. I *always* get what I want."

"Even if someone has to die? Even your own mother?"

Cordell shrugged. "You know how many people I've killed over the years? How do you think I became a billionaire, by being *nice*? I barely remember half of their names. Years from now, I won't remember yours, either."

The earth shook as one of the hydra's heads slammed to the ground, slashed and dead at the end of a limp neck. Jason hit the grass and rolled, dodging out of the way as another open drooling mouth plunged down at him.

"Thank you," Lionel said.

Cordell squinted. "For?"

Lionel unzipped his jacket. His shaky hand pulled one side open, to show Cordell the slim black box of the Cosmo 98 body mic. The tiny microphone was clipped to his shirt lapel.

"I borrowed this. Hope you don't mind. And my people took over the AV trailer about fifteen minutes ago. I needed them ready to commandeer the speakers."

The singing from the lawn had stopped. Fallen silent.

"I'm pretty sure you just made a full confession in front of...well, how did you put it?" Lionel's bloody lip twisted in a smile. "You did say you wanted the entire world to be watching tonight."

Cordell's rage deflated like a pinpricked balloon. His face fell, slowly, blood draining, becoming a mask of abject terror.

Lionel reached down and clicked the transmitter off. This next part was for Cordell alone.

"My girlfriend told me something that stuck with me," he said. "She said that it's almost impossible for a mortal to destroy a hero...but a hero can destroy himself. All you needed was a little encouragement. But, hey, congratulations on a job well done."

Cordell took a halting step away from him. Then another. His muscles were locked, body rigid, as if he thought he could dig his heels in and stop this from happening. The end of his myth, unfolding before his eyes.

Then he turned and ran, tearing toward the Great Lawn.

Lionel groaned and shoved himself to his feet. The earth shook one last time, almost knocking him back to his knees. Maddie's lighter was nestled in the grass. He scooped it up.

The hydra was dead. Jason lay slumped against one of its fallen heads, broken teeth still gripped like daggers in his ravaged fists. The air smelled like hot tar, and the stone and grass sizzled under the beast's bloody wounds.

Jason didn't look much better. He was covered in burns, his clothes in seared tatters, some of his wounds so deep Lionel could see the exposed bone beneath. One of his eyes was sealed shut under a lump of bruised-black flesh; the other, milky, struggled to focus. His lungs rattled as he took a breath.

"You," Jason rasped. "Did you see?"

His fist thumped the hydra's hide. His arm jerked, muscles losing control, and fell limp at his side.

"I bagged a big one."

"Sure did," Lionel said.

"You're a bard, right?"

"I'm a reporter."

"Close enough." Jason leaned forward and coughed. Flecks of blood spattered his legs. "Need you to do something for me. Please."

"Name it."

"Tell my story," he said. "Spread it far and wide. I need them to hear it. I need them to believe it. I need them to—"

He leaned into another racking cough, hacking up blood as his shoulders shook. Lionel waited in silence, listening.

"Tell them," he said, "that *this* was the fate of Jason of Thessaly. Tell them that I fought. Tell them that I was brave. Tell them that the goddesses granted me a second chance at glory, and this time I didn't fail."

"I will," Lionel said. "I promise."

Jason offered something like a smile. He sagged back against the dead beast's hide.

"It's a better ending this way," he said. "Just going to…rest my eyes a moment."

His lungs stopped rattling. His chest fell, one last time, and never rose again.

~~

Cordell stood on a silent stage. Thousands of eyes fixed on him like a heat lamp. He looked to the teeming crowd, to their upturned faces. He saw confusion, sadness. Disgust.

"I—" he said, cringing at a squeal of feedback. He tapped the microphone.

"I...that was...that was a demonstration of a new...immersive...dramatic presentation, being put together by my, um, new media division..."

This wasn't working. Nothing was working. He couldn't win them back, not now. Not now that they'd seen who he really was. Movement at the left side of the stage turned his head.

Detective Mathers was waiting for him, along with a pack of uniformed cops.

He slowly eased his way right, still babbling into the microphone, barely hearing his own voice as he scrambled to put together a plan. He could get out of this. He always did. The world bent the rules for heroes.

He looked right and froze. On the other side of the stage, Maddie was waiting for him.

She held up the white clay flask.

He understood what she was offering him. Maybe the last choice he would ever get. For the first time in his life, he had to face the consequences of his actions.

She'd allow him to choose his judge.

Shoulders slumped, Cordell turned the other way. He walked offstage, down into the group of waiting officers. He didn't fight, didn't even speak, as Mathers cuffed his hands behind his back and led him away.

CHAPTER FIFTY-FIVE

Lionel sat in the back of an ambulance, wincing as a paramedic—a silver key dangling around a delicate chain at her throat—taped his ribs.

"I need to stop getting my ass kicked," Lionel said.

Maddie tilted her head at him. "Is that a plan, or a goal?"

"Probably more of a goal, to be honest."

The street was flooded with people, most of them wandering off, shell-shocked and confused...but alive. Some of them held on to one another, walking a little closer, clinging a little tighter than they used to. Agnes stepped over to the open back door of the ambulance, cleaning her bifocals with a handkerchief.

"You two need to go to ground and stay there until things calm down." She shot a glare at Lionel. "*Especially* you. The authorities would like to have a word with you about tonight's events, and Detective Mathers can only distract them for so long."

"What about the hydra?" Lionel asked.

The pedestrians cleared for a trio of city sanitation trucks, spitting exhaust as they rumbled into the park.

"Being handled," the lawyer said. "Also, good news from

our huntress-worshiping friends. The first batch of poison has been synthesized, and teams are already on the move to deliver it. By tomorrow night, all six of the remaining hydras will be neutralized."

"Almost seems wrong," Lionel mused, wincing again as the bandages drew tight. "I mean, it's a life-form like nothing else on earth, and we're just...wiping it out."

"If there was any safe way to preserve it, we would," Maddie said.

Agnes nodded. "Eventually, it would break free again. And the consequences next time around...let's just say there's a reason such things were scoured from this world once before."

"Last of the old monsters?" Lionel asked.

"Oh, no," Agnes said. "*Plenty* of old monsters still around. But only the ones who have learned to change with the times. The hydra is a relic of the age of heroes, young man, and the age of heroes is over."

She put her glasses on. Then she smiled at him, her sharp eyes glinting in the dark.

"It's our turn now."

~~

They needed sleep, and safe harbor. When they got into the cab together, Lionel knew the address before Maddie said it out loud. Stranded for the night in Manhattan, there was really only one place they could go.

Back where their story began.

The cab wound through the sleeping streets of Chelsea and let them off on Tenth Avenue, outside a low stone wall and the red-brick spires of what had once been a seminary. A sign over the entry gate, white letters on black, read "The High Line Hotel."

Maddie took his hand, and they walked inside together.

A clerk was alone in the empty lobby. She turned and offered them a smile. That, and a gray folio with a pair of black key cards nestled inside.

"Ms. Hannah? Mr. Page? Regina Dunkle called ahead and asked us to have your room ready. Suite three, your usual."

They shared a glance.

"I'm not even capable of surprise at this point," Lionel said. "Way too tired."

"Roger that." She took the keys.

The suite was the same as they'd left it. Lionel looked to the rug, where Maddie had taken him on a journey into a tarot card, his first initiation. To the bed they'd shared. Maddie scooped up the remote control from the antique writing desk next to the door and perched on the edge of the mattress.

"I have to see how much trouble we're in," she said.

Lionel ambled over to the minibar. He hefted a slim blue bottle and wriggled it in his hand. "Bombay Sapphire?"

"Hell yes," she said.

He poured the gin. She flicked through the channels. Every station was covering the event, with mixed levels of confusion, processing the story through captured video from the live-stream and jumpy cell-phone footage. Nobody was entirely sure what had happened in Central Park, only that the sound system had suddenly broadcast an "explicit and shocking" confession from the beloved Cordell Spears. One channel was showing a clip of Lionel at center stage.

"WABC-TV has identified this man—who sounds like the same person interrogating Cordell Spears on the captured audio—as Lionel Page, a veteran reporter for a Chicago news station. Reached for comment, station manager Brianna Washington responded: 'Lionel is currently on a field assignment. He is a seasoned journalist with a proven nose for a story, and we hope that the authorities give this emerging situation their full attention. We have nothing more to say at this time.'"

"Oh, she's *pissed*," Lionel said, coming over to sit beside Maddie.

"You sure?"

"I know Brianna. Trust me. She'll be burning up my phone in about—"

His phone started to buzz.

"There we go. I'll call her back in the morning, when she hates me a little less."

They clinked glasses.

"In Holyoake, Florida," the anchor said, "local authorities have pledged to reopen the investigation into the homicide of Leticia Spears, Cordell Spears's mother. Representatives from Cordell's law firm say that at this hour, they have no comment—"

She flipped the channel.

"So what about Cordell?" Lionel asked.

"Depends on him. He knows we've got the flask. It's a sword dangling over his head by a very thin, golden thread. If he owns up to what he did and takes his punishment in the mortal courts, we might not use it."

She leaned back on her hands and kicked her shoes off. They bounced across the dark hardwood planks.

"Then again, we might anyway. Sisterhood's going to have a meeting. Something like this has to be a group decision."

That seemed fair. They drank their nightcap, scrolling through the channels, enjoying each other's company and a little bit of peace. Eventually, they made their way into bed and clicked off the lights. They held each other in the dark.

Maddie felt restless in his arms. Not sleeping. And he wouldn't sleep until she did. There was one subject they hadn't broached, and he felt it weighing on her.

"Do you want to talk about...him?" he whispered.

She stirred, turning, spooning back against his body.

"Did he die well?" she asked.

"He did. I need to write it all down. I promised I'd tell his story."

"Tell me," she said.

So he shared the story. Grew the myth. Only by one person, but he supposed myths had to start somewhere.

"I don't think he'll be back," she said.

"Appropriate ending?"

"Even had a moral," she said. "A handful to choose from, really."

"What do you think the moral was?"

"I think..." She trailed off for a moment. "I think that sometimes people make mistakes in life. Bad mistakes, even terrible ones. And I think that sometimes...sometimes they get a second chance to get things right."

She slept after that.

~~

Lionel woke up in bed alone.

His hand rested on rumpled, empty sheets. His blood turned to ice. His eyes snapped open—

—and there Maddie was, standing next to the bed, her

phone to her ear. She made an apologetic face and held up one finger while she listened to the muffled voice on the line.

"Yes, my queen. Of course. I won't fail you."

She hung up, set the phone on the end table, and sighed.

"Was that..." Lionel asked, uncertain.

"*Her*. No rest for the wicked, and there's a situation that needs handling." She glanced at the clock. "Just enough time to grab a shower and maybe coffee, then hit the road."

His heart sank, but he tried not to show it. He'd just found her again, and now she was going to head off on another mission, another ride into the darkness. And he'd be waiting.

"I get it," he said. "That's just...how it works."

He closed his eyes, listening for the sound of the shower.

Instead, a pillow bounced off his face.

"Well?" she said, standing over him with her hands on her hips. "Get up, sleepyhead. You don't get to nap on the Lady's time. You gave up that life. Too late to complain now."

He blinked. "You're...taking me with you?"

"Come on. Shower. With me. Now." She tugged him by the hand, out of bed and into the bathroom. "Of course I'm taking you with."

They stood there, face-to-face, and shared a silent gaze. Her fingertips brushed his chest, tracing the sunken scar there.

"We're a team, aren't we?"

"Yeah," Lionel said. "I like the sound of that."

She pointed. "Then. Get. In. The. Shower. Wait, first, get naked. Then get in the shower. Besides, I obviously can't leave you behind. You are *way* too dangerous to be left to your own devices."

"I confess a slight proclivity for trouble," he said. "So where are we going?"

She twisted the tap. Water rumbled down, kissing the air with curlicues of steam.

"West," she said.

"Just…west?"

"We'll figure it out on the way," she said. "Come on, let's have an adventure."

AFTERWORD

There almost wasn't a sequel. *Ghosts of Gotham* was originally conceived as a stand-alone, one-shot story. That said, I loved visiting haunted New York, and heard from a lot of readers who felt the same way and wanted more. And while I knew what happened next — that Lionel and Maddie would inevitably reunite after parting ways in Montauk — I wanted to get it down on the page.

Also, this year has been a cosmic dumpster fire and I wanted to close it out with something optimistic. With the endless parade of doom and gloom in the air, some folks need a reminder of just how powerful they really are, and how much they're capable of.

If you think I might be talking to you, I probably am.

Of course, I couldn't do this alone. Special thanks to my editor Kira Rubenthaler, my cover designer James T. Egan, my wonderful audiobook narrator Susannah Jones, and my assistant Morgan Blake.

Want to know what's coming next? Head over to http://www.craigschaeferbooks.com/mailing-list/ and hop onto my mailing list. Emails go out to announce new releases. Want to reach out? You can find me on Facebook at http://www.facebook.com/CraigSchaeferBooks, on

Twitter at @craig_schaefer, or check out my Patreon page at https://www.patreon.com/craigschaefer (where, at the time of this writing, I'm serializing a side story set in the *Ghosts of Gotham* universe.) And thank you so much for reading!

Made in the USA
Monee, IL
06 December 2020